The Ungovernable series:

Zero Day Threat
Jailbreak
Time Bomb
Insider Threat
Firewall
Trojan Horse
Security Incident
Threat Agent
Attack Path

TROJAN HORSE

R.M. OLSON

ISBN-13: 978-1-990142-01-7

To Michelle, whose morning conversations keep me
sane.

TROJAN HORSE:

Malicious code or malware designed to trick system users into loading and executing it by deceiving the user of its true intent

Important note:

Dear readers,
As you will have surmised from the previous book, this book takes place on a pleasure planet. It's … not a nice place. So please be aware that, while I have tried to make sure anything too disturbing happens off-screen, the story does contain implied sexual violence, implied violence (sexual and otherwise) to minors, and a scene with a somewhat gruesome injury.

1

Jez leaned up against the wall, gasping for breath, her heart pounding a hole in her chest. The walls of the small, darkened corridor off the gambling rooms pressed in around her claustrophobically, and she cradled one arm close to her body, the dull ache of it almost unnoticeable under the pounding glow of adrenalin.

Had she lost him? She wasn't certain. She closed her eyes for just a moment, sucking in a deep breath of air that smelled of sweat and stale alcohol, trying to slow her heart rate.

"There you are."

Her eyes snapped open, and she bit back a curse as her involuntary movement jolted her arm.

A small, wiry man stalked around the corner, and even in the dim light, she could tell his expression was one of cruel satisfaction.

He might have been handsome, when he wasn't looking like he'd sucked on a damn lemon, but his fine clothing and dapper appearance marked him out as someone who didn't know much about brawling. Not someone she'd generally be worried about, honestly. Probably could knock him over with one very satisfying fist to the face.

But then again, it was harder to knock someone over when they were holding a laser gun on you.

He had another gun loose in his other hand. Her gun. Which, with Ysbel's mods, was pretty much enough to leave a Jez-shaped charcoal stain on the wall behind her.

She grinned at him through the pounding of her heart. "Well, guess I was wrong. I thought you were a stupid, slow bastard. Turns out you're a stupid fast one."

His eyebrows lowered. "And I thought you were supposed to be smart. Not so smart now, are you?" His smile turned slightly mocking. "If your com was working, I might worry about that mass murderer friend of yours. But then, that's why I never travel without my EMP blocker."

"Maybe I already put a call out," said Jez, with as much snark as she could muster. "Anyways, if she did want to come after you, she could probably find you by smell. Ever heard of a shower, you scum-eater?"

His smile didn't falter, but his expression hardened. "I suppose I will have to shower after this," he said. "I hear ash is hard to get off your skin."

"What, planning on setting yourself on fire?" Her arm throbbed, and she could see the murder glowing through his expression, but hell, she figured she was in deep enough anyways at this point.

"Sit." He gestured with his gun. For a moment she debated jumping him, but … well, satisfying as that would feel, it would probably be fairly short-lived. Considering she'd probably have a hard time feeling anything with a hole burned through the middle of her gut.

Slowly, she sat.

His smiled widened, slow and ugly. He'd come a couple of steps closer, but still too far for her to be able to lunge for him.

Probably on purpose. He seemed the type that would think about that kind of thing.

"Alright, Solokov," he purred. "Looks like you've finally begun to see reason."

"Hey now, I know you're a useless plaguer, but I have things to do. Can we get whatever the hell this is over with? I'm kind of a busy woman, to be honest with you."

"Ah Jez," he said, almost fondly. "I expect that your options of places to go and things to do may have just gotten a lot smaller."

Her heart was pounding even harder now, her grin stretching across her face, a prickle of panic crawling up her spine, mingling with the cold of the corridor wall against her back.

The gambling ship was big. And yes, she'd taken that into consideration, but at the same time—

Well, at the same time, he might just straight-up kill her. And he might just be able to.

"So," he said, in a conversational tone. "You've been wreaking havoc on this ship for the last week, rumour has it. Gambling, cheating, drinking, whatever it is you've been doing. And I don't know what happened a week ago, with the fire alarms and everything else, but it wouldn't surprise me at all if you had something to do with it. And when I went to look you up—" he shook his head. "I'd expect shame from most people. Smuggling. With Lena, to boot. And the kind of things on your record, I was almost ashamed for you. But here you sit, Jez, and you're not ashamed in the slightest."

"Nope," she said, managing a smirk. "Figure it could be worse. I could look like you, for one thing. And besides—"

"Shut up, Solokov," he growled, raising his laser gun meaningfully.

She'd read up on his record, too. He wouldn't hesitate to use it.

She shut up.

"So," he continued. "Here we have a smuggler, a gambler, a drunk, and a cheat. And you got an invite to this conference, for some reason, or else you and your friends managed to forge your way in. And I decided it was time someone put an end to this."

"You sure that's what it was?" she asked. She was pretty sure she should actually shut up, but her mouth didn't usually pay attention to considerations like that anyways. "Because I figure it was because I cheated every damn credit off you three games in a row before you figured out what the hell was going on." She shrugged. "I mean, gotta hand it to you, it takes skill to be that plaguing stupid, but—"

The laser gun burned a smoking hole in the dirty carpet beside her, and she gave an involuntary yelp.

"The only reason that didn't hit twenty centimetres to the right is that you're going to do something for me, Jez. You're going to give me my credits back, and you're going to do it right now."

"Which chip do you want?" she drawled. "The one I cheated off you, or the one I stole off you?" Every muscle in her body was tight, and her brain buzzed with a heady mix of fear and anticipation.

He glowered at her. "Don't think I'm stupid. I saw you transfer the credits into your chip."

"Yeah? Well hell, I'd love to give those credits back, since you asked so nicely. But—" She shrugged regretfully. "You hit my com with an EMP blocker. So I can't just send it over."

"Take out the chip and toss it to me."

She shrugged again. "I could, I guess. You'd never get inside it, because it's set to my biometrics, and I figure you don't have a hacker friend who's nearly as good as mine."

"You'll give me that money back, Solokov," he said in a flat voice.

"You'll figure out a way, or I'll take my chances with a hacker friend."

"Well, here's the thing," she said. "I do have a way. I just don't think you're going to like it."

He narrowed his eyes. "Tell me."

She gave him a look of wide-eyed innocence. "Old-fashioned way. You hook your com into mine, and you can transfer the funds right over, easy peasy."

He looked at her for a long moment, eyes narrowed. He was probably making the same calculations she was—she was taller, and probably stronger, and a hell of a lot more experienced at brawling. But then again, she was injured, and he had a gun.

At last, reluctantly, he nodded. "Alright. That's what we'll do. But —" he raised his gun again. "I know what you're thinking. You're thinking you'll be able to jump me, take off, go find your friends." He gave her a grim smile. "Before you embarrass yourself, I've been checking. All of your friends are on the other side of the ship, and I have people who'll let me know the moment one of them moves. And if they do, you're dead. You aren't the first person who's underestimated me. The difference here is, you're still alive. Let's see if you can keep it that way." He gestured with his gun. "Go on. Legs out in front of you, hands on the wall behind you."

Reluctantly, she did as he asked.

Be hard to lunge at him from this position, which was probably the point.

Still—maybe she wouldn't be able to jump to her feet, and maybe her hands were over her head on the wall, but if he was right in front of her, maybe—

He stepped closer cautiously, as if she were a wild beast that might snap at him. She gave him her toothiest grin, but his expression just took on a tinge of disgust.

He was right in front of her now. He'd have to put one of the guns down to hold his com up to hers, either that or keep a gun in his com hand while he transferred the credits.

The adrenalin rushing through her veins was almost enough to make her dizzy, and she was grinning like a complete lunatic.

"Alright," he said, crouching in front of her so he was at her eye level. "You're going to lower your com hand, nice and slow, and then —"

She didn't wait for him to finish, just brought her good hand down so the edge of her palm would connect with the side of his neck—

He caught her wrist in his hand and shoved it out of the way, and with his other, slammed the butt of Ysbel's modded gun into her injured arm. She bit back a whimper of pain as he twisted her good arm up behind her back, doubling her over, and then the muzzle of the laser pistol was jammed into her ribs.

"You think I was born yesterday, Solokov?" he hissed into her ear. "Now, let's try that again. Give me your com hand."

Reluctantly, painfully, she held out her injured arm. She had the brief hope that he might let go of the gun for an instant in order to touch his com to hers, but he somehow managed to keep the muzzle steady against her ribs and twist his wrist so the two coms made contact. She could hear the faint, steady *click* of credits transferring over, and she swore and gritted her teeth against the tears of pain forming in her eyes as he pulled her arm up tighter.

At last, the clicking stopped.

"Thank you, Jez," he said mockingly. "I couldn't possibly have done it without you. And it looks like I took a little more than what you owed me, but I thought it was probably fair payment for the trouble you put me through."

The pressure on her arm released abruptly, but before she could gather her wits, he'd stepped back, the gun trained on her. He'd switched weapons now, and this time he was holding Ysbel's modded heat gun.

"But I wouldn't worry about that," he continued conversationally. "I'm pretty sure you're not going to need credits where you're going." He aimed, and she lunged to her feet, because he was going to pull the trigger anyways, so what did it matter—

He fired.

The gun clicked.

She grinned at him. "Where do you think I'm going, you bastard? Back to my room?"

He cursed and yanked out his laser gun, levelling it at her, but she pulled a small tube out of her pocket and clicked it before he could pull the trigger.

"Didn't even notice your EMP blocker was missing," she said, tossing it into the air and catching it in her palm. "Bit of an innocent, aren't you? Bet you get your pockets picked in every damn zestava you visit."

He was glaring at her now, clearly too angry to be alarmed.

She grinned to herself and tapped her com against her thigh. "Hey Galina, you feel like some target practice?"

The man's face went suddenly bloodless. "What—what are you doing? That com doesn't work. I used the—"

"Like I said," she drawled, leaning back against the wall. "I have a tech-head friend."

"Hands up," came a woman's voice from down the hall.

Slowly, the man raised his arms.

"Now," said the woman, "Drop your weapons. Turn around slowly. And get the hell out of here. I don't like it when people hit

Jez."

She was about half a head shorter than Jez, with wavy black hair falling half-way down her back, high boots, and a short dress that showed off her curves to admirable advantage.

And a heat-pistol, of course.

Jez sighed dreamily.

The man did as he was told, lowering his gun gently to the ground, then turning and sidling past the woman, who was holding her gun in a no-nonsense way.

Jez grinned at her. It was honestly incredible how hot knowing how to manage a heat pistol could make someone. And, to be fair, Galina was pretty damn hot to begin with. As hot as Jez had remembered from the night she'd met her in the casino, after Masha had sold them out, and she'd almost walked in on Lev—

Actually, probably better not to think about that.

Anyways, and considering how drunk Jez had been at the time, that was actually fairly impressive.

When the man was gone, Galina lowered her heat pistol and strode over to Jez, concern written across her face. "Are you alright?"

Jez grinned at her, despite the throbbing in both her damn shoulders now. "Yep. Bastard took the bait and swallowed it whole."

Galina looked her over quickly. Her eyes caught the way Jez cradled her arm, and she frowned.

"Jez. You're hurt." She reached out and ran a practiced hand down Jez's arm, and Jez couldn't hide her wince. "What happened?"

The concern on Galina's face made something strange and slightly uncomfortable twist inside Jez's stomach. Because hell, she was used to a lot of things, but it would be a long time before she got used to people being concerned about her.

Still, she managed a snarky grin. "Well, he decided he was going to try to break my arm before he shot me. But he's a damn amateur. I've been beat up plenty of times before, and I can tell you—"

"That doesn't make it better. I don't like you getting hurt." She leaned in and kissed Jez gently, and for half a moment Jez completely forgot about her arm.

Because if she'd learned one thing about Galina in the past week, it was that she was a very good kisser.

"Alright you big hero, let's get out of here," Galina said fondly, stepping back.

Jez blinked at her for a moment before the words penetrated the fog in her brain, then she grinned. "Did I ever tell you you're damn hot when you're holding someone at gunpoint?"

Galina laughed. "How about you tell me tonight? Come on. We'd better get out of here before he figures out what you just pulled on him."

2

"Hey kids! Time to move!"

Tae looked up in time to see Jez jog onto the main deck. There was a broad grin spread across her tawny face, her tousled black hair was even more disheveled than usual, and she was holding her arm like it hurt her.

Galina was close behind her, heat-gun still in her hand, concern on her face.

He stood quickly. "Jez? Are you—"

She winked at him. "Relax, tech-head. All good. But I figure we've worn out our welcome. Better get moving." She glanced behind her. "I'd give us maybe five standard minutes before that plaguer decides to spend some of his new credits, and finds out they're forgeries. Maybe a little longer than that before he realizes that from the moment he touched his com to mine, we had a mirror copy of every damn thing on his info chip." She winced slightly as she brought her com up, popping the chip free. She tossed it to Tae, and he caught it.

"She's hurt," said Galina. "Her arm needs to be looked at. Is there a first aid kit anywhere I can—"

Jez turned to her with a grin. "Here's the thing, Galya—usually we fly first, and deal with first aid and crap later. Tae? Everyone on board?"

He nodded, and she disappeared down the hallway towards the cockpit.

Galina looked around uncertainly.

"Strap down," said Tae, face grim. "Doesn't matter where, just strap down."

Galina, to her credit, didn't ask questions, just slipped into the nearest seat and hit the restraint. Tae gave one final glance around the cabin, then grabbed for the pile of tech he'd just finished laying out on a table.

He barely had time to realize Jez had already used her code to hit the doors on the hangar-bay airlock open when the ship shot forward. He lost his balance and his footing as he was flung backwards, and gritted his teeth against the inevitable impact with the damn deck—

And then someone caught him, strong arms arresting his fall and holding him steady, and instead of the hard deck, the ship's momentum shoved him against someone's warm chest.

"Easy there," came Ivan's low, slightly amused voice in his ear, his short-cropped beard brushing against Tae's cheek. "You alright?"

A small, pleasant shiver ran through Tae's body, his tight muscles relaxing at the warmth of Ivan's arms around him, and he found for some reason he was smiling.

Even aside from keeping him from landing face first on the damn deck, like he seemed to do every time Jez decided to go somewhere in a hurry, something about Ivan did that to him.

Which was dangerous. He damn well knew better.

"Yeah," he said after a moment, when he realized he hadn't actually answered Ivan's question. "Yeah, I'm—I'm fine. Thanks."

He wasn't entirely sure why his legs had gone slightly shaky, but it was probably just relief that for once in his life, he wasn't going to have a new set of bruises from Jez's takeoff.

The ship steadied on course, and at last, cautiously, Ivan loosened his arms from around Tae.

Tae took a deep breath, strangely reluctant to step away.

"Hey tech-head!" Jez sauntered back onto the main deck, grinning. "You and Ivan decide to do this instead of making out on the couch, like last time I wasn't here to supervise?"

He scowled at her, straightening quickly. "For the millionth time, Jez, that was a damn distraction."

She gave a snort of laughter. "Yeah? Who was more distracted, you or Ivan?"

"Jez—"

She snickered and dropped into one of the seats, hitting the button to release the mag lock and tipping it back so it balanced on two legs. She leaned back with her hands behind her head, and he glared at her.

"Anyways," she said, "find anything on that chip I got you?"

"If I could work without you bloody well trying to knock me onto my face every time you get into the cockpit—" he muttered.

She shrugged. "Hey, thought you'd be glad I got you out without getting us shot at. Anyways, that bastard Masha said to get us to some nice, safe coordinates so she could talk with Olyessa over the com, which I did. So not sure what you're complaining about."

"Speaking of getting shot at," said Galina, releasing her restraints, "you need to get that arm seen to." She stood and turned towards the cupboard with the first-aid kit.

Jez gave Galina a wink. "Hey Galya, you can look at any part of me you—"

"Jez—" said Tae through his teeth.

Ysbel came through the door a few moments later. With her shaved head and muscular build, she would have looked intimidating even if you didn't know she was a mass murderer. "I heard our lunatic pilot talking in here, so I assumed it was safe to stand up," she grumbled.

"Jez?" Lev stepped out onto the deck behind Ysbel, his scholarly air and slightly disheveled appearance forming a stark contrast to that of the demolitions expert. Tae caught the slight stiffening in his posture at the sight of Galina, but to his credit, it disappeared almost as quickly as it came. "Are you—"

Galina looked up from where she was bending over Jez's injured arm and shook her head, still looking concerned. "She says she's fine, but—"

Lev smiled reluctantly. "Ah. I understand."

Jez had stiffened as well when Lev entered, and was clearly avoiding his eyes.

Lev sighed. "Masha is going over some of the final aspects of our plan, or at least, that's what she told me. I'm fairly certain she knows we want to talk without her, and it sounds like she's willing to respect that, for the moment, at least." He paused. "Jez. Did you get the information?"

"Yep," Jez drawled. "Who do you think you're dealing with, genius-boy?"

"Good." There was a long pause, and then Lev turned with an obvious effort to Galina. "Galina. Did everything go alright on your end?"

She quirked an eyebrow at him, but nodded. "And I'm not nearly as stoic as Jez, so you can believe me, I'd tell you."

"Good. That's good. I'm glad things worked out. And we're very glad to have you on board," he said, with a sort of dogged politeness.

There was another moment of awkward silence, and Tae exchanged glances with Ysbel.

Finally, Lev shook his head and took a seat at the table. "Alright. So. What have we found out so far?"

Tae sighed. "Nothing, yet. I'm just pulling it up now."

"Alright. While you do that, let's go over what we do know, so Galina is up to speed." He paused a moment. "Masha's plan, at least what she's told us of it, is pretty simple. Grigory's going to come after us. She's ensured that. His finances are hurting right now—he banked a great deal on being able to pull off the coup, and when we stopped him, and killed a large percentage of his people in the government, it dealt him a serious blow. So he won't be able to ignore another threat to his income. And as long as we have the patronage of Olyessa Janovik, he won't dare simply gun us down."

He paused a moment.

Tae glared down at his holoscreen as he worked his way through the security on the chip Jez had copied onto her com, trying to ignore the sick feeling in his chest.

It seemed like every time someone mentioned Masha these days, that same empty nausea rose inside him.

She'd betrayed them.

They'd all trusted her, and she'd lied to all of them, and set all of them up, but—well, but somehow it felt far too personal.

Because he'd honestly thought that no matter what happened, no matter how much she wanted something—she wouldn't do something to hurt them.

And instead—instead, she'd listened to the plans that they told her in full confidence, and worked against them. She'd withheld information that had almost gotten all of them killed. And she'd set them up. They'd killed fifty people, without realizing what they were doing. He'd been trying to bloody well save lives, and instead, they'd killed fifty people. And the sickest part of it was, those people had died just so Masha could give Grigory a black eye, so he'd come after them, and the crew would have to help her with this job.

"The pleasure houses?" said Galina at last. "That's why you brought me along, right?" There was a hard edge to her voice, and Tae glanced up.

Jez put an arm around Galina, and was watching her with a hint of concern.

Galina's expression was like stone.

"Yes," said Lev. "The pleasure houses. The majority of Grigory's income derives from there. We're going to set up a fake pleasure house in competition to his, convince him to invest his funds in the hope that he can take over the loan and then call it and ruin us, and then, once his funds are in the account Tae sets up—" he spread his hands. "He'll lose everything."

"That's not all, though," said Galina in that hard, quiet voice. "That's not the only thing we're doing. We're taking down the damn pleasure planet itself, right? Because that's the whole reason I agreed to this."

Lev gave her a small smile. "Yes. As I mentioned, I've studied Grigory's finances in depth. If we can convince him to invest in our fake house, he'll have to leverage his properties in order to do so. And the only assets he can easily leverage that would give him the funds he'd need are his pleasure houses. Once he's been taken down, he'll lose them, and if Grigory's pleasure houses go under, the entire place will implode."

"Good," said Galina quietly. "It's about time."

Jez pulled Galina in a little tighter and whispered something in her ear, her face still cut with concern. Galina turned to her with a small smile, and Jez kissed her softly.

Lev noticeably avoided looking at them. "Tae," he said. "Did you get into the chip?"

Tae nodded, and hit a button on his com. "I just sent the information through to the rest of you." He paused. "I don't know why Masha wanted it so badly. There's not a lot here that seems relevant. The bureaucrat Jez conned must have had connections with Olyessa, like Masha suspected—not surprising, since he was on Grigory's kill-list. We have her entire organizational structure here," he tapped his holoscreen and spread his fingers, enlarging the screen. "And then here," he swiped across to a new screen, "we have intel on all of Olyessa's big players, at least the ones connected with the government. But why we'd need to know this for the job we're pulling—" He trailed off, shaking his head.

Ivan pulled up his own holoscreen and looked down at it, frowning. His black hair curled across his forehead, and his short-cropped beard stood out against his olive complexion, a small line creasing between his eyebrows, but his face still held the mild good humour and cultured air had struck Tae when he'd first met Ivan in prison, and Ivan had stepped in to save Tae from the prisoner who'd been intent on beating the hell out of him.

Tae dropped his eyes quickly. He'd been watching Ivan longer than he'd meant to.

At last Ivan glanced up. "Lev, you probably have more inside information than I do, since you were working in the government until a year or so ago. But my family's in government, and I grew up hearing about who was in charge of what, and who was in or out of favour. This name right here, Veronika—" he tapped a name in the top of one column, "she's been rising in the ranks for some time now. She's the head of a cabal that doesn't always agree with the administration, so it doesn't surprise me that she's working with Olyessa rather than Grigory. Which means, there'll be a power struggle within the government soon. It's certainly useful information."

Lev nodded thoughtfully. "I hadn't been thinking of the political side of things, but you're right. Olyessa's mafia outfit has always been Grigory's rival, but she's never had the influence to be much of a threat. Until we pulled that job on Vitali, of course. If her people are gaining power, that will tell us something about her position, and by implication, her finances, and since we'll be working with her for as long as we're working this job, that's not bad information to have, I suppose. As far as we know, she still deals with Vitali, correct?"

Ivan frowned. "I hadn't heard—" he stopped, glanced at Tae, and gave a rueful smile. "Tae. One of these days, you'll have to finish telling me the story of what you lot have been up to."

"It's—a long story," Tae murmured.

"The short version is, Vitali won't work with either Grigory or the government, because Masha double-crossed all of them on our first mission as a crew," said Lev. "And if Olyessa wasn't implicated in that, she's gained significant power and influence in the interim. Which means she'll have plenty of credits, but she'll owe plenty of favours. And there will be people from Grigory's team who are itching to take her down. We may be able to use that in the future, although as Tae said, I'm not certain why it's relevant at the moment." He paused, and glanced around. "I'd like all of us to take a look at it. Look for anything you think would be useful. We're going into this blind, and Masha's proven she's willing to use us for her own ends. I'd like to have as much information as possible."

Tae bit down hard on his molars, fighting back another wave of sick anger.

He'd been stupid enough to trust her.

Lev sighed. "Alright. Jez, how close are we to the coordinates Masha gave you?"

Jez shrugged. "A little less than a standard hour, I guess?"

Lev nodded, and pushed himself to his feet. "Alright. That will put us in Olyessa's airspace, which I don't like. However, I suppose Masha's correct—even if Grigory's already hunting us, he won't come after us there. In the meantime, I'd better go talk with Masha."

Tae glanced up. "Shall I send the information through to her?" His voice was tight.

Lev paused a moment, then finally nodded. "Yes. I suppose we'll have to."

He turned and left, closing the door behind him.

"Well," said Jez, to no one in particular. "Guess I'll head back to my cockpit, if we're done here." She sighed, with the slightly euphoric expression she always got when she was thinking about flying, gave Galina a lingering kiss that made Tae turn his head away, and turned out the door.

When she'd left, Galina glanced around. "I—should go with her, I guess," she said, sounding for the first time somewhat unsure.

Ysbel shook her head. "Galina," she said, her tone slightly amused. "You're part of the crew now. You can go sit in that cockpit with Jez if you want, but if you want to go make sure your things are stowed, you can do that too. No one's going to throw you off."

"I'm—afraid I make things a bit—uncomfortable," Galina murmured, with a wry glance in the direction Lev had left.

Ysbel chuckled. "No, he and Jez make things uncomfortable. That's not your fault. And, to be fair, he is trying very hard." She paused. "He's not doing a very good job. But he is trying."

This time Galina did crack a smile. "Thank you." She paused a moment. "I don't know what happened, and I'm not going to ask. But I don't blame him for liking Jez. She's something special."

Ysbel snorted loudly. "Well, yes, she is. Depending on how you define that word. But I'm glad the two of you get along. Now, go."

Galina gave her that wry smile, and, after a moment's hesitation, turned to the passageway that led to the cockpit.

Once she was gone, Tae and Ysbel looked at each other. Ysbel was clearly trying to hold back a smile.

Tae rolled his eyes and shook his head. "Well, like you said. He is trying."

"You do have to give him that," said Ysbel. "Do you think everyone on this ship will survive the next few weeks?"

Tae chuckled reluctantly. "You know, once upon a time, when I first joined this crew, I thought the thing I'd be most worried about was the fact that people always seem to be trying to kill us?"

"Yes," said Ysbel nostalgically. "We were all so innocent back then." She shrugged. "But, she seems like a nice girl, anyways. I was a little surprised. I assumed whoever Jez brought back would be able to kill her with bare hands."

Tae shook his head, smiling slightly. "Who knows? Maybe she can. She knows how to use a heat-pistol anyways."

Ysbel snorted. "Can you imagine our pilot getting together with anyone who didn't?" She shook her head and stood. "I told Tanya I'd be back shortly. You sent the information to her com as well?"

He nodded.

"Good." She paused. "I—expect she'll be doing more in this job than I will. She has much more experience with this type of work."

Despite the tightness in his chest, Tae smiled as she stepped out the door. He'd noticed the strain between Ysbel and Tanya on Grigory's ship. But it seemed to have eased in the last few days.

Finally, it was just Tae and Ivan in the room, sitting at the table.

"Tae," said Ivan at last, pushing back his chair. His face was serious.

"Yes?" Tae looked over at him.

Ivan gave him a searching look. "Are you alright? Really?"

He sighed. "I—I'm fine."

"Tae." Ivan ducked his head until he caught Tae's eyes. "Honestly."

Tae gave a reluctant smile. "Yeah. I—" he paused a moment and blew out a breath. "I—honestly didn't think Masha would do that," he said at last, in a low voice.

Ivan watched him for a few moments. "I know," he said at last. "I'm sorry."

Tae shook his head in frustration. "I should have seen. Out of all of us, I was the only one who hadn't agreed to her plan. I should have seen, or guessed, or something." He sighed, and dropped his gaze. "We killed fifty people, Ivan. For no reason. We listened to Masha, and she used us to kill them. I—I knew better, I should have been watching her more closely, but—" He shrugged helplessly, and trailed off.

Ivan was still watching him, his face sympathetic. "I'm sorry, Tae," he said at last. "I wish I could have done something."

Tae gave a short, humourless laugh. "That's the thing. You couldn't have. You couldn't have known. But I lived on the streets for how many years? I knew damn well that not paying attention could get someone killed. And—and I bloody did it anyways."

"Tae," said Ivan softly. "You can't do everything on your own. And you shouldn't have to try."

Tae shook his head sharply, finally meeting Ivan's eyes. "Then who will? My whole damn life I couldn't ever afford to let something slide. If I did, my friends would die. And I bloody forgot that these past few months. I can't do that again. I—" He stopped quickly, choking back the lump in his throat, and turned away.

He'd wondered, for a few brief, stupid moments back on Grigory's ship, if Ivan might actually care about him as more than just a friend.

But—well, but he knew better. He wasn't the boy who Dmitri had somehow fallen for in the university, someone who could afford to laugh, and sleep in, and actually relax, have fun. He'd been stupid enough to be that person for a while. And then he'd damn well learned his lesson.

He wasn't someone anyone would fall in love with anymore. He couldn't afford to be. He was just the worried, stressed, overtired kid he'd been his whole damn life, trying to keep the people he cared about alive. And Ivan was kind enough to care about him anyways, like he cared about the rest of the damn crew, because Tae had helped him back in prison. And he was a good friend, but that was all, and Tae bloody well had to stop pretending it might be anything else.

Ivan studied him for a long moment, then gave a small smile. "Tae. Listen. You can't do everything. No one can. It wasn't your fault." He held out his hand, and after a moment, Tae took it and pulled himself to his feet.

But the sick knot that had been there since he'd pulled up his holoscreen on Grigory's ship and discovered what Masha had done, still sat heavy and cold in his stomach.

3

Jez tapped her fingers restlessly against the controls, her whole body tight.

She was plaguing flying her ship. She should feel more comfortable than she'd felt in ages. But somehow, the tight unease wouldn't go away.

"Jez? Are you alright?" asked Galina.

Jez glanced over at her. Galina was seated on the edge of the copilot's seat, like she wasn't entirely sure where she should be sitting.

"Yeah," Jez said, managing a small smile. "Yeah, I'm good. Just a bit—" She gestured vaguely.

"I know. You hate waiting for things, don't you?"

Galina had dimples, which should have been sweet, but on her were actually ridiculously hot.

"I—" Jez swallowed, and Galina's smile deepened.

It wasn't like they were actually in a relationship or anything. When Jez had staggered out of the gambling hall a week ago, she hadn't actually expected to see Galina again. And when Galina had called the next day, asked if she wanted to grab lunch, she'd mostly only agreed because she couldn't handle being in the same room as Lev right then. And she and Galina'd had a very long talk that evening, and Jez had made it clear that relationships weren't her thing, and this would only last until she had to leave in a couple days. And Galina had just gotten out of a disastrous relationship of her own and wasn't looking for anything long term anyways. So that had been that. But then Galina mentioned she knew people who'd gotten out of the pleasure planet, and when Jez had brought her aboard the *Ungovernable* and told the others, Lev had asked Galina, surprisingly politely, if she would be willing to come along to help.

And anyways, now here they were, at least until this job was done. And Galina was smiling up at her through her lashes, and the thing was, Jez might have been absolute crap at relationships, but she knew a come-on when she saw one.

She wasn't exactly sure how long they'd been kissing, but they were both in the pilot's seat and tangled together so thoroughly that she wasn't sure anymore where Galina left off and she began and also wasn't sure it mattered, when someone cleared their throat behind her.

Reluctantly, she pulled away from Galina just enough to glance over her shoulder.

Masha stood in the doorway, one eyebrow raised.

"Kinda busy here," Jez drawled.

"I can see that," said Masha, disapproval and amusement mingling in her tone. "However, I was wondering if you could spare the attention to tell me when we might arrive."

Jez winked at her and turned to the holoscreen, pulling Galina a little farther onto her lap, one hand settled firmly on Galina's very nice butt.

Galina didn't seem to mind in the slightest.

"About—" Jez frowned and peered closer at the screen.

Five red dots, that hadn't been there a few moments before, were coming in fast.

"Just a sec, Galya," she murmured, tapping the holoscreen and enlarging it for a closer look.

Short-haul ships, and they looked to be heavily armed.

Galina glanced at the expression on her face and slid off Jez's lap. Reluctantly, Jez let her go.

"I'll get out of the way," she whispered. "I'll wait for you on the main deck when you're done."

She gave Jez a quick smile and slipped out the cockpit door.

Jez looked after her fondly for a moment.

Galya was a surprisingly good friend, even without taking the kissing into account. And the kissing was a definite bonus.

"Those are Olyessa's ships," said Masha quietly, coming to look over her shoulder.

"Yeah? Well, I thought we were coming out into that bastard's airspace so it would be nice and peaceful while you chatted with her. Doesn't look like that's going to happen. So these plaguers better hope their ships are fast, because I'm about to do a hyperdrive jump."

"Wait," said Masha, putting a hand on her arm. "I think perhaps it would be best if we spoke with them. Olyessa clearly sent them, and we can't afford to lose her support."

Three other ships had appeared on her other side. Jez gritted her teeth.

"Paging Masha Volkova," came a harsh voice over the com. "Please stand by."

Jez mashed the com. "You'd best stand by your damn selves, you plaguers. Or else I'll ask my gunner if she wants to use something as ugly as you for target practice."

In response, a shot cracked out from the lead ship. Jez swore through her teeth and jerked back on the controls, and the shot skimmed the edge of their shields.

No using the hyperdrive, then. Couldn't risk an off-balance jump, not a second time.

She slapped the internal com. "Ysbel, get—"

Masha hit the com as well. "No," she snapped. "Stand down. We can't risk shooting at Olyessa's ships."

"Well, they don't seem to be playing by same damn rules," Jez growled, yanking the ship out of the way of another shot. "You want me to just play hopscotch with them while we sit around and talk this over?"

Three more ships appeared on her holoscreen, then two more. Jez closed her eyes for half a second, letting her fingers go loose on the controls.

Her heart was pounding, because hell, she'd been flying crap with people shooting at her for her whole life, and honestly, this was usually the part that made everything worth it.

But there was an unfamiliar tension in her muscles, a tight knot in her stomach. Because the last time she'd been shot at, she'd almost lost her ship, and honestly, she wasn't sure she could handle that again.

Another shot cracked out, and she shoved their nose down, letting it pass just over their heads. Then she spun the ship lightly and punched the accelerator, and the *Ungovernable* shot through the narrow gap between two of the ships.

If she couldn't fight back, she could damn well make them work for it.

"Whenever you feel like it, Masha," she said. Even with the nausea churning in her gut, there was a grin spreading over her face.

They weren't shooting to kill. The blasts weren't strong enough for that. They were trying to disable her.

Well, they could damn well try.

There were two more ships in front of her, and she spun the *Ungovernable* and aimed straight for the nearest of them. They fired off panicked shots as she dove at them. She dodged, and at the last second twisted between the two ships, the *Ungovernable's* body almost scraping their hulls. The other five ships were after her, but they weren't firing, because at this point, any shot risked taking out one of their own.

She spun and dived back into the middle of them, and as they scattered in panic, she tipped the *Ungovernable* on its end and shot upwards.

"Masha, coordinates," she said through her teeth. "Or else I'm just going to make us a path for deep space."

"Pilot, stand down. You're surrounded," the voice through the com snapped.

She hit the com. "Yeah? Well, from what I can see—"

"Jez, please," said Masha, sliding into the copilot's seat. There was a faint tension under her words. Honestly, Jez was aching to either run or fight right now, she didn't even care which, but—

She took a deep breath and loosened her hands on the controls, and Masha hit the ship's com.

"This is Masha Volkova," she said blandly. "I was intending to speak with Olyessa, as she and I discussed earlier. We have an arrangement."

"She's changed the arrangement," came the rough voice. "And she'd like to speak to you in person."

Jez glance down at her screen.

With Ysbel in the gun tower, she was pretty sure she could give them something to remember them by, because there may be a lot of them, but hell, she was flying a ship that had Tae's shields and Ysbel's guns, and her as a pilot, and anyways—

Masha shot her a meaningful look that clearly meant 'please keep your damn mouth shut.'

"If you will put her on the line, I'm happy to discuss matters with her," Masha said, voice still bland.

"No. You'll follow us in."

There was a moment's pause, and then Masha said, "As I said, I'm happy to discuss the issue with her on a private com line—"

"You'll do as you're told," the speaker snapped. "You'll come, or —"

A shot flickered out from one of the ships, but hell, Jez had cut her teeth flying smuggler runs for Lena, and she'd been watching for it. She bumped the control stick lightly, and the ship dipped gracefully beneath the bolt of energy like a dancer taking a bow.

"Shall we show them what Ysbel can do?" asked Jez in a low voice.

"I don't think that will be necessary, Jez," said Masha pleasantly.

A moment passed, and then another. Jez's foot was tapping a beat against the cockpit floor, her fingers smoothing the control panel, and she almost wished they'd just damn well shoot again.

"If you'd like us to come, I suggest you send the coordinates through to our ship," said Masha, voice still calm.

"You'll follow us."

Jez opened her mouth to respond, caught Masha's quick glance over her shoulder, and somehow managed to shut it again.

"Very well," said Masha at last. "We'll follow."

Jez clenched her hands into fists as the ships gathered around them, hemming them in.

She could still get out if she wanted to, she was pretty sure of it anyways, and if she could use her damn guns—

"Lock onto my ship, pilot," said the voice.

Masha gave her a meaningful look, and finally, gritting her teeth and muttering curse words, Jez did as she was told.

"I damn well hope you know what you're doing, Masha," she said.

"As do I," said Masha, her voice still pleasant. "But it appears Olyessa is highly motivated to meet us in person. That may end up working in our favour." Masha gave her a sharp glance. "Jez—"

Jez rolled her eyes. "I know, I know. You don't want me to call Olyessa a bastard or anything. Fine. But just saying, if someone needed a picture of an absolute damn bastard, I'm guessing she'd be their model."

Masha's lips twitched slightly. "I don't necessarily disagree. However, working under the assumption that both you and I want everyone on this ship to survive this encounter, I'm asking that you refrain from stating that in front of her."

Jez grinned. "Just for you, you bastard, I'll give it a try."

"Thank you," said Masha, a small answering smile on her own face.

There was a tap at the door, and Lev stepped inside. Jez looked away quickly, but she caught the tightness around his eyes and the corners of his mouth.

"Masha," he said quietly. "You agreed to bring us onto Olyessa's base."

Masha nodded, but her posture had stiffened slightly. "Yes, Lev. Considering how badly we need her cooperation, I thought it best to acquiesce."

"Without consulting the rest of us?" he asked, in that same quiet tone.

"There was not an opportunity for consultation."

Lev raised an eyebrow, and Jez glanced between the two of them, her stomach tightening.

Because—well, Lev was right. Masha had used them once already. And Jez had tried not to think too hard about the fact that she and Lev had killed fifty people, blown them to shreds, because they'd trusted Masha and she'd lied to them, but it still woke her up at nights sometimes.

And she should probably agree with Lev, and hate Masha like everyone else in the crew did, but—but somehow, she couldn't seem to. Because she couldn't bring herself to believe that the damn plaguer didn't care about them, didn't care about Tae and little Misko, and—well, and her. She couldn't believe that Masha would actually hurt her. At least, not on purpose.

Despite everything, somehow, she actually trusted that Masha was trying to do the right thing.

And so instead, she swallowed down the sick feeling that came every time she thought about what Masha had done, and the sick feeling that came every time the others discussed how to protect themselves against her, and she tried to pretend that everything was fine, and honestly, that may have been the reason why sitting still, even in her own damn cockpit, was making her completely crazy.

"I'm coming with you when you talk to Olyessa," said Lev at last, his voice still deceptively calm. "You're playing a game with us, Masha. You planned for this, and I intend to find out why. And when I do—" he let his words trail off.

There was a moment of strained silence.

"I would never have believed you would do otherwise," said Masha at last, her bland smile returning, but there was a tension behind it that hadn't been there before.

4

Lev closed his eyes for a moment as the ship lowered gently to the floor of the massive hangar bay. He couldn't actually pinpoint the moment when they landed—Jez was far too skilful a pilot for there to be any sort of a jolt—but he kept his eyes closed for a few seconds even after he was certain that they must have touched down.

Masha was waiting by the loading dock. She didn't say anything when he approached, just gave him that bland smile, and he found his heart beating faster than usual, a heady mixture of anger and worry.

Either Masha had planned for Olyessa to bring them here, and she wasn't going to tell him why, or else she hadn't planned for it, and Olyessa had found a way to throw her own wrench in their plans.

He wasn't sure which possibility was worse.

But at least he could keep an eye on Masha. And if he didn't know what she was planning, at least he could get enough information to hopefully make a contingency plan.

He smiled at her in return, but it didn't reach his eyes. "Masha. I'm almost surprised you waited."

She raised one eyebrow at him. "I certainly hope I'm not that much of a villain."

"Well. I had also hoped you wouldn't play us for fools back on Grigory's ship, but then, we don't always get what we hope for."

Her smile didn't falter, but he thought he detected a flicker of something in her eyes.

If it had been anyone but Masha, he might have said it was regret.

She watched him a moment longer, then turned back and hit the loading ramp controls. The ramp hissed, and steam from the releasing pressure curled around the edges as it tipped open. It lowered gently to the ground, and he followed Masha out.

The hangar bay was large, the air hot and so dry he had to choke back a cough as he stepped off the ramp. As in Grigory's ship, there was a loose half-circle of boyeviki waiting for them. The colours of their jackets were brown and orange, as opposed to Grigory's blue and gold, but their expressions were an identical grim.

The leader gestured to two of the boyeviki, and they stepped forward, patting Masha and Lev down for weapons. When they were satisfied, the leader stepped forward. "Follow me," she said.

Lev glanced at Masha, and they followed the woman through the hangar bay doors and into the attached compound.

The compound itself was breathtaking. The floor sloped gently downward, while the ceiling sloped up. The result was a massive, airy room that felt almost like being out of doors. Small ponds dotted the grounds, and running fountains made a low, soothing murmur, filling the air with the scent of water and warm growing things. Plants lined the ponds, and although the few skylights were nothing but grey masses of whirling sand, the artificial lights glowed with the pleasant tinge of sunshine. Flowers bloomed on trees and bushes, and the smell was light and sweet.

It should have felt refreshing. But the hiss and whine of the blowing sand against the skylights grated on the edge of his hearing, and the strangely shifting shadows from the natural light were a constant reminder that this entire place was one crack, one mistake, one miscalculation away from a force that would rip it to shreds.

It set his teeth on edge.

He shook his head, and tried to force his thoughts onto more practical matters, tried to ignore the way the boyeviki had moved closer around them, not even pretending to hide their weapons now.

He couldn't imagine Masha making a miscalculation grave enough to get them both killed, and he assumed she still needed him, at least for the present.

He glanced around again. The amount of credits it would take to maintain something like this on what was clearly a desert moon was almost unthinkable. How much of this had come in the past two months, he wondered, since Masha had first declared war on Grigory and the government by double-crossing them both and blowing up their relationship with Lev's weapons-dealer uncle?

They walked down a winding path, then through a smaller doorway that led to a hall with polished stone floors and an arching ceiling painted in airy colours. They must be underground now, because the whine of blowing sand and the eerily shifting shadows had been left behind. But he could still feel the palpable sense of unease.

He smiled to himself wryly. Of course, that could potentially have been influenced by the fact that he was completely defenceless, and surrounded by armed guards who looked distinctly unfriendly, and walking straight into the compound of a woman who could order his death with the raise of an eyebrow or the gesture of a hand.

When they reached the door, the man leading them touched his com and muttered something into it, and the door slid open almost soundlessly. Their guide beckoned them inside, and for the first time since leaving the ship, Lev was suddenly, acutely aware that both he and Masha were unarmed.

It hadn't escaped his notice that Masha hadn't protested when they'd been asked to disarm.

Masha hesitated for the briefest moment, and for just that moment he saw the stiffness in her posture, the strain under her casual expression.

Whatever it was she'd planned here, she wasn't a hundred percent certain it would work.

And then it was gone. She smiled and stepped into the office, and warily, Lev followed.

The room was large and comfortable, with sitting cushions placed strategically throughout, and a small fountain bubbling in one corner. In the centre of the room was a simple desk made of a light, polished wood. It was expensive, of course, built out of the best of materials, but it didn't scream opulence like Grigory's had. It was intentionally understated, a kind of folksy charm in the design that might have been at home in a small, comfortable cottage in the woods outside Prasvishoni. And behind the desk, a woman, with a wrinkled, grandmotherly face, who he immediately recognized as one of the most cold-blooded killers in the system. Another of them, anyways. At this point, he was well on his way to being on a first-name basis with every power-hungry, conscienceless murderer in the damn Svodrani system.

"Masha Volkova," she said, in her rustic accent. She was smiling, but Lev could see the cold calculation under those warm brown eyes. "And who might your companion be?"

He met her gaze cooly. "Lev. Formerly of Prasvishoni."

"I see. And why did the infamous Masha choose to bring you onto her crew, Lev?"

He didn't drop her gaze, kept his expression bland enough that Masha would have been proud. "I'm good at remembering details, I suppose."

She knew every last detail of his file, he was certain. But if she wanted to play this game, he would oblige.

She smiled, her face wrinkling into comfortable smile-lines, but the expression looked ever so slightly off. Then he realized what it was. The smile-lines around her mouth were deep and obvious, but the smile-lines around her eyes were all but non-existent.

This was a woman who smiled often, but not a woman who was easily amused.

"A pleasure, Lev." She studied him for a moment, then turned back to Masha. "Masha," she said again, as if tasting the name in her mouth. "It's good to finally meet you in person. Negotiating over holoscreens and coms just isn't the same. I was so upset when I heard you'd gone to meet Grigory first. He's always been a quick one, that Grigory." There was a hint of humour in her voice, an old woman laughing at her own foibles. "But I guess I should count myself lucky that I wasn't the one on your bad side."

Masha shrugged slightly. "Grigory killed my parents. When I was a child," she said, in that calm, even tone of hers. "I felt it was only just that I should take something in return."

Lev just managed to stop himself from turning to stare at her.

She was probably lying. She must be lying. Why would—

And then he remembered the look on Jez's face, before they'd ever set foot on Grigory's ship, every time they mentioned Grigory's name, the way her eyes would dart towards Masha and then away.

She must have known. Masha must have told her at some point. And that didn't mean it wasn't a lie, but—well, but Jez wasn't the kind of person who would be easily taken in by a lie.

And he was slightly surprised at the pang in his chest as he realized he had no idea what Jez knew and what she didn't. Because this entire time, he'd always been so damn sure he knew everything that he'd never bothered to ask. He'd somehow never imagined that she'd know something important and not simply volunteer it.

He frowned. Had he always been this much of a damn stuck-up idiot and just not noticed it, or was he actually getting worse?

He wasn't sure which option he liked least.

Olyessa watched Masha, and she didn't seem surprised in the slightest. "My condolences," she said, and a calculating note glinted through her folksy rural accent.

Lev studied Masha from the periphery of his vision. The only reason he could see the slight tension in her posture was the fact he'd known her for so long, worked together with her over and over in situations where seconds seemed like hours and minutes passed like days and their lives and the lives of the rest of the crew hung in the balance.

But it was there.

"I appreciate the sentiment," said Masha. "However, I'm sure you wouldn't have sent your boyeviki to shoot at us unless you had something you wished to discuss."

Olyessa smiled, that smile that was meant to be homey, but didn't quite reach her eyes. "You're right. There is something I wanted us to talk about."

She leaned back in her chair, as if contemplating her next words. Her eyes were half-lidded, and if you didn't see her posture, the small hints of readiness under the placid exterior, you might have mistaken her for an old woman laying back to enjoy the sunlight.

But he'd seen the coldness in her eyes, and he'd read her file.

"You told me you planned to open a pleasure house to compete with Grigory. Or at least, that's how you want it to look. You've bated Grigory to make sure he'll come after you, and you needed my credits to set up, and my protection to keep him from just knocking you off."

Masha nodded.

"And I agreed. But then, just now, you robbed one of my people and stole the information off his chip, and it made me think. The reason you've kept yourself alive when you've made so many enemies, Masha, is that you never leave things to chance. And here I was, leaving things to chance."

"You requested a tracking device on our ship, and a security interest in the property I purchased," Masha said, raising an eyebrow slightly. "I wouldn't say that's entirely leaving things to chance."

Olyessa chuckled. "But you would have been much more careful, wouldn't you?" She leaned forward. "So here's the new arrangement, Masha. I'm sending fifteen of my people down there. They'll arrive on the pleasure planet shortly after you do. And I'll need collateral. Something that's as valuable as the funds I'm lending you, and as you know, that's a large sum." She smiled slightly. "There's only one thing you have that might possibly match that— your ship."

Lev felt ice forming in his stomach.

No one other than the crew knew how valuable the *Ungovernable* was, that it contained Sasa Illiovich's lost tech. At least, no one should know. Vitali knew where the ship had come from, but he had a vested interest in not broadcasting the fact that a gang of five ragtag ex-convicts had managed to rob him blind. And even if he did let that slip, he hadn't known what it was he had, or that Sasa's tech was on board.

This had been Masha's doing, he was almost certain of it—on purpose or not, that was the only way Olyessa would know.

And yet again, he had no idea what Masha's endgame was.

Ysbel looked up from her holoscreen and glanced around the cabin quickly. "Olya, my love, where's your brother?"

Olya glanced around the cabin as well, and shrugged. "I don't know, Mama. I think I heard him open the door a few minutes ago."

Ysbel swore under her breath and pushed herself to her feet. "You stay here, please. I'll go find Misko."

There was a tension in her muscles she couldn't get rid of.

They were on Olyessa's base, in Olyessa's hangar bay. And Masha and Lev had been gone for what seemed like a very long time now.

She wasn't used to sitting back and waiting while someone else made the decisions.

Tanya was on the main deck with Tae and Jez, likely preparing for whatever their backup plan was if things went sideways. And Ysbel was trying to track down her son, who'd likely stolen sweets and then hidden so he could eat them without being found out.

She took a deep breath.

Perhaps this was how Tanya had felt since they'd broken her out of prison.

Misko wasn't difficult to find, mostly because she could simply follow the trail of discarded ration pack wrappers. She found him huddled under the table in the mess hall, hands and face a sticky green, mouth full. He managed to mutter something about 'dirty plaguing scum-sucker' as she grabbed him by one arm and dragged him out.

She narrowed her eyes, and his expression went from sullen to mildly terrified. Which, she'd learned, was the only possible emotion that would motivate him not to swear, and considering Tanya's views on curse words for children, and Jez's unwavering determination to ensure Misko's vocabulary was at least as colourful as her own, was probably a prudent fear to instil in him if he wanted to reach adulthood.

"Come here, you," she said, wetting a cleansing cloth at the ship sink and mopping his face.

"I'm hungry, Mama," he said sullenly, as soon as his mouth was empty enough that he could speak.

"Yes, well, I have some vitamin rations for you then. You don't get to eat only sweets. It will make you sick."

He glowered at her. She glowered back, but the look that had in the past brought prison gang leaders into stammering submission had no effect whatsoever on her son.

"Ysbel." Tae's voice came through the headpiece. "Stand by. Lev and Masha are coming back on board. They'll be here in a couple minutes."

She glanced helplessly between her son in one hand and the damp, slightly sticky cloth in the other. "I'll—be there in a minute," she said through her teeth.

"Uncle Tae's a scum-sucker!" Misko shouted.

She tapped her com off against her thigh and glared at him. "And you are coming with me right now, you little terror," she said.

By the time ten minutes had passed, Ysbel was still in their shared cabin. She had, however, disciplined Misko twice for swearing, explained to Olya how antigravs worked, explained to Olya how force fields worked, explained to Olya how a heat gun worked, explained to Olya why the Svodrani system was named what it was, explained to Olya how space squid moved, explained to Olya the origins of the word "scum-sucker", disciplined Misko for sneaking off and stealing more dessert ration packs, fed Misko, fed Olya, fed Misko again, and explained to Olya how ration packs were packaged.

When Tanya slipped back through the door, smiling slightly at the scene, Ysbel shook her head wearily.

"My love," she said, "I don't think I've ever been so happy to see you in my life."

Tanya's smile widened, and she kissed Ysbel's cheek. "Good. I came to give you a hand. Everyone else is on the main deck already, and I think Masha has something important to say."

"She always does," Ysbel muttered sourly.

Tanya gave her a wry smile, then turned to their son, shaking her head. "Come on, you," she said affectionately.

Which was a good thing, as Ysbel was rapidly running short on affection at the moment.

By the time all four of them were assembled on the deck, the others had clearly been there for some time. Ysbel took a long breath, trying to force herself calm.

There was no reason that an entire day alone with two small children—her own two small children—should raise her blood pressure to the point of a potential heart attack, but there you were.

She glanced quickly around at the others.

Tae looked worried, and Ivan stood protectively just to one side of him.

Despite everything, she had to bite back a smile.

Tae was very smart in most areas, but … well, it was a good thing that Ivan seemed like the patient type.

Jez was leaning up against one wall, grinning casually, one arm around Galina's waist. Masha was as pleasantly expressionless as always.

And Lev—

There was a grim, worried look on his face, and he was watching Jez, and for some reason, Ysbel was almost certain that his concern had nothing to do with the fact that Jez and Galina didn't have enough room between them to let water through, and had a lot more to do with—well, with Jez.

With whatever Masha was going to tell them.

She frowned.

Masha glanced around at the crew gathered in the small space. "Well," she said in her blandest tone. "The good news is, our plans have not changed significantly. Olyessa does not want out of this deal, as she sees the potential benefits for herself as clearly as I had hoped she would." She paused.

"But?" Ysbel prodded.

Masha took a long breath. "She has two conditions. The first is, she is sending her people with us. That may not be a bad thing, all things considered. At the very least, it will make Grigory hesitate before he sends someone in to assassinate us. And second—"

She paused again, and Ysbel caught her quick glance in Jez's direction.

"And second, she—requests a security. On the *Ungovernable*."

The only sound in the room was Jez's sharp intake of breath. The pilot's face had gone completely bloodless, her expression stricken.

"What kind of security?" she whispered.

"It will be a physical tracker, installed on the ship," said Masha. "If our job fails, she'll own the ship. And to ensure we bring it to her, the tracker will allow her—"

"It would let her wipe the ship completely," Tae said quietly.

Jez turned to Masha.

Masha nodded. "I'm sorry, Jez. It's the only way Olyessa would agree to this."

There was a long moment of silence.

A cold anger was spreading up through Ysbel's chest.

All of this stank of a setup.

The ship was a thousand times more valuable than any amount of credits. It was priceless.

And Masha had put them in a position where it was impossible to refuse Olyessa's request. Ysbel had known that the moment she'd seen their ship turn and start after Olyessa's fighters to head back to her base.

They were on Olyessa's ground, and she'd take what she wanted.

Since that moment on the casino ship, when she'd learned what Masha had done, she'd known she'd never be able to trust this woman. But Jez—that ridiculous idiot Jez—still trusted her. And of course Masha knew that. And Ysbel wasn't entirely sure that Jez would survive this.

"Jez?" Galina whispered into the silence.

Jez closed her eyes for a moment.

"Listen," Lev said abruptly. "I won't agree to this."

"You're right," said Ysbel, looking away from Jez. She made no attempt to hide the anger in her voice. "We're not going to—"

"No." Jez's voice was barely audible. She swallowed hard. "Masha," she said with an effort. "Is—is there anything else we could do? Maybe ... maybe I could stay instead. As security, I mean."

"You can't," said Masha quietly. "We'll need you if we want to pull this off."

For a few more moments, Jez said nothing. She was breathing too quickly, and there was panic in her eyes.

Ysbel pressed her lips together tightly.

"Do you—do you promise we'll get her back?" Jez was almost whispering now.

"Jez," said Masha in a low voice. "I promise you. You won't lose your ship."

Jez didn't take her eyes off Masha. At last, she took a deep breath. "Alright then," she said, her voice almost choking. "Fine. We can— we can do it, I guess. If—if everyone else is OK with it."

She turned abruptly, and disappeared through the door to the cockpit.

Galina shot Masha a look of controlled anger and turned to go after her.

For a few minutes, no one spoke.

At last, Lev drew in a long breath. "Masha," he said.

"Yes?" Her tone was still fighting to be pleasant and calm.

"Masha. If you hurt Jez—" he broke off, voice choking.

Masha looked around the deck, the weariness in her face suddenly very apparent. "I don't ask you to trust me," she said. "But at least believe me when I say, there is tech on this ship I don't intend to lose, and I certainly don't intend to leave in Olyessa's hands. Perhaps that will give you some measure of comfort."

"Very well," said Lev in a quiet voice. "But if you do this to Jez— if you make her lose the *Ungovernable*—you'll lose us. Every last one. Because I will take my chances with Grigory over working with you, and I can guarantee that Tae and Ysbel will say the same. So. I suggest you think very, very hard about the choices you make."

"I always do, Lev," she said quietly. "I don't think you understand just how much."

"Masha," said Ysbel finally, letting her voice go completely emotionless. "Any favour you think I owed you was paid when I didn't kill you on the casino ship. So don't think I'd let anything stop me."

Tae said nothing, but the look on his face was one of someone who'd smelled something rotten. Ivan placed a hand gently on his shoulder, and Tae closed his eyes for a moment and took a deep breath.

"I am sorry," said Masha, her voice still calm, but there was a strain under it that hadn't been there before. "However, I was telling Jez the truth. I fully intend to keep the *Ungovernable*. Tae, I'm going to need some help from you to get everything ready."

Tae looked at her, his face still slightly twisted in disgust, then turned on his heel and stalked out of the room. After a moment, Masha followed.

Lev shook his head, face grim, and went out after them.

"Is Aunty Jez going to be alright?" asked Olya in a small voice.

Ysbel looked down, startled out of her reverie. Olya was watching her with a concerned expression.

Ysbel gave her daughter a small smile. "She will be fine, Olya. You know that pilot girl won't let anything happen to her ship, so you don't need to worry about it. Besides, I won't let anything happen to her, and nor will your Uncle Tae or your Uncle Lev. So it will be fine." She paused. "Let's go. You still haven't cleaned up your room."

When they'd reached the cabin, and the children were arguing sullenly in their bedroom about who's turn it was to make the bed, Ysbel turned to Tanya.

"I don't like this," she said quietly. "There's no way Olyessa should have known enough about this ship to want to use it for leverage. That has to have come from Masha. But I don't understand why."

"I don't like it either," said Tanya, shaking her head. "I don't know what Masha's playing at, and I don't like it."

They were quiet for a few moments. At last Ysbel said, "My love. I —I know I haven't been good before at asking your opinion. But— I'm worried about Masha. And I'm worried that there may come a time that it will be a matter of her life or ours."

Tanya studied her for a long time. There was that trace of hardness in her face that Ysbel recognized from her years in prison. At last, slowly, she nodded. "Ysi," she said. "On this, I believe you and I agree perfectly."

5

"Jez."

She looked up from the controls, and managed to paste a smile on her face.

Lev stood in the doorway. He looked almost as awkward as she felt. "Do you mind if I … I have the coordinates, if you'd like me to —"

"Yeah. Thanks. That'd be good." She looked away from him quickly, fixing her gaze out the cockpit window.

Lev sighed, and slipped through the door. A moment later, she heard the slight creak of the copilot's seat as he slid into it, and the sound of him letting out a long breath. And for a moment, something stung at the corners of her eyes, a knot rising in her throat, because once upon a time that sound had been maybe the most comforting thing in her life, the sound that meant that everything was as it should be. Back before—well, before everything had gotten complicated. Before she'd stupidly let herself get into a sort-of-almost relationship with him, and then broken up with him, and hurt him, and wrecked every last damn thing, before she'd opened the door to the suite a few days later and seen him half-undressed, kissing a woman she'd never seen before. And hell, he had every right to kiss whoever he wanted to, but somehow she'd still felt like someone had punched her in the gut.

He pulled up the holoscreen in front of him, and for a few moments they sat in silence. Finally, he said quietly. "Are you alright? I mean, with the ship and everything?"

"Yeah," she said. "'Course. I'm always alright."

He shook his head. "Galina told me that she was worried you were going catatonic."

Jez bit down hard on the back of her teeth, because there were damn tears trying to form in the corners of her eyes, which was absolutely ridiculous. "Nah. I'm fine. I just—I—"

He was watching her now, and she felt her grin falter.

"It's alright, Jez," he said quietly. "I don't know if it helps, but I think every last one of us threatened Masha with some sort of violence if she screwed this up. We're not going to let you lose the *Ungovernable*."

She stared at him for a moment, and this time she did have to blink back tears. "Yeah," she said softly. "Um. Thanks."

He was still looking at her, and she forced her gaze to the cockpit window in front of her, heart rate jumping.

Damn.

She'd been very careful, this whole past week, that no matter where she went or what she did, she wouldn't be alone with Lev. Because—well, because she'd quite frankly rather go up against every last damn one of Olyessa's fighter ships all at once than try to untangle that much crap.

"Jez?" he said at last, and there was something in his voice, something tentative and unsure, that made her glance over at him without meaning to.

"Yeah?" She wasn't actually sure how she managed to get the

word out.

"Jez." He paused, looking down at his hands. Finally, he glanced up again and caught her eyes. "I—I wanted to apologize."

She frowned. Her heart was beating so damn fast that maybe she'd just misheard.

He gave a small, wry smile. "I'm—afraid I made a mess of a lot of things over the past few weeks."

"I—I mean, I'm—" she swallowed hard. "I'm glad you found someone. I mean, we agreed, right? So I'm glad you … I'm glad you found someone you liked. She, um, looked like she's probably good for you."

The words stung in her throat, but hell, they were the truth.

He gave a rueful smile. "We're not actually together. But thank you. I'm—I'm glad you're happy as well. Galina is a lovely woman. But—well, but I could have handled things a lot differently, and I'm sorry. I. Um." He looked down again. "You—told me you didn't want us to be together because you didn't know how to do relationships. I—well, I suppose I don't either. I don't even know how to be a friend, apparently. I've screwed up a lot of things lately, I think." He looked up wryly. "Ysbel had to yell at me, and she was right, to be honest. But Jez," he paused, and there was something strangely vulnerable in his expression. "I—I'd like to learn to be friends, if—if you want. I'd like to try to be friends with you again. I won't ask you for anything more, I promise."

She stared at him for a long time, something painful swirling in her chest. And for a moment she was tempted to tell him she didn't actually want anything to do with him, because it was too much, and she couldn't handle it, and she didn't know if she even wanted to handle it at this point.

But—

But, well, the truth was, she missed him. She missed their companionable silences, she missed turning in the pilot's seat and seeing him there, bent over his holoscreen or staring out the front window. And she hadn't realized how much she missed him, not until that very moment, and the missing him rose up in her throat until it almost choked her.

"Yeah," she managed finally. "Yeah, I guess we could try that."

He smiled at her, for a brief, unguarded moment, and there was a sort of undisguised happiness and relief in his face she hadn't seen there in a very long time.

"Thanks, Jez," he said at last. "I—missed you."

"Yeah," she muttered, wiping at her eyes. "I missed you too, you bastard." She found she was smiling too, and something heavy and sick that had been sitting on her chest, almost choking the life out of her, had lifted, replaced by a sort of lightness.

She turned back towards the cockpit window, glancing down at the coordinates he'd sent to her com, and for a few minutes they sat in a companionable, comfortable silence.

And she honestly hadn't realized how badly she'd needed this. How much the thought of losing Lev had ripped away at her insides, and how having him back was like a heat-kit on a blast wound, soothing and cooling and somehow putting her back together.

He bent over his holoscreen again, and a few moments later, the landing coordinates popped up on her screen.

"That's the pleasure house Masha's purchased," he said. "I believe it has a small hangar bay. If you were anyone else, I'd say set down somewhere outside, but I'm certain you can put us down there if you want to. There's a gate in the city force field just a few streets down, I'll put that through to your com as well."

She nodded, and he looked up at her and smiled, and—and, well, it was a nice feeling. That she could just smile back without worrying about any of that other crap.

Her fingers tightened on the controls as she brought the ship down through the atmosphere on the planet. She'd never actually liked this place, and the same tightness in her stomach she'd felt the first time she came here reasserted itself.

She took a deep breath.

This time, though, it was different.

This time, they were coming to take the whole damn place down.

When she saw the city glimmering in the distance, she hit the throttle, and the ship leapt forward. She twisted them up on one side without slowing to skim through the force-field entrance, then yanked down the choke and dropped them neatly through the doors of a cramped hangar bay in the overgrown back garden of a huge, tumbledown building.

She pulled down the power to the ship, then turned to grin at Lev. "See, genius? You're getting better at this. One of these days you're not even going to look like you're about to throw up every time I fly."

"I'm—not certain you're correct," he muttered. "But one can only hope."

She winked, and he cracked a reluctant smile in return. Then she turned back to the cockpit window, a familiar weight settling over her.

It had been a long time since she'd been here, but somehow it had never totally left her mind, niggling in the back of her brain, popping up in her nightmares. The emerald green of the long grasses, the heat of the sun, the smell of dust in the air.

The girl's scream, as Jez ran down the cobbled streets.

She hadn't done anything back then. There hadn't been time, and besides, there was nothing she could have done, except maybe get herself and the rest of the damn crew killed.

But this time—This time, she was damn well going to do something. They all were.

She glanced over at Lev. There was a distant look in his face and a tight set to his mouth that told her he was thinking some of the same things she was.

She pushed herself to her feet and took a deep, steadying breath.

Anyways, might as well get it over with.

The others were gathered and waiting for them when she and Lev arrived on the main deck. Masha looked as calm and unruffled as ever, but there was a tinge of grey in her normally brown complexion, and a hint of exhaustion behind her eyes, and Jez frowned slightly.

It had been a while since she'd seen Masha look tired. She hadn't actually really thought, in the tangled, confusing mess that was Lev, and Galina, and Masha's betrayal, and everything else, about what this must mean to Masha.

Grigory had killed her parents, when she was just a kid. And this, now, was Masha paying a long-held debt.

Jez repressed a shiver.

She wasn't afraid of many things. But after the past few months, she was very glad that she wasn't on the ledger of people Masha wanted revenge on.

Well, at least not for anything big.

Masha turned to them, ignoring the venom in the glances of the others.

"This is what we'll be turning into a pleasure house. We're situated outside the pleasure district, and on the very outskirts of the city, which will make it much more difficult for Grigory to track who comes in and out, and should make it simpler to secure. However, I will caution you—it will take a great deal of work to turn this into anything resembling a viable pleasure house, and we do not have much time." She glanced around at them. "With that in mind, does anyone have questions?"

There was a moment of silence.

"I believe we've said all there is to say," said Lev quietly.

Masha nodded at Jez. "Very well. Jez?"

Jez hit the control panel, and the door hissed open.

The light from outside almost blinded her, and she blinked a few times before she ducked out the door and jumped from the slowly lowering ramp to the courtyard below. She rubbed her eyes hard, and looked around.

Then she whistled.

"You weren't kidding about this place being a piece of work," she said, turning in a slow circle.

From the air, the building and the courtyard surrounding it looked slightly decrepit, but still in decent shape. From the ground, though, she could see the tangles of rotting vegetation in what must have once been a garden, the broken stones of the fountains, the crumbling rot in the luxurious false front of the building, half-collapsed and exposing the dirty prefab blocks underneath.

"Believe me, I've been in worse," said Galina from beside her. Her voice was hard, and there was a grim tightness around her mouth.

"You OK, Galya?" Jez asked, turning.

Galina looked up and gave her a tight smile. "I'm fine. Just— brought back some memories."

Jez took Galina's hand, trying to force down the creeping sick nausea that standing on this damn planet brought. "Hey," she said quietly. "If you need to stay in the ship for a bit, take some time—"

Galina squeezed her hand and smiled up at her, and Jez's heart skipped strangely. Because hell, she didn't know how to handle crap like this, that was basically the exact reason she didn't do relationships. One of the reasons, anyways.

But the way Galina looked at her—like she trusted her. Like Jez was the place she felt safe.

From somewhere behind her, someone cleared their throat loudly.

She looked up, glaring.

Ysbel stood there, looking amused. "Come on, you two. We have work to do."

"Fine," Jez grumbled. "What are we doing?"

Ysbel gestured with her head to Masha. "Ask her. I'm on Misko duty right now."

Jez rolled her eyes and strolled towards Masha, not letting go of Galina's hand.

"Jez," said Masha dryly. "I'm glad you were able to join us. I'd like Galina's thoughts on the interior of the building."

Jez glanced quickly at Galina. Galina's face tightened momentarily, but she nodded.

"Alright," said Jez. "Let's go then."

They stepped through the doors into what had once been a spacious lobby, the high ceiling rising the full three stories of the decrepit building. On each of the two floors above, a falling-down balcony surrounded a wide walkway that overlooked the lobby, and behind it, Jez could see hallways leading away, lined with doorways on either side.

Galina's hand tightened in hers, and she glanced over. Galina's face was set, her eyes haunted, her expression hard.

"Galina," said Masha quietly. "I assume you have a working knowledge of what needs to be fixed up?"

Galina paused a moment, her eyes not moving from Masha's. "I agreed to help," she said at last, in a low voice. "But before I do, I need to know something. You're turning this into a decoy pleasure house. Who will be working in it?"

"The only people inside this house will be people who come of their own accord. I promise." Masha's voice was the same low calm as Galina's, but there was a serious note in it.

"And will they be safe?"

This time, Masha cracked a small smile. "As safe as it's possible to be, when the goal is to take down the mafia. I'll only allow people who can take care of themselves to act as entertainment. They'll have an emergency alarm, and we'll have an extraction plan in place before we let them go up. And they'll each carry a weapon as a last resort, in case things go in a direction we had not anticipated."

Galina studied Masha for a long moment, and Jez could feel her tension through their clasped hands. At last she nodded. "Alright," she said, and that strange hardness was back in her voice. She loosened her hand from Jez's and pulled up her holoscreen, frowned at it for a moment, then began sketching quickly. "These sections I'm marking we'll need to repair. Whatever I leave unmarked, we won't need to worry about. The courtyard will need to be repaired, of course, and the outside facing the street. I have some ideas."

Masha watched, a frown of concentration on her face, and Jez glanced around again at the empty, decaying building.

Dust settled thick in the air, cut through here and there with a bright shaft of light that illuminated the dust motes like sparks. The air smelled musty, as if it had been sitting undisturbed for far too long, and held the sharp, bitter undertone of something dead and long decayed, probably a rat carcass in a corner somewhere.

She shivered slightly.

She hadn't known Galina for long. But Galina wasn't a woman who was easily unsettled, and Jez was pretty damn sure that whatever they were dealing with, it was something she really, really didn't want to know the details of.

By the time Galina and Masha had moved to a dusty, half-broken bench shoved up against the wall to continue their conversation, Jez was almost climbing out of her own damn skin. She took a deep breath and tried to keep from tapping her foot against the floor. She'd already counted every one of the balcony railings that were still intact, and she'd calculated how far she'd have to stand back to take a running jump to hurtle the railings. Probably survive the fall, too, if you were lucky and landed rolling.

"Jez?"

She looked up quickly.

Galina was watching her, a small smile on her face even through the obvious strain. "I'm going to be here a while, I think. But at some point we'll need to get a sense of the streets outside. It will affect how we set everything up. You may as well do that, instead of dying of boredom in here."

Jez could have kissed her, and almost did.

Then she hesitated. "You … going to be OK here?" she asked.

Generally in a situation like this, her first instinct would be to run as far and fast as she could. But—there was something in Galya's face that made Jez want to stay. To—well, to protect her, somehow, which honestly, when you thought about it, was a bit crazy, since Galina was definitely the kind of girl who could take care of herself.

Still, there was something about that haunted look in her eyes that made Jez want to kiss the hurt away, not because she enjoyed kissing Galya, although she did, but just because she wanted to see her smile again.

"I'll be fine, Jez," she said, her dimples appearing, and damn it to hell, now Jez wasn't totally sure she wanted to leave. "I just—this brings back some memories. That's all. I told you about … about my friend—"

Jez nodded, something twisting uncomfortably in her chest. "Yeah. I—look, I'm sorry. You sure you don't want—"

"Jez." Galina cut her off with a small smile. "I've known you long enough to know you're about to drive yourself crazy. Go on. I'll be fine, I promise."

Jez paused a moment, torn between the probably ridiculous desire to make sure Galya was alright, and the desire to move before she honestly lost her damn mind.

"Go," Galya whispered. She stood and came over and kissed Jez gently on the lips. "I told you. I'll be fine. I'll call you on the com if I need you."

"Alright," Jez said, when she caught her breath. Damn, that woman could kiss. Honestly, it was almost a pity they were going to go their own ways after this was done. "As long as you're sure."

"I'm sure." Galina's smile was genuine this time.

Jez was already half-way out the door when Masha called, "Please don't get into trouble. I don't want to make our presence here any more obvious than it has to be until we're in a slightly less vulnerable position."

Jez half turned and grinned over her shoulder. "Come on, you bastard, I never get into trouble."

She pulled the door open and slipped out before she could hear Masha's response.

6

The feel of sunlight on her face, and of finally being able to move after standing still for what seemed like a million years, combined with the nervous unease that still lingered in the back of Jez's brain every time she thought of Olyessa's damn lock plugged into her sleek, lovely ship, made stepping outside feel like drawing in a first breath of air after almost drowning.

The streets outside were busy, foot traffic and skybikes mingling on the narrow, cobbled streets. The outsides of the buildings were painted bright colours, and the people walking past wore clothing cut in the latest style, colours a million years away from the drab practicality of Prasvishoni. Jez took a deep breath and stepped out into the bustle.

She wandered down the street, making cheerfully rude gestures at skybike drivers who cursed her for getting in front of them, and looked around curiously as she walked.

When she'd come here last time, they'd come in on the other side of the city, into the pleasure district. It had been crowded with foot traffic as well, but there it had been the rich scum-sucking bastards who were the customers, and their damn bodyguards and hangers on. These people looked like the kind of people who lived here, worked here, made a living on the streets. Alleys were packed with crates, and with people dressed in practical working gear unloading them from ships or loading them into buildings, and in the skyways under the city forcefield, small short-run in-atmosphere cargo haulers crossed the skies in a packed jam of ships and passengers. Some of the pilots shouted curses out the open cockpit windows at the other drivers, and she smiled at the comfort of the familiar sound. The smell of sunlight on stone and too many people packed into too small of a space mingled with the city smells of ships and food and cooking and engine oil.

Might look like a stretch, getting the high-class bastards out here to a pleasure house, but honestly, Masha's idea hadn't been that bad. There wasn't any ID in the forcefield gates, probably because no one who came here wanted anyone to know about it, and there was that cut in the field just a street or two down from their new place of business. Easy to slip down a street without attracting too much attention, if that's what you were after, and the streets themselves were wide enough that a whole group of bodyguards could follow you if they wanted to.

She passed a stairway at street level leading down to a dimly lit doorway. From the darkened entrance, she caught the sharp scent of alcohol, and the sweet, sticky scent of something distilled from manka-leaf, and a slightly mangled tune filtered through the cracks in the door.

She paused, and drew in a long, satisfied breath.

Looked like this damn city had places a person could entertain themselves even if they weren't a messed-up scum-sucking plaguer.

She turned down a slightly narrower street. There were more of the street-level entrances here, and the smell of alcohol and manka-leaf was thicker in the air, mixed with the smell of stronger drugs.

She could feel her grin widening, and she placed a hand on the heat pistol at her belt.

This was more like her kind of place, honestly.

Someone cursed from behind her, and she glanced back to see a skybike barreling towards her.

"Get out of the way, you plaguer," the driver shouted.

"Learn how to drive, mud-eater!" she shouted back with a grin.

She barely had time to notice the small sound before instinct made her throw herself against the wall. Three more bikes whipped past, and as she scrambled to her feet and dived into the nearest alley, one of the riders drew a long heat gun, raised it, and fired a long spray of heat at the bike in front of him. The man riding it caught a blast squarely in the back just before he rounded the corner a few metres ahead of Jez. He screamed and jerked the handles of the bike wildly as the air above him and around him blistered with heat, then slumped, falling hard and rolling to come face-up in the mouth of the alley where Jez had taken refuge. His bike hit the wall of a building with a sickening crunch as the three pursuing skybikes shot past.

Jez rolled to her feet and peered out the entrance to the alley.

The three skybikes pulled up hard at the end of the street, and the man who seemed to be the leader drew his heat pistol, a grim, satisfied look on his face.

The man on the ground groaned weakly, blood running down his face. He blinked, his eyes rolling in panic, then focused on Jez.

"Please," he whispered. "Help me."

It was a bad idea. Honestly, it was a terrible idea, because they'd just got here, and she was pretty damn sure Masha didn't want to get into any fights with the street gangs.

Still—

Three to one wasn't very fair odds.

And hell, bad ideas were kind of her specialty.

She grabbed the man by the sleeve, and he gave a strangled scream as she yanked him into the alley.

"Can you walk?" she hissed.

He groaned and shook his head.

"Then you'd damn well better learn how to fly," she whispered, tucking his arm over her shoulder and starting off down the alley as fast as she could manage.

The three on skybikes hadn't seen her grab him, she was pretty sure, but she was also pretty sure they'd put two and two together quickly enough.

The damn plaguer she'd rescued was heavy, and he wasn't helping much, but she managed to get him through the alley and out into the next street, just as she heard the sound of skybikes idling past the alley's far entrance.

"They're going to come after us," the man groaned.

Jez rolled her eyes. "Figured that out already. Come on!" She glanced around quickly, then dragged him into a stairwell set into the street, shoving him down so neither of them could be seen from street level.

The skybikes idled past a few moments later.

"Where the hell did he get to?" the leader growled.

Jez chanced a quick glance up over the railing.

He had his pistol drawn, and he didn't look happy.

"There was someone in the alley when we hit him," snapped the woman riding on the bike behind his. "Must have been one of Katya's people. She probably dragged him clear."

"Boss isn't going to like that he survived the hit," the leader said, and then they were out of hearing range.

Jez ducked back down into the stairwell.

The man she'd rescued slumped back against the wall, eyes half-closed, and Jez winced in sympathy.

Honestly, he didn't look good.

Then, from behind her, a hand slipped around her arm. "What have we here?" a voice crooned.

Slowly, Jez straightened. Her heart was pounding loudly in her chest, and honestly, she'd been wanting a fight for so damn long that her hands were practically aching for it.

She took a long, blissful breath, and in one quick move, jerked her arm free of her assailant's hand and drew her pistol as she spun and shoved him backwards. He took a staggering step back, missed his footing on the stairs, and put out a hand to stop his fall. She grabbed his elbow, spun him around, and shoved him up against the wall, her pistol pressed hard into the hollow under his chin.

"Hey now," she whispered. "Careful who you talk to on the street. Not all of them are as nice as I am."

He was a little shorter than she was, muscular, but not bulky, and a thin beard covered his chin. His dark brown skin had gone an unhealthy colour, and his eyes were crossing to see the tip of the gun.

She smiled at him. "Hey you plaguer, just realized you shouldn't pick a fight with someone if you don't know who they are? Don't feel bad, we all have to learn sometime."

"I—" His voice was blustery, but there was fear under it. She pushed him harder against the wall and shoved the muzzle of her pistol harder under his chin, so that it wobbled when he swallowed.

"So," she said, in a conversational whisper, "here's what we'll do. You're going to shut up. And you're not going to move so much as your damn eyeballs until I tell you to. And if you do that well enough, you might just be able to walk out of this without your insides cooked to well-done. Deal?"

The gun was digging too far into his throat to allow him to speak, but he nodded frantically.

"Good," she said, letting the pressure off the pistol slightly. "Always nice to deal with a reasonable person." She glanced around quickly.

The stairway they were in was narrow, and if he hadn't figured out how to signal to the people inside for help, he would soon. If he did, her options were a bit limited, seeing as she was on foot.

Still, she'd think of something if it came to it. Usually did.

From the corner of her eye, she could see the man she'd rescued whispering something frantically into his com.

Possibly another ambush—hell, whoever he was might have plenty of reasons to kill anyone who saw that crap in the street—but then again, what was life without a few chances?

"Alright," she said to the man in front of her. "You're going to walk back down those stairs and close the door behind you, and you're going to forget you ever saw me, OK?"

He gave a quick, nervous nod, but she noticed how his eyes flicked to the door.

She grinned wider. "Figure someone's coming out of there to save you? Because they could try, sure. It would just depend if they could get through that door and fire off a shot faster than I could pull the trigger. And I'll be honest, I'm pretty damn fast."

He swallowed. "I—don't know what you're talking about."

"Good," she said. "So—"

Abruptly his face tensed, and he hooked the toe of his high boot around her ankle and jerked it forward, just as the door slammed open and two figures appeared in the doorway.

It would have knocked her off balance and shoved her into their guns, but then she'd been expecting something like this. She threw herself to one side, her hip connecting painfully with the hard prefab stairs, and used her momentum to pull her captive around between her and the heat guns. One of them went off, and the man screamed as the sleeve of his white shirt turned to ash, then she shoved him backwards. One of the armed figures stepped back to avoid the tumbling body, and the other stepped forward to catch him, and in the confusion Jez scrambled to her feet, pulled the man she'd saved up after her despite his whimper of protest, and took the stairs two at a time, hauling him after her. Heat rippled the air over her head as they reached street level, and the man beside her stumbled, pulling her to one side.

She swore through her teeth, dropped him against the wall, and yanked out her own heat pistol, aiming for the first head to show above the stairwell.

And then three other bikes burst out of an alley, and as the first of her pursuers scrambled up the stairwell, the air crackled and hissed as the three on the bikes fired.

The man abruptly dropped back down, and a moment later, Jez heard a door slam hard.

She grinned to herself, and turned to face the new players.

The bikes that had appeared from the alley surrounded the fallen man, and one of the bikers jumped down and knelt beside him.

"He's alive," she reported, her voice grim. "Barely."

"Get him back to the boss," snapped one of the men still on his bike. "She's going to want to know about this. Those were Adric's thugs."

Then she stood and turned to Jez, face cold, heat pistol steady. "And who are you?" she asked, ice in her voice.

"She's crazy, whoever she is," the fallen man said weakly. "Pulled me out of the way of Adric's people and almost got both of us shot."

The woman turned back to Jez, expression thoughtful. "I assume you're looking for a reward?" she asked at last.

Jez shrugged, still grinning. "Dunno. What you offering?"

The woman narrowed her eyes, and Jez gave her a wink. "Hey now. Maybe I just figured three on one wasn't great odds." She paused a moment. "What the hell was that all about anyways?"

The woman gave her an odd look.

Jez shrugged. "New in town."

"We're Rims," the woman said at last. "The Blood Riots are trying to take this street, but it's our territory."

Jez raised an eyebrow. "OK, but I thought Grigory Korzhakov and Olyessa Janovik ran this place."

The woman scowled at her. "You think they run the streets? The Rims break for Olyessa, the Blood Riots go for Grigory."

Jez grinned at her. "Well. Figure that's a stroke of luck. Guess I do have a favour to ask after all."

By the time she got back to the pleasure house, she felt about a million times better.

You just needed something like that every so often, honestly. And, she figured having a street gang who'd agreed to watch out for Grigory's people and pass on the word would be something even Masha would be happy about.

But she almost forgot her coup when she stepped through the broken-down door of the pleasure house.

A hoard of construction workers had descended on the place like a plague of rodents, and the dust of something long abandoned had been completely replaced with dust from prefab and cut wood. The noise was almost enough to make her put her hands over her ears.

Galina stood beside Masha, directing the workers, and Jez

watched her for a moment, a fond smile on her face.

OK, so maybe she'd gotten together with Galya because she was damn hot, and in fairness, she was. But—well, but it felt good to see her like this. She looked like she was in her element, giving orders, shouting out instructions, consulting her holoscreen every now and then and calling out a correction.

She looked like she'd been born for this.

It had been a while since Jez had actually wanted to know the life story of the person she was sleeping with. Wasn't usually all that relevant, to be honest. But—well, for some reason, she was looking forward to a quiet talk in Galina's room almost as much as she was looking forward to what would hopefully come afterwards.

Galina looked up and noticed her. She said something to Masha, then closed down her holoscreen and crossed the wide open room to Jez.

"Jez!" she shouted over the noise. "Is everything alright?"

"Yep!" Jez shouted back. "Just learning about the place a little."

Galina nodded, opened her mouth, then shook her head. "Our rooms should be ready by tonight. We'll talk then." She paused a moment and glanced down, a hint of sharpness to her expression. "And I want to hear about how you got hurt. Do you need a first aid kit?"

"Nah, just a bruise," Jez shouted back. She paused a moment. "You—look like you're enjoying yourself."

Galina cocked her head to one side, then laughed and squeezed Jez's arm. "I suppose we each have our thing. Yours apparently is getting into fights, mine is yelling at construction workers."

Jez was still smiling as she watched Galina cross briskly back over to Masha.

7

Tae scowled down at the list of names on his holoscreen.

It was a compilation of everyone any of them could think of who might be willing to help out in this crazy scheme of theirs, which meant most of it was comprised of people Ivan or Tanya knew who they'd broken out of prison.

He was acutely aware of Ivan, sitting beside him and leaning to see over his shoulder.

"There," said Ivan quietly, reaching out to touch a name on the screen. "I think I can figure out a way to contact her. She'd come, I'm sure of it. And I have a handful of other friends who were arrested with me at the protests. She'll know how to get a hold of them."

His arm brushed Tae's as he drew it back, and Tae bit the inside of his cheek hard.

There was absolutely no reason why every damn time Ivan was sitting this close to him, his mind should keep going back to that moment on Grigory's ship, where the mafia boyevik had stepped into the room and Ivan had pulled Tae onto the couch and leaned him backwards, the warmth of Ivan's lips on his, the feel of his hands, the way the world had gone slightly hazy …

He gave a quick shake of his head.

They had plenty to do, and no time to do it, as usual, and this was the absolute last thing in the system he needed to be thinking about right now. He couldn't bloody afford any distractions, he'd thought he'd finally learned that lesson.

Anyways … anyways, last time he'd let himself fall for someone, it had just about broken his damn heart. And between Dmitri and Masha, he wasn't sure if he could handle having his heart broken again.

He gritted his teeth and tried to bring his focus back to the holoscreen in front of him.

"What about Radic?" asked Lev, from across the table. "Would he come?"

Tanya looked up and caught Ivan's eye, then turned to Lev with a wry smile. "I don't think we could stop him from coming. Even if we wanted to."

It was late, and they'd turned on the artificial lights after pulling down and fastening the heavy blackout blinds. When you were being hunted by the krestnaya of one of the most powerful mafia organizations in the system, making yourself a silhouette against a window wasn't the wisest plan.

A week into their stay on the pleasure planet, between Galina and Masha, they had a small suite of rooms that, if not comfortable, were at least livable. The floors were still bare prefab blocks, as were the walls, but the doors were solid, and they'd set up makeshift cots for everyone, as well as a slightly rickety table and chairs in the main room. They were gathered around the table, all except for Masha, who was doing whatever it was she did in the hours she spent pouring over her holoscreen, Ysbel, who was with the children, and Jez and Galina. They'd been here until about an hour ago, when Jez had stood and informed everyone in no uncertain terms that she and Galina hadn't had any time alone for the past five days, and now that they had doors on the rooms, they intended to remedy that.

Lev, to his credit, had hardly reacted beyond a slight stiffening of his posture, and had politely bid them goodnight. And if there had been a trace of grimness to his expression since then, Tae couldn't exactly blame him.

"Alright," said Lev, making a mark with his forefinger on his own screen. "If we can get Radic and Anya, that brings us up to fifteen. Ivan, you said you thought Anya could get you in touch with some of your other prison friends?"

Ivan nodded. "I'd say at least five, maybe up to eight or nine, depending."

Lev nodded. "Tanya? Do you have any connections you could use?"

Tanya looked up from her own holoscreen. "I believe I do. I could probably get … maybe ten more. Not much more than that, honestly."

Lev frowned down at the screen. "Alright. So Ivan, if everyone you think you might be able to contact made it, and Tanya was able to bring ten more—" he paused a moment. "That brings us to twenty-eight or twenty-nine." He bit the inside of his lip, still frowning. "That may be enough, barely. But we'll have to play some of the parts ourselves, if that's the case."

"I could play a part," said Ivan, and Tae didn't have to look at him to see the smile on his face. "I have some experience as a server, anyways. And as an added bonus, I'd be able to pick out most of Grigory's people, at least the ones who were on the ship with us, and I doubt they'd recognize me. That's the advantage of being a server —you're interchangeable for anyone else in the same uniform."

There was that familiar mild good humour in his voice, and Tae wasn't sure why his stomach clenched at the thought of Ivan in danger.

Actually, no, he knew exactly why. Because the last damn time he'd seen Ivan working as a server had been the time he'd been seconds away from being blown into bloody pieces if Tae hadn't solved the puzzle Zhenya, the mafia pakan, had set for him. And he'd solved with only seconds to spare.

Even the thought still had the power to make him shaky.

"You alright?" Ivan whispered in his ear in his kind, concerned tone, which did nothing to help with the shakiness.

"I'm fine," Tae whispered back, trying to keep the sharp worry from his voice.

"Alright," said Lev at last, putting a hand over his com to shut down the holoscreen. "I guess that's all for tonight. We'll put the call out first thing tomorrow morning." He turned to Tae. "How's the tech coming?"

Tae sighed and shook his head. "I'm wiring in the sound and camera systems, and the emergency alert system Masha asked for. I'm getting there, but it'll take time."

"Tae, listen," said Ivan, turning to him. "Don't run yourself ragged, alright? I've seen you when you get working. You need to sleep sometimes, too."

"Agreed," said Lev, and there was a touch of amusement under his voice. "Ivan, I'll put you in charge of making sure our tech-head gets enough sleep to be able to do his job."

Tae rolled his eyes, but he didn't dare look at Ivan, because it was late and he was tired and he was pretty sure that his brain would start doing things he really didn't want it to do if he looked over and saw the small smile-creases that formed around Ivan's eyes, and the concern in his face.

He had enough damn things to worry about right now. Like trying to keep all of them alive.

"Alright then," said Tanya, standing. "If that's all we're doing tonight, I'd better go. I don't know if Ysbel will survive Misko much longer than this."

Tae bit back a small smile, despite everything. Ysbel was right, this was Tanya's expertise at the moment. But the thought of the gruff, taciturn mass murderer being run ragged by her six-year-old was more amusing than it probably should be.

Four days later, Lev stood on the balcony beside Tanya, looking down over the open lobby below.

It was almost unrecognizable from the place it had been a week ago. Every trace of decay and rot had been swept away, replaced by a decadent grandeur.

What he'd always imagined a pleasure house would look like, honestly.

The courtyard outside was the same, the grass short and soft, the bushes and trees covered in blossoms that released a thick, heavy scent that was almost oppressively sweet, and gilded alcoves walled off tastefully here and there.

And, of course, the part he was least happy about.

The cages, displayed in the centre of the room, the bars gilt an opulent rose-gold.

A place to display the entertainment.

He'd felt slightly sick the first time he'd realized what the workers were constructing. He still felt sick just looking at them, if he were being honest.

"So," said Tanya quietly. "What do you think?"

He closed his eyes and took a deep breath.

It had been just under a week, and they'd all been working hard enough that they probably could have fallen asleep standing up. Galina, especially, had been working herself ragged, to the point that Jez had intervened and told her that if she didn't get some rest, Jez was going to lock the damn bedroom door and sit outside it to make sure she didn't come out.

He pressed the heels of his hands into his eyes for a moment. The list of things that absolutely had to be taken care of felt like it was tattooed into the backs of his eyelids, but he was so tired that he wasn't sure he trusted his memory.

He looked up at Tanya, and saw the same weariness behind her eyes.

"In a perfect world, we'd have a year to set this up," he said. "Even six months would be something, although that would be pushing it."

"And we've had a week," said Tanya, that quiet humour in her voice.

He nodded with a wry smile. "Yes. That's about the size of it. But —considering our time frame, I think we're as ready as we're going to be."

Tanya nodded, and they looked out over the lobby again.

The vaulted ceiling stretched up in a huge dome, heavy with gold paint. The floors were smooth, polished stone, a light grey marbled with gold. Yes, it was just a thin layer painted over prefab blocks, but from here it looked genuine, and absurdly expensive.

Tae was huddled in one corner, working, Lev hoped, on getting the security system up and running.

And in front of every door, one of Olyessa's grim-faced boyeviki stood, weapons displayed prominently in holsters.

They were taking no part in the proceedings, and for that, Lev was heartily grateful.

Yes, he understood their necessity. But the fact that they were under the constant watchful eyes of at least six people with the firepower, and probably the inclination, to murder them all, was not comforting.

He turned back to Tanya.

She gave him a small smile. "Well?"

"I suppose there's no point in putting it off longer," he said.

She gestured him ahead of her, and he crossed over to the long, spiralling staircase. There were lifts, of course, but right now there was a tight knot of nerves in his chest, and he'd much rather be moving.

He tapped his com. "Masha?"

"Yes, Lev?" Her voice was as calm as always.

"Could you meet me in the lobby, please?"

"Of course." Her line clicked off, and he took a deep breath and crossed the wide, open space to where Tae sat in the corner.

Tae glanced up at his approach, still scowling in concentration.

"How's it coming?" Lev asked.

Tae sighed and shook his head. "I'm getting there. It's a complicated system if we want it to do everything you and Galina asked for."

Lev nodded, and for a moment they were silent. At last Tae sighed, familiar worry in his face. "We're going to put the word out?"

Lev nodded. "Time to let Grigory know we're here."

Tae paused a moment, reluctance clear in his posture. "You know once we do this, we're committed. Whether we're ready or not."

Tanya raised an eyebrow. "Well, on the bright side, I imagine Grigory has already repaired his ship and started to look for us. So either way we're about to be hunted by a mafia krestnaya whose entire reputation depends on how gruesomely he can kill us. I don't know that there's all that much to lose."

Tae stared at her for a moment, then shook his head, smiling reluctantly. "I'm not sure how I ever managed to sign on with a crew that thinks that's the kind of thing that will make me feel better," he muttered. "Alright, let's get it done, I suppose."

Masha was waiting for them over by the grand lobby check-in. She was dressed, as usual, in her worn pilot's coat, and the strain and exhaustion under her expression were barely visible, unless you knew her as well as Lev and the rest of them did. And for a moment, Lev felt a strange pang. Because if he were being honest with himself, he'd valued Masha's insights. He'd never completely trusted her, but he'd believed her. And he'd enjoyed working with her.

That had been what she'd wanted, of course, because that was the only way she could have betrayed them like she had.

But he hadn't expected how much losing that friendship—if that's what it had been—would hurt.

He gave her a pleasant smile as they came up to her. "Masha. I believe we're ready."

She smiled back. "I expected nothing less." She glanced at Tae. "Something subtle, I think. He needs to know what we're doing, and who is doing it, but if we make it too obvious—" she shrugged. "He's an intelligent man. I'd hate to insult him."

Tae gave a brief nod, his lips pressed tightly together. Lev glanced at him from the corner of his eye.

Tae had taken Masha's betrayal harder than any of them, and he hadn't spoken more than a handful of words to her since that evening on the casino ship. If Lev hadn't known Tae like he did, he might have thought it was anger. But he could see the sharp hurt behind the kid's stoic expression, and he was certain Masha could as well.

"I'm turning the com to the general channel," Tae said quietly. "It will be in with the rest of the chatter, but I've tagged it just a bit. Not enough to be noticeable, but enough that this will rise to the top of the noise, and replay a few times." He paused a moment. "Start talking. I'll hit the com part-way through the conversation."

Lev nodded and took a deep breath. "Alright." He turned to Masha. "How close are we, do you think?" he asked in a low voice. From the corner of his eye, he noticed Tae hit the com button half-way through his sentence.

"Close enough," said Masha, in the same low tone. "I think this will be everything we need it to be. I have a feeling business will be flocking to our section of town. This should be a very profitable endeavour."

"In addition to its other advantages," said Lev. He paused a moment. "Well, at any rate, I suppose we may as well get the word out. No point in keeping it secret much longer."

Masha hesitated. "I'd prefer to wait until we're no longer vulnerable," she said at last. "But, as you say—" She sighed. "I doubt that particular vulnerability will go away until we've been running for a few months' time. So I suppose you're right."

Half-way through her last sentence, Tae tapped the com off, and gave them a quick nod. Masha stopped speaking, and she and Lev turned to him.

"Well," said Tae after a moment. "Every word you said is out there now. And if what you guessed is correct, and he's got someone scanning the general lines, there's no way he misses that."

For a moment they were quiet, looking at each other. Masha's face was unreadable as ever, Tae's expression was hard, and Tanya's eyes were narrowed, her face slightly grim.

"And you think we can pull this off," Lev said, turning to Masha.

"You do, at least," she said. "Or you wouldn't have followed me here."

"There's a difference between necessity and reasonableness," said Lev. "You didn't give us much choice."

"Well," said Masha briskly, "at the very least, you believed that this had a higher chance of success than simply letting Grigory hunt you down. Based on my past experiences with this crew, I would say that gives us a higher chance of survival than ought to be possible for this sort of endeavour." She paused. "At any rate, we don't have time to worry about it now. I give it a week before he contacts us, maybe less, and we have plenty left to do in that time."

She turned briskly and strode off, and Lev watched her go.

"Well, we know she'll survive it, at least," Tae said under his breath. His tone was sharp and bitter.

Lev turned to him, and managed a slight smile despite the worry clenching in his chest. "I suppose then, it's up to us to make sure the rest of us do as well."

8

Tae was just stepping out of his room, blinking against the light and tying the laces on his tunic, when someone clapped him on the shoulder hard enough that he almost staggered.

"Tae!" said a familiar voice, and he turned in surprise to see Radic.

The lanky man was smiling broadly. His face was burned three shades darker than it had been in prison, his dark hair longer than the regulation prison length and the scar on the corner of his eye lending a rakish look to his appearance.

"When did you get here?" asked Tae, smiling despite himself. "What have you been doing since prison?"

Radic winked. "Keeping busy. Like usual. Honestly, it's just as well you called me, because I happen to have gotten on the bad side of the police on the planet I was lying low on."

Jez's door opened, and Jez stepped out, grinning broadly. "Radic, you dirty cheating bastard! Thought the police would have thrown you back in prison ages ago!"

"Hey kid, who you calling a cheat?" Radic said. "If I recall correctly, you were the one who cheated me out of my lunches for a week when they punished me by sending you as my cellmate." He crossed over to her in two strides and grabbed her in a bear hug. "I see you're as scrawny as ever."

She hugged him back. "Yeah? Well, since you're as ugly as ever, guess that's only fair."

They were both grinning delightedly, and Tae shook his head in a sort of bewildered amusement.

There was a soft chuckle from beside him, and he turned to see Ivan standing next to him, smiling.

"Between those two, I'm not sure any one of us will make it through this alive," he said in a low, amused voice.

"Well, there certainly won't be a dull moment," said Tae wryly.

Ivan chuckled again. "He got in this morning. He said there should be a few others coming in on the transport ship later today, but he hitched a ride on one of the cargo ships."

Galina emerged from Jez's room, blinking, and Radic turned to her, raising his eyebrows. "Alright Jez, introduce me to your friend."

"Sorry you bastard, she's taken," said Jez with a grin, slipping her arm around Galina's waist. "Also, she's your new damn boss, so you'd better learn some respect. Galina, this is a skinny plaguer I met in prison and taught how to play fool's tokens."

"Hey kid," said Radic in mock offence. "I'm not sure that 'cheating someone blind' is in the definition of teaching. And whatever the hell you were playing, pretty sure it wasn't fool's tokens."

Tae rolled his eyes at Ivan. "Come on, let's get some breakfast. Those two will be insulting each other for at least another twenty minutes."

By the time breakfast was finished, three more of Ivan's and Tanya's prison friends had arrived. Tae smiled at one of them, a young woman with a wide smile and a businesslike air. "Hey Anya.

It's good to see you."

She grinned back at him. "Good to be working with you again. I know tech, but I've never seen anyone do what you do. I'd have come just for the chance to watch you, maybe pick up some tips."

Ivan was greeting the others. He turned to where Tae and Anya stood, a broad smile on his face. "Tae. I'm not sure if you remember these two. This is Artur and Lia. Artur, Lia, Tae. The one who saved all our lives in that prison breakout."

Tae looked down, heat rising to his face. "It's—nice to meet you again," he muttered. "Um. I think Lev wanted everyone up in the conference room." He turned to Anya. "Have you eaten yet? Grab some breakfast and come up when you're ready."

For some reason, though, the sight of Radic's and Anya's familiar faces seemed to have loosened the tight knot in his chest that had been there since they landed on this damn planet.

By the time they were all up the stairs and gathered in the conference room, their number had swelled by another four.

Lev was bent over his holoscreen, frowning, and Masha sat beside him, wearing her usual bland smile. Lev glanced up as they entered, then shut down his screen and stretched, wincing slightly.

"Alright," he said, when everyone had taken their seats. Jez and Radic were in the back of the room, swapping increasingly unbelievable stories and increasingly offensive insults, both of them grinning broadly. Galina came in after them, but Lev beckoned her over and cleared his throat.

"Alright," he said, into the silence that was punctuated only by Jez and Radic's whispering.

He cleared this throat again and scowled in Jez's direction, and finally she looked up, gave him a wink, and stopped talking.

"Alright," Lev said again. "This is Galina Drosdova. She's going to be organizing this. Masha and I have asked you to come because of skills you have that we may need. However, we have limited resources. No matter how valuable you may be as a hacker or a pickpocket, we'll need you to take a role. We don't have the time or space for people who can't. Galina will give you the parts each of you is to play. I don't need to tell you how vital it is that what we do here looks completely genuine. The people we're working against will not hesitate to kill every last one of us in very painful ways if they for one moment suspect anything is off. So I'll need your commitment to work as hard and as long as it takes to make this perfect, understood?"

He glanced around the room, and Tae followed his glance. The looks on everyone's faces were serious, but there was an air of repressed excitement.

"This will be dangerous. As you all know, we're pulling a sting on Grigory Korzhakov. And we intend to take him down completely," Lev said into the silence. "You'll be paid, but there's no way to compensate you for the kind of risks we'll all be taking. Do this because you believe in it, or don't do it at all."

"Or," said Ivan quietly, "do it because there are people here you believe are worth the risk."

Tae didn't dare look at him, but he felt his face heating again.

Ivan wasn't talking about him, damn it. He was talking about the fact that these people were old prison friends, and he'd damn well better remember it, and honestly, he had no idea what was wrong with him these days.

And he couldn't afford to forget himself like this.

He could feel Ivan's quick glance in his direction, but he wouldn't meet his eye.

"Nothing's happened yet," Lev continued. "If you want to back out, we have the funds to pay your return passage. So now is the time to speak up if you're having second thoughts. But if you stay, things will start happening quickly. We need to convince Grigory that we're serious. The best way is to make him think the big spenders have changed who they're loyal to. There's a conference booked in the Strani house in a week's time, with some of the biggest spenders in government. We're going to get them to back out, and then we're going to spread the word that they came here instead. We'll do that in two ways: first, a couple days before the conference, Ysbel is going to set off an explosion in the grounds near the Strani house. And then Jez is going to Prasvishoni to convince the marks that Grigory's called it off because it's not safe. After that—" he spread his hands. "I expect after that, we'll get a visit from Grigory's people."

There was another long silence. Lev looked around the small group one last time, and at last he nodded. "Alright. Galina, go ahead."

He sat, and Galina stood, a grim, businesslike expression on her face and an intensity in her eyes that Tae didn't remember seeing there before. For the first time since he'd met her, he realized that she was actually slightly frightening.

Jez must have noticed the same thing, because her grin went dreamy.

Tae shook his head, and beside him, Ivan gave a low chuckle.

"I wonder daily how your pilot is still alive," he whispered.

"Alright," said Galina in a brisk voice. "Here's what we need. First, there's the serving staff—food servers, cleaners, people to check customers in at the desks. For those positions, we'll need people who can blend in, and who can remember details. No one notices a server —or at least, no one should notice a server. Second, customers.

You'll be weapons dealers, criminals, wealthy government officials. The type of house we're running caters to only the wealthiest, so whoever you are, you're important and you're used to getting your way. And finally, we'll need the—" she paused for a moment, distaste evident in her voice. "The entertainment, as they call them. We won't be putting you with paying customers, because we won't have any, other than Grigory's people—if people call in to book, we'll tell them we're full. And for those who go with Grigory's people, we'll have measures in place to keep you safe. However, this will be the riskiest position by far.

"If you get nerves, or if you break down under pressure, this isn't for you. You'll need to be able to play your part right up to and until you think a customer is about to slit your throat just for the fun of it. That said, this isn't going to be the kind of house that uses disposable entertainment. You'll be trained for the various positions, so I'll need those of you who have some physical dexterity—if you've ever danced, or played an instrument, or done any type of sex work, that would be helpful. And you need to be good with a weapon. I won't let anyone play an entertainer who can't shoot a heat pistol." She glanced around. "Does anyone have questions?"

No one spoke, but their faces were grimmer than they had been.

"Good," she said at last. "I'll be here. Lev will tell each of you what he needs from you. Then come see me, and we'll figure out which part you can play."

There was a murmur of assent from the gathered company, and slowly, people stood and made their way over to Lev or Galina.

Tae stayed where he was, worry churning in his stomach. "Do you think they know what they've signed up for?" he asked quietly, turning to Ivan.

Ivan smiled without humour. "I don't know. But I do know these people. They hate Grigory and everything he stands for. So whether they know or not—this is something that they believe in. Enough to … well, enough to risk their lives over it."

Tae heard the words he'd been about to say, and hadn't. "Enough to die for it."

He shivered slightly. Because it could very well come down to that.

9

"Misko bit me!"

Olya's voice was much louder, and much more shrill, than Ysbel had imagined could come from a person of her size.

Ysbel looked up from where she'd been cutting the dessert ration packs into two exactly identical-sized pieces, and lowered her eyebrows at her son. "Misko," she said in her sternest voice. "Don't bite your sister. You know better than that."

Misko glared at her, unimpressed.

"And," Olya chimed in self-importantly, "she's going to give me a bite of your dessert. Right Mama?"

Misko's face collapsed into utter despair, and he began wailing.

"Misko!" Ysbel bellowed over the noise. "Please stop that before this entire building comes down, or else I go completely crazy."

Misko kept wailing.

"Or I eat your dessert myself."

The wailing abruptly stopped, stifled into a hiccuping, sniffling silence.

Ysbel gave a short sigh of relief. "Thank you, Misko. Now, go sit down, both of you."

The children obeyed.

Ysbel studied Olya as she picked up the dessert rations and handed them to the children.

That girl had Tanya's brains, that was for certain.

Behind her, the door to their quarters opened, and she turned quickly, hand going to her heat pistol.

Tanya smiled as she slipped inside. "Ysi. How are you, my heart?"

Ysbel smiled back despite herself, the tension from the last three hours draining away at the sight of her wife.

Tanya looked—happy. Not just happy. Purposeful. She had that look to her that Ysbel had fallen in love with so many years ago, when they were both just children, really, that look of someone who was doing something she loved and was good at, and was determined to see it through.

It had been a long time since she'd seen Tanya look like this.

A faint pang of guilt stirred in her chest at the thought.

Tanya had been right. Ysbel had forgotten what it meant to be married. And Tanya had given everything, and had kept giving everything, because Ysbel was taking it all.

But—well, the thing was, she'd told Tanya the truth, back on the casino ship. This marriage was worth putting back together. Even if three hours with Misko the hellion and Olya who had to know everything about everything was almost enough to send her curled up and weeping into a corner.

"How is everything going out there?" Ysbel asked, kissing her wife's forehead.

Tanya drew back and looked at her, face serious. "Good, I think. But it's time for your part now."

Ysbel tried to hide her expression of relief, but Tanya chuckled and shook her head. "Things are going that well with the children, then?"

"It's not the children, specifically," Ysbel grumbled, keeping her voice low enough that Olya hopefully wouldn't overhear.

Olya, she'd learned through sad experience, had very sharp ears.

"I love the children very much. It's the fact that at any given moment, I'm being pulled into the middle of a fight between someone and someone else. I think Misko would pick a fight with the table leg if Olya weren't around. But when she is, she's more than happy to oblige."

Tanya shook her head, smiling softly. "I'm sorry, my heart. They are in a new place, and they aren't used to being looked after by anyone but me. We'll all get used to this sooner or later, I'm sure."

"You're assuming I survive that long," Ysbel muttered, but she was smiling as well.

Tanya ran a hand over Ysbel's shaved head and trailed her fingers down the back of her neck. "Anyways, you'll have a reason to get away for a little while now. Come on, I'll finish up with dinner. You go get ready."

Ysbel nodded, took Tanya in her arms, and kissed her tenderly. Then she shot a mock scowl at the children. "You behave, alright?"

"I always behave, Mama," said Olya primly.

"I never behave," Misko said exuberantly through a mouthful of crumbs. "And I'm never going to behave. I'm going to be a grownup soon, and I'm going to do whatever I want! And I'm going to eat dessert every single meal!"

"Finish chewing before you talk, my heart," said Tanya absently. She turned back to Ysbel. "Good luck, Ysi." She paused a moment. "I—know this isn't easy for you. And I—"

Ysbel shook her head and pulled her wife back into her arms. "Tanya," she said quietly. "It wasn't easy for you, either, I just didn't see that. I told you. I want to make this work. Seeing you happy is worth everything to me. And I should have done this a long time ago."

Tanya looked at her fondly, and for a moment, Ysbel forgot the combination of stress and boredom that had become her entire life these past few days, forgot everything but how much she loved this woman.

"Go on," said Tanya, kissing her lightly. "I'll wait up for you."

Ysbel took a deep breath, smiled at her wife, and made her way down the hallway to her workroom.

She was almost finished her preparations when there was a light knock at the door.

"Come in," she called, and Lev stepped inside.

"Ysbel," he said quietly. "Galina's ready. She's waiting by the bikes." He paused. "You've decided what you're going to hit, I assume?"

"Yes," said Ysbel. She pulled up a map of the pleasure district, and tapped an open area near the red mark that was the Strani house. "There's a park here. It shouldn't attract too much attention, but should still make people uneasy." She paused a moment. "Also, it shouldn't kill anyone. Tanya believes that killing people should be done only as a last resort, and I support her in this."

Lev raised an eyebrow.

"I didn't say I agree with her," said Ysbel. "But she is my wife, and I support her."

"Ah." Lev nodded, clearly trying to fight back his amusement. "Well. In this case, at least, I believe Tanya is correct. As you say, we don't want to cause injuries, just enough of a stir that people might think twice about visiting the pleasure district." He paused, and gave a small smile. "It won't escape Grigory's notice that we're far enough away from the pleasure district that anyone who still wanted to attend an establishment would be perfectly safe here."

Ysbel smiled. "Well, as safe as you can be, if your entertainer is a trained assassin. How is Tanya doing?"

Lev smiled. "She's a natural, to be honest with you."

"I knew she would be," said Ysbel, with a fond smile. "She is very good at anything she puts her mind to."

He chuckled. "And Jez running the gambling hall was a stroke of genius. She's in her element there."

Ysbel studied Lev for a moment. "You're—doing well with this," she said at last. "You're not a terrible person around Galina, and I'm glad. Because she's a nice girl."

Lev looked at her, startled, then gave a small, wry smile. "Is it that obvious?"

"Well, yes. But you are trying, that's the thing. And our pilot girl can see that too." She paused again. "And you know, I think she missed you. Maybe she doesn't want a relationship, but that doesn't mean she doesn't care about you."

"I—know," said Lev, in a soft voice. "I missed her, too. I hadn't realized how much. And—and I'm happy for her. Galina's better for her than I ever was." He gave a soft, rueful laugh. "I don't think I realized how much of a complete ass I was to her."

"Well, yes, you were," said Ysbel philosophically. She shrugged. "I mean, in fairness, she can be very irritating, but—"

Lev gave a small smile. "Well, I'm glad she found someone who can manage not to be a complete ass. And—I'm working on it. Since she actually gave me a second chance, which I didn't deserve."

"It will hurt less, eventually," said Ysbel quietly, a pang of pity stirring in her chest. "It will get easier, I promise."

"I—hope so." His voice was quiet, and she heard the tinge of heartbreak under it. Then he shook his head briskly. "Anyways, I'll let Galina know you're on your way." He gave her a small smile, then turned out the door.

She looked after him for a few moments, shaking her head.

He'd survive, and honestly, this was probably good for him. That boy thought a little too highly of himself, and a little too low of everyone else, for his own good. And Jez would be a good friend for him, if she decided she wanted to be. Still—well, she knew how it felt to have a broken heart.

All things considered, he was doing alright.

When Ysbel reached the skybikes, Galina was waiting for her. Ysbel looked her over critically. She was dressed in a dark grey outfit, with a hood pulled up over her head. Her face was tense, but she relaxed into a slight smile when she saw Ysbel.

"Your wife told me what to wear," she said.

Ysbel smiled back. "Yes, Tanya is good at that sort of thing."

Galina nodded, and Ysbel was struck suddenly by how young she was. A couple years older than their crazy pilot, maybe, but no more than that.

"Alright," Ysbel said, swinging her leg over a skybike. "Let's go. I'll let you lead the way, since Lev tells me you know this place better than I do."

Galina gave her a tight smile. "I don't know it personally. I have a friend, though. She—knew it very well. And she described it to me enough times that I know more or less where we're going."

"I see," said Ysbel quietly.

Galina turned away hurriedly and swung up on her own skybike, and Ysbel followed her out the small hangar bay door.

They rode through the dark streets without speaking, even over the coms. The air on the planet had cooled now that dark had fallen, and it brushed across Ysbel's face, sending a small shiver down her back.

The streets weren't deserted, but they were much less busy than they had been in the day. Flickering artificial lights hung in orange globes over the streets, but they cast almost more shadows than light, and the people who walked the streets did so in small clusters, with the nervous movements of people constantly looking over their shoulders, or with the swaggering confidence of people who were the ones being looked at over shoulders. From below street level, through the small stairwells that led to darkened doorways, there rose snatches of music and boisterous voices, and every so often a shout or curse. As they passed one doorway, the door was flung open, a shaft of yellow light cutting through the dimness of the streets, and a woman staggered out, as if she'd been pushed. She cursed, picking herself up, and, leaning against the wall, made her unsteady way back up to the street.

"We're not going directly into the pleasure district," said Galina in her earpiece. "I think it will be better if we park the skybikes out of the way."

The streets they rode down were growing gradually dirtier and narrower, the artificial lights dimmer and less frequent. The smell from the streets was that of garbage and human waste.

"Are you sure you know where you're going?" Ysbel said into the com.

Ahead of her, Galina gave a short nod.

Ysbel shrugged. It probably didn't matter, honestly. She doubted that anyone in this filthy city, crime boss, mob leader, or boyevik, could possibly match the level of destructive power she was carrying in the padded bag around her neck.

At last they stopped in the entrance to a small alley. Galina paused a moment, then slid off her bike, leaning it up against the filthy wall.

Ysbel came to a halt and did the same.

"Where are we?" she asked quietly, looking around. The smell from the alley behind them was foul enough that a whiff drifting out in the still air was enough to make her cough.

Galina sighed. Her posture was so tense it was almost painful to look at. "This—is where the entertainers and the servers live. When they're not being used. Or when they've been used up."

There was a bitterness to her voice that surprised Ysbel, and she frowned at the girl.

"Tell me, Galina," she said in a soft voice. "It—wasn't just your friend, was it?"

Galina stiffened further. "I—don't know—"

Ysbel shook her head. "Listen. I'm not stupid. You don't have to tell me if you don't want to, but there's no need to keep it secret. It's not something shameful."

Galina stayed where she was for a few moments, face turned away, body stiff with tension. At last, though, her posture drooped tiredly.

"You're right," she said in a low voice. "I—once upon a time, a long time ago, I was here. I—I was only a kid. I didn't know—I didn't know what was happening to me. They didn't tell me—" She broke off again, and for a long moment, she was quiet. At last, she said, "I got out, smuggled myself off in one of the cargo ships. I was one of the lucky ones." She gave a soft, bitter laugh. "But there were people who took care of me, protected me. And I never came back for them. I—I was too afraid." She turned to Ysbel, and even in the dim light, Ysbel could see the haunted look on her face. "I've felt guilty over that my whole life. My whole life, it's eaten me up from the inside. The people here, in this part of the city—the servers, the cooks, the street cleaners, the entertainers—they're bought and sold like damn animals. And they last about as long as animals, too.

Everyone who helped me is dead by now."

For a few moments, her words hung in the air. Neither of them spoke.

There was a faint sickness coating the back of Ysbel's throat.

She'd known about the pleasure planet for as long as she could remember—she could remember as a child her mother speaking of it in hushed tones to her father. And she'd known about the trafficking. It was an open secret in the system—if you were wealthy enough, you could visit the pleasure planets as a guest. Your parents have enough bad harvests, so that they have the choice of letting one child go or letting all the children starve, or you're a lone street kid without a gang of other kids for protection, and you end up on the pleasure planet as something else—a server, a cleaner, an entertainer. And some of these houses were notorious for having disposable entertainment.

She'd known that, ever since she was a child, and the knowledge had always sickened her. But it wasn't until she was here, standing in the entrance to this filthy alley and looking into the sickened, guilt-ridden face of this girl, that she actually realized what it meant.

"I'm sorry," she said at last. "I don't know if this makes you feel better. But—I'm not sure many people would have come back at all."

Galina managed a small smile. "When—when Jez told me about the rest of you, what you were doing, I—I almost ran for it. But—" she paused, closing her eyes for a moment. "But the thing is—well, the thing about Jez is, she—has this way of making you believe you can do things you never thought you could. I've seen her scared before. But she does it anyways. And—I guess I couldn't run away."

"Does Jez know?" asked Ysbel quietly.

Galina nodded. "I told her, back on the casino ship. No one else knows, though. She said she wouldn't say anything unless I wanted her to. She said I didn't have to come, that if I wanted, I could just wait on the ship and she'd come back for me when you were all done. But—" she shook her head and managed a small smile. "But I couldn't. I couldn't let her come here, and lose my one chance to do something to make things better."

Ysbel swallowed down something in her throat. "Well," she said at last, "I've never thought of myself as a coward. But I don't know that I would have been able to do what you're doing right now. And don't worry. I won't say anything unless you want me to."

Galina gave her another faint, grateful smile. "I'll—tell them tomorrow. When we get back. I think Masha and Lev have probably already guessed."

Ysbel nodded, and Galina turned back to the street in front of them.

"I guess we should get going, then," she said. "Follow me. I know a path from here into the pleasure district."

They made their way silently through the unlit streets. Most of the bulbous artificial streetlights were broken, although here and there one gave an anemic orange flicker. Ysbel had spent enough of her life around Tanya to know how to get somewhere without making much noise, and Galina could be surprisingly quiet as well.

There was a large wall built around the pleasure district, but Galina led them unerringly to a small gateway. It wasn't guarded, and when Ysbel expressed her surprise, Galina gave her a grim look. "It's because some of the guests want to find their entertainment in the wild, they call it. If they have enough bodyguards, they don't have much to worry about. And like I said, everyone in the slum district belongs to someone. There isn't much they can do."

Ysbel closed her eyes for a moment, and tried not to let Galina's words paint a picture in her head. She wasn't certain she would be able to get it out again.

Stepping out of the slums and onto the streets of the pleasure district was like stepping onto a different planet. Here, the street lights were a soft gold, their lights illuminating the cobblestones with a brilliant glow. The streets here were as busy as they'd been in the daytime, on that day months ago when Ysbel had planted an explosive in the Strani House as a distraction when they were kidnapping a weapon's dealer to steal his identity.

Now that she thought about it, it had been a long time since she hadn't been part of a crazy plan that almost certainly should have killed her.

Still, she hadn't had the time to look around much back then, considering the circumstances. And alright, perhaps this wasn't all that different, but you did become accustomed to it eventually.

Galina pulled back her hood, and was walking in a purposeful way that made people step aside for her almost unconsciously. Her long hair bounced against her back, and her clothing was just drab enough not to attract attention, and just nice enough not to attract comment.

Ysbel had never had to worry too much about that—she found a scowl was generally enough to inform people that staying out of her way was their best option, at least if they wanted to keep all their body parts attached. But, to each their own.

The lights of pleasure houses glowed and flashed in bright, garish colours, and raucous laughter and shouts rang out from the open doorways. Galina led them quickly past them to a large, open park. Or at least, it looked open. As Ysbel got closer, she realized that the maze of bushes and half-walls made it into a series of small enclosures. On a gilded bench outside the maze, a couple sat pressed together, clothing disheveled, eyes half-lidded, the sweet smell of street-drugs recognizable even from here.

Galina paused a few meters away from the entrance. "This is the place you showed me on the map."

Ysbel frowned. "There will be people inside that."

Galina nodded, chewing the inside of her cheek. "Maybe somewhere farther down the street. If we keep an eye out—"

From inside the structure came a sharp, shrill scream, abruptly cut off.

The two women exchanged grim looks.

Ysbel reached inside her jacket pocket, pulling out a small canister. She handed it to Galina. "How is your throwing arm?"

Galina frowned, face still tense. "Alright, I guess."

"Throw this as far into the middle of that hell-hole as you can," said Ysbel shortly. "It won't do any permanent damage, but if anyone stays in the place after the gas starts to disperse, it will be because they're dead."

"Then what?"

Ysbel gave a small smirk. "Then you stand back. Far back, please, because I think Jez would be upset if I brought you back in pieces. I'll give the people inside time to get out. And then—" she shrugged.

Galina gave a tight nod and started off around the other side of the park. Ysbel stood back, eyeing the place critically. She smiled to herself, and strolled over to one corner of the maze of bushes.

She'd almost finished planting her explosives when she heard the small *pop*, and then the hiss of releasing gas. She set the last explosive in place, then straightened and wandered back towards the crowd, keeping an eye on the maze entrance.

A few moments later, coughing, choking people began to stagger out, tears streaming down their faces.

Galina appeared a moment later, her face set.

Ysbel sighed and handed her a mask. "Go on," she said. "This will keep you from breathing it, anyways. And you're going to go in to make sure they're all out, no matter what I say."

"Just the entertainment," said Galina quietly. "I don't care about the others."

She slipped the mask over her face and ducked through the coughing people crowding the entrance to the maze. When she emerged a few minutes later, she caught Ysbel's eye and nodded. Ysbel gestured her out of the way with a quick jerk of her head.

Already, she could hear police bikes whining up the streets, over the sounds of people shouting and backing away from the clouds of gas hanging over the park.

She shook her head regretfully. As much as she'd like to wait until the scum-sucking police officers pulled their masks on and went into see what had caused the disturbance, Tanya had asked, and she'd promised Lev. So when they were close enough that the blast would at least give them a shock, she hit the controller.

The noise was so loud it almost ceased to be a noise and became a physical force, and she squeezed her eyes shut against the brilliant flash that wrote itself across the back of her eyeballs.

When she opened her eyes, the park, with its maze of bushes, was gone. In its place, a smoking crater yawned open. Police officers, flung back by the blast, shook their heads and slowly pushed themselves up on their elbows.

"Ysbel," Galina whispered, and Ysbel turned to find the girl at her elbow.

She wore a fierce, hard expression, and even Ysbel would hesitate to cross her right now.

But there was something in the girl's face as they walked back through the slums, and something in her posture as they mounted their bikes, that made Ysbel wish she could give Galina a hug.

But then, she was fairly certain that Jez would take care of that. And that somehow, the restless, snarky pilot would know what to say to Galina to make everything just a little more bearable.

When had she become so certain of that?

She wasn't entirely sure if Jez had changed, or she had.

10

Jez bounced on the balls of her feet, eyes closed, fingers flexed.

"Jez? You alright?"

She looked up. Galina stood there, with Lev beside her.

Jez gave Galina a grin that did nothing to hide the relief coursing through her body. "Yep. Been too long since I've been in my damn ship, that's all."

Galina smiled at her fondly. "I wanted to come see you off, at least. I'd come with you if I could. But—they need me here."

"I know." Jez caught Galina's hand and pulled her in for a long kiss. Galina's body was soft, and her curves almost reminded Jez of her beautiful ship, and she smelled of soap and sweat and sawdust, and for a moment Jez wished Galya would be flying with them, so much she could taste it.

But Galya was right, they needed her here, and—well, and the fact was, if Jez couldn't get back in the sky, she might actually go completely crazy. So at last, reluctantly, she released Galina and grinned at Lev.

"You ready, genius?"

Lev sighed, a tinge of strain in his expression. "I'm ready. You?"

"Born ready," she said, smirking at him. "Get in and strap down."

They climbed the loading ramp, and Jez sighed in a sort of desperate relief.

There was something about stepping into her ship that made the whole world feel right again.

She slid into the familiar comfort of the pilot's seat and rested her hands on the controls, letting the feeling of them seep up through her fingers like water into dry soil, then she hit the ignition. Lev strapped in to the copilot's seat beside her, she touched the controls lightly, and the ship lifted gracefully off ground.

They rose smoothly out of the hangar and over the wall that surrounded their courtyard. From the corner of her eye, she saw the wary apprehension on Lev's face turning to a sort of cautious relief. And then she hit the throttle, and the ship shot forward, flipping on its side to slide through the opening in the planet's force-field, and streaked towards the blue-black line that marked the end of the thin band of atmosphere holding them down.

With the hyperdrive, the trip only took an hour or so, and when she brought the ship in through the atmosphere and swooped low across the evergreen forests and swamps that surrounded the city, it was close to evening.

She grinned. Perfect timing.

She'd never actually liked Prasvishoni all that much, but on days like this, with the evening sun glinting across the branches of the evergreens, lighting the frosty tips below her like a thousand sparkling stars, she couldn't help but feel a grudging fondness for the place.

Lev took a deep breath, and let go his chokehold on the arm of the copilot's seat. "I'll send coordinates through to your com," he said, voice shaking only slightly. "We'll be landing at one of the public docking bays. The shielding spoof Tae set up should stop them from tracking us." He paused. "Jez. You … know what you're doing, right? I just want to go over this one more time."

She gave him a skeptical look. "Listen, genius. If I don't know, I'll figure it out as I go, OK? Not like I haven't done it before."

Lev took a long, steadying breath. "Jez," he said at last. "These are the government officials who've planned a convention on the pleasure planet. The big spenders. We need Grigory's people to see you talking to them, and then they have to not show up at the Strani House. The second part we've taken care of, between Ysbel's explosion yesterday and the fact that Tae hacked in and will cancel all their bookings tonight. But Grigory needs to believe you talked them into coming to our pleasure house instead."

She rolled her eyes. "You're acting like I've never even heard of this plan."

Lev took another long breath. "I'm sorry. So you know what you need to do."

She shrugged. "Nah. I wasn't actually listening to what you eggheads were saying. But I might have been. So not like you should just assume."

The sound of Lev sucking in a sharp breath through his nose was as familiar and comforting as the hum of a running ship.

She laughed. "Relax, genius. Yes, I know what I'm doing."

She steered them in through the city gates, then turned towards the docking bay Lev had indicated on her holoscreen. She pulled into docking bay forty-seven, and as she powered the ship down, something tightened inside her chest.

She hadn't been in a docking bay since the last run she'd made as a smuggler. It seemed like yesterday, and a lifetime ago—when she'd been running completely free. No one to worry about, no strings, nothing but her and her ship and deep, deep space. None of this crap about saving the system or taking down the government or taking down Grigory Korzhakov.

No strings, no one to worry about.

But there'd been no one to worry about her, either.

She swallowed hard and gave a quick shake of her head.

OK, so it was different than smuggling. And yes, maybe she missed that sometimes, the freedom of it. The way she could go wherever she wanted, and do whatever she wanted.

But, well—she wouldn't trade it, honestly.

At the entrance to the docking bay, Lev paused. He checked his heat pistol, placed it carefully in its holster, and turned to her with a grim expression on his face. "Alright, Jez, this is your plan. So. What are we doing?"

His voice said he wasn't sure he really wanted to know.

She grinned. "Well, they're expecting someone from Grigory to show up, right? So that's what I'm going to give them." She paused a moment to enjoy the look on his face.

"If—if you think that's a good idea," said Lev after a moment, in a slightly strangled tone.

"Damn right I do," she said, still grinning. She checked her own pistol—well, pistols, since she had about three of them, and a couple of Ysbel's explosives.

No point in coming to a party unprepared.

"Is that—all?" he asked, after a long breath.

She rolled her eyes. "What else do you want to know? You're coming in as backup, so you don't have to do anything, just sit there and tell me if someone comes in who wants to kill me. I'll tell the government idiots I'm from Grigory, and tell them this whole thing is a bad idea and they'll probably get blown into a million pieces if they try to come."

"Jez. Why don't I tell them that, and you be the backup? I spent more time with Grigory than you did, and—"

"Two reasons, genius," she said, holstering her weapons. "First, you can't gamble like I can. And second, you hate being shot at."

"How—why do either of those things—"

She winked at him. "Watch and learn." She turned and started off down the narrow, filthy dock streets. A moment later, she heard Lev's footsteps coming after her.

"Jez," he whispered as he caught up with her. She half-turned, prepared to argue, but he just shook his head, a tight, strained expression on his face. "Good luck," he whispered at last. "I'll be in the back if you need me, and I'll be listening in on the com. I'll give you any information I have that might be helpful."

She almost stopped walking to stare at him.

He managed a reluctant smile. "What?"

She shook her head and turned back to the street in front of her. "You aren't going to fight with me?"

His smile grew a little more genuine. "Well, first off, it wouldn't change anything. And second—" he paused a moment, his voice growing quieter. "Second, you—well, your plans are mildly unconventional. But—they've always worked. And I supposed it's stupid of me to argue with you over something you've clearly already thought through, just because it's not how I'd do it."

She almost stopped walking again, not entirely certain she'd heard him right.

He stopped as well, and turned to look at her. "Jez. Listen. I know I've been a complete ass basically the entire time you've known me. If it makes you feel better, I'm coming to realize I've been a complete ass basically my entire life. But—well, but I don't fight with Ysbel every time she comes up with a plan with her explosives. And I don't argue with Tae when he's talking about tech, because that's what he does. And I'm not sure why I thought I should be able to argue with you when you're doing something you're clearly better at than I am." He paused. "Like I said. I know I'm crap at being a friend. But—I'm trying, alright?"

She stared at him, and something prickled at the corners of her eyes. She blinked hard, and tried to smirk at him, but it didn't seem to work the way she wanted it to. "Um," she said. "I."

He was smiling, just a little. "You don't have to say anything," he said. "Honestly. I'm sorry you've had to deal with me for so long."

"Um. Yeah." She blinked again, and gave him a quick smile. "If— if it makes you feel better, I—I'm not used to having friends. Much. I don't—you've—" She took a deep breath. "Look. You're one of the first people in my whole life that ever made me feel like they actually wanted me around, OK? So maybe you're not such a crap friend."

He smiled back, a wide, genuine smile this time, and for a moment they stood there grinning at each other like idiots, and she honestly didn't even care.

Because even if that whole disaster that had been them trying out a relationship hadn't worked—well, she hadn't lost him. She hadn't lost him forever, even though she'd been pretty sure she had, and hell, if it meant never kissing him again she'd take it just to see him smile like that.

Finally he shook his head and turned. "Alright. We'd better get going, or we'll miss our friends."

"Yeah," she said quickly, turning back to the street in front of her. "Better get going."

They didn't speak again until they were almost at the club, but it was a comfortable silence, somehow, and she almost didn't want it to end.

It was strange how just walking down the dirty, familiar streets of Prasvishoni, Lev beside her, without anyone waiting to sleep with her or try to kill her—well, OK, the jury was still out on that second one —could send a giddy, relieved happiness bubbling through her brain like alcohol.

"We're almost there," said Lev quietly, as they turned onto one of the busier streets. The citizens of Prasvishoni who through some combination of necessity and bad luck were out on the grimy streets, had their scarves pulled up over their heads, shoulders slouched forward like they were walking into a heavy wind, huddled against the evening chill. Jez and Lev had done likewise, but honestly, Jez had never been good at blending in, here or anywhere else.

"Yeah," she said, glancing down quickly at the coordinates he'd sent through to her com. "OK, look. You go in first, get settled down. Don't want people thinking we're together. Once you've found a place, tap your com and I'll head in."

He nodded, the strain from earlier back on his face.

She bumped him with her shoulder. "Hey. Genius. Relax. We've done crap like this before, and we all lived through it."

He drew in a deep breath and gave her a tight smile. "You're right. However, your equanimity in the face of the prospect of either getting shot or getting the actual hell beat out of you has always been better than mine."

"Nah. I wouldn't let them beat the hell out of you," she said with a grin.

"Well, I'm not certain I would be able to prevent someone beating the hell out of you, although I'd certainly try."

"Well, figure you won't have to," she said, patting the pistol in her hip holster. "At least, probably," she amended. "Anyways, better get in there."

"Yes," he said, looking at the narrow alley that held the doorway to the club, a grim expression on his face. "I'll let you know when I'm in."

He straightened, tugged on his jacket to smooth it, and strode forward, disappearing into the alley entrance.

Jez wasn't actually the nervous type. You dealt with the crap in front of you, and there was enough of that that you didn't actually have time to worry about the crap that was waiting for you. At least, that's how she usually lived her life. But ... well, but waiting had always been a special kind of hell. Besides, she couldn't get out of her mind the worry on Lev's face, before his expression had smoothed over into one of casual confidence and he'd stepped forward into the alley that led to the club.

Yes, her plan should work, in fact she was pretty damn sure it would, wouldn't have suggested it otherwise. But—well, but Lev was right, he'd never really been good at fighting, and yes, maybe neither of them really knew how to be a decent friend, but hell, if he got himself shot now when it looked like they were finally figuring things out, she might actually—

"Jez." His voice hissed through her earpiece, and she jumped.

She tapped her com. "Yeah? You OK?"

"I'm fine. I have a place over in the corner, the club owner thinks I'm waiting for my friends to arrive. Our targets are on the main floor, in the gambling area." He paused. "How—did you know they'd be—"

She grinned. "Hey genius. You're not the only one who can read, you know." She paused. "I mean, I didn't actually read the crap you sent. But bunch of big government spenders, where else are they going to be?"

There was a moment's pause, which was probably Lev sighing.

Then he tapped his com back on. "Well, you were right. You can come in any time. They don't seem to suspect anything."

"On it. See you in a sec." She pulled the scarf from her head and shoved it into her bag, then pulled out another scarf Galina had lent her and looped it casually around her shoulders, unbuttoned the top few buttons of her coat to show off her expensive-looking white tunic, and sauntered around the corner to the entrance to the club.

When she pulled the door open, the two bouncers glanced her up and down, obviously taking in the fineness of her outfit.

She grinned at them.

"Weapons?" the woman grunted.

Jez raised an eyebrow. "Hey now, how's a woman supposed to protect herself around here? Anyways, these are for decoration."

The woman still looked skeptical.

Jez winked, and leaned in closer. "Don't like it, you can take it up with Marina Kaschak. Or with the Krestnaya. He probably won't be too happy to hear from you, but you could take your chances." She paused a moment. "Or, you could just wink your eye and let me past, and I'm pretty sure I have a thank-you gift here for you, from Grigory himself."

The two bouncers met eyes over her head, then at last the woman nodded. "How much of a gift, did you say?"

"Hold up your com, you'll see," she said.

They did so, and Jez let a generous amount of credits click over.

Hell of a lot nicer to spend money when it wasn't yours. Even better when it belonged to a bastard who'd taken a security interest in your damn ship. And anyways, no point in looking cheap right now.

"Go on, then," said the woman at last, waving her forward. Jez gave her wink and strolled into the club, glancing around quickly.

"The five over there. To your right," came Lev's low voice over the com, and she turned to look in the direction he'd indicated.

A group of people lounged around one of the tables, laughing. There were gambling tokens and drinks on the table, and she grinned to herself.

"On it, genius," she whispered, and sauntered in the direction of the table.

They didn't look up at her approach, but when she pulled up a chair and straddled it, resting her elbows on its low back, the woman who seemed to be in charge glanced up at her in annoyance.

"What exactly do you think—" she began.

Jez grinned at her, watching her eyes take in the obvious quality of her outfit, the colours hidden subtly in the weave of the scarf. "Hey now, you always so rude to a co-worker?" she drawled.

The woman frowned. "Did Grigory send you?" she asked, her voice sharp and skeptical.

Jez shrugged easily. "Careful how you throw names around," she said. "Don't know where you grew up, but where I grew up, we watched what we said."

The woman's frown deepened. "I don't know—"

"That's fine. No point in getting this off to a bad start." She stood and swung the chair around, and sat so that she'd joined them at the table.

"What does Grigory want?" asked a man. "Lady knows we've bent over backwards to make sure he gets what he asks for."

She glanced at the table. "What you playing, lady in the park? Go on, deal me in. Easier to talk if we're playing a nice friendly game."

"Behind you." Lev's voice was tight. "One of Grigory's boyeviki. She just walked in."

Under the table, Jez tapped out a pattern in pilot's code onto her com. *Then you'd better keep her busy. I'm just getting started.*

The man who'd spoken dealt the tokens grudgingly, and Jez turned hers over with a casual flick of her wrist. "So," she said, placing a token down in the centre of the table. "Guess you heard about what happened out at the pleasure planet last night."

The woman looked up, frowning. "No. What happened?" She glanced down at her pile of tokens, then dropped one beside Jez's.

Jez grinned. "Explosion. In the park two streets down from the Strani House. A bunch of saboteurs, they think, but they haven't caught them yet."

A tall man, with a full beard that made him look a little like a swamp rat with its cheeks full, scowled. "What happened? Have the authorities done anything?"

"Nah," she said, glancing over the pile of tokens in the middle of the table. "Not sure they want to, to be honest. They haven't been looking too fondly on Grigory since whatever the hell happened up on his private ship."

"His private ship?" asked a short, pale-skinned woman with long blond hair.

Jez raised an eyebrow. "Not sure I should tell you, to be honest. But I'm just saying, might not hurt to look into what happened at Grigory's last conference, is all I'm saying."

They were all watching her now. She gave a meaningful glance at the pile of tokens in the middle of the table, and the bearded man frowned and pulled out a token absently, throwing it into the middle of the pile.

"Anyways," she drawled, "hate to be the one to break bad news. Thought you'd have already heard of it. But the conference is off. Actually, I'm surprised one of the boyeviki didn't come by to let you know, considering how much the boss man paid for you." She winked broadly at them.

The woman who'd first spoken scowled at her coldly. "I resent the insinuation—"

Jez spread her hands palm up. "Hey now, not insinuating anything, just passing along some news." She glanced down at her tokens and, after a moment's consideration, pulled one out of her pile that had definitely not been in the pile when the woman had dealt.

Although honestly, she was pretty sure she could have pulled the token out of her boot, spit-shined it clean, and dropped it right into the centre of the table and got away with it, with the amount of attention these idiots were paying to the game.

"Guess the least I can do is buy you all a drink. You know, something to wash bad news down with. What are you having?"

She stood and gestured a server over.

Out of the corner of her eye, she could see Grigory's boyevik, a thin woman with a look to her face of someone who probably killed people for fun. But she wasn't watching them. Instead, she was frowning down at her com, her expression slightly confused.

Jez cast a quick glance at Lev, who'd pulled up the holoscreen on his com and was typing something surreptitiously.

He looked up and gave a quick wink, and she almost fell over with surprise. Because honestly, she'd been expecting him to be glaring at her like he couldn't wait to give her some sort of talking-to when they got out of this.

She cleared her throat and turned quickly back to the server, who'd approached and was now waiting patiently. She gave him an easy grin. "Get everyone here what they ask for. And me—" She paused a moment, with a slightly dreamy smile. "I'll have a glass of golden murder."

The server stared at her.

Everyone at the table was staring at her.

She shrugged. "Hey, you don't have the good stuff, that's fine, you only have to say so."

"That—it's just, not many people ask for that," said the server, seeming to recover himself. "We mostly use it for decoration, to be honest. It's … a little strong for most people."

She grinned at him. "Well, I'm not most people. And I'd like a glass of it, please. Hell, bring the bottle."

He gave the slightly stunned shrug of someone who'd done his duty to warn and couldn't be held responsible for any consequences, and turned to go. Jez leaned back in her chair and surveyed her companions, who were still staring at her. "Well, you going to throw your tokens? Because I just did, and unless the rest of you want to fold—"

The server returned a few minutes later with the drinks, and the others at the table politely fought back coughs at the sharp sting of alcohol wafting from the open bottle. She grinned at them and poured a generous amount, then raised her glass. Finally, they raised theirs in return,

They'd finished three games and were about one round from the end of a fourth when Lev whispered, "Jez. I have the one boyevik distracted. But another just came in. I think there's going to be trouble."

How the hell are you distracting her, anyways? She tapped quickly.

"Doesn't matter," he hissed. "The point is, you're about to be in the middle of a shootout if you're not careful. I'll do the best I can, but I'm not sure how effective this is going to be."

What are you going to—

"Doesn't matter. Just watch your back."

She looked down at the table, pretending to concentrate on her tokens, but out of the corner of her eye she was watching the door.

Sure enough, a moment later, a man stepped inside, and Lev rose smoothly to intercept him, putting a hand on his arm. The man turned in annoyance, and Lev said something in a low voice, and soon the two men were conversing in quiet tones. The woman boyevik glanced up from her holoscreen, but didn't seem unduly alarmed.

And then another man, with the discrete colours that marked him as Grigory's woven through his scarf, stepped into the room.

There was something faintly familiar about his face.

Damn. She turned back to the table, rummaging through her tokens.

If they recognized her and Lev, this could go sideways quickly.

Then she paused.

On the other hand …

She grinned and pulled a token out like a trophy. "Well, guess this is my final bid," she said cheerily, loudly enough that her voice cut through the muted conversation and laughter of the club. She dropped it into the centre of the table with a flourish, then leaned back, raising her glass tipsily.

Her partners threw in their own tokens, with the loud laughter of a group of previously staid government officials who'd been introduced, for the first time, to golden murder.

She grinned. They weren't faking their tipsiness. Honestly, as good as the stuff was, she didn't envy them the headache they were going to wake up to.

"Well," she drawled, letting her words slur just a little, "let's flip tokens and see who won."

The man she'd recognized was staring across the table at her, with an expression of someone who can't decide if he's seeing a ghost, or if he's seeing someone he intends to make a ghost by the most expeditious means possible.

What the hell are you doing? Lev was tapping out pilot's code as well now, obviously still trying to hold the attention of the boyevik he was speaking to.

Just keep your head down, and get ready to run. Might get a little hot in here in a couple minutes.

She was grinning so wide it hurt.

The woman who'd taken de facto control of the group of officials, and who was possibly a smidgen less drunk than the others, flipped the remaining tokens in her hand. The others followed her lead, and for a breathless moment, they all stared down at the table.

"That's not possible," said the woman after a moment.

The man next to her gave a drunken grin that broadened into a loud, delighted laugh. "I won! I bloody won!"

"Yeah? Well done, then," said Jez jovially, clapping him on the back.

Behind her, the boyevik's glare had turned to pure ice.

She was pretty sure she remembered cheating him out of at least three months' worth of wages. Probably more, honestly.

He took a step forward, and Jez half-turned, letting her movements go slightly uncoordinated. "Well," she slurred, "guess you took me on that one. Thought I was going to win for a bit there. But what're a few credits between friends?"

"Nothing! That's what," said the man emphatically, and she grabbed his sleeve as if to catch her balance, pulling him casually between her and the enraged boyevik at the entrance.

The other government officials were still grumbling, but Jez shot them her best grin. "Come on, we're all friends here, right? You know, all on good terms and all? Hell, sit back down, might as well finish off the bottle."

Grumbling, they subsided, dropping back down into their seats. She poured another round of Golden Murder, and looked with regret at her own glass, still half-full from her first pour.

Well, they all had to make sacrifices.

"Anyways," she said, her voice still too loud, "guess we all know where to go for a good time these days."

They were all drunk enough that they didn't even question her statement, and she grinned at them.

Some people just couldn't hold their alcohol.

From the corner of her eye, she saw the boyevik making his way over to their table, a determined look on his face.

"Well," she said, standing and catching herself on the back of the chair, "we'll have to try this again next time. Not every day you get gambling partners like the group of you."

She'd tucked her scarf with its mafia colours carefully into her bag. No point letting Grigory's boyeviki know she'd been impersonating them.

"We'll see you around, then?" slurred one of the bureaucrats.

"'Course you will," she said, with a loud, drunken cheerfulness. "When you all come out to see us on the pleasure planet."

The man who'd won was still between her and the boyevik, which was a damn good thing, honestly, because if the sheer hatred he was glaring in her direction could have killed her, she'd probably already be dead.

"Hope you're ready for this," she muttered into the com. And then she stepped out from the table, weaving drunkenly, and grabbed the boyevik, as if trying to keep her balance. He stumbled, pulled off balance, and she slid her hand along the holster at his side and neatly extracted his heat gun before he had time to realize what she was doing.

"What, sorry you couldn't get in on the game?" she whispered to him. Then, before he could gather his wits to shout, she brought the butt of his gun down hard on the base of his skull.

He slumped to the ground without so much as a groan, and she stepped back, letting him land hard. "This damn drunk was trying to damn well rob me," she slurred at the top of her voice.

Two of the servers, and several of the patrons, turned at her shout, and she was mildly gratified to see her group of government officials turn too, in drunken indignation.

"Hey, you leave her alone," the woman shouted.

The boyevik Lev had distracted by doing ... something to her com, whatever the hell it was, glanced up, then swore and leapt to her feet, drawing her gun.

If she didn't recognize Jez from Grigory's ship, she'd recognize her after this.

The man Lev was talking to jerked his head up as well, and grabbed for his own weapon.

Jez shot them a cocky grin.

"There's a back exit," Lev hissed into her earpiece. "Comes out two streets over. Get behind the bar and into the kitchen, I'll meet you there."

"First, duck."

To his credit, he didn't ask questions, just hit the floor. She aimed, and fired what, for someone who was supposed to be about three quarters of the way to flat out drunk, was a pretty damn good shot, at the boyevik who'd been coming up behind Lev. The woman shouted in pain, grabbing her scorched shoulder, and Jez hit her com. "Alright genius. Now run."

He rolled to his feet and ran for the bar, dodging the two bouncers who'd come to see what the commotion was all about. Jez fired off another shot, narrowly missing another of Grigory's people—how many of the bastards were in here, anyways?— and then leapt a tipped-over chair, bumped hard into a table, sending tokens and drinks across the floor into the path of her pursuers, and started after him.

Someone grabbed her by the arm, and the force of her momentum whirled her around. It was one of the boyeviki she didn't recognize, an expression of grim triumph on his face.

"You Jez Solokov? Because I've heard—"

She glanced around, snatched a bottle from the nearest table, and broke it over his head. He staggered, blood running down his face, and Jez shoved him backwards, vaulted a table, crashed down in between two men locked in an amorous embrace, then slid around the bar and pelted down the hallway crowded with servers towards where Lev had said there was an exit.

"Jez," he said into her earpiece, his voice surprisingly calm. "When you come around the corner, duck."

"Got it," she panted.

There. That must be the corner he was talking about. She skidded on the floor wet with spilled alcohol and slippery with shattered glass, caught herself against the wall, and dived through a swinging door, keeping her head low. There were footsteps pounding behind her, but Lev grabbed her arm and yanked her around behind the door frame. He held a finger to his lips, and she swallowed down her question.

Three boyeviki appeared in the opening, and as they stepped through, a crackling blue line shot like lightning across the entrance, right at neck-level. The man in front screamed and dropped, and the two behind him fell to the ground convulsing.

She shot a glance at Lev, who had a slightly smug look on his face.

"I switched two of the wires on the lighting system," he said. "It will keep sparking every time someone comes through there until they figure it out. It's not enough power to kill anyone, but it will probably put them to sleep for a few minutes. Come on, let's get out of here."

The back door was large and heavy, but a couple blasts from Ysbel's modded heat-gun was enough to melt even a very large and heavy lock, and moments later they were back out in the dark Prasvishoni streets, snow drifting down around them like dirty ash, their breaths puffing out white steam in the flickering orange glow of the grimy street lamps.

She was laughing almost too hard to breathe, and Lev was laughing too, and for a moment they clung to each other, panting and laughing and trying to catch their breath enough to run. Then there was the *hiss* of a heat-gun blast through icy air, and she grabbed his jacket, and, still laughing helplessly, they pelted down the street as fast as their feet would take them.

Lev had the map of the city memorized, because of course he did, and he led them through narrow alleyways and down back streets until they reached the hangar. By the time they slipped inside, they'd stopped laughing, mostly because they didn't have the breath for it any longer.

"Get inside, genius," she panted, as the loading ramp began to lower. She vaulted inside the moment there was a space wide enough to admit her and reached down. Lev grabbed her hand, and she hauled him in as a cluster of Grigory's boyevik skidded through the door of the hangar, already firing. Lev hit the controls to close it as she threw herself into the pilot's seat, and the *Ungovernable* shot through the partially opened doors, sending boyeviki sprawling, and then they were out into the city.

"They'll be coming after us with ships, I'm almost certain of it," said Lev grimly. He'd been thrown backwards by their precipitous escape, but he'd managed to catch hold of the seat back, and now pulled himself into the copilot's seat and strapped down.

"Figure it wouldn't be much fun if they didn't," she said with a grin, running her fingers along the controls. "You ready for some flying?"

His expression turned, if possible, grimmer. "Just tell me you didn't actually drink as much as it looked like you drank."

She turned long enough to wink at him. "Come on, genius, you think that would slow me down?"

"Slow you down? No," he muttered. "That's not what I'm worried about."

She flipped the ship on its side and dived into a wide strip between the buildings, the light haze of snow turning the front window into a hypnotizing blur of streaking white. Ion-cannon shots blasted off the walls behind them, and she turned down the narrow dock streets to the nearest force-field entrance as chunks of prefab sprayed out like slightly thicker snow behind them. They shot through the gate past the astonished guards, and she pointed their nose for the sky.

"They're going to be after us still," said Lev grimly. "Grigory's not going to give up that easily."

She leaned back in her seat, basking in the luxurious feeling of flying, and shallow space, and ship's controls beneath her hands. "Well," she drawled, "figure they might try. But they're going to have a hell of a time of it. Seeing as we have hyperdrive and they don't."

By the time she'd pulled out of hyperspeed and spun them around behind a floating bank of space junk, just in case their pursuers followed them through the nearest wormhole, Lev looked like he might lose his streak of not throwing up.

She grinned at him. "Hey genius. Figure we did alright back there."

He swallowed hard and closed his eyes for a moment. Then, to her shock, he began to chuckle.

She stared at him, but as his chuckle became an actual laugh, she joined in without meaning to, and for a few moments they were laughing as hard as they had been outside the back door of the club. At last Lev subsided, wiping his eyes and shaking his head.

"Jez," he said, "did you actually let those government officials win at tokens?"

She grinned at him. "Yep. Sure did." She paused a moment. "Of course, while they were putting in their bids, I managed to tap their credit chips and rob them completely blind. But they did win the game. Anyways, if they remember anything at all after they wake up tomorrow, they'll think it was Grigory's goons. You know, like the one who was trying to rob me while I was helpless and drunk?"

He was shaking his head, still chuckling. "I've certainly seen you drunk, Jez, but I've never in my life seen you helpless." He paused a moment. "So you weren't actually drunk."

She rolled her eyes at him, still grinning. "'Course not, genius." She let a moment of regret filter through her happiness, remembering the half-empty glass she'd left at the table. "Although it's a damn shame to waste that kind of alcohol. I'll get some for you one of these days, then I figure you'll understand the kind of sacrifices I make for this team."

He shook his head ruefully. "I smelled the alcohol in that bottle from across the room. I'm actually not certain how you could pour something that strong without it vaporizing on contact with the air. I think I'll leave that particular drink to you."

She shrugged, still grinning, and brought the ship out in a wide arc towards the coordinates of their pleasure house. "Your loss."

He smiled at her, and she smiled back at him, and for a moment something choked in her throat.

"Thanks," she said quietly, when she could speak again.

He raised an eyebrow, then gave her a soft, rueful smile in return. "I'm sorry I was such a complete bastard that you thought this was something to say thank you for," he said. "But. Um. Thanks for giving me another chance anyways."

And as they burned through the atmosphere, she honestly couldn't remember how long it had been since she'd felt this happy.

11

Tae pinched the bridge of his nose, fighting off a headache.

If Lev had calculated right—and Lev almost always calculated right—Tae should be hearing from one of Grigory's people any day now. And he had a sinking feeling he knew who was going to be contacting him.

He'd hardly been able to sleep for the last two nights, worrying about it.

At last he opened his eyes and glared down at his holoscreen.

"Masha," he said through his teeth, without looking up. "I've set this up the way you asked me to. Anyone who looks at it will think it's an account at the Svodrani National Bank. You have everything you damn well need. But I have things to do if we want this finished before Grigory gets here." He slapped his hand down on his com, and the holoscreen disappeared. "I'll send the information through to your com later, when my program's finished running," he muttered, shoving his chair back and standing. "Anything else?"

"No, Tae," said Masha quietly. "That's all. Thank you."

He didn't bother to respond, just left the room and closed the door firmly behind him.

Once he was outside, he leaned against the wall of the broad hallway, breathing in deeply.

She'd never told them everything. He'd always known she was hiding things.

But—well, but he'd always believed, deep down, that she wouldn't actually go as far as outright betrayal. She might walk up to the edge, yes, but he'd been certain she'd never actually step over. And when she had …

The look on her face months ago, when they'd been cellmates in that forsaken prison. When he'd realized he'd miscalculated, and he couldn't get everyone out, and she'd told him it wasn't his fault. That everything didn't have to depend just on him, and that he should actually get some sleep, for once.

That had been the first time he'd believed she actually looked at him as a person, not just something to use and throw away. The first time he'd started to believe that maybe he could trust her, that despite everything, he could depend on her to keep his friends safe.

And he'd been wrong.

He straightened, shaking his head. It didn't actually matter right now. What mattered was, he could stand to be around her for long enough to give her the tech she needed. And he could stand to work with her for long enough to keep his friends alive. That was the important part.

And until the call from Grigory's people came in, he may as well help get things ready.

When he reached the main lobby, Galina stood in one corner, with four or five of their motley group of ex-convicts gathered around her. When she saw Tae, she looked up and gave him a quick smile.

"Tae. I need to talk to you. Give me a minute to finish up here."

He nodded, and took a seat on one of the luxurious chairs that lined the sides of the lobby.

Around him was the bustle of people readying for their roles—crates were being dragged across the floors, a man in a skin-tight uniform was practicing some sort of dance moves over and over against one wall, and a woman dressed like a weapons dealer was bent over, fixing a knife into a holster on her boot.

He didn't realize he was looking for someone until Ivan stepped into view, dressed in a server's uniform, his mild face with a slight smile on it, his figure as contained and elegant as always. Tae found his eyes following his friend as he walked across the floor, every movement somehow both unassuming and graceful. He paused to talk to someone, and the woman laughed, and even though Ivan kept his face solemn, Tae saw the smile-wrinkles form around his eyes and at the corners of his mouth.

It wasn't until Ivan had left out the opposite door that he realized Galina was standing beside him.

"Tae," she said, and there was a small smile on her face. "We need to discuss your role. Hopefully you can stay in the background, but we need you assigned to something, just in case. I've talked to Masha and Lev—you'll need to be as free as possible to run the tech, but there may be times when you'll have to step in."

Tae nodded absently.

"I was thinking of making you a customer."

He jerked his head around and stared at her.

"Galina, listen," he said, when he'd regained his voice. "I'm not sure what you know about me. But I'm a damn street kid, alright? Put me as a cleaner, if you want, or one of the staff. I can't—"

Her face was serious. "Listen, Tae. I understand, believe me. Ivan originally suggested that you work as a server with him."

Tae tried to ignore the way his face heated.

"But a server wouldn't be able to move around as freely as you'd need to. If someone ordered you out, you'd have to go. This is the best solution we could think of."

Tae closed his eyes. "I—I can't—"

Galina sighed and shook her head.

"Tae." Tanya had come up to join them, and was giving him an appraising look. "You don't have to do anything that makes you uncomfortable. You don't have to touch the entertainment or anything. Just look at them like you want to, that's all we need you to do."

"I—" His face was hot, and he could feel his hands shaking. "I can't—I—" He blew out a long breath. "My friends were street kids," he said at last, in a low voice. "You think I don't know that it could be any one of them here, if we weren't lucky? I can't do this."

Tanya studied him for a moment, then at last she nodded and turned to Galina. "He's right, I think. Tae is possibly the only one in the entire crew who's actually a moral person all the way through."

"I'm—sorry," Tae muttered.

Tanya gave him a long look. "That's not a bad thing, Tae. But," she turned back to Galina. "It does mean that we have to come up with a new plan."

Galina was frowning. "We could try him as a server, I suppose," she said at last, dubiously. "It's not ideal, and it may leave us in a bad spot, but possibly—"

Tae sighed and tipped his head back against his chair. "Listen," he said through his teeth. "What if—" he blew out a breath. "When we were in the university, Jez started some rumours about me. That I'd been a model citizen, and—and I'd had—"

"A boyfriend on every planet, I remember," said Tanya. She wasn't smiling, but the corners of her mouth twitched slightly. She turned to Galina. "That might work, you know. He's seen so much he's bored by all of this?"

Galina raised her eyebrows, staring at Tae. "I—suppose that would—Jez said—why did Jez—"

"Because she thought it would—look, it doesn't matter, alright?" he ground out.

She shook her head again slowly, considering. "It—could work, honestly." She turned back to Tae. "We could spread your backstory around, and then all you'd really have to do is lounge around and look bored. That could work."

Tae sighed heavily.

At this point, it hardly seemed worth trying to fight it.

Tanya gave him a sympathetic look, but she was still obviously trying to fight back a smile. "I'm not sure if this makes you feel better, Tae, but I'm part of the entertainment."

He gave her a skeptical look. "How many of the customers are you going to kill?"

She laughed. "None, I hope."

He sighed again, and glared at the two women. "Fine. I'll do this. But neither of you had better tell Jez—"

"Tell me what?" Jez sauntered over. "Hey tech-head. What are you going to be?" She turned to Galina. "You know what Tae would be good as? Some player boy. I mean, he already has that reputation pretty much everywhere he goes."

Tae gritted his teeth. "Jez. If you so much as—"

A notification dinged on his com, and he glanced down.

Then he felt the blood drain from his face.

Zhenya.

Of course it would be Zhenya.

From the corner of his eye he saw Jez's expression turn from a smirk to one of concern, and Tanya and Galina both frown at him.

"Hey. Tech-head. You alright?" Jez's voice came from what felt like a hundred kilometres away.

He took a deep breath and shook his head to clear it.

He'd been expecting this. They'd all been expecting it. Counting on it, really.

Still—he couldn't get out of his head the last time he'd sat with Zhenya, and the mafia pakan had sat back in their chair and casually told him that Ivan was walking to his death. He couldn't forget the frantic, desperate panic that he wouldn't solve their puzzle in time and Ivan would be blown to bloody pieces in front of him and there'd be nothing he could do about it.

He looked up at the circle of concerned faces, and tried to force a smile onto his face.

"It's … it's the call we were waiting for. Zhenya. They want to see me. And they'll kill Caz and Peti and the rest of them if I tell any one of you."

Tanya nodded grimly. "Good. That's what we planned for, yes? Come on. I'll call Lev, and we'll get you ready. When do they want to meet?"

"Tonight," said Tae softly.

The rest of the day was spent in hurried conference with Lev, Tanya, and Masha. Jez haunted the room, her usual snarky grin cut with worry, and Ivan kept poking his head in to see how they were doing, and bringing something for them to eat when they'd all forgotten it was long past mealtime.

By the time the streets were darkening, there was a knot in Tae's stomach large enough that he wasn't sure he'd be able to keep down the food he'd eaten earlier, but they were as prepared as they could be.

"The bug in your com is undetectable, right?" asked Lev for the hundredth time, as they sat in the conference room.

Tae nodded. "It's not really a bug. It's a recording device, but it doesn't send anything out, so it won't be easy to catch. If I'm killed, it will trigger the com to send everything, but as long as I still have a pulse, nothing goes out."

"So if they just knock you unconscious, or put you in a coma—"

Tae gave Lev a tight smile. "Don't worry. I'll find a way to kill myself if it comes to it."

"That's—not what I meant," said Lev. His voice was sharp with concern.

"He's got a tracker on his com, anyways," said Tanya grimly. "If there are strange movement patterns and he's not back when we expect, I'll be able to find him."

Lev nodded, but the worry on his face didn't subside. He turned back to Tae. "Alright. He's going to think he has Caz and Peti and the others somewhere he can get at them. We've got their records tied to another apartment building several streets away from the one they're currently in, and where they are currently is protected by Olyessa's people. So even if Zhenya does discover our trick, there's no way Grigory's boyeviki can get in to hurt them, right Masha?"

"That's correct," Masha murmured. She'd been uncharacteristically quiet, only speaking when necessary, and Tae had the uncomfortable feeling she was doing it because she didn't want to make this any more difficult for him than it had to be. Which only actually made it worse. If she'd bloody well be a jerk about it, it would be easier to hate her, instead of feeling like someone had ripped out a piece of his heart and then tried to sew over the empty spot.

He stood quickly, pushing back his chair. "Alright. I'd better get going. I don't want to be late."

"You have your weapons, yes?" asked Tanya. "There's no way you bring them in to the meeting, I think, but at least to keep you alive on the way there and back."

He nodded, checking his holster for the modded heat-gun Ysbel had supplied.

"Good," she said. "I don't know that there's much else we can do."

Tae nodded again, trying to fight down the sick worry, then turned out the door.

"Good luck, tech-head," said Jez as he stepped through the doorway, clapping him on the shoulder. He had to bite back a sharp response.

She was just worried about him.

He thought she'd walk with him to the hangar bay, but instead she gave him a knowing wink and strode off down the hallway in the opposite direction. He looked after her for a moment, shaking his head, then turned towards the skybikes.

He'd wanted to be alone, of course. But for some reason, stepping into the darkened hangar without any of the others even to see him off made his heart drop, just a little.

Which was ridiculous. He wasn't a kid, and he didn't need someone waving goodbye.

"Tae."

He spun.

Ivan stood by the bikes, waiting for him, and the concern in his voice was almost enough to crack Tae's fragile composure completely.

He stepped over and grabbed Tae in a tight bear hug. "I didn't want to miss you before you left."

Tae felt himself relaxing into the warmth of Ivan's embrace, leaning into him unconsciously.

"Are you alright? Really?" Ivan whispered. "If—if I can go instead, if there's anything I can do—"

Damn it to hell, he couldn't afford this. He had enough to do to keep everyone alive, and he couldn't afford to get distracted.

"Tae?" Ivan pulled back slightly, peering at him with a worried expression on his face. "Honestly. Are you alright?"

"I'm—I'm fine," he managed, his voice shaking just a little.

Ivan didn't let go of his shoulders, and didn't look away, and his eyes were dark and concerned and as deep as deep space, and Tae was about to get lost in them if he didn't look away right now.

He managed to tear his gaze off Ivan's. "Anyways, I'd—I'd better get going."

"Yes. I guess you'd better." Ivan let go of his shoulders with something that was almost reluctance, and there was a wry tone in his voice.

Tae took a long breath and blew it out slowly, trying to steady his heartbeat. "I'll be back as soon as I can, and I'll let you know what happens. This is what we planned for, so there's nothing to worry about."

He wasn't sure if he was trying to convince Ivan, or himself.

Ivan smiled at him, but there was still that sharp concern in his eyes, the lines of worry around his mouth. "Alright. Just—be careful, OK?"

"Yeah," Tae mumbled, turning to the skybikes. He threw his leg over one quickly, before he could lose his nerve and look at Ivan again, and started it up. It rose gently, and he couldn't resist one final look over his shoulder as he leaned slightly forward and the bike idled out the hangar door.

Ivan was still watching him, a dark silhouette against the light from inside the building, as he turned down the street.

By the time he approached the place Zhenya had set for a meeting, he'd somehow managed to slow his heart rate down to almost its normal speed, and his hands were only trembling a little. The cool of the night air had helped, at least, to clear his tangled thoughts, and now most of his shakiness was only due to the fact that he was coming to meet Zhenya, who had easily outsmarted him the last time they spoke, and the fact that if he made one wrong move, he'd be killed.

After what he'd dealt with over the past few months, the thought that if he messed up it would be only him who would die for it was refreshingly calming.

There were people waiting outside the entrance to the small, dark doorway, lurking in the meaningful way of people who wanted to be seen while appearing not to want to be seen. He'd seen enough of the unspoken threats on Grigory's ship that this had an almost comforting air of familiarity to it.

He idled his bike to a stop, dismounted, and leaned it up against a stair-railing, locking it in place with a mag lock. The lurkers had moved closer, ever so slightly, and he allowed a hint of his nervousness to show in his movements.

He couldn't appear too calm. If he honestly thought Zhenya would be able to hurt Caz and Peti—well, he was pretty sure he'd actually vomit on the street corner before he managed to get inside.

He laid a reassuring hand on the holster of his heat gun as he walked carefully down the steps to the darkened doorway, and with his free hand, pulled the door open.

The light that streamed out almost blinded him after the cool dark of the evening, and the music and warmth inside, along with the thick smell of sump cut with the sharper smell of other liquors and the sweet cloying scent of various street drugs he could probably identify if he took the time to sort through them assaulted his senses. He blinked and took a step inside, and it wasn't until he'd blinked a couple more times that he felt the cool, hard pressure on his ribs that had to be the muzzle of a heat-pistol.

"Tae Bezdomnikov," said a quiet voice beside him. "It's good to see you again."

He turned, and saw the vicious smile on the face of a woman who he recognized from Grigory's ship.

Her expression told him she was only glad to see him because she had a pistol at his ribs.

"I'm here to—" he tried to make his voice sound more bold than he felt.

She smiled mockingly. "Here to meet with the pakan, I know. Now, here's what we're going to do. You're going to move your hands somewhere I can see them. Then you're going to let my friend here remove your pistol and do a quick scan. And once we're both satisfied that you're unarmed, you're going to walk ahead of me, nice and easy, exactly where I tell you to."

He stood still while the man beside her, another boyevik who he vaguely remembered, pulled Ysbel's modded pistol out of his belt, and did a quick scan for weapons. He found the knife in Tae's boot, and confiscated that as well. Then the woman gestured him forwards, keeping the gun jammed painfully into his ribs.

"Go on," she said. "Get moving. Don't want to keep Zhenya waiting."

He gritted his teeth and did as he was told.

No one in the club looked up as he walked past. The boyevik holding the gun was clearly experienced—she walked in a casual manner, her gun hidden beneath her jacket, her posture relaxed, as if she had her hand on his back because they were friends, or maybe lovers. He closed his eyes for a moment, collecting himself.

If he died here, no one would be any the wiser. Even if Lev and Tanya realized something was wrong, there'd be no way they'd get to him in time. And they hadn't dared send an escort. If Zhenya caught one whiff that he wasn't alone, he was as good as dead, and their plan was shot.

The boyevik beckoned him up a short flight of stairs and through a doorway into a private room. He stepped through reluctantly, and glanced quickly around the small space.

Zhenya sat at the end of a long table, leaning back in their chair. Their posture was the same as it had been on Grigory's ship, a mixture of casual confidence and the sort of alert readiness that came from being raised on the streets. They half-stood as he entered, a small smile spreading across their face.

"Tae," they said, gesturing to the seat beside them. "I'm so glad you were able to get away."

Their smile was predatory, but there was something genuine about it too, as if Zhenya was honestly happy to see him.

The boyevik prodded him forward, and reluctantly, he crossed to the chair, his movements stiff.

"What are you going to do to my friends?" he asked in a low voice, the moment he was close enough. "Why are you threatening them?"

"Patience," Zhenya said, with a lazy smile. They waved a hand at the two boyeviki who had brought Tae, and both of them backed out the door, closing it behind them.

"You'll get your weapons back, don't worry," said Zhenya, glancing over at him. "I have no intention of taking anything of yours."

"Why did you bring me here?" he asked again, his voice harsh with the strain. "And what are you going to do with my friends?"

Zhenya sat back in their chair, watching him appraisingly. For a few moments they didn't speak, just looked at him, as if he were a puzzle and they were trying to find a solution.

"Tae," they said at last. "You and your friends—outwitted us. Outwitted me. What you did was exactly what I was supposed to protect against. Grigory doesn't blame me, of course—who could have predicted what you did on that ship? In fact, I think he was impressed that I was able to shut you out of the systems in the first place. But," Zhenya leaned forward slightly. "But Tae. I'm upset with myself. I'm upset that I wasn't able to foresee that. Because that's my job. That's what kept me alive on the streets all those years. And I don't like failing."

Tae watched them, his teeth clenched painfully.

He needed this. The whole crew needed this. But the moment he'd walked into this room, he'd remembered why he'd felt that gut-deep dread at the sight of Zhenya's name on his com.

Because Zhenya was smart. They were a survivor, and they were smart, and they'd already outwitted him once.

"I watched you, you know. While you were on the ship. I had my people watch you. You're not the outsider you pretended to be. But you're not completely aligned with the rest of them, are you? I noticed that. You care for them, certainly. But you're not really one of them. Your street family, though—they're the ones who kept you alive, kept you from ending up on a planet like this as entertainment. And you gave up your own rations and your own blanket on the coldest nights, didn't you? Kept them alive, too, when there was no way they would have survived without you. That kind of bond, Tae

—it means something. Maybe more than your alliance to a group of people who might have your back, or might, possibly, not. Hard to tell sometimes, isn't it?"

Tae's heart was pounding. "What do you want, Zhenya?" he asked again, the strain roughening his voice. "You brought me here. Tell me what you want from me."

Zhenya smiled. "I want to win my self-respect back. A petty thing, maybe, but there it is." They leaned forward on the table, and there was a gleam in their eyes. "I want you, Tae, to tell me how to beat Masha. And in return, I'll keep your street kid friends safe. That's what I want."

Tae bit down hard on the back of his teeth.

This was what he and Lev and the others had wanted. This was exactly what they'd wanted, and Zhenya had played right into their hands.

He wasn't sure why his palms were sweating and his mouth had gone dry.

"Why—" He swallowed, and tried again. "Why should I help you?"

Zhenya raised an eyebrow. "I thought I'd explained that."

"How do I know you aren't bluffing?" he kept his voice low.

He had to appear suspicious. He had to appear reluctant, because one wrong move now and everything went to pieces.

Zhenya smiled, a small smile that was almost fond. "You're right, of course. Anyone could have looked up your background, at least what was replaced on your file after it was wiped. They could have tracked down information, found out the names of your friends, of the brother and sister who are holding everything together in your absence. Caz and Peti. They could have found the file the police have on them as well—although I'm not sure if you've seen that yet.

It's surprisingly extensive. Apparently, your antics have made the government very interested in your friends. They could have read all about little Mila, the youngest child in your gang. She's what, only just seven? This month, I think, as far as the information we have on her suggests. You know, I believe I have some idea why she keeps getting fevers. But then, I'm not a doctor, so I could be wrong."

Tae's heart was beating out a quick, frantic pattern in his chest, like the wings of a trapped bird.

This was all part of the plan. Zhenya was right, anyone with sufficient resources and contacts could have learned all of this. But hearing his friends' names in their mouth, the intimate details of their lives—

Zhenya leaned a little farther forward, placing their hands on the table, and their grin widened slightly.

"But Tae. Even if I had access to the best hackers money could buy—could I know what you said to them last night, when you called them on your com?"

Tae froze.

"Caz," Zhenya recited, leaning back slightly as if trying to remember the exact words. "Keep them safe, OK? Just make sure everyone stays inside as much as possible. I don't want any of you getting into trouble. It will only be for a little."

A cold numbness was spreading through Tae's entire body.

Those were the exact words.

That link was untraceable. He'd have bet his life on that.

He had bet his life on it, and the lives of all the other kids.

"You didn't want them to be used as bait, did you?" asked Zhenya softly, studying him. "I commend you."

"I—" he couldn't get words out. He couldn't seem to breathe, couldn't seem to remember how to make his muscles move.

"It wasn't your link, you know, if that's what's worrying you," Zhenya said. "I'm actually impressed at how you managed to do that. No, we got that recording because of the bug I had my people plant in their apartment. While Caz was out yesterday getting food. I'm afraid Peti is a little more anxious to go out these days, and I'm afraid that's our fault. Well, not mine specifically. I was always as kind as I could be to the girl. But she's a street kid, and she's smart. Smarter than Grigory realized, I think. He never had to survive on the streets, like you and I did."

Tae still couldn't speak. His muscles felt paralyzed.

Zhenya was still talking, seeming hardly to notice Tae's horror. "Were you thinking maybe I'd believed they were at the dummy address you planted?" they asked pleasantly. "You almost did fool me there, honestly. I consistently underestimate how clever you are. But what you didn't realize?" They let their smile broaden slightly. "How could you have known that I was friends with one of Olyessa's people? Of course you didn't know that. No one does, or he and I would probably both be dead. But it's to our mutual advantage. And he knows the people who watch that complex. He was able to track down your friends from the descriptions I gave." They gave a small shrug. "If it makes you feel better, no one other than me would have been able to do that. So your plan was more or less a success."

"I—please. Leave them alone." Tae's voice was a desperate rasp. "They're just—they're kids. They—"

"They need you?" Zhenya asked softly. They held Tae's gaze, and he couldn't look away, like he'd heard you couldn't look away from a sand snake before it struck. "Yes, Tae. They do. They need you to keep them alive. Your crewmates don't. If this plan of theirs goes badly, they lose a chance at revenge, perhaps, but that's all. Grigory will still come for them. He'll always come for them. I may be able to keep him from coming for you, because you weren't involved, thanks to me. You didn't blow up his ship and ruin his chances. But your crewmates either stay under Olyessa's protection, or they die, and pulling this off won't affect that one way or the other. Your street friends, though, Tae. The ones who do need you. I'm holding them in the palm of my hand right now, and all I'd have to do—" they brought one hand up, palm open, and clenched their fist in an abrupt motion.

Tae closed his eyes for a moment, swallowing back the sickness in his throat.

"What do you want?" It was his voice, but he couldn't remember saying the words.

Zhenya studied him, their face almost sympathetic. "I want, Tae, to know what your friends here are doing. I want to know how Grigory can beat them."

Tae took a long breath, then another.

Zhenya had found Caz and Peti. They could kill the street kids as easily as they'd said they could, he had no doubt of it.

But …

Lev's worried face, Ivan's concern, Jez, haunting the hallway outside the room while they were discussing strategy, even though he couldn't imagine it not driving her completely mad.

He opened his eyes at last. He didn't have to fake the haunted look on his face. "Alright," he said quietly. "I'll tell you."

Zhenya smiled. "I'm glad."

"They—Masha is trying to get a pleasure house going, you're correct." He still wasn't sure how he was talking, how the voice that sounded like his was coming from his mouth. "She—plans on sabotaging the Strani House and all the other houses that pay a cut to Grigory. There was that explosion in the pleasure district—that was us."

"We'd assumed that," Zhenya murmured with some amusement.

"And we've been able to get some ins with the wealthier politicians. She figures if enough of them take their business to our pleasure house, she'll be able to hurt Grigory enough to cause the Strani House, at least, to go under."

Zhenya nodded slowly. "That is what Grigory had assumed," they said. "But Tae. I'm surprised at you. You're going along with operating a pleasure house? That's not something I would have assumed you'd agree with, with what I know of you."

"There's a lot of things Masha does I don't agree with," he said, and he didn't have to fake the bitterness in his voice. "But at least this one won't use disposable entertainment. Maybe it's bad, but it's not as bad as the Strani House, and if it means the Strani House closes ..."

Zhenya smiled slightly. "You always surprise me in the best of ways. I wish more people had your morals. This system would be a better place." They paused a moment. "How is Masha funding this? That must take a staggering amount of credits."

Tae nodded. "It does. And she has to undercut Grigory's prices, so there's no way she makes it back. Olyessa's helping, and she put in the funds. Masha put in all her own funds, including the ones she stole off Vitali."

"And that was enough?" Zhenya prompted, their eyebrows raised delicately.

Tae sighed and shook his head. "I—I can't—"

"Who are you more loyal to, Tae?" asked Zhenya softly.

Tae closed his eyes.

The thing was, it wasn't a question of who he was most loyal to. That question didn't have an answer.

The only question now was, did he trust that Lev and the others could pull this off? Because if he answered what they'd planned for him to answer, they pulled it off, or Caz and the others died.

He took a deep breath. "No," he said at last, his voice sounding distant in his own ears. "Olyessa's wealthy, but not that wealthy. We're—Masha's opening an account with the Svodrani National Bank, asking for funds. She has the account set up as an investment, and she's hoping someone with deep pockets will come along. She's got a block on the account, so you can only buy in if you have sufficient credits. She needs it all at once, not something coming in a trickle at a time, and she thinks that will protect us." He didn't have to think about the words, he'd practiced them so many times. But when he'd practiced them, his voice hadn't trembled, like it was now. "If the Strani House goes down, and if she can sabotage the Pleasure District with a few well-placed explosions, sow some terror —well, she's the only game in town, really. It's not that risky of an investment, as investments go."

Zhenya watched him, eyes narrowed in thought. "I see," they said at last. "And you say she needs those funds."

Tae hesitated a moment, then reluctantly nodded. "Yes," he said at last. "She needs those funds, or she goes under."

"When?" asked Zhenya, still watching him.

He hesitated again. Zhenya shook their head, a faint smile on their face. "Tae. I know this is hard for you. But I will find it out, sooner or later. I'm very clever. And if you tell me, you'll be giving me all sorts of reasons to keep Peti and the others safe. I know you don't agree with this pleasure house anyways."

He sighed heavily, shoulders slumping in defeat. "Soon," he said, his voice barely audible. "She'll need it soon. Probably within the next couple of weeks. Certainly not long after the convention."

Zhenya nodded slowly.

"Are you going to try to block her account?" he asked. He didn't have to fake the dull hopelessness in his voice.

"I'm not certain yet what I'm going to do," said Zhenya. "I hate to make snap decisions. But you've given me a great deal to think about." They smiled again. "And Tae. I haven't told Grigory anything about your friends' whereabouts. I'm the only one who knows it, at this point. You see, I have no interest in hurting street kids if I don't have to, and I respect you far too much to wish harm on your friends. If I were to tragically die, of course, that information would be broadcast to the entire mafia, but in the meantime, it's a secret between you and me." They smiled wider. "And I appreciate the consideration you've showed in return. I've checked. This entire building is under a field I had set up, and I've been monitoring it. I doubt even you could hack around it. So I know you're not broadcasting our conversation to your friends. If you had, Caz and Peti and the rest of them would be already dead, but I knew you wouldn't take that chance. I gambled on it." They gave a gentle smile. "In a manner of speaking. I suppose we could say your friends unwittingly gambled on it. So I once again commend your intelligence, and your sense of fair dealing."

Tae said nothing. He was shaky with relief that at least he'd gotten this right, at least he'd foreseen this, even if he'd foreseen nothing else this whole damn evening.

Zhenya stood, pushing back their chair, and held out a hand.

Tae hesitated, then, forcing back a shudder, took it.

Zhenya smiled and helped him to his feet. "It's always a pleasure working with you, Tae Bezdomnikov. You turned down my offer last time I made it, and I suspect you'll turn it down again. But I say this in all sincerity—I would be honoured to work with you. I'm quite fascinated by you, Tae."

Tae didn't let himself react. He wasn't sure what he would have said or done if he had let himself react, because the sick, cold numbness that had come when Zhenya had quoted the words of his conversation with Caz the night before was still spread over him like a blanket.

He stood slowly, motions heavy and uncertain, and turned for the door.

"My people will take you back out to your skybike," Zhenya said. "I may call you again if I need you. If I do, please do remember how discrete you were this time, and how much I appreciate it."

He nodded without looking at them.

Perhaps being rude to one of Grigory's pakans was suicidal, but he somehow had the feeling that Zhenya wouldn't kill him, at least not right now. He was still a useful tool, after all—Masha had used him, and now Grigory wanted to. And there was no point in breaking a tool you still intended to use.

The two boyeviki from earlier were waiting outside the door. They escorted him to the door of the club and handed him back his weapons without a word. The woman was still looking at him with a seething hatred, but then, that hardly mattered.

Somehow he mounted his bike, and somehow he found his way through the streets back to the pleasure house.

Before he reached it, he did a quick scan of his com. There were no bugs there, only the small one that had been encrypted in Zhenya's original message to him. He'd built a wall around it, so it wouldn't show them anything he didn't mean for them to see.

Other than that, he was clean.

But then, that wasn't a surprise. Zhenya had him exactly where they wanted him, and they knew it.

He parked his bike, dismounted, and hung his helmet on the spike on the wall. When he turned to go back into the main building, he almost tripped on something, and he swore quietly. The something jerked upright, and he realized it was Ivan, and that he'd been sitting in the doorway waiting for Tae the whole time.

Tae stared for a moment, and for the first time, something penetrated the icy cold that had been sitting in his chest since the moment he'd seen Zhenya's face.

"Tae?" Ivan pushed himself to his feet, blinking. "Sorry. I—" he rubbed the sleep from his eyes and gave Tae a rueful smile. "I was going to wait up for you. Let the others know when you got back. I'm not sure if you realize this, but every member of this crew was driving themselves crazy the past couple hours. Me as much as any of them." He put a hand on Tae's shoulder, and despite himself, Tae felt his muscles relaxing at the touch.

"So. How did it go?" He peered closer at Tae's face in the darkness, and his own face creased with a sudden concern. "Tae. What happened? What's wrong?"

Tae gave an exhausted shrug. "I—I think we'd better call the others. It's—not good."

When everyone was gathered at last into the conference room, Tae stood up from where he'd collapsed on a chair in the corner.

"What happened?" asked Masha, her voice sharp with worry. "Ivan said something went wrong."

"Nothing went wrong from your perspective," said Tae bitterly. "I told them exactly what you wanted me to. I saw the wheels turning in Zhenya's head, and if they don't tell Grigory that he should invest in your company, I miss my guess."

"What did go wrong, then?" asked Lev quietly. He was watching Tae with concern, and for a moment Tae almost couldn't stop the tears of frustration and strain and exhaustion from coming to his eyes.

"They—they found out where Caz and Peti really are," he said finally. "Zhenya knows where they are. And they'll kill them if we make one misstep."

There was a long moment of silence. He almost couldn't bear to look at Masha, in case he caught a glimpse of triumph on her face. But he looked despite himself.

Her face had gone bloodless, and he wasn't sure if even she could feign the shock, half-hidden under her expression.

"How—that's not possible. How did they find out?" Lev's voice was strained. "I checked everything a thousand times. There's no way—"

Tae gave a small, bitter smile. "Except there was something we didn't plan on. Zhenya has a friend in Olyessa's organization who passed on the information. At least, that's what they told me."

He didn't look at Masha, but he didn't have to. She was smart enough to have heard the accusation in his words.

"Tae," she said at last. "I know you don't trust me, which is your right. But think, at least—I have no reason to want you under the thumb of Grigory, or Zhenya."

He did turn to her, finally. He didn't honestly think she'd done it, but then there'd been a lot of things he hadn't thought she'd do. "Of course," he said quietly. "You have no reason to want that. At least, no reason we know about. Right?"

She didn't say anything, but there was something in her expression that made him turn away quickly.

He didn't need to bloody well feel sorry for Masha, on top of everything else.

"Well," she said at last, turning back to the others. "This

complicates things. We're going to have to pull this off perfectly. There's no room for error. But I still believe we can do it."

"You're just going ahead with it, then?" asked Ivan softly, from where he'd taken a seat beside Tae. "This changes nothing?"

Masha turned to look at him, and her gaze was challenging. "Tell me, Ivan. What should it change? If we back out of this now, do you think Tae's friends are safe? If we stop this, Zhenya will know that Tae's told us. And they told Tae, one word of this to anyone else and those children die. Believe me. I know Zhenya. I've known them for years. They wouldn't hesitate for an instant." She shook her head. "No. We go on, because there's nothing else we can do." She looked around the room, her expression challenging.

Finally, Lev nodded. There was a tightness around his eyes, but his face had somehow settled back into its usual facade of calm. "I believe Masha's right," he said quietly. "There isn't an option at this point. We go forward." He closed his eyes for a moment and drew a deep breath, then turned to Tae. "I'm sorry, Tae," he said softly. "I should have foreseen this."

"It's not your fault," said Tae dully. "It's not anyone's fault."

It was, though. It was his fault. Not directly. But hadn't that been what he'd promised himself when he'd first taken the job with Masha, so many months ago? That he wouldn't put his friends in danger again?

And then Peti had been kidnapped by Grigory, and now this—it seemed he was a danger to them no matter what he did.

And Zhenya was right. Those kids needed him. They needed him to protect them from the consequences of his own stupid decisions. And he wasn't completely sure he could.

12

Once Masha had gone and he'd heard the door to her bedroom latch shut, Lev stood abruptly from where he'd been sitting on his cot.

He'd asked for the room beside Masha's for a reason. He suspected she knew that reason, but she hadn't said anything, and nor had he. And the click of her lock was her telling him that whatever they were going to do behind her back was safe for him to do.

He didn't know how much she knew, or how much she suspected. To be quite honest, he didn't care. She'd proven they needed to protect themselves against her. And perhaps she thought she had a tight enough stranglehold on them that it wouldn't matter. But what mattered right now was only that she didn't know the details of their plans.

That was all he needed at the moment.

He tapped his com. "Ysbel. Are you awake?"

There was a moment's pause, then Ysbel's voice came over his earpiece, groggy with sleep and faintly irritated. "Well, I am now. What do you need?"

"Did Tanya tell you what happened tonight, with Tae?"

"Yes." She sounded slightly more awake now.

"Good. Are the children asleep? Can you talk?"

"For the moment."

"Alright. I need everyone—you, Tanya, Jez, Tae. We'll meet in the conference room."

There was another pause. "And I assume this meeting will be without Masha present?"

"Yes," he said grimly.

"Alright," she said after a moment. "I'll get the others together."

It was only about fifteen standard minutes later that they were all gathered around the large conference table, blinking sleepily. Lev waited until everyone was inside and the door was shut. Then he said quietly, "You all know what happened to Tae."

They nodded without speaking. He could see the worry on their faces, the haunted fear cut deep into Tae's expression.

"I'm not going to let that happen," he said. "We're not letting Tae's friends die. So." He paused a moment. "We need a backup plan. Insurance if Masha isn't playing straight with us."

Jez gave a short, sharp shake of her head. "Lev, look, I get it. You're worried about Tae's friends. I am too. But Masha's not going to—"

"I don't know what Masha's going to do," he said quietly, meeting her eyes. "I wish I did. And Jez, I know you trust her. I know you have your reasons, although I admit I don't know what they are. But —even if she honestly doesn't want Tae's friends to get hurt, and I'm willing to give you the benefit of the doubt that she doesn't, what then? She will play this through to the end. You know that. And it's not like she's never made a miscalculation before."

Slowly, Jez nodded, her eyes still locked with his. He could see the struggle on her face, and the fact that she wasn't sure whether she trusted him or Masha more cut him deeper than he'd expected it to.

Still—well, he hadn't been particularly trustworthy himself recently, doing whatever he thought was necessary to keep Jez safe without even bothering to consult her. Working with Grigory on a plan he knew would sicken Jez if she knew about it.

At last, though, she said, "Alright. Alright, genius, I agree. We'll make a backup plan. You're right, no one is bloody well hurting those kids as long as I can do anything to stop it. But—we won't use this backup plan unless we have to. Right?"

He took a long breath and glanced around at the others. They were watching the two of them, no one speaking. He closed his eyes for a moment.

Masha was dangerous. Masha was probably the most dangerous person he'd dealt with, and that included Vitali and Grigory. She'd been on their side, or at least brought them onto her side, for long enough that he'd grown accustomed to working next to her, had actually come to believe she wouldn't pose a threat to them, even if she did to the rest of the system.

He'd been disabused of that belief on Grigory's ship.

But—well, but Jez still trusted her.

He hadn't realized, until he'd been forced to take a look at himself, how he'd grown accustomed to treating Jez. Like someone who had to be watched to keep her from hurting herself or tripping up the stairs. But she wasn't a kid, and she wasn't an innocent. She'd been thrown out of her home at fourteen, she'd told him that, had survived in one of the most vicious smuggler gangs in the system, stolen the crew boss's ship, and kept ahead of the consequences for years before he met her. She was whip-smart, she'd never have survived otherwise. And … well at this point, after their job in the university, she knew Masha maybe better than any of them.

If she trusted her—

At last he opened his eyes and met Jez's steady gaze. "Alright," he said quietly. "Only if necessary."

She nodded once, and stood. "Listen. I'm going to bed. I'm not letting those damn kids get killed, so if you need me, I'll be here. But I don't want to be part of this. I don't want to know about it unless I have to." Her voice was uncharacteristically grave. "Anyways, just— just remember what I said, OK?"

He nodded, and she turned and left the room, closing the door behind her.

Lev looked around at the others. "What about the rest of you?"

"I'll do whatever you need me to do," said Tae, his voice strained. "You know that. But—but I may have to meet with Zhenya again. The less I know, the better."

Lev nodded. "I agree. Go get some sleep, then."

Tae nodded, but Lev was fairly certain from the grim set to his face that the kid wouldn't be sleeping anytime soon.

"Go on," he said more gently. "At least try to sleep, OK? We'll figure this out, I promise. Your friends won't get hurt if there's anything I can do to prevent it."

Tae gave him a faint, strained smile, then turned for the door, exhaustion written in every line of his posture.

At last it was only Lev, Ysbel, and Tanya.

Ysbel looked up at him, raising one eyebrow. "Alright, Lev. What do you want us to do?"

Lev sank back into his chair and rubbed his hand over his face. "Honestly, I have no idea."

She looked at him for a long time. "You really think that Masha will let those children die?"

He looked up, not bothering to hide the exhaustion on his face.

"I'm not willing to bet their lives that she won't."

She nodded.

For a few moments, they were quiet. At last Ysbel said, "How far are you willing to go for this?"

He sighed.

That was the question, really. That had always been the question.

"I … don't know," he said at last. "I don't know."

There'd been a time, not too long ago, where he thought he had known. On Grigory's ship, with the memory of his onetime professor's attempt to kill Jez fresh in his memory, he'd thought he'd been willing to do anything at all.

And then he'd seen exactly what being willing to do anything at all looked like.

Oh, it would have been for a good cause, certainly. He would have done whatever it took to keep his friends safe. To keep Jez safe. But in the end, it wasn't what you were doing it for that counted. It was what you did.

Grigory had tortured a man to death in front of Lev, because he'd thought Lev would enjoy it.

And Lev had become the kind of person who Grigory might think would enjoy that.

He almost had been. Not someone who'd enjoy it, perhaps, but condone it anyways. He'd been almost willing to kill hundreds of innocent people, in order to stop the person who had the power to kill his friends. He'd been a hair's breadth away from it. A hair's breadth away from losing his damn soul, if he had a soul in the first place.

A hair's breadth away from losing Jez forever.

Because in the end, he'd been willing to do whatever it took to get what he wanted, just like Grigory was.

And he couldn't be that person again. He couldn't.

Ysbel was still watching him, but there was a look on her face that said she'd guessed what was going on inside his head.

"There are things I won't do, Ysbel," he said at last. He managed a wry smile. "I'm—still working out what those are. But to answer your question, I'll go as far as I can without making Tae and Jez ashamed to be in the same room as me."

She watched him for a few moments. At last she said, "One day, that's going to have to come from you. What you believe. Not what they believe."

"I know," he said softly. "But it's a step."

She nodded, and they were silent for a few moments. At last Ysbel said, "Well. If that's the case, then, I suggest you leave what needs to be done to Tanya and me. I have some ideas."

He nodded. There was a strange feeling in his stomach, a sort of dread mixed with relief. "Alright," he said. "I won't ask what you're doing."

"Don't. Please. I know you don't want to keep anything from Jez, and I'm glad, because that would make you a very terrible friend. She doesn't expect me not to keep things from her, though, and if she asks me, I will tell her to piss off."

He managed a chuckle.

"I will need one thing from you, though," she said.

"Yes?"

She gave him a small smile, and suddenly he was very glad that he wasn't in Masha's shoes right now. "I will need you to introduce me to someone."

"Who?"

"Your uncle. Vitali Dobrev."

He stared. When he'd recovered his power of speech, he said,

"Ysbel. What in the system are you thinking? First, he'd kill all of us on sight, and second, he's—"

"Here. On the pleasure planet. I've checked into this. I'm not surprised you didn't know, because he's been keeping his whereabouts confidential since we pulled our little heist. There are a lot of people who don't like him, and most of them he doesn't like back. But he's here. My father was a famous weapons designer, you know. I have plenty of contacts in that world, and no one who deals in weapons is stupid enough to lose track of a man like Vitali Dobrev."

"I—" for the first time in a long time, Lev was unable to come up with words.

"He'll talk to you. I promise. I don't think you understand how obsessed with you he is. You're his brother's son, and you outwitted him, twice. He's not the kind of man who forgets someone like that."

"I'm—fairly certain that he's only interested in me insofar as it helps his ultimate objective of actually killing me."

"Well yes, he does want to do that. But don't sell yourself short. That isn't the only reason he's interested in you."

"It's a relatively important one, as far as I'm concerned!"

She smirked at him. "At any rate, you know there are people thinking about you."

"Again, because they want to kill me."

She shrugged. "Anyways. You can believe me when I tell you, he may want to kill you, but he will talk to you if you ask. And if you introduce me to him, he'll talk to me. My father knew him."

"And what do you need to talk to him about?"

She looked at him. "And that, Lev, is what I would like you not to ask me, if you truly don't want to be hiding things from Jez."

Reluctantly, he nodded.

She was right—it was probably better for him not to know, at least until he was sure what he was and wasn't willing to do.

"Send me what you have on him," he said at last. "I'll find a way to speak with him."

"I suspect that will not be as difficult as you are imagining," she said with a grim smile.

"As I'm hoping," he muttered.

Her smile only widened.

13

"My heart. You will be alright while I'm gone?"

Ysbel looked up, startled out of her reverie.

Tanya was watching her, concern on her face. "Is everything alright, Ysi?"

Ysbel sighed, and tried to smile. "Yes. I—was just thinking about Vitali."

Tanya nodded, and, after a moment, sat down on the bed beside her. "Do you think he'll call you?"

"He'll call me. If Lev contacts him, he'll call me. I don't think he'll be able to resist."

"And you think he'll take you up on your offer?"

Ysbel paused a moment, then gave a short nod. "I'm quite sure he will."

There was something tight in her chest at the thought, though.

She sighed again. "Anyways, you don't need to sit here and listen to me worry. They need you out there. You go, I will take care of things here."

Tanya kissed her fondly and slipped out the door, and Ysbel looked after her with a foolish smile on her face.

She suspected she was as stupidly in love with Tanya as she'd been at fourteen, but then she deserved it now, after however many years of marriage.

"Mama!"

She bit back a sigh at the shrill shout, and turned to where her son was dragging something out of her bedroom.

She looked closer, then cursed under her breath, grabbing for him. "Misko! Where did you get that? Those are mama's explosives. You know you're not supposed to play with mama's explosives."

"I want to! I want to blow things up like you do!"

"No." She snatched the bundle of components out of his hands. "You are not to blow anything up until I have time to teach you how to do it safely, do you understand?"

He scowled at her. "I want to."

"Yes, but I said no. So you can't." She paused a moment. "Why do you want to? Is there someone you are angry at?"

"No," he muttered, dropping his gaze. "I just want to blow things up like you do."

She frowned at him. "Why?"

"Because. Because I want to be like you when I grow up."

She stared at her son, something strange stirring in her chest. "You—you do?"

"Yes," he muttered.

For a moment, she almost had to grab the wall to steady herself.

"Well," she heard herself saying. "Perhaps then we should sit down one of these days. Because if you want to learn about explosives, you need to be able to hold still so you don't kill yourself while you're putting them together."

He looked up at her, sudden hope gleaming in his face. "I'm going to learn how to blow things up?"

She smiled past the lump in her throat. "Well, we can try. But remember, you have to be able to sit still."

His whole face transformed when he smiled. She hadn't remembered how much, maybe because he'd spent most of the last weeks sulking. But he was smiling now, like a sun had lodged behind his eyes and was shining out of them, and he grabbed her around the legs in an over-enthusiastic hug.

"Careful! You'll knock me over and I'll land on top of you," she grumbled, but there was a lump in her throat. "You go finish your chores, and maybe after that we can sit for a little, and I'll start to show you some components."

His face fell again at the mention of chores, but he went, grumbling to himself.

Ysbel watched him go with eyes that were slightly misty.

She would never have thought it, honestly. A six-year-old proclaiming he wanted to be like her.

She'd lost them, five and a half years ago. But maybe, for the first time—maybe she was getting them back again after all.

She hardly noticed the sound of the door opening, several standard hours later. When she looked up, Tanya stood in the doorway watching them, a soft smile on her face.

"Hello, my hearts," she said. "You look like you've been having fun."

Ysbel glanced around. Misko had settled himself on her lap, and Olya was sitting across from her, organizing the explosives components in front of her into neat piles.

"We've been very busy," said Ysbel, trying to keep her face solemn. "Misko almost blew this entire place to dust before we decided that maybe I should help him."

"I didn't need help," Olya volunteered. "Mama told me what needed to happen, and I figured out how to keep the pieces separate until I got the ratios right."

"She did, you know," said Ysbel, glancing at her daughter fondly. "She's very good at this."

"She will be quite the threat, then," Tanya murmured, coming over to stand beside them. "She's already very good at what I do. She's a fast learner."

"I'm also a very good gambler," said Olya importantly. "Aunty Jez says so. She said I would be able to out-cheat her in a couple years, if I practice very hard."

Ysbel bit back her chuckle at the look on her wife's face and turned to her daughter. "Yes, well my love, perhaps that's something that should wait until you're a little older."

Olya gave her a skeptical look. "If I'm good at it, I should probably work on it right now. Mamochka says it's good to work on your talents."

"Well—" Ysbel paused and glanced up at Tanya again. "Perhaps we should talk about this later, Olyeshka."

Olya sighed and rolled her eyes, then reached for another component. "Anyways, I'm going to have a bomb that I made all by myself."

Ysbel watched her fondly. It was the simplest of bombs, but then she remembered how proud she'd felt, sitting in her mother's workshop with her very first explosive. It could hardly have blown the roof off their cottage, but it was hers, and that was all that mattered.

"When you're finished, I'll let you come into my weapons room and test it, alright?" she said, and Olya gave her a look that was almost hero worship.

She stood, taking Misko carefully off her lap. He clung to her for a moment before she put him down, and there was something about his small hands on her arms that made something expand in her chest until she wasn't sure there was room for it. She kissed him lightly on the cheek and set him down on the bench. "Only the components I gave you, alright? What happens if you touch one that mama didn't give you?"

"I go to my room," he muttered sullenly.

"And?"

"And you get to eat my dessert after dinner," he said, his eyebrows lowered threateningly, eyes narrowed in disgust at the injustice.

"That is right," said Ysbel impassively. She turned to Tanya. "Alright, my love. Tell me what is happening in the rest of the world."

Tanya glanced at the children. "Will they be alright alone for a moment?"

Ysbel looked at Olya. "Olyeshka, will you watch your brother?"

"Yes mama," said Olya primly.

"And if he tries to take any of the components that he's not supposed to?"

"I'll take them away from him and call you."

"And?"

"And grab him and run as far away from the table as I can and hide behind a door, in case something blows up."

Ysbel gave her a fond smile. "That's right. Good job." She turned to Tanya, who was wearing an expression of mild concern. "Don't worry, my love. I was younger than this when I started working with explosives. Besides, there's nothing here that would blow up anything bigger than this room, so if they're behind the door, they'll be safe."

"I—know that," said Tanya. "I suppose they just seem younger when they're your own children." She sighed, and stepped into the bedroom, and Ysbel followed.

They sat on the mattress, and Tanya reached out, taking Ysbel's hand and pulling it into her lap. For a few moments she just sat there, looking at the way their fingers twined together.

"What is it?" asked Ysbel.

Tanya looked up, as if startled, and then smiled ruefully. "I'm sorry. It's just—we got word on Grigory. They've been monitoring his communications, since Lev broke the code. He'll be sending people to check out the pleasure house in the next few days, and I'm not certain we're ready."

Ysbel frowned. "That soon?"

Tanya managed a slight smile. "It's a good thing, I think. This is what we've been waiting for. He's not going to risk money on something that isn't legitimate, and he's got to find out what's happening somehow. But it does mean we let Grigory's people in here, and—" she shook her head. "I don't know what he's capable of. I don't know if he wants us dead badly enough that he'd be willing to risk a quarrel with Olyessa. But it's not something we can discount."

Ysbel nodded thoughtfully. "Masha's not worried, I assume. But then, why would she be? She always has an escape plan. What about Lev?"

Tanya shook her head. "He's worried. He's trying not to show it, I think, but he's worried. And Tae looks like he hasn't slept since he came back from talking with that Zhenya."

"He'll be fine," said Ysbel, leaning over to kiss her wife on the forehead. "I don't think you realize how little that boy sleeps when we're on a job. I keep expecting him to fall over, but he hasn't yet."

Tanya gave her a small smile and sighed. "You know, that Ivan—"

"Would be good for him, I know. Do you think we should tell Tae that Ivan's completely off his head for him, or do you think he'll figure it out at some point?"

This time, Tanya gave a reluctant chuckle. "He's a good boy, you know."

"I know," Ysbel said softly. "I know he is."

They didn't speak for a few moments. At last Tanya said, "Ysbel?"

Ysbel opened her mouth to respond, but a small noise from her com stopped her. She glanced at it, then frowned suddenly, stomach tightening. "Just a moment, my love," she said quietly. "I think this is important."

She tapped her com. "Hello?"

"Ysbel." It was a man's voice, rough, but with a genteel accent.

She recognized it immediately.

"Vitali Dobrev," she said.

"Yes." He paused, and there was a trace of humour in his voice when he continued. "I suppose I should be swearing at you right now, or threatening to kill you. But to tell the truth, I'm intrigued. I got a call recently, from a long-lost nephew. And he asked me to call you, although he wouldn't tell me why. I was curious, and so I looked you up. Imagine my surprise." He chuckled, and there was a menacing quality to the sound. "I had no idea who you were when I had you locked in my cells a few months back. I wish I'd known. I wouldn't have missed the opportunity to talk shop with you. And now, here we are. I can't track you, because I imagine that hacker kid you had with you last time did something to your com. And whether or not you know where I am, you can't get at me. So, since neither of us can kill the other, I suppose we talk."

Ysbel was silent for a moment.

Whatever she said to this man, she'd have to weigh every word.

Vitali Dobrev. The weapons dealer. The man they'd stolen the *Ungovernable* from, in what seemed a lifetime ago. Lev's uncle. Even if she hadn't known that, his brilliant mind was readily apparent in every one of his vicious, deadly creations.

She glanced quickly at Tanya. Her wife's face was strained, but she gave a short nod. They'd discussed this, for hours.

"Vitali. I have a proposition for you," she said at last.

"Yes?"

"Suppose I told you I could give you Masha Volkova. Is that something you'd be willing to bargain for?"

There was a long pause over the com. When Vitali spoke again, his tone was calm, but she could hear the pulsing hatred under his words. "I don't think you realize how badly I'd like to kill you all, really. It would be a great pleasure to kill any one of you. But Masha Volkova? I would burn down the system to kill her."

"That's what I thought," said Ysbel, letting a hard edge show in her own voice. "I don't know yet if it will be necessary. I may as well tell you, Vitali—you are my backup plan only. But I believe this is something that could possibly benefit both of us."

There was another long pause. "Ysbel," he said at last. "Your father was many years older than me. And I don't believe he ever approved of my work, even though my dream was to emulate him. But he'd never have insulted me like that."

"Then perhaps you'd best learn who you're dealing with," said Ysbel, letting all the emotion drain from her tone. "Because my father was a very kind man. He would not have blown up a shuttle station and killed thirty-five people, or blown Lena's ship into space dust with her crew aboard. He probably would not have stolen your ship, and he'd certainly not be threatening to kill you right now. So I would like both of us to be very clear. You are not dealing with my father. Right now, I am working with Masha. There may come a time in the near future when I am not. If that time comes, I am giving you an opportunity to take your revenge. If you feel that's insulting, shut off your com now."

"You're willing to give me Masha Volkova, if she stops being useful to you," he said at last. "And what's your price?"

"I assume," said Ysbel quietly, "that if I asked you to send your people to protect some children in Prasvishoni, you could do it?"

"There is only one thing I would accept in trade for something like that," said Vitali, his tone back to a faint amusement. "Fortunately for you, it's what you've offered me."

"Good," said Ysbel. "Then let's discuss details."

When she finally shut off her com, she met Tanya's gaze. Both their faces were grim.

"Do you think it will come to that?" asked Tanya.

"I don't know," said Ysbel.

"You hope it doesn't," said Tanya softly.

Ysbel paused for a moment. At last, reluctantly, she nodded. "You're right. She betrayed us once, and she could easily do it again. But—you are right." She closed her eyes for a moment, fighting back the sick feeling in her chest. "And you, my Tanya? You are the one with the conscience. Am I doing the right thing?"

For a long moment, Tanya didn't speak. At last she said quietly, "We can't let those children die. So—yes. I believe you are."

For some reason, Tanya's words did nothing to quell the tightness in Ysbel's chest.

For a few moments they sat in silence. Then Ysbel said, lightening her voice with an effort, "So. You said you need to be able to find a way to protect us from Grigory's people, yes?"

"If things go badly, it would be nice to have a backup plan," said Tanya.

"I have a good idea," came a small voice from behind Ysbel, and she jumped, biting back a curse.

"Olya," she said, once her heartbeat had slowed sufficiently to allow her to speak. "I thought I told you not to sneak up on me."

Olya gave her a superior look. "I didn't sneak up on you, Mama. I just came over. I'm very quiet."

"Yes, well, I've noticed that. Good job. Please say something when you come through the door next time, though."

Tanya was fighting back a smile.

Olya sighed heavily. "Alright. If you really want me to."

"If you want your mama to live long enough to see you grow up, yes, I want you to," Ysbel grumbled.

Olya started to roll her eyes, noticed Tanya, and stopped herself mid-roll. "Anyways, Misko went to get some food, and I got it down for him, so he's eating right now. And I came to find you, and I heard you saying you needed a backup plan, right?"

"Yes, that's correct," said Ysbel warily.

"Well, I have an idea. What if we put a smoke bomb in the rooms? And if something goes wrong, you can set it off and yell fire, and then they'll have to get out."

Ysbel raised an eyebrow and exchanged glances with Tanya. "That's—not a bad idea, actually," she said, her tone thoughtful. "Let me think about it." She turned back to her daughter. "Thank you, my Olya." She paused. "You are very smart, you know. I think I've been missing out when I didn't use you to help me before. I—" She paused a moment, swallowing down something in her throat. "You were very young when I—when we got separated. So I suppose I'm not used to having someone around to help me when I need it. I'm sorry."

Olya smiled, but there was something pinched and worried in her face. "Mama?" she said at last, her voice small.

"Yes, my love?"

"Why did we come here? You never told me."

Ysbel sighed. "My love. You remember Grigory, yes? We're trying to stop him from killing us. And—" She paused. "And also, my Olyeshka, there are people in this place, on this planet, that … hurt people. They hurt people like your mamochka and your aunties and uncles. People like you. We're going to try to stop it."

Olya looked up at her, face pale and grave, and there was something in her look that told Ysbel she knew much more about this place than Ysbel had told her. "And you will stop it, right mama?" she asked.

Ysbel gave her a small smile. "Yes, my love. With your help."

The look Olya gave her then wasn't hero worship. Instead, it was something like adoration. Ysbel reached out her arms, and Olya allowed herself to be hugged, conscious of her dignity at first. And then she gave in, wrapping her arms tightly around Ysbel.

"I love you, mama," she whispered.

"I love you too, my Olya," Ysbel whispered back, through the lump in her throat.

14

"They're going to be here soon." Tae's strained voice came through Jez's earpiece, and she grinned reflexively.

"They'd damn well better," she murmured back. "Because honestly, I'm going to get bored pretty soon here, and considering I'm running a damn gambling hall with a damn bar attached—"

"Jez." Masha's voice was icy.

Jez gave a snort of laughter, and someone on the general line let out a long-suffering sigh. Normally she would have guessed it was Lev, but … well, but something had changed with Lev. She still wasn't sure how to react to it, but he wasn't harassing her nearly as much as he had been.

It was—well, it was honestly kind of nice. Nicer than she'd expected. Having him on her side, rather than trying to logically point out all the flaws in her plans, which, honestly, had never actually worked mostly because she started ignoring him the moment he opened his mouth to argue with her, but still … Anyways, knowing that he wasn't going to be pointing out all the flaws in her plan somehow made her look at them a little more closely to begin with, which might or might not be a bad thing, depending on how you looked at it.

She sighed heavily, glancing quickly around the dimly lit gambling hall, then took up her place at the back of the hall, on a tall stool set up against the wall-length mirror.

She always preferred cheating when there was a mirror in place. Gave her idiot partners a false sense of security.

The hall itself was not nearly as fine as the hall on Grigory's ship. Still, Galina had overseen it, and it was actually pretty damn impressive. That woman knew how to make something look nice. It had the ambiance of a small kabak in a backwater dirt-eater zestava, but the rough trappings were stylized and somehow elegant—the ubiquitous folding aluminum tables replaced with tables of something silvery and expensive-looking, polished to an old-metal sheen, the rickety stools replaced by stools of the same shape, but with comfortable seats and discrete back supports for people who planned to spend an evening gambling. The stereotypical rough bar was made of blocks of stone cut to look like prefab, but the soft gleam of them made it obvious that it was only a facade, and the counter was polished worked wood instead of rough-cut timber. And honestly, the collection of dark, elegant bottles behind the counter told you everything you needed to know. Yes, she'd gotten smashed on sump plenty of times in her life, but there was something distinctly different about getting smashed off something that would cost you enough credits that you could start your own damn smuggling cartel.

It was dimly lit, but her people were in place. Radic, at one of the tables, gave her a reassuring wink. She'd set him up to get the games running, and he'd agreed on the condition that she teach him how she cheated.

Wasn't going to show him all her tricks, but she'd given him enough to get him started, and from the wide grin she'd seen on his face while he practiced, he was very happy with the arrangement.

"You got this, Radic?" she said into her com in a low voice. He gave a brief nod. His face was tense with anticipation, but she could see the hint of a grin under his expression.

"Good," she said. "I'm going out. Figure they might need a hand. Besides, wouldn't be bad for me to be seen. Got a bit of a reputation on Grigory's ship. May as well let the bastard know that we're all here."

"Good luck," he said into the com.

She shot him a jaunty grin, and strolled out of the gambling hall.

Galina was waiting for her outside the door, and she straightened as Jez stepped out.

Jez looked her up and down in appreciation, letting her eyes linger on the very attractive curves that Galina's new outfit showed off to admirable advantage. She was dressed like a weapons dealer who'd made a hell of a lot of money—tight thigh-length boots, a soft, intricately embroidered black shirt, a fitted black vest. She had at least three heat pistols Jez could see, and probably a hell of a lot more that she couldn't, as well as a set of very sharp gutting knives attached to her belt, and honestly, she looked like she could walk into the middle of a crowd of people and gun down every last one of them.

It was a look Jez had always found completely irresistible.

She gave a low wolf-whistle. Galina dimpled—damn it, those dimples almost did Jez in every time, honestly—and gave Jez a wink. "Well," she said. "Are you ready to run your very own gambling hall? This is every dream you've ever had coming true, right Jez?"

Jez put her arm around Galina's waist and pulled her in for a moment, grinning, and ignored the small pang in her chest.

Because yes, running a gambling hall, not to mention a gambling hall that's only purpose was to pull a job on Grigory Korzhakov, and hopefully, in the process, cheat his boyeviki out of every damn credit they had, was actually something she was very much looking forward to.

But—

But to get here, she'd let Olyessa put a lock chip on her ship.

Even the thought of it felt like a splinter of metal in her lungs, making breathing difficult and relaxing impossible.

The *Ungovernable* was every dream she'd ever had come true, and the thought of losing her was like a piece of herself being ripped away.

"Well, you look like every dream I've ever had coming true," she said, making her voice light somehow. "You look like you could kill me without breaking a sweat."

Galina gave her that fond smile. "You, Jez, are probably the only person I know that gets off on people looking like they could kill you without breaking a sweat."

"Their loss," said Jez with a smirk.

Galina chuckled softly. "Well, according to Tae, our visitors should be here any minute now. I'm going to get into position."

Jez followed her out into the lobby, but there was still that ache in her chest, and she couldn't decide it had to do with her ship, or Galina, or what had happened between Masha and the rest of them, or all of it combined.

When she reached the lobby, she stared around her in frank astonishment.

She'd been focusing on her gambling hall, which, fair enough, because first of all, it was a gambling hall, and second, she was running the place, and third—well, third, she had no desire to know about the kind of entertainment that would take place in places other than the gambling hall. Even if they were all fake.

But what they'd done to the lobby almost took her breath away.

It was disgustingly, decadently opulent. Gold dripped from the chandelier, and gold coated the walls, and it wasn't even trying to be tasteful, just filthily rich. The chairs were upholstered in wine-red fabric that looked as soft as a warm bath, their legs the buttered glow of polished wood, and even the polished-stone floor was veined with gold.

It was light-years away from the rowdy construction site it had been the night before. Which was a good thing. A very good thing. But—

Well, but for a moment her stomach turned slightly. Because this looked too much like something real.

She took a deep breath and crossed over to where Masha was standing.

She steadfastly refused to look at the cages. Because hell, she'd seen a lot of crap in her life, but watching living, breathing human beings locked into cages was something she wasn't planning on experiencing if she could help it. She'd been avoiding the lobby ever since they installed the damn thing, honestly, and that had been before there'd been people locked in it.

She forced her mind away from the thought of other pleasure houses, other cages whose occupants didn't have an emergency key to get out any time they needed to.

"Hello, Jez," said Masha calmly. She was dressed resplendently, her trousers and vest brightly coloured and heavily embroidered, and her nondescript hair, usually pulled back in a simple rat's tail, hanging loose around her shoulders in soft waves.

Jez raised an eyebrow. "What, you decide to try for a model citizen role?"

Masha gave her a small smile. "No. I decided to dress the part of the proprietor of a pleasure house. Because, as you may remember, if we mess this up, we will all be murdered in very unpleasant ways."

Jez grinned. "Wouldn't be much fun otherwise, would it?" She turned and surveyed the room, still consciously averting her eyes from the cages.

Galina had settled herself into a chair across from the cages and was studying the actors inside with a critical eye. Across from her, another customer lay back on a couch, eyes half-lidded with the glazed expression of someone who was higher than the damn atmosphere, and had been for a long time. One of the "entertainers" was draped across his lap, her own eyes glazed. Part of it was the eye drop solution that Ysbel had come up with, but most of it was acting, and they were doing a good job of it, as far as Jez was concerned.

Although in fairness, any time Jez had been that high she had exactly zero recollection of how she'd looked.

A few other customers were scattered throughout the room, in various attitudes of debauchery, some with entertainment, others without, and the small, discrete chart of open rooms placed behind the desk was visible if you were looking for it, most of the rooms marked in a deliberate bold red as occupied.

She glanced over at the gambling hall. She'd taken care of that, she and Radic, anyways. He was a good man to have close when you were trying to set up a gambling hall and bar, to be honest. Although after having tasted the crap he'd distilled back in prison, she wasn't sure she trusted him with stocking the place.

"You know what you're doing, right Jez?" Masha murmured.

Jez grinned. "Know exactly what I'm doing. You want someone to cause havoc, figure I'm basically an expert."

Masha didn't respond, but her lip twitched slightly in what might have been the beginnings of a smile.

Jez's chest tightened again, because … well, because she still wasn't completely sure how she felt about Masha, and this wasn't making it any easier.

And then the doors slid open, and two people walked through.

Probably, if you didn't know who they were and you didn't have someone like Tae who'd been tracking every single one of Grigory's people on the planet for the past three days, you might have thought they were regular customers. But Jez had spent long enough on Grigory's ship to notice all the little tells—the way their eyes moved restlessly, taking in the room. The way they glanced at Masha, then glanced back again surreptitiously, as if wanting to watch her without being watched in return. The handles of weapons poking out of pockets and holsters. The stiffening in their postures when they saw Jez.

She grinned at them.

They glared back at her, the animosity in their gazes hardly disguised.

She looked them up and down insolently. No one she recognized, but then Grigory would hardly send someone they'd recognize.

What he'd sent was a man and a woman, both wearing fine clothes, both looking ever so slightly uncomfortable in their fine clothes, like you might if you'd practiced wearing them, but only for long enough to put on an act. The woman was pale skinned, with hair so light it was almost white, the man's complexion around the same colour as Jez's, his long, straight black hair hanging around his shoulders.

"You the proprietor here?" the man asked, looking Masha over and ignoring Jez.

"Yes," said Masha smoothly. "I am, as a matter of fact." She gestured around the room. "As you can see, we're quite busy. But tell me what you're looking for, and I'll see what I can do for you."

"I heard you were the new game in town. We wanted to come see," said the woman lazily.

"Of course," said Masha. She turned. "Jez? Would you do the honours?"

Jez winked at her and turned to the two, who'd stiffened palpably.

The sight sent a warm flood of satisfaction through her chest. Honestly, it was nice to know you'd made enough of an impression that people told their friends about you. Honestly, she'd cheated so many of Grigory's damn boyeviki out of their credits she could probably have set up shop on her own, if that was what she got off on.

"Guess that means Masha likes you," she said in a stage whisper to the two people who were eyeing her with something approaching loathing. "Not to brag or anything, but I'm pretty damn important around here. But hell, I like Masha, so I do her a favour now and again. Come on, I'll show you 'round."

They followed her, and she brought them out the back way into the gardens.

On our way back, she tapped out in pilot's code, her com resting casually against her thigh.

Ready, came the reply.

She held her com to the panel in front of the doors, and they slid open.

The gardens, like the lobby, had been transformed. The bushes and shrubs were arranged artfully, blocking off secluded alcoves from which slurred voices and wordless moans emanated. Flowers, garishly coloured and too large to be natural, drooped from trellises, their thick, heavy scent smothering in the warm air.

"Here's the garden. Can't get in unless you have a guest token, which means making nice to Masha," she said over her shoulder. She led them through a maze-like passageway, glancing around surreptitiously.

Supposedly, she was supposed to stumble over someone right about in the centre of this hell-hole, but she was pretty sure she'd passed the centre already.

Damn it, what's happening? She tapped out.

Sorry, came a hurried reply, but nothing else. She narrowed her eyes.

The damn flowers were already giving her a headache.

Then three people tumbled out through the bushes and into the path in front of her. She jumped back, cursing, and grabbed for her gun before she realized that she recognized all three of them. Two were dressed as entertainment, one was dressed as a customer, and they all looked slightly sheepish.

"Hey, you bastards," she snapped, "you want to use the garden, you can damn well stay where you've booked."

"I'm—sorry," said the woman dressed as a customer, straightening and brushing dirt off her dress. She cleared her throat and seemed to be trying to regain her dignity. "You two," she snapped at the two "entertainers" who were still on the ground. "You heard that. Get up."

They rose, heads bowed meekly, but Jez caught just the twitch of a grin at the corner at one of their mouths. The "customer" jerked her head, and they followed her back through the newly created hole in the bushes.

Jez glanced over her shoulder. The two boyeviki were watching in faint confusion.

She grinned at them. "Like Masha said—get all types in here."

"Take them up the right-side path," came Lev's voice in her earpiece, that sort of measured calm that he always used when he wasn't at all calm. "We're having some issues with the pavilion. If they get in there, I'm not sure—"

On it, she tapped out.

"What's over here?" asked the boyevik man as they exited the maze of bushes. He was pointing to the left, where a huge pavilion stood, obscured by the greenery and draped with luxurious-looking vines that still gave Jez the shivers, honestly.

Jez shot him a lascivious look. "Hey now, some things you don't get to see until you pay your dues, if you know what I mean." She paused and glanced over at him, raising an eyebrow. "Actually, now that you mention it, maybe I should take you over in that direction. You look like a man who appreciates pain."

His eyebrows shot up before he managed to force his face into something approximating unconcern. "What—do you—"

She grinned and winked. "Not sure I want to spoil it for you. You know, there are people who are into that, and we've only had—" she paused a moment, as if thinking. "Two deaths in there so far. To be totally honest with you, I'm a little surprised, but I guess some of our guests have the constitution of a swamp-ox. Couldn't kill them with a thirty-centimetre gutting knife." She paused again. "Or maybe it was a thirty-five centimetres? I don't remember what she used."

"I thought Masha said this house didn't keep disposable entertainment," the woman snapped.

Jez grinned wider. "Oh, I didn't say it was entertainers that died. Masha would have had a fit."

The man was looking at her in open horror now.

"Come on," said Jez, turning towards the pavilion. "Figure

adventurous customers like you, you'd fit right in. Bet Masha would even give you a discount on the price if you came in hurt badly enough. Looks like a merciless bastard, I know, but she's got a soft spot when people are bleeding all over her nice polished floors. You know why she wanted them stone, right? Hell of a tough thing to wipe that kind of blood off wood."

"I—" began the man. "I'm not certain—"

"I don't think we'll require a tour of the pavilion," said the woman, her tones icy, but the mild horror underneath clearly apparent. "I'd rather head back and look at the entertainment, if—"

Jez clapped a hand on her shoulder, and she flinched back in distaste.

"Who said anything about a tour? Thought I'd give you a taste of what you can buy around here. Like I said, your buddy there looks like the kind who likes a little pain."

"Take us back inside," snapped the woman.

Jez shrugged, raising her eyebrows. "Well, guess if you want to waste a good offer—" She hesitated, then turned up the narrow path along the right side of the garden, and the visibly relieved boyeviki followed close behind.

The walls of the pleasure house were a brilliant white, and at this time of day, the sun beating against them made the reflection almost blinding. Jez closed one eye completely and squeezed the other to a slit, and took a few moments fumbling at the door.

The better the shock between the outside and the dark gambling hall, the better for everyone.

Radic, we're coming in, she tapped inconspicuously on her com as she worked.

We're ready for you, he tapped back.

She pulled the door open, and gestured inside with a flourish.

"Don't usually let customers come this way, but hell, make an exception for you," she said. "This goes straight into my gambling hall. Usually you have to go around through the lobby. Don't want anyone sneaking out without paying their debts, if you know what I mean." She gave them a broad wink.

Both boyeviki glared at her, and then the man ducked inside, followed by the woman. Jez stepped in after them and closed the door, opening both her eyes as the light from outside was abruptly cut off.

Even with the precautions she'd taken, it took her a moment of blinking to make out anything in the dim room. When she could distinguish shapes again, she saw Radic lounging against the far corner of the bar, pouring out a drink and chatting in a low voice to an obviously inebriated customer.

Around them, the muted *clink* of tokens tapping against a table, the murmur of voices, the thick, expensive smell of alcohol that cost a hell of a lot of money, enveloped them like a blanket. She closed her eyes and sighed in contentment, then stepped forward.

"Come on, you two," she said over her shoulder. "Can't have people thinking you're copping a peek at someone's tokens. Get you killed in a place like this."

"Your pleasure house seems like an exceptionally dangerous place to be a customer," said the man, his expression stiff. From the way he was blinking, his eyes couldn't have adjusted to the light yet.

Which was exactly what she wanted.

"Well, we've been pretty busy, so guess not everyone is as timid as you two," she said in a jocular tone. He glared, still blinking, and she led them purposefully close to the tables.

"Got every game you've heard of here, and probably a couple you haven't," she said as she walked. "Figure you could probably learn a couple things if you sat in here for a while. Might lose a few credits though."

"And how would we know that someone," he placed an entirely unnecessary emphasis on the word, "wouldn't cheat?"

She turned her head to shoot him a quick grin. "Person in charge of the gaming tables would shoot them dead," she said nonchalantly. "We put in the atmosphere of a kabak, might as well put in the rules."

"Cheats get away with that in kabaks, sometime, though," said the man softly. His voice held an edge of menace.

She shrugged, grinning. "Well, guess you could always try. Figured you'd be a little too timid for that, though. After what I saw in the garden, you don't seem like the type who could handle himself in a kabak. Probably best that you two stick to the lobby, honestly."

The man opened his mouth to protest, and Jez winked at the woman at the table next to her, stumbling slightly. The man behind her stopped short to keep from bumping into her, and the other boyevik stumbled into him, and Jez nudged the table with her hip at the same time.

The woman at the table jumped to her feet, grabbing the boyevik man by the shoulder of his jacket. "You filthy plaguer," she hissed. "You cheating for this bastard playing against me? Wouldn't put it past him. But he's damn well going to have to—"

Jez grabbed the woman's wrist in a vice-like grip, grinning. The woman winced, her fingers loosened on the man's jacket.

Honestly, Jez wasn't holding her that hard, but they'd practiced enough times in the last week that she probably had bruises.

"No fighting in my gambling hall," Jez said, in a tone that was as menacing as she could make it while she was trying very, very hard not to laugh.

The woman stared at her for a few moments, expression dangerous, then jerked her arm away in disgust.

"Pour her a drink," Jez called to Radic, who'd busied himself behind the bar. "On the house. And if she tries to start something again, throw her out."

"You got it, boss," said Radic, turning to pull a bottle from the collection behind the bar.

Jez turned back to the woman, who was glaring at her.

She was actually a pretty good actor, honestly. Or it might have been her bruised wrist.

"My hall, my rules," she said softly, keeping her voice as menacing as possible. "One chance. But you don't get any more. Just be damn glad I caught you before you'd hit my guest."

The woman narrowed her eyes and turned away, muttering, and Jez turned back to the boyeviki and gave them a wide grin.

The man was looking around him uneasily.

"Well," she said, "you two know how to make friends fast. Better get you back to the lobby before you get killed." She gestured casually around her. "Floor in here is great for gambling, but cleaning blood off it is hell. Don't want to do that again anytime soon."

The rather subdued boyeviki followed her out of the hall. She made a point of pulling the doors open wide, so their eyes, now adjusted to the dim lighting in the gambling hall, would be flooded with the golden glare from the lobby.

"Come on, don't got all day," she said impatiently, as they blinked against the light. "Masha's at the desk, but I don't know if she'll be for long. We're pretty full right now, so if you like what you've seen, you'd probably best get over there."

They walked past her, still blinking, and she leaned against the doorway, grinning.

By the time they reached Masha, they were too far away for their voices to carry, but Masha's com, like the rest of theirs, was set to the general line, and Jez could hear the conversation distinctly through her earpiece.

"And did you enjoy your tour? I hope it impressed you. Jez is a rather unconventional tour guide, I know, but—" Masha shrugged. "She is fairly skilled in certain areas, and I wanted to make sure you weren't inadvertently killed."

"I find it difficult to believe that people frequent this house if it's so dangerous," said the man, his voice gruff.

Even from here, Jez could see Masha's bland, amused smile. "Well, it's not dangerous for everyone. Most of it is very safe. But there is a rather large market of people who are looking for things on the more adventurous side, and when you ask to be shown around, you risk running into things that are perhaps a little more than your sensibilities are prepared for. I do apologize. I should have warned you, but I took you for customers with slightly more experience ..." she trailed off delicately, letting the finely barbed insult hang in the air. "Of course, I only serve customers here who like what I have to sell. If you aren't interested, I'm happy to recommend one of the ... tamer houses."

Jez glanced over to where Radic had joined her, leaning up against the gambling hall walls out of sight of the boyevik. He caught her eye and raised an eyebrow. She gave a quick shake of her head.

The ideal situation, of course, was that the boyevik left without asking to use the entertainment. But the merest whiff of hesitation on Masha's part could spell the end of their plan, so they'd have to be bloody well begging to leave.

"We'll stay," said the woman sharply, and Jez glanced back to the scene.

"I want you to book us a room, please, and show us the available entertainment."

"Of course," Masha murmured, lowering her head, but her slight smile was clearly visible. "A word on the house rules—entertainment here is of the highest quality. It's not disposable. So please keep that in mind. If it comes back damaged beyond a couple days' recuperation, you'll be paying a fine, and damaged beyond repair, along with the fine, you'll not set foot in here again. Your recreation, beyond getting intoxicated, happens in the private rooms or in the garden, please—if you want to make a public display we have places for that, but it's reserved in advance." She reached down and pulled out two chips, set into expensive-looking necklaces. "Once you pay, I'll give you these. They're your access chip while you're here, although I'm the only one who can unlock the entertainment—I don't want fights from people who've reserved one."

"Very well," said the woman coldly. There were a few moments where Masha took their credit chips, and Jez found herself wishing very much that their plan hadn't involved her keeping the plaguers out of her gambling hall, because her fingers were practically aching with the desire to cheat the bastards out of every last credit they owned.

She gave a long, regretful sigh, and Radic grinned at her. "If it makes you feel any better, kid, I'd pay good money to watch you cheat them blind."

She grinned at him. "Figure they don't know me well enough to want to kill me yet. But I bet I could change their minds pretty quick."

He chuckled and shook his head. "I still don't know how you lived to grow up."

She rolled her eyes good-naturedly, then turned back to the lobby.

She'd have to look at the cage now, if she wanted to see what was going to happen next, which was honestly a dilemma. Because even knowing what she knew, the cage made her want to vomit.

Still—

She took a deep breath, and let her eyes be pulled where every line of the setup of the room wanted to pull them.

She was pretty sure from what she remembered of their meeting the evening before, at least the part of it she was paying attention to, that there were going to be five or six people in the cages when the boyeviki first came in. Now they were down to two, as planned—a man and a woman. The man lay on a couch, wearing a robe that was falling enticingly open, but there was nothing at all enticing about the magnetic cuffs on his wrists and ankles. At least, nothing that she damn well got off on.

Although apparently there were people who did find that enticing. And hell, she could maybe see that if they were dressing up for fun. But people liking that when the cuffs were real, and the people inside them terrified and desperate?

The thought made her swallow back bile.

The woman was leaning up against the bars of the cage, her back to the boyeviki. Her outfit was a loose shift dress, hardly revealing, but the expensive fabric clung to her slender form. Even facing away from them, even chained, she had an obvious presence and grace.

Both boyeviki couldn't seem to take their eyes from the woman.

Honestly, Jez could hardly blame them.

"We'll take that one," said the woman boyevik.

"Very good," said Masha. "You have excellent taste. I'm honestly surprised she's available right now, but I believe she just got finished with another customer. You're lucky." She paused. "Are you certain? House rules are, once I've unlocked them, you can't change your mind. I've had too many issues in the past. So I'd advise you to inspect carefully before you make a decision."

"We've inspected enough," said the man, his voice tinged with annoyance. "We're not innocents. No use trying to convince us to take the lesser goods."

Masha shrugged slightly. "Lady forbid. If you're certain, then …" She tapped her com against the bars, and the lock clicked open. She tapped it again against a control on the floor, then straightened as the woman's restraints fell away.

"You," said Masha, her words a short command. "Come. You're wanted."

The woman turned, and Jez bit back a grin.

Tanya had always been good at looking at you like she could murder you seventeen different ways before you realized you were dead. Jez had been on the receiving end of that look enough times to thoroughly appreciate it. And the way she'd made up her face and arranged her clothes—she didn't look particularly seductive, except in the sense that the almost-palpable air of danger she carried with her was seductive, but there was something about the way she stood watching the two boyeviki that was unutterably compelling. In the way that a plains-cat crouched in the long grass watching a helpless newborn marsh-gritha was compelling, but still …

Tanya turned her thoughtful gaze on the man, and Jez saw his adam's apple jump as he swallowed nervously.

Radic grinned at Jez, and she grinned back.

Honestly, this was spectacular.

"You say she's … quite popular?" asked the woman, the sharpness in her tone doing nothing to conceal her sudden nervousness.

"Of course," Masha murmured. "She's perhaps the most popular entertainer I have. As I said, I do tend to attract clients who are on the more adventurous side."

"And she—she's restrained, correct?"

Masha chuckled in faint amusement. "Of course. If she wasn't, I assume not a single person in this lobby would be alive right now. Although she's very good at working within constraints. I have not had an unsatisfied customer yet." She paused. "At least, the ones who were still able to speak were all complimentary. My understanding is that two are still recovering in the medical facility here. We've only lost one. And I'm fairly certain the one she just came from will walk again, with proper treatment."

The boyeviki looked at each other.

"I've changed my mind. I want the other instead," said the man quickly.

Masha shook her head. "I'm sorry. House policy, as I explained. We're extremely busy, as I told you. But if you try her and don't like her, I promise you a full refund."

The woman made an obvious effort to steel herself. "And she's good for anything?"

Masha gave a small smile. "As I said, this isn't a house with disposable entertainment. But within those constraints, yes. Do take care of her, please, she's very expensive." She paused, glancing down at her com. "I've booked you into room 223."

"Very well," said the woman, turning. "Come on, you." She jerked her head at Tanya. Her companion fell into step beside her, and Masha said in a low voice that, even over the com, was obviously just loud enough to be overheard without sounding intentional, "We've talked about this. Please avoid killing them. It reflects poorly on the house."

Tanya gave a brief nod, and Jez caught the glint of amusement in her face as she turned to follow the boyeviki up the stairs.

There were a few moments of silence as they ascended, and then over the com on Tanya's wrist, they heard the room door click shut.

"Well," said Radic into his com, "you want to take bets on who needs the emergency alarm first, Tanya or the boyeviki?"

"Believe me, no one will take you up on that," said Ysbel, her voice low and amused. "I know my Tanya. They'll be begging for their lives before she has time to do anything other than look at them."

"I'd put my bet at—" Lev paused a moment, as if calculating something. "Five standard minutes."

"You think?" asked Radic. "You didn't see them when Jez was bringing them through the gambling hall. I give them two minutes at the most."

"Possibly," said Lev. "However, I'm taking into account the fact that they'll probably be too frozen with fear to move for at least four and a half minutes."

In total, it was three standard minutes and fifty-two seconds before the boyeviki emerged from the room, their expressions those of people who've stared death in the face.

"Your house is lovely, but I believe we'll be checking out," said the woman, in a tone that did not invite discussion.

The man appeared almost catatonic.

Masha raised an eyebrow. "Are you certain? I'm sure I have other things here I could tempt you with, if you'd just—"

"I said, we're checking out," said the woman tersely.

"Very well," Masha murmured. "I do hope you'll recommend us to your friends."

The boyeviki didn't bother to answer, just handed in their key chips, collected their credit chips, and left.

After the door had closed behind them, Jez began to count slowly. She'd reached eighty-seven before Tae's voice came over the com.

"They're gone. I'm tracking them, but they're halfway back to the pleasure district, driving like the seventeen demons themselves are chasing them, so I think we're safe."

Jez turned to meet Radic's gaze, and both of them burst into laughter. Over the coms she could hear Ysbel chuckling as well, and Lev's quiet sounds of amusement.

"You can stop pretending to cheat each other," Radic called back into the gambling hall. "Laslo, do you even know how to play three blind beggars? You had seven tokens in your hand the whole time."

The man lounging on the bench in the cage sat up, hitting the button on his wrist com to pop the cuffs free and pulling his robe closer around him, and the customer and the entertainer who'd been passed out on the couch sat up as well, shifting away to give each other space and blinking the eyedrops from their eyes.

"Well," said Masha, looking around as the actors from outside trickled in, and Lev and Tae appeared on the staircase. "It appears our first outing has been a success."

"What I'd like to know is what exactly you did to those boyeviki," said Ivan wryly, glancing at Tanya, who'd come to stand beside the counter.

She gave him a small smile. "I don't know what Jez did to prep them. But—" she shrugged. "By the time I'd pulled the first gutting knife from my boot, I thought they were both going to faint. I was worried at first that I'd be locked in there for half a standard hour before they got up the nerve to try to get away from me."

Ivan chuckled, and Jez snorted.

"Well, could have told you those bastards had a pretty good sense of self-preservation," she drawled. "Bet they'll give Grigory the most glowing report they can dream up, just to avoid being sent back here again."

Masha held up a hand, although she couldn't hide her faint smile. "Good work, everyone. But we won't know if we were successful until we know Grigory's reaction. Tae, I assume you'll let us know if another boyevik is being sent here?"

Tae nodded, without looking at her.

"Good. Then I suggest we close this down for the day."

Jez caught Lev's eye across the room and raised her eyebrow, and he picked his way through the crowd over to her.

"Jez. You did well," he said when he reached her, and there was a genuine warmth to his tone she hadn't expected.

She smiled at him. "Yeah? Well, you did pretty good yourself, you and Tae." She paused. "So. Now what?"

Lev glanced down at the com on his wrist. "I've been monitoring the account Tae set up in Masha's name. So—" he looked up and gave a faint shrug, with just the hint of tension in it. "Assuming that Zhenya told Grigory what we wanted them to, and assuming Grigory came to the conclusion that we expected, and assuming the boyeviki fell for our act—we wait, and see if he takes the bait."

15

Lev turned restlessly in his bed, staring up at the ceiling.

It was later than he wanted to think about. He'd found some excuse or another for staying up, checking his com surreptitiously every few standard minutes.

Grigory's boyeviki hadn't returned since they'd left early that afternoon, and Tae hadn't been able to detect any chatter over the com lines that Grigory was sending more. It wasn't confirmation, of course, but it likely meant that, one way or another, Grigory had come to a decision. Either he'd had seen through their ploy, or he'd been taken in by it.

Lev squeezed his eyes closed, suddenly, unaccountably, wishing for his cot on the *Ungovernable,* the slight, barely perceptible hum of the ship underneath him, the comfortable knowledge of exactly where each other member of the crew was.

He smiled wryly to himself.

Jez would laugh her head off to hear him, of all people, say that.

Jez—

Damn it. He wasn't going to think about this, he wasn't ready to think about this, damn it to hell—

But the thought had already, somehow, wormed through his

defences, and now it flooded over him, hot and heavy and suffocating.

Jez. Her swaggering walk, the careless way she tipped back her chair when they gathered to discuss plans, balancing it on two legs as easily as if it were built that way. The sick expression he'd seen on her face whenever she glanced in the direction of the cage in the middle of the floor. She didn't lie awake in the middle of the night deciding if she was going to be a good person or not, and pondering what that meant. She swore, and cheated, and got into fights, and said the most outrageous things, and she couldn't stop herself from being a good person even if she tried.

And he loved her.

Damn everything, he loved her, he'd loved her since he'd first caught a glimpse of who she was, under the snark and the insults and the bravado.

And it might actually kill him.

He sat up, shoving his blankets off.

Ysbel said it would get better. And he had no idea whether she was right or how she'd actually know, considering she was married to the woman she'd loved her entire life, but he was clinging on to her statement like a man drifting in space clinging to his oxygen line.

It would get better. Somehow it would get better, and he would survive this. His heart would stop feeling like it had been ripped from his damn chest, leaving a pulsing wound that couldn't really heal. Because it wasn't possible for something to hurt this much forever.

He leaned back and breathed in deeply, once, then again, then again.

He remembered the look on her face when she'd agreed to his tentative offer of friendship. The sudden, undisguised relief, the spark of happiness in her expression that he hadn't seen there for far too long, at least not while she was looking at him. The way she'd looked at him today, when he complimented her on her work, the slight shock, quickly concealed. The way they'd laughed, breathless and leaning on each other for support, outside the club in Prasvishoni, before they'd turned and run for their lives. The silent gratitude in her face when he defended her in front of the others.

She honestly hadn't believed he'd do that.

Yes, he loved her, at least, he'd always told himself he had. But—well, the truth was, he'd been an idiot the whole time. Too caught up in his own damn self-importance to wonder what it was like for her. Too quick to condemn every little failing and roll his eyes at every mistake, and use his care for her as a bludgeon, an excuse to tell her what to do and be upset with her if she didn't do it.

The thought made him feel slightly ill. He'd always managed to shove it away before, but now, in the middle of the night, when there wasn't any noise to block out his thoughts, he couldn't seem to stop it.

But—maybe Ysbel was right after all. Maybe that's what she'd meant. Because for the first time in a long time, Jez seemed happy to be around him. She didn't flinch unconsciously when he entered the room, tense when she met his eyes. And as much as the empty ache in his chest hurt, so badly he thought he might drown in it—there was something about seeing that spark in her again, that careless grin, the familiar ease of being in her company that made it bearable.

He tipped his head back against the wall and ran his hands over his face.

He'd make it through this somehow. Because maybe he was still the same selfish bastard he'd been months ago. But one thing, at least, had changed.

He wanted Jez happy.

Even if it bloody killed him, and it honestly might, he wanted her happy, and he'd damn well learn how to be a decent friend, even if he couldn't be a decent anything else. He'd somehow learn how to be a decent person, whatever that meant.

He closed his eyes for a while, listening to the silence around him, letting his heart beat slow back to its usual pattern. He'd been clenching his hands so tightly that his palms stung where his fingernails had dug into them.

He almost didn't hear the small *ting* of a notification coming through on his com, his eyes half-closed, his thoughts far away. And then he did, and he jerked upright, pulling up the holoscreen.

He stared at the notification, scarcely daring to breathe, then tapped it to open a screen.

For a long while, he just looked at it, trying to be sure he was seeing what he thought he was seeing.

And then, slowly, he cupped his hand over his com. His heart felt like it would beat its way out of his ribcage.

He tapped over to a private line. "Tae," he whispered.

For a moment there was no answer, then Tae's groggy voice came through his earpiece.

"Lev? What's wrong?"

"Tae," he said. He must sound dazed—he felt dazed, honestly.

Because he hadn't honestly believed they'd actually pull this off.

"I just got a notification from the account you set. Grigory's transferred in a pledge. I followed it through, and it looks like he's leveraged his pleasure houses. He's transferring in the full amount we said that Masha needs to fund this."

There was a long moment of silence on the other end of the com.

"You're—certain?" asked Tae, sounding much more awake. "He

pledged the whole amount?"

"It won't come through until he gets the funds secured against the houses. But—yes. The entire amount. He took the bait."

There was a long sigh of relief through the com. "I—" said Tae, then paused, and Lev could almost see him shaking his head, that faint, disbelieving smile on his face, like he was pretty sure he was dreaming but he wasn't certain he wanted to wake up. "I guess we'd better tell Masha," he said at last, and this time Lev could hear the smile in his voice. "We can probably wait until morning to tell the others, but she'll want to know."

"I'll talk to her," said Lev. He was grinning himself, and he doubted he could have stopped it if he wanted to. He hadn't realized how much strain he'd been under until it was suddenly released, and he felt like he was floating. "You did it, Tae. Not that I should have worried—you always pull off the impossible."

"We did it, you mean," said Tae. He paused a moment. "Thanks, Lev."

Lev laughed softly. "Go back to bed, if you can. But I thought you might want to know right away."

"I did. Not sure I'll be able to sleep now, but—" Tae's voice choked slightly.

"It's OK," said Lev softly. "Caz and Peti are safe. At least for now, at least until we have to deal with next steps, they're in the clear."

"I know," said Tae, clearing his throat. "I know."

Lev tapped off the com and leaned his head against the wall, eyes closed, letting the rush of relief flood over him.

They might just pull this off after all. It was just possible they'd pull this off, and they'd all survive it after all.

16

"—and honestly, you should have seen their faces when Tanya turned to look at them," Jez was saying through a mouthful of food. "I thought they'd actually pass out."

Tae caught Ivan's eye and smiled slightly. The festive atmosphere had lasted all through the morning, and would probably last the rest of the day at least. Grigory had taken the bait, and now it was just a matter of keeping up the facade until the money transfer came through.

He still felt light with relief.

Something dinged on his com, and he sighed. He'd been getting calls all morning from people who had been in the back and wanted to watch the video footage from the lobby again.

It dinged again, and he shook his head, swallowing down the last bite of his breakfast. They might be finished, but he wasn't, because an account like the one Masha had wanted him to set up needed constant maintenance if it was going to look genuine.

"Never a quiet moment," said Ivan with an amused shake of his head, and Tae glanced down at his com as it dinged a third time.

It took a moment for his brain to process what he was seeing.

And then he felt like he'd forgotten how to breathe.

"Tae?"

He barely heard Ivan's voice, the sudden concern in it.

He closed his eyes for a moment and drew in a long breath. Then he stood.

Whatever the expression on his face, it must have been bad, because the noise and laughter faded as the others in the breakfast room turned to look at him.

"Everyone back in costume," he said quietly. "I just got a message from Jez's gangster friends. Grigory's sent another group, and they'll be here in twenty minutes."

There was a moment of shocked silence. "Are you sure—" someone began.

Jez turned to scowl at the speaker. "Listen, tech-head says something's happening, it's damn well happening. Get moving." She stood. "Come on Radic, you bastard, we've got work to do."

"I'll get Lev and Galina," said Ivan, standing quickly and putting a hand on Tae's shoulder. Tae nodded, and Ivan slipped out of the room.

Jez caught his eye. "Look, tech-head," she said, just loud enough to be heard over the sudden chaos. "It'll be fine. We've done it once, we know what we're doing now."

He managed a brief nod, and then she was gone as well.

Tae glanced down at the notification on his com again, something hard and tight in the pit of his stomach.

There was only one reason he wouldn't have seen this coming earlier. Considering the tracking he had on every communication coming to or from Gregory, there was only one way.

These were Grigory's people, he was certain of that, but it wasn't Grigory who'd sent them.

And he knew damn well who it had been.

Zhenya.

When he reached the lobby, it had transformed into an organized chaos. Galina was waiting for him at the base of the stairs, Lev beside her.

"Tae," she said shortly. "We don't know who's coming, do we?"

He shook his head grimly. "But it was Zhenya who sent them. Whoever they are, they'll be looking for the slightest thing out of place."

Galina nodded, and he knew from the look on her face that she understood the consequences of failure as well as he did.

"The tech is set, right?" she asked briskly. "Then I want you in costume. We'll have you start out in the back room, but if there's an emergency, I need to be able to call you down."

"Yeah." He tried to fight down the sickness in his stomach. "Yeah. I'll be ready."

She nodded, then turned and strode towards the centre of the chaos, calling out orders over the noise.

He bit back a curse.

"Tae?"

He spun. Ivan was there, already in his server's uniform, a small smile cutting through the worry on his face.

Ivan had spent years in prison, and Tae had seen the look on his face when he talked about what put him there. If Ivan hadn't seen friends killed or tortured, Tae missed his guess. But even so, there was something about the way he smiled that made Tae believe that maybe things would turn out after all.

"I think we're about ready," said Ivan. He paused. "You OK?"

"I'm—fine," said Tae, swallowing down his panic.

Ivan watched him for a moment, then squeezed his shoulder sympathetically. "Good luck," he whispered.

Something fluttered in Tae's stomach, and he only managed a flustered nod before Ivan turned back to his work.

He took a deep breath.

This was ridiculous. He had things to do, and he had plenty to worry about. He shook his head to clear it, and made his way out of the crowded lobby.

He'd barely gotten into costume—fine, high leather boots, a pair of soft trousers, and a shirt and vest that were so heavily embroidered they were stiff to the touch—and dropped into his seat at the table in the conference room, pulling up his holoscreen, when Jez's voice came over his earpiece.

"Hey tech-head. They're here." She paused a moment. "It's not anyone we've seen before. At least, it's not anyone who I cheated at gambling, and it's not anyone who tried to kill me, so I think that basically covers everyone on Grigory's ship. So they shouldn't recognize us. And if you wiped the vid feeds on Grigory's ship like you said, they won't have pictures to go by either."

"Thanks, Jez," he said shortly.

His stomach was a tight knot. He pulled up his holoscreen again and expanded the screen, then pulled up three more screens so he could monitor all the feeds.

Behind him, a door opened, and he glanced over his shoulder as Lev stepped into the room.

Tae gestured to the seat beside him. "Jez said they've arrived."

Lev joined him, and Tae hooked the screens into the camera feeds.

They heard the murmur of voices off-screen, but it wasn't coming through nearly as clear as it should be—

He felt suddenly sick.

Damn it.

Damn it to hell.

Damn Zhenya to hell.

"What is it?" asked Lev quickly.

"Shielding. On their coms. It's messing with my feeds." He stood quickly, hitting his com. "Galina. I've got to get in there. They've got something on their coms that's disrupting my feed. It's going to mess with our emergency systems."

"Give me a sec." Galina's voice was tight with strain. "OK," she said after a few moments. "Come down on the third-floor lift, the one on the right side. You've been here since the night before last. You're not hungover or drunk, so don't worry about that, just act the part of a bored government brat."

He blew out a quick breath.

Easy. Just act the part of a bored government brat. Someone who'd never gone hungry a day in his life, who saw people as objects for his personal entertainment.

And if he screwed up, his friends died.

Nothing simpler.

His palms were sweating by the time the lift doors slid silently open, heart beating out a rhythm against his ribcage.

Galina lounged in a corner by the cages, and hardly glanced up as he stepped out into the lobby, the hard soles of his boots clicking off the polished stone of the floor.

He kept his eyes on his destination, a chair in the corner, because that way he didn't have to look at the cages.

If he saw them, he might actually vomit.

Thank goodness Galina was spreading rumours about him, anyways. He could just pretend it was boredom, not disgust, that influenced his choice of seat.

A small cluster of people stood at the front desk, and Masha was playing the part of hostess.

"As you can see," she was saying, "we provide only the very best in entertainment." She turned, and let her eyes linger on one of the entertainers, a younger man with pale skin and light hair, his outfit clinging to his body, his wrists manacled.

Tae looked away quickly.

"I can see that," said the woman, smiling. "Well. I'm so glad to have met you, Masha."

"And I'm delighted to welcome you," said Masha, returning the smile. "Please. Take your leisure. We have servers who will bring you whatever you ask for—your chip will summon them. There's a gambling hall through that door, fully staffed, as well as a wide selection of intoxicants. This isn't a house with disposable entertainment, so weapons stay outside the room."

"Of course," said the boyevik, with a slight, knowing smile, and Masha handed each of them a necklace containing a control chip.

Tae slouched in his chair in the corner, and pulled up his holoscreen.

Lev. What's the plan here? he tapped in pilot's code.

"We're going to try to get as many as we can into the gambling hall," came Lev's low voice through his earpiece. "Jez will keep them busy. We can't use Tanya again—too much of a coincidence—but all the entertainers are people who can take care of themselves. The plan is to keep the boyeviki distracted for long enough to get Ysbel's emergency protocols in place before they take the entertainment up to the rooms."

Tae gritted his teeth and glanced quickly through the specs on his screen. He'd been right—there were blockers set into the coms of all the newcomers.

He cursed again under his breath, and typed in a command,

delicately prodding at the system.

This had to be Zhenya's work. Which meant he had to be absolutely certain that getting through the blocker would leave no trace.

He hesitated.

There was no avoiding it. He'd have to get close enough to one of the boyeviki to get a physical scan of their com system, and to do that, he'd have to be inside the radius of their blocker.

He took a deep breath and stood.

Most of the boyeviki had moved towards the gambling hall, but three of them were still in the room, standing near the cage and watching with unbridled salaciousness.

"She's right," said the woman boyevik, letting her eyes linger on a caged woman. "You can always tell the higher-quality entertainment when you see it."

The man beside her grinned, but there was something about his expression that made Tae's stomach twist. "Come on, Branka. We all know you like the houses with disposables."

She raised her eyebrow at him. "Sometimes you need class, and sometimes you need the dregs. That's just life."

He laughed loudly.

Tae bit down hard on his teeth and stepped closer, pretending interest in what was inside the cages.

The man turned on him in annoyance. "Who are you?"

Tae ignored him.

"I said," the man began, his voice gaining a rough edge.

Galina's smooth voice interrupted him. "I'd be careful," she said lazily. "That's Nikita. His mother's a minister. Not the kind of person you want to offend."

Tae managed to bump the scanner on his com surreptitiously,

hardly deigning to glance towards Galina. He glanced instead at the man who'd addressed him, letting his eyes run dismissively from his hair to his boots. "What do you want?" he asked at last, trying to keep his tone bored instead of horrified.

The man glowered at him. "Nothing. I was—mistaken."

Tae raised an eyebrow. "Good."

"He was one of the model citizens a few years back," Galina continued in a languid whisper. "They say he had a boyfriend on every planet, and about fifty others who wished they were his boyfriends. Masha's been running herself ragged trying to find something that will impress him."

The light on his com was still blinking. The scan had to be close to done. How complicated was this damn blocker?

He turned back to the cage, fighting back the sudden, urgent need to vomit.

The boyeviki were casting curious glances in his direction.

"So," said the woman. "Which minister's son are you?"

He shrugged and turned to her, grateful for the excuse to look at something other than the cages. "I try to keep my mother out of things like this."

The woman laughed. "You don't think that something like this would drag her name through the mud, do you? You of all people know how many officials visit this place every year."

He gave a one-shouldered shrug. "She pays me enough to keep myself busy, and I promise her I won't give her a reputation. That's the only arrangement we have."

His heart was beating so quickly that he almost couldn't hear them speaking through the pounding in his ears.

"So," said the woman. "You've gone through all the entertainment here, and none of it impressed you? That's unfortunate."

He shrugged again, and forced himself to meet her eyes.

He didn't recognize her, but he recognized the hardness in her face. He'd met plenty of people like her, in his years on the streets.

This was a person who killed for fun. Who enjoyed causing pain like he enjoyed a warm jacket on a cold evening.

She was watching him too, and he let his eyes narrow slightly. "Honestly, I didn't see the point," he said, gesturing with his chin towards the cage. "They're all attractive, if that's the sort of thing you like, but if you've seen one of them, you've seen all of them. Nothing new. I was hoping with a new house they'd have found a way to bring in something fresh, but—" He lifted a shoulder again. "I'm sure Masha's doing her best."

Something flashed on his com, and he had to fight the urge to glance quickly down at it. He brought his hand to his mouth as if covering a yawn.

The light on the scanner was a solid green.

Done.

He managed a slight smile. "Best of luck. Perhaps you'll find something to your taste," he said, turning to go. "Take your time looking. They don't bring in the quality stuff until later in the day, usually."

"Wait," said the woman.

Reluctantly, he paused.

"You know," she said thoughtfully, studying him. "I've been where you are. Jaded about the state of the system. It's always more fun if you can find something unexpected. And I think you've inspired me, honestly." She smiled, and something in her smile made him shiver. She reached down and tapped her pendant.

"What are you—" the man said.

She smiled at him. "Calling in a server. Of course."

Tae felt suddenly cold.

Damn.

Damn, damn, damn, they hadn't prepared for this.

From the corner of his eye he saw the door swing open as one of the servers came though, their gait quick and professional.

"Yes? How can I help you?"

Tae's head jerked up at the familiar voice, and he felt his insides turn to ice.

Ivan stood there, head lowered deferentially, his posture the picture of graceful professionalism.

Tae's palms were damp with sweat, and he thought his legs might actually give out.

Ivan hadn't looked in his direction, but Tae knew him, and he was certain Ivan had been the one to come because he wanted to make sure Tae, of all the damn people in the system, was alright.

Damn him. Damn Ivan to hell, why couldn't he bloody well look after himself for once?

"You," said the woman, placing her hand on his arm. Ivan was too much the professional to jerk away, but his posture stiffened slightly. "I'd like you. You're certainly a quality specimen, at any rate."

"No." Tae's voice came out harsher than he meant it to.

The woman turned to stare at him.

"That one's mine," he said, stepping over.

This couldn't happen, he couldn't let this happen. This woman would kill Ivan for fun, and happily pay the fine afterward, and they didn't have a contingency plan for this—

The woman looked down at his hand on Ivan's arm, right above hers, and then up into his face. She arched one eyebrow in amusement. "Really. You've laid claim to one of the servers already? I suppose I'm not as original as I'd thought."

"I paid for him. This morning," said Tae tersely. He didn't meet Ivan's eye, because he couldn't. Because if he looked at him, he'd panic.

Tae.

The word came through his earpiece, tapped out in pilot's code.

He cut his eyes quickly to one side to see Galina, leaning back on one of the thick couches. She was watching the scene, her fingers tapping casually against her com as if considering what her next move should be. She caught his eye and gave a small shake of her head.

You can't put up a fight. She'll get suspicious. You already told her there's nothing here that interests you.

He could see the strain on her face, under her lazy expression.

She was as worried about this as he was. But he couldn't—

Tae. Listen to me.

Somehow, he forced himself to turn back to the boyevik.

She was giving him a slightly triumphant smile. "Well, I see I've found something that you want. That wasn't hard, was it?"

He couldn't stop himself from glancing at Ivan. His friend's face was strained, and there was fear behind his expression, but he gave a quick shake of his head. "Go," he mouthed.

Tae made himself raise his eyes and meet the woman's gaze once more, forced his grip on Ivan's arm to loosen.

Galina was right. There was no way out of this without someone he cared for getting hurt, but they had a chance, at least, to save Ivan. Caz and Peti would be dead the moment Zhenya suspected something amiss.

"Well," he said with a shrug. "You can't say I didn't try to warn you. This one isn't worth much as far as entertainment goes."

"I see," said the woman, watching him. "You don't mind if I try him, then?"

Tae managed a scoff. "You think this would hold my attention?"

He tried to ignore just exactly how much Ivan managed to hold his attention.

"Take it, if you want. But I did warn you, if it's excitement you're looking for, this isn't going to qualify."

The woman turned back to study Ivan, and the way she looked at him made Tae's skin crawl. "Maybe I'm not as picky as you are," she said at last, turning back to Tae with a knowing wink. "It's not really the entertainment's job to provide the excitement, after all. I can make my time with him as exciting as I'd like." She paused a moment. "You're welcome to come watch. You might learn something."

Tae's pulse pounded in his ears, but somehow he managed a slight, world-weary smile. "Oh, I doubt that. Disposable entertainment just doesn't do anything for me, to be honest."

She gave a small shrug. "Suit yourself. But I've found my morning's activities, at least."

Tae managed to stay upright until he reached his chair, and then he collapsed into it.

Why the hell did it have to be Ivan?

He yanked up his holoscreen, looking over the scan feverishly.

Behind him, he heard a voice he recognized as Masha's.

"No," she was saying, "I don't sell the servers, unfortunately. I use only the best, and they're hard to come by on this forsaken planet."

He bit back the desperate hope rising in his chest, because right now he needed to figure out this blocker, and he couldn't afford to be distracted by anything else.

"I want this one," said the woman. "I'll buy it from you right out."

"It's not for sale," said Masha. "I appreciate your generous offer, but—"

"Why in the system not?" The woman was beginning to sound annoyed. "I told you, I'll pay market price for him."

"It's not that simple, getting someone in—" Masha was clearly wavering.

He swore under his breath.

She was only wavering because she was on the edge of risking suspicion herself, and one wrong move could bring this whole plan down. But somehow it felt like another damn betrayal.

There. He was almost certain he could see it now, a way in.

He had to get this working, he had to. There was no other option.

"Well then, I'll let you keep him at the end of it," the woman said. "If there's any use left in him, it's all yours."

"We don't—"

The woman waved her hand airily. "No disposable entertainment, I know. Don't worry, I'll keep the house rules."

Masha sighed reluctantly. "Very well," she said. "But full price, and there's a fine if you break him beyond repair. Double if he dies within a week."

The woman nodded.

Tae's chest was so tightly constricted he wasn't sure how he was still breathing. He needed to figure this out, needed to give Ivan a chance, at least—

"Here," said Masha. "I'll get him outfitted."

"No," said the woman, and he could hear the anticipation in her voice. "Leave him like this. It's different, and I like it."

"Suit yourself," said Masha, with a slight shrug. "But he needs a wrist restraint. That I insist on. I won't have it be said that we're lax about precautions in this house. It's as much as my reputation's worth." She turned to Ivan. "Hold out your hand."

She'd given him an emergency device, which was something, but it wasn't, actually, unless Tae could crack this damn blocker.

He glared at the holoscreen in front of him, the readout from the program he'd grabbed from the boyeviki's com and the 3D holo-image rotating gently next to it.

"Is that it?" said the woman, tightening her grip on Ivan's arm. "Good. Book me into a room, please. I've decided how I'm going to spend the morning."

Masha nodded pleasantly. "Give me a moment. I'll get a room arranged."

Damn it, he was pretty sure Ysbel hadn't set the smoke bombs in the rooms yet, because this wasn't supposed to happen until this afternoon.

The woman nodded. Out of the corner of his eye, he saw her beckon with her head. "Follow," she snapped, and Ivan, the worry evident in the stiffness of his posture, hesitated the briefest moment. The sound of her slap carried across the room, and Tae almost bit through his lip.

He squeezed his eyes closed.

They'd kill Caz and Peti. If he moved, they'd kill Caz and Peti.

He was swearing softly to himself, hardly noticing the words he was saying, hardly noticing the iron tang of blood in his mouth.

The scan hung suspended on his screen, and he rotated it with two fingers.

Damn. Damn everything.

He blew out a steadying breath, and then sucked the air back in sharply and began frantically typing.

He'd have to be careful, but he was pretty sure ... he prodded gently at the edge of the system, where he thought he'd seen an opening.

Yes. There it was. He could get through without detection. Now he just had to write the splice and send it through to the rest of the devices.

He was typing feverishly, desperately.

I'm sorry. That's the best I could do.

He didn't bother to look up at Masha, but he heard out of the corner of his mind her words as she handed over a room key. "Remember, you pay for anything you damage. And I'm sorry, I have to insist that weapons stay here."

He'd have another couple seconds while she did the weapons scan, and then—

And then he heard footsteps ascending the stairs.

He couldn't stop himself glancing up. Ivan followed behind the three boyevik, head bowed, but Tae could see the tension in his posture, the way his hands clenched and unclenched.

He was afraid.

Tae had faced death with Ivan more than once, but this was the first time he'd seen his friend truly afraid.

He turned back to the holoscreen in front of him. It would take them a few moments to get to the top of the stairs, and then a few more moments to find the correct room. And surely there would be a moment or two after that before things started to go bad. Surely—

Above him, he thought he heard the faint hiss of a door unlocking, and then a moment later, locking again.

It could have been just his imagination. He probably hadn't actually heard the door, it was too far.

The seconds seemed to stretch to an absurd length.

Almost finished. Almost …

He glanced down at his com as he hit the last keystrokes.

How long had it been?

Six and a half standard minutes.

Ivan had been alone with the boyeviki for six and a half standard minutes.

He swallowed back a fresh wave of nausea and hit the button that would push the patch through to all the devices.

To Ivan's device.

Instantly, a red light flashed on the side of his com. Galina stiffened, and Masha looked up, her movements casual, but her face betraying her worry.

The emergency alert from Ivan's device. And Tae had no idea how long it had been going.

17

Jez stepped quickly through the door into her gambling hall and surveyed the scene.

OK, none of their actors were professional gamblers, but they'd done a damn good job at faking it. You'd have no idea that half a standard hour ago, this place had been as dead as a long-haul with no oxygen reserves. They had a decent grasp of the most common games, and she'd taught them one or two of her more obvious cheats. Really, she'd stack the tables how she wanted them, but wouldn't hurt if her people knew how to turn a game if they needed to. Honestly, she'd much rather be sitting at one of those tables herself, letting the smooth coolness of the tokens slide between her fingers, but there was work to do.

"Listen up, you plaguers," she said in a low voice. "They're here, and they'll be coming in in about five minutes, I'm guessing. Get your games where you want them, and if you're supposed to be drunk, at least smell like it."

The ragged assortment of gamblers turned quickly back to their tables, a few of them gargling their drink and letting it spill down their shirts, splashing it across their faces like cologne.

She grinned to herself as she took her place at the back of the hall.

Her time on Grigory's ship had taught her some very useful things about some very expensive liquors, and if Grigory's damn plaguers managed to leave this gambling hall without becoming very talkative indeed, she should probably just hang up her hat and go home.

The more they knew about what was happening, the better.

The boyeviki pushed their way into the gambling hall a few minutes later. She scanned them quickly as they came in, and swore softly.

Six of them, and none of them had taken off their weapons. Not that she'd particularly expected them to, but that wasn't the problem. The problem was, that left three in the lobby.

Not much she could do about that right now, though.

She grinned, and stood as they entered. "Hey there. Showed up at the pleasure house and found your way in here, did you?"

One of the men turned, and gave her a long, menacing look. "Watch your tone," he said in a low voice.

Jez shrugged, and perched back onto her stool. "My hall, my rules. The ones who want to gamble bad enough put up with it. Right, you bastard?" she turned and addressed her remark to a woman who sat at the table closest to her, her mouth fixed in concentration as she studied her tokens. She looked up and gave Jez a brief smile, then turned back to her game.

Jez leaned back expansively. "There you go. So, what'll it be? My hall my rules? Or you don't gamble one damn token in this place?"

"Your hall, your rules," said a woman, with a slight smile. "We can live with that. If you can throw in a drink to make your rules go down a little easier."

"Figure I can at that, you plaguer." Jez slid off her stool, still grinning. "And I figure you and me should get along just fine." She jerked her head towards the inside of the hall. "Go on in, then. But this is a place for people who know what they're doing. Don't say I didn't warn you when you leave here with nothing but your damn socks."

The man who'd first spoken shot her a glare, but they filed into the gambling hall and one by one, chose their game. Jez watched for a moment before she strolled over to the bar and emerged with a bottle and a handful of glasses. It wasn't Golden Murder, mostly because there were probably about three people in the entire system who would purposely accept a drink of the stuff without being at least three-quarters drunk already, and anyways, she knew Grigory kept his boyeviki pets on a tight leash. Probably best to ease them into it.

She set the glasses on the table and poured a generous amount of alcohol into each, then slid them across to her new customers. "This one's on the house. Next one you pay." She reached under the table and picked up a bag of tokens and passed them around, like you always did in kabaks. She wasn't completely certain this was custom in fancy halls like this one, but, her hall, her rules.

Besides, they'd decorated it to look like a kabak, so couldn't be that shocking.

They examined the tokens carefully and handed them back, and she tossed a handful face-down across the table in an easy gesture. No one asked to see the bag again, and she grinned to herself as she dropped it back in its place.

Any mud-eater who was too innocent to ask to see the bag after the dealer cast deserved every last one of the extra tokens she'd palmed from the inside pocket of her jacket and slipped into the deal.

It was almost insulting, honestly. At least on Grigory's ship she'd had to try.

Not that she was planning on skinning them, even though she wanted to. But it was always nice to have control of the game, in case things started going sideways.

"Well," she said, "Go ahead. I'll be keeping an eye on the floor."

She turned and sauntered back to her stool. At a table at the far end of the room, one of the ex-cons looked up and caught her eye, and she cut a quick glance at the table with three of Grigory's boyeviki.

She'd let them win a couple games first, just to get their confidence up. But if she was going to get them completely smashed and pump them for information, it was going to be more than a one-person job.

The man she'd signalled waited the full ninety standard seconds before he stood and stumbled towards the bar. He swayed as he passed the table she'd indicated, bumping it heavily. The boyeviki and Jez's people all jumped back, swearing, as tokens scattered across the floor and drinks spilled across the table, and one of the actors grabbed the man by the collar.

"Hey," Jez called across the room, not bothering to stand. "You throw one punch and your sorry butt isn't coming back through those doors, got it?"

The gambler turned, scowling, not loosening his grip on the hapless drunk. "Did you see what this mud-sucker did?"

Jez grinned. "Guess he's buying you all a round." She stood, then stopped abruptly.

The small red light on her com, the one that signalled an emergency, was blinking.

She shot an easy grin across at one of the servers. "You. Get over there and serve them. Make sure that drunken idiot pays. Got to take care of something outside."

He gave her a faint frown, but did as she asked, and she slipped out through the doors, her stomach suddenly tight.

"Tae," she whispered into her com the moment she was out of sight. "What's happening?"

"They took Ivan into a room," he said, his voice tight.

She stared at her com, then swore. "We were supposed to have a few hours before anyone picked up entertainment."

"I know!"

She stepped into the lobby and glanced around quickly. Tae stood beside Masha and Galya, every line in his posture betraying his horror.

She gave him a tight grin from across the floor. "Guess you'd better let someone who's good at this take care of it, then."

Ivan. This wasn't good.

"Radic," she hissed on the private line, starting towards the stairs. "Get in here. Your damn prison buddy's about to be killed."

"What?" He answered immediately. "Kid, what's—"

"Lobby," she whispered. "I'm heading up to the room." She hit the general line. "Masha, what number?"

"Jez, what are you—"

"Give me the damn number, Masha."

There was a moment's pause. "203," said Masha at last. "Jez—"

"Leave her alone. She knows what she's doing."

She stared at her com. It had sounded like Lev's voice, except she was pretty sure she'd never heard Lev—

"What do you need, Jez?" he asked.

"Tell Tanya if Radic and I don't come out in five standard minutes, burn the room down," she said grimly.

Radic slipped out the gambling hall door and sprinted across the lobby, catching up with her as she reached the stairs.

"What are we—" he began, falling into step beside her.

She jerked a heat-gun out of her pocket. "You're trying to kill me, because you lost all your credits at tokens and you think it's my fault," she said, shoving at him.

He raised an eyebrow. "You want them to think I'm stupid, kid? I know better than to pick a fight with someone who fights dirty."

She grinned at him, dread and anticipation pounding through her blood in equal measure. "Well, maybe I fight dirty, but here's the thing—I usually win."

He gave her an amused glance that did nothing to hide the worry in his face. "I have a distinct memory of one time in prison when you were only on your feet because Lev and Tae—"

She rolled her eyes. "That was on purpose." They'd reached the landing, and she looked around quickly, trying to get her bearings.

"First hallway to your left, second door on the right," said Lev into her earpiece, his voice tight.

"On it," she said. She turned to Radic. "Go on, hit me. Need a black eye at least."

He hesitated, then drew back his fist, took a deep breath, and punched from the shoulder, turning his face away at the last moment. She staggered slightly at the blow, cursing loudly.

"Need to work on your punches," she whispered, leaning up against the wall.

He gave her a relieved look, then shouted, words slurring slightly, "You dirty scum-sucker! You expect me to believe you took that many credits off me without cheating?" He pulled out the pistol she'd handed him, raised it, and deliberately put a blast into the wall behind her. She cut her eyes quickly to one side.

203. Right door. At least, it damn well better be, because she

wasn't sure how many doors she could go crashing through in a row and make it sound natural.

She swore again and lunged at him, and he caught her.

"Through the door," she whispered, and he nodded, and shoved her. She stumbled back against the door, putting her weight into it, and at the same time the heat blast from the modded gun she'd handed him melted through the lock.

The door swung open, and she fell inside, and Radic crashed in after her, gun still raised.

She took in the composition of the room in a glance. Ivan stood against one wall, tension in every line of his body, but he was alive. That was all she needed to know at the moment.

But she couldn't help but see the torn line of his thin server's shirt, the bright line of blood that circled his throat and ran half-way down his bare chest.

She exchanged a grim look with Radic. Then she exploded to her feet, managing to jam her elbow into the sternum of the woman holding the knife. The woman staggered backward, swearing, and Jez stomped on the toe of her boot, knocking her off balance. She went down hard.

"What—" one of the men began.

"I'll teach you to cheat at tokens," Radic growled, lunging at Jez. She ducked, and he slammed full-on into the man who'd started to speak. She noticed with a grim satisfaction that he managed to catch the man in the throat with his shoulder, and the man went down, gasping. Jez turned, stepping backwards quickly and grinding the heel of her boot into the downed woman's wrist. The woman gasped in pain, and Jez yanked a heat-gun out of her holster and snapped off a shot that was nominally in Radic's direction, but somehow managed to hit the wall so close to the third man's head that she could smell scorched hair.

"My hall, my rules," she ground out through her teeth. Somehow she was grinning, and she couldn't stop it. "Might want to think before you call me a cheat."

Radic rolled to his feet, planting his knee in the solar plexus of the man he'd bowled over. The man, who'd been struggling to rise, fell back with an agonized wheeze. Jez stepped back again deliberately. The woman on the floor must have been a quick learner, because she tried to roll out of the way, but Jez had anticipated that. She stumbled, falling backwards and landing hard, elbow first, into the centre of the woman's stomach. Radic had grabbed the one man who was still upright, using him to haul himself to his feet. Radic's foot caught behind the man's knee when he was almost up, and the man went down with Radic on top of him.

"You damn drunk! Learn to plaguing hold your alcohol before you try going after someone," Jez called.

The woman shifted underneath her, and then there was the shriek of an alarm, pounding against her ears.

She caught Radic's eye, and they exchanged a grimly satisfied look.

Then she hauled herself to her feet, careful to inflict the maximum amount of pain on the woman below her, and was standing sullenly when the door burst open. Three bouncers stepped into the chaos, clipping everyone's hands behind their back with mag cuffs.

Masha was waiting for them when they were frog-marched down to the lobby.

"Jez Solokov," said Masha, eyes icy. "I suggest you learn to control yourself. What happened here?"

Her voice was so convincing that Jez's muscles tensed

involuntarily, like they would have months ago at the sound of Masha's voice.

"This idiot was trying to shoot me," she muttered. "What the hell was I supposed to do?"

"She cheated me!" Radic slurred loudly. "She took me for everything I have. Her tables are rigged."

Masha turned her cold glance on him. "I suggest," she said, her voice sharp enough to cut steel, "that you sober up. You will not be welcome here a second time."

She turned to the boyeviki. Jez noticed with satisfaction that all of them were limping. From the way the woman was holding her wrist, Jez might have actually broken it.

"I'm so very sorry," Masha said, her voice going from hard to apologetic. "Please. Come with me. I'll get someone to bring a first aid kit, get your injuries treated." She turned to the bouncers. "These people did nothing wrong. Let them go at once, please."

Once their cuffs were off, she led them into the medic room, apologizing profusely.

Jez glanced at Ivan as they left. He was looking straight ahead, but a muscle worked in the corner of his jaw and the blood from where he'd been cut pooled in his shirt and dripped in a steady, monotonous pattern onto the stone floor.

She narrowed her eyes.

With any luck, the man they had playing medic would manage to inflict a little more pain as he was bandaging the plaguers up.

The door closed behind Masha, and Ivan's shoulders slumped in relief. The bouncers unlocked their handcuffs quickly, and Radic crossed over to him in two steps. "Ivan. Are you alright?"

Ivan let out a long breath and managed a shaky smile. "I'm fine, I think. At least, no permanent damage. Remind me never to get in the middle of a fight between you and Jez."

Radic chuckled reluctantly, then Tae pushed past him. His face was grimmer than Jez had seen it in a long time.

"Ivan," he said tersely. "Come with me. We need to get that bandaged." He turned over his shoulder. "Jez, make sure they get out."

"On it, tech-head," she said. "Worry about Ivan. We've got the rest."

He nodded, and took Ivan's arm in a gesture that was almost painfully tender. Ivan didn't protest, just let Tae steer him upstairs towards a free room.

"Hey, genius," Jez whispered into the com. "Need you on the screens. Tech-head's busy."

"Is Ivan alright?" Lev asked, voice tense.

Jez glanced to where he and Tae were disappearing down a hallway and managed a grin. "Figure he probably is now."

"I'll pull up the monitor screens." There was a moment's pause, then he said quietly, "Thank you, Jez. I—didn't have a backup plan for that possibility."

"Sure you did," she said. "Had me, didn't you?"

"I—suppose I did." There was something like a smile in his voice.

She let out a long breath and glanced at Radic. "Guess I'd better get into the gambling hall. They're going to miss me in a few minutes here. You'd probably better make yourself scarce." She paused a moment. "Thanks, by the way."

He gave her that lopsided grin. "Wouldn't have missed it, kid. If I'm going to risk my life doing something absolutely ridiculous, you're the person I'd do it with."

She gave him a wink, then took a deep breath and turned back towards the gambling hall, trying to ignore the ice in her stomach.

Probably better hurry up with getting the plaguers drunk, because she was pretty sure they'd all be leaving earlier than scheduled.

But the sight of Ivan, standing against the wall, defenceless, body stiff, beads of blood forming and trickling from the cut on his throat like jewels in a necklace, made her swallow hard against the taste of vomit in the back of her throat, and she wasn't completely sure she could trust herself with tokens until her hands stopped shaking.

18

"How did we let this happen, Masha?" Ysbel stood slightly from her seat at the conference table. Her voice was steady, but she was certain Masha could hear the anger under it. "I thought you'd considered every possibility."

"Unfortunately, Ysbel, as you are well aware, it is not possible to plan for every possibility."

Masha's tone was sharper than usual. Ysbel narrowed her eyes.

The woman was clearly shaken.

They were all shaken, honestly. She's seen the look on Tae's face, when he'd slipped out of the medic's for a few minutes to check through what his monitors had picked up. Ivan wasn't hurt badly, but that wasn't the point.

The point was, they were very lucky he was alive at all.

Masha took a deep breath and looked around at the rest of them, gathered around the table in the conference room. "At any rate, it wasn't a complete disaster. Jez was quick enough on her feet to keep anything from going too badly sideways, and we got some information from the boyeviki in the gambling hall, I believe. Nothing substantive, but enough to know that Tae's guess was correct—Zhenya was the one who sent them, likely without

Grigory's knowledge. This lends credence to the idea that Zhenya may not have told Grigory about the whereabouts of the street children. I believe that is at least a point in our favour, however slim."

Lev shifted slightly in his seat. "Jez and Radic were good, and their actions almost certainly kept Ivan alive," he said quietly. "It was our best option. But we can't know whether the boyeviki saw through it."

Ysbel drew in a long breath.

She hadn't been down there. She'd been with the children, reading them a story to keep them quiet, and she hadn't known what had happened until it was over.

And if she was being honest, that was the thing that had shaken her the most. She hadn't even known there was a threat.

Like that evening so many years ago, back on her small farm. When she'd tucked her children in bed and kissed her wife, and then stepped outside to bring in the last of the harvesting tools.

And her next view of her home had been the flames leaping from the door and licking up the roof, Tanya's terrified face at the window, the children's screams.

She closed her eyes for a moment, trying to compose herself.

"You've been watching the account, Lev?" Masha was asking.

"Yes." Lev's voice was grim. "Nothing's changed. Grigory's pledge is still in place. But until he can cash in the security on his pleasure houses and actually deposit the funds, which will likely be a few days at best, we're vulnerable. And as you said, Zhenya may not be telling Grigory everything at the moment. They could be keeping their secret until the time it would hurt us the most."

"Well, there's nothing we can do about it at present," said Masha finally. Her lips were pressed tight, her expression grave. "We'll carry on. Galina and I are working on emergency protocols for all the actors now, although hopefully we won't need it again." She sighed. "In the mean time, this house needs to look busy. Word will get around if it's dead. So we'd best get to work keeping it looking busy. Galina will be working with Lev to set up shifts of people coming in and out, and we'll need to keep the place lit and noisy enough that it doesn't arouse suspicion. So." She glanced around at them once more. "I suggest we get to work."

Slowly, the others rose from their seats.

Ysbel caught Tanya's eye, and Tanya gave a quick nod. Once the others had left, she turned to Ysbel.

"What is it?"

Ysbel shook her head, face still grim. "We can't afford another mistake like this. It was only luck that those two idiots got Ivan out before he was killed, and who knows who it will be next time?" She sighed. "Why wasn't Ivan armed? I thought we'd armed all the servers."

"He was," said Tanya, in a low voice. "The whole time, he had a heat pistol in his boot. He could have shot them dead, at any moment."

Ysbel turned to stare at her wife. "Why didn't he?"

Tanya gave a brief, humourless smile. "He knew if these people suspected anything, Tae's friends would die. I've known Ivan for a very long time, you remember. Believe me when I say, he would have let himself be killed."

Ysbel closed her eyes, feeling suddenly cold.

That was the problem with this whole thing. They couldn't afford anything to go wrong. Not a single thing. They were balancing on the edge of a knife, and one slip in either direction, and people they cared about would die.

For a moment, she pictured the merciless expression on Vitali's face.

Lev had been right. The backup plan was necessary, whether Jez believed it or not. Because they couldn't afford to slip.

She pushed herself to her feet. "Can you take the children for the rest of the day, please? We're setting off another explosive in the pleasure district tomorrow night to keep the pressure up on Grigory. I'd like to make sure everything is ready."

Tanya looked up at her, frowning slightly. "You need to do that tonight? Olya told me you'd promised to finish reading the story to her, and Misko will cry if I tell him you aren't going to put him to bed. It should only take an hour, if that, and you can work on it the rest of the evening."

Ysbel shook her head tersely. "No. I don't want to take any more chances."

That wasn't the real reason. The real reason was, she wasn't sure if she could bear sitting in their snug room, the children cuddled in her lap, holoscreen in front of them with the story in letters big enough that Olya could read along, and not see, every time she closed her eyes, her last evening with them in their little cottage on their small farm.

Tanya was watching her quietly. "I'll tell them, then," she said. "They'll be upset, I'm afraid."

"They'll be fine, I'm sure," said Ysbel, trying to keep the harshness from her tone. "They're more used to you anyways." She paused, then leaned down and kissed Tanya's forehead. "I'm sorry, my Tanya. But this is important."

"Of course," said Tanya quietly.

19

"Jez. You're sure you're ready for this?" Ysbel's expression was unaccountably grim.

Jez gave her an easy grin. "Born ready."

Ysbel snorted, and gestured with her head. "Well then, get going. We don't have all night."

Jez smirked at her, and sauntered out towards the hangar bay.

Alright, maybe she wasn't totally sure she could go back to the pleasure district without absolutely losing her crap. Maybe there was something inside her stomach that was clenched so tight it was almost painful, and maybe every damn time she closed her eyes she could see the lines of blood trickling down Ivan's neck and his bare chest and pooling in his ripped tunic and dripping onto the floor, the sick, haunted, horrified look on Tae's face. Maybe all of those things were true.

But honestly, right now all she wanted was to move, do something, fly her skybike fast enough that the wind whipping across her face and tearing through her hair and dragging at her clothing was enough to make her forget what had happened yesterday.

It wasn't being in danger. She'd been in danger plenty of times before, hell, every member of the crew had been almost killed more times than she could count, and yes, she always hated it when someone she cared about might be killed, but—well but there was something different about this. Maybe it was the fact that Ivan had been standing there, hands cuffed together, not fighting, not even moving. Trapped.

And the woman with the knife had liked it. Jez had seen the look in her eyes as she and Radic had burst through the door, the echo of the expression before it turned to one of shock and outrage.

She'd been hurting him, and she'd enjoyed it, because she'd enjoyed seeing him scared and helpless. That was what was making the nausea twist uneasily in Jez's stomach.

She'd almost let herself forget, all this time, that she was on a pleasure planet. That this same damn city where she and Radic slipped into speakeasies and laughed and joked with the alley-porters and the dockworkers and the gangsters around the bar held a pleasure district, and the pleasure district was the engine that fed the rest of this damn place.

"Are you alright?" asked Ysbel quietly, mounting her bike.

Jez smirked at her. "I'm good. Don't plan on driving slow for you, though."

Ysbel was still watching her, expression far too perceptive. "I know you don't like this. I'd bring Galina again, but—"

Jez turned, swallowing hard against the sick in her throat. "Ysbel. I know. They need Galya here. I'll be fine, OK? Grew up in a damn smuggler crew. I'll be fine."

Ysbel studied her a moment longer, then nodded and pulled her own helmet on over her shaved head. "I'll meet you at the coordinates Lev sent to your com, in case we get separated."

Jez swung up on her bike and shot one last grin at Ysbel over her shoulder. Then she hit the controls and shot forward, leaning until she was almost parallel to the bike, the wind dragging tears from her eyes.

By the time she arrived at the coordinates, her fingers were numb and stinging from the cold, and tears pulled out by the wind streaked backwards across her face and wet her hair. She drew in a long, shaky breath and shook her head, actually looking around her for the first time.

She'd stopped at the mouth of a narrow, filthy alley, which was probably where Ysbel wanted her to wait.

Speaking of Ysbel—she dismounted and pulled up her com, then rolled her eyes.

Ten standard minutes at least. Maybe fifteen, at the speed she was flying.

For a moment, she was tempted to swing back up on her bike, come back when Ysbel was a little closer. But, considering this was a stealth mission, probably better not to advertise their presence by flying down the alleyways fast enough to curl the paint off the walls.

She sighed heavily and leaned up against the wall, pulling off her helmet and wiping the tear-streaks from her face with the back of her sleeve.

It was dark in this corner of the city. The sputtering artificial street lamps barely illuminated the small circle of air around them and served only to cut her night vision, making everything seem even darker than it was. The alley where she stood was cool, and the sharp scent of decaying flesh wafted in on the air stirred by her passing.

She glanced behind her quickly.

Hopefully a dead rat, but honestly, in a place like this she couldn't be certain.

The noises of the street were muted and furtive, like whoever was moving there didn't want to be heard. Jez leaned against the filthy wall and tapped the heel of her boot against the slimy pre-fab blocks.

Ysbel could damn well learn how to fly a little faster, honestly.

She glanced down at her com, and suppressed a groan.

Nine more standard minutes at least.

She swore under her breath and looked around again.

Footsteps hurried down the street outside, their quick patter a testament to a fervent desire to pass by as quickly as possible. Jez straightened and moved cautiously to the edge of the alley, peering outside at the darkened streets.

Damn the street lights. With them glowing sickly in the periphery of her vision, it was almost impossible to make out the shapes in the streets outside.

She put a hand to the reassuring smoothness of the heat pistol in its holster on her belt, and drew in a slow breath.

No one here would be able to see any better than she could, so it wasn't like she was at a disadvantage. But she bloody well felt like she was at a disadvantage, naked and exposed in the dim light, unable to see to protect herself.

Not even sure what she thought she'd need protection against.

A small movement made her glance down, and she jerked back and swore, heart pounding.

The thing she'd mistaken for a heap of garbage on the street had stirred, and now she could make out the huddled shape of a person —probably a child, from the size of the ragged bundle of blankets covering it.

She stared, feeling vomit rising in her throat, then, reluctantly, she forced herself to crouch down beside the bundle of filthy rags.

Honestly, what she wanted to do was run as far and fast as she could in the other direction.

"Don't—don't hurt me." The child's voice was dull and rasping, as if it hadn't been used in some time. "Please."

Jez's hands were shaking. The smell from the blankets was even worse than the smell from the alley behind her, that thick, clinging scent of rotting flesh.

"Hey, I'm not planning on hurting you, kid," she whispered. "You OK?"

The child stared at her, as if unable to comprehend her words.

It was hard to see in the dim light, but he looked young. Maybe Olya's age, or maybe a year or two older. His eyes were too big for his face, cheekbones jutting out of sunken cheeks.

Tae's street kid friends had looked something like this the first time she'd met them. But they'd had a sharp wariness about them that spoke of a desperate struggle for survival.

This child's eyes were dull and hopeless.

His words to her hadn't been the plea of a child begging for his life, just the exhausted entreaty of someone who only wanted to avoid more pain.

Jez swallowed hard and fumbled in her jacket pocket, pulling out a slightly battered rations pack. "You want this?" she asked, holding it out.

The boy just looked at it, uninterested. She ripped the packaging open, and held it out again.

Surely the kid knew what a rations pack was.

"Go on," she whispered. "Take it. It's to eat."

Finally, he reached out a hand and took it from her. As he moved, the blanket shifted, and Jez thought she might be sick.

There was a gaping wound on the boy's leg, open and rotting. Flies crawled through it, and the stench made her gag.

Damn. Damn, damn, damn. There was nothing on her bike that

would help, nothing in the tiny emergency kit to deal with something like this.

The boy still held the rations pack, as if unsure what to do with it. He looked up at her with those dull eyes, void of curiosity or life or hope. "I'm going to die," he said. "They put me out here because I was going to die. You can't use me for anything else."

Jez almost did throw up at that, almost emptied her entire dinner on the filthy street. "I don't want to use you for anything," she said, and the words came out harsher than she'd meant for them to. The child quailed back instinctively, and Jez closed her eyes and drew in a long, steadying breath. "I'm sorry," she said, more quietly this time. "Look, I don't want to use you for anything. I don't do that, OK? But—if there's something I can do to help you—"

He looked at her with a vague curiosity, as if he didn't understand her words, and Jez turned away for a moment, swearing softly to herself.

"Jez?"

She jumped and spun around, hand on her weapon. Ysbel stood there, looking down with a mix of pity and concern.

"Ysbel, this kid—they—" she swallowed hard, and found she couldn't say anything else. Wordlessly, Ysbel crouched beside her. Her face, in the dim light, was grim, but she clearly wasn't shocked. Not like Jez had been shocked.

She'd known about this. The rest of them had all known about this. And she had too, sort of. At least, she'd heard rumours of the pleasure planets when she was working with Lena, but they were only vague rumours, winks and nudges between some of the more unsavoury pilots. And when she'd come here before, when she'd first started flying with Masha and the others, Lev had given a brief explanation, when pressed.

But this?

Somehow, the last ten minutes had taught her more about this pleasure planet than she'd ever wanted to know. And the sight of the gangrenous, rotting wound on the kid's leg mingled with the memory of Ivan's face, set and afraid, the blood running down his neck and chest.

Except this kid hadn't had someone to step in.

Ysbel was speaking with the child in a quiet voice, and now, gently, she pulled the blanket back. Jez could see the way her posture stiffened at the sight and the smell.

Gently, carefully, Ysbel replaced the dirty blanket and stood. "I'm sorry, Jez," she said quietly. "There's not much we can do."

"Damn it to hell," Jez spat, standing abruptly. Her heart was pounding, and tears threatened to squeeze themselves out between her eyelids, but she blinked them back.

"I'm sorry," said Ysbel. She was still crouched beside the boy, and her hand on his skinny arm was gentle, but she was looking at Jez.

"Let's go then, get this done and get the hell out of here," said Jez through her teeth.

She wanted to hit something. She wanted to bloody shoot someone.

They walked quickly through the streets. Ysbel led the way, looking carefully around them before turning onto a new street, staying far enough away from the alley entrances that no one could grab them unawares.

Jez was too damn angry to care.

There were other people in the streets, furtive, ragged figures, many of them limping or maimed, others huddled in alleyways like more dirty bundles of rags. Like the kid they'd left in the alley. The kid who was bloody well going to die, and there was nothing they could damn well do about it.

When they reached the archway that marked the entrance to the pleasure district, Jez swallowed down the sick in her throat a second time. The clean cobblestones looked dirty, somehow, and the shadows cast by the bright, garish lights reminded her of bloodstains.

She didn't speak, and neither did Ysbel, as they slipped through the entranceway and started off down the street. Ysbel's posture was casual, her hood thrown back, the lights flashing from the pleasure houses lining the streets casting harsh reflections across her pale skin.

Jez was as taut as a strung wire. She ached to grab one of the bastards strolling down this street and plant her fist in the middle of their damn smug face.

"Jez," said Ysbel warningly, casting a quick glance over her shoulder. "I know how you feel. But getting into a fight isn't going to do anything."

"I know," Jez replied, her voice low and harsh. "It's not damn well going to do anything. Look at this hell-hole. There's a million kids like that kid in the alley, I get it, and we can't help them. But—what the hell is the point, then?"

Ysbel stopped a moment, considering her. Then she took Jez firmly by the arm and drew her back into a space between two buildings. "Jez," she said in a low, grim voice. "Right now, all we can do is try to keep the rest of the crew from being killed by Grigory. That's what we're doing. That's all we're doing. Do you understand?"

"Yeah?" Jez shot back. "And what about that kid in the alley? Who cares enough to save him?"

Ysbel just looked at her steadily, and finally Jez jerked her arm free and turned away.

"Fine," she said through her teeth. "Fine, Ysbel. Let's keep our own damn friends safe and happy, and to hell with everyone else, right?"

Ysbel didn't answer, but Jez heard a long sigh from behind her. "Believe me," Ysbel said in a low voice after a moment. "I don't like this any more than you do."

Somehow Jez managed to hold herself in check as they wound their way through the streets to where Ysbel and Galina had decided would be the most effective place to plant the explosive.

Thinking of Galina made it worse somehow. Because Galya had lived here. Galya had worked in the damn kitchens during the day, and spent the nights chained in the cellar, and she'd escaped, and she was alright.

But she was one of a very, very few.

They reached the place, a tall building shaped like a palace. Ysbel handed Jez a small smoke bomb. "Around the back," she whispered. "Throw it inside, and sound the alarm. I'll wait until everyone's out before I detonate the explosive." She paused. "This is a gambling hall. So don't worry. There's no one in cages here."

Jez gave a tight nod.

When she reached the back of the building, she hurled the smoke bomb, and it sailed through the glass window with a satisfying crunch. "Fire!" she shouted at the top of her voice. "Fire! The damn place is burning down!"

Despite everything, it was immensely satisfying to hear the screams from inside.

Let these bastards be the ones screaming, for once.

She headed back around the side of the building, and met Ysbel. Ysbel jerked her head wordlessly, and Jez followed her at a quick pace down the street.

And then there was a *crack* that seemed to shatter her eardrums, followed by a low, ominous rumble. When she glanced over her shoulder, the gambling hall was gone. In its place, a pile of debris settled into a massive hole blown into the ground.

But somehow, it wasn't enough. It wasn't ever going to be enough.

She almost didn't notice, as they approached the arch that led back into the filthy squaller of the slum town, the motion near the gate, until Ysbel put up a warning hand.

Jez came to an abrupt halt and frowned, something cold stirring in her stomach.

A group of people stood there, laughing and joking. They were all clearly wealthy, and clearly here to enjoy themselves, and they were flanked by a handful of menacing-looking bodyguards. One of them had a heat gun, but most had the long, thin, elegant gutting knives that she'd come to hate the sight of.

"Let's go, then," one of the men said, and started through the gates, and the others followed, the bodyguards bringing up the rear.

"What's—" she began, turning to Ysbel, but the look on the woman's face stopped her.

Ysbel paused a moment. "It's nothing you want to know about, Jez," she said quietly.

Jez sucked in a quick breath. "Ysbel," she said, biting off her words. "Look. I hate this, alright? I bloody hate this, and if I could I'd burn this whole planet down. But I'm not an innocent. I don't need to be protected. And you're damn well going to tell me what's going on."

Ysbel paused for another long moment. At last, she nodded heavily. "Alright. But I did warn you. Galina told me, last time we were here. That gate—there's a reason it's not locked."

Jez had already guessed what Ysbel would say next, but hearing her say it somehow made it worse.

"Jez?" Ysbel's voice seemed to come from far away.

"Yeah," Jez said, distantly. "Yeah. Thanks for telling me. Guess—guess we should be getting back now."

Ysbel studied her for a few moments, and there was probably concern on her face, but honestly, Jez didn't really care.

"If you're sure you're alright," she said quietly. She turned, and somehow Jez made her legs move, made herself follow Ysbel through the archway and into the dirty streets.

They hunted them. Like animals. The pleasure houses weren't enough, so they'd follow them out here to where they tried to hide and lick their wounds.

And they thought it was exciting. It was a game to them, just another diversion in a planet full of diversions.

She hardly noticed the feel of the street under her boots, or the cool of the night air on her skin.

It didn't really matter. Because for the first time in her life, she realized the truth—this was too big, and too terrible, and too overwhelmingly sick and wrong for any of them to make a difference.

No matter what she did, no matter where she went, no matter how long she lived, she'd never scrub the filth of this place off her skin.

And then there was a shout up ahead, and every muscle in her body tensed.

And then another sound, a small, raspy voice she recognized, crying out in fear, and Jez was running, heat pistol in her hand, before she even realized what she was doing.

She rounded the corner and took in the scene at a glance—one man bending over the boy, an unpleasant smile on his face, three of his companions standing behind him, watching with lascivious interest, the bodyguards standing slightly back.

Her first shot hit the bent-over man squarely in the chest, which was actually pretty impressive since she hadn't even bothered to slow down.

He swayed for a moment, then fell soundlessly, a look of surprise plastered grotesquely onto his face.

There was a moment where everyone was looking at him and no one had looked up yet to see where the shot had come from.

And then she bowled into the three people who were still standing.

One of them, a woman, fell hard against the wall. Jez caught herself, spun around, and grabbed one of the remaining men by the collar, jerking him forward and planting a fist into the centre of his nose. He shouted, a fine spray of blood spattering Jez and his companions and the wall beside them, and Jez jerked him around, his body forming a shield between her and the bodyguards.

The woman who'd been thrown against the wall had recovered herself and grabbed Jez by the throat. She was reaching for her gun, but Jez twisted free and kicked as hard as she could, planting the heel of her boot hard into the woman's kneecap. The woman shrieked in pain, and the gun skittered across the dirty alley.

Jez was grinning, but there was still that hard, vicious knot in her chest. Sure, she was going to die, right here, but she'd damn well rather die than let this happen.

The other man grabbed her wrist, wrenching her grip from his companion's shirtfront, and hit her hard in the face. She staggered, but managed to grab his hair with her free hand, jerking his head down as he grunted in pain. He tightened his grip on her wrist, twisting hard, and she could feel the bones about to break, and then she managed to bring her knee up. It was awkward, and not nearly the kind of blow she was hoping for, but her knee connected with his nose and he dropped his grip and stumbled backwards. She spun—

The other two had stepped back. The five bodyguards were spread in a half-circle around her, weapons aimed, expressions hard.

"Get back," one of them said to the man, who was holding his face and muttering curses.

He complied.

Now it was just Jez.

She grinned at the bodyguards, her heart jumping like a damn desert rabbit, her pulse pounding in her ears.

She hadn't honestly thought she'd die in a dirty street in a slum on a pleasure planet, but hell, you take what you get.

And then, through the sick anticipation that flooded through her like a drug, she heard Ysbel's voice, two terse words.

"Get down."

There was something about Ysbel's tone that made Jez's muscles obey automatically, and she dropped to the ground like she'd been hit over the head. There was a spray of something with a familiar sharp, chemical scent, and the part of her brain that was still somehow trying to keep her alive recognized it, and she was already rolling out of the way, grabbing the terrified bundle of rags that was a child as she did so, and then the world went white.

When it cleared, she was braced against the wall of the alley, her body sheltering the kid from the shrapnel.

Cautiously, she raised her head.

Ysbel stood across from her, expression grim.

Jez didn't bother to look down at what remained of the customers and their bodyguards, because she was pretty damn sure she didn't want to see that. Instead, she got shakily to her feet, leaning against the wall of the alley for support. A sharp pain in her wrist reminded her that she'd been in a fight a couple minutes ago, but she was pretty sure that wasn't the reason her legs were shaking like she'd drunk a hell of a lot more than she could handle.

"Are you alright?"

It took a moment for the words to penetrate her brain, then she nodded shakily. "Yeah. Yeah, guess I am. Thanks."

Ysbel took her by the shoulders, her grip surprisingly gentle, and turned her around, looking her up and down critically.

"You've got blood all over you," she said.

"Don't think most of it's mine," said Jez, attempting a grin. She wasn't sure it turned out, considering the look on Ysbel's face.

"Are you going to be able to get back home?"

The question finally snapped Jez out of her daze. She blinked a moment, then managed a snarky grin that felt a little more successful than the last one.

"Ysbel," she said. "Who do you think you're talking to? Do I look like I'm actually dead?"

Ysbel raised an eyebrow. "I'm not completely sure I would be able to tell the difference at this point, but since you're standing, I'll assume that no, you're not dead."

"Well then," said Jez with a smirk. "Guess that answers your question."

"Fair enough," said Ysbel wryly.

Jez took a deep breath to steady herself. Then she crouched down in front of the child.

"Hey. Kid," she said softly. "You OK?"

The boy's face was blank with terror, but at last he managed a small nod.

"Good," she said. "Look, I promise I won't hurt you. At least, I'll do my damndest not to. But this isn't a place for children, OK? I'm going to pick you up, is that alright?"

His expression froze, his whole body trembling.

"I promise. I'm not trying to hurt you," she said softly, and she found her voice was trembling too, just like her hands and her legs and her whole damn body.

Finally, finally, the child gave a small, terrified nod.

"What are you—" Ysbel began.

Jez didn't look up at her, just scooped the bundle of blankets and child gently into her arms and straightened, somehow managing not to stagger. The kid weighed almost nothing, and when she looked down, his face was twisted in silent agony.

"You got painkillers in your first-aid kit?" she asked, still without looking up.

"Jez," began Ysbel, after a moment's pause.

"I said, you got any damn painkillers?" Jez asked through her teeth.

Ysbel sighed heavily, and there was the sound of someone rummaging through a handful of small items.

"There are these," Ysbel said at last, crossing over to stand beside her. "They're for a full-grown adult. But if you give him just a half, it should cut the pain."

Jez took the proffered half-tablet, and propped her knee up on her bike, supporting the impossibly light weight of him. Gently, she pulled back the bit of filthy blanket that had covered the boy's face.

"This will make it hurt less," she whispered.

The kid's teeth were clenched so tightly she wasn't sure if he could open his mouth if he wanted to.

"It will dissolve quickly if you can get it into him," said Ysbel quietly.

Biting back nausea, Jez pulled his lip down gently and tried to pry the chalky tablet between his teeth. In the end she had to settle for dropping it into his bottom lip and letting his mouth pinch closed again.

"We should go," said Ysbel, her voice still quiet. "Someone will come looking for the others sooner or later."

"How long does this take to work?" Jez asked, her voice tight.

From the corner of her eye, she saw Ysbel shrug. "I don't know. Fifteen minutes, maybe? Longer than we can wait."

"Yeah." She swallowed hard.

"Jez," said Ysbel after a moment, and her voice was painfully gentle. "I'm sorry. That boy isn't going to—"

This time Jez did look up, and hell, maybe there were tears in her eyes, but she couldn't actually help it right now, and her arms were too full to be able to brush them away.

"I don't care," she said in a low, vicious voice. "I don't actually give a damn, OK? Because I'm not leaving him here. I'm not bloody leaving him. Maybe I can't save him, but I'll be damned to every hell in existence before I'll just leave him like this."

"Alright," said Ysbel at last. "Then I suppose we'd best get going."

Steering the bike, even with the achingly light bundle in her arms, wasn't difficult. She'd been telling Ysbel the truth—she could probably ride the thing if she was unconscious, because her muscles knew what to do even without any input from her brain. But she rode slowly, trying not to jostle the kid.

She could tell the moment when the painkillers finally kicked in, because his stiff body went gradually limp in her arms, which, on one hand, was a relief, and on the other, made her whole body seize up with terror, because through the blankets she couldn't tell if he was still breathing or if he'd finally just given up.

Ysbel must have radioed ahead, because when she pulled into the hangar bay, Galina and Tanya and Masha were all there, waiting for her. She slid off the bike and handed her bundle over to Galina, who took it gently and laid the boy on the floor. Jez could see the emotion flit across her face as the blankets fell back, horror and resignation and pity.

"Masha, I need a full first aid kit," she said, words terse. "Tanya, help me."

Tanya knelt down beside her and sucked in a quick breath.

"There's no way we save him," she said quietly. "Not with a wound rotting like that. I'm sorry."

"I know," said Galina, voice tight. "But we can at least make him comfortable." She looked up. "Ysbel, go wake up Ivan and ask him if anyone here is a doctor."

Jez leaned up against the bike and closed her eyes. Every part of her felt shaky and sick, like when she was a kid and had come down with something that she'd thought might actually kill her, and she'd puked her guts out for three days and hadn't been able to stand up without falling over for a week after that.

She wasn't a kid anymore, though, and she wasn't hurt, at least, not really, and—and—

"Jez?" Lev's voice was warm and concerned, and then his arm was around her shoulder. "Jez," he said again, and she collapsed against him, and he just held her.

She leaned into him, feeling the familiar rise and fall of his chest, the warm circle of his arms, and closed her eyes, trying to gather enough strength to stand up on her own legs again. Finally, when she thought she could stay on her feet without falling over, she straightened.

"Jez, you're hurt," he said quietly. "Let's get that taken care of. Come on, neither of us can do anything here, but I've patched you up enough times I can probably handle that, at least."

She managed a weak grin, somehow. He left his arm around her waist, as though he could tell that her steadiness might give out at any moment, and led her from the room. She glanced back over her shoulder once, to see Galina and Tanya and Masha and a man she didn't recognize crouched beside the filthy bundle on the floor. Galina looked up and shot her a quick, strained smile before turning back to her work.

"They'll do everything they can," he said, his voice soothing somehow. "Come on. You can't help here right now."

It was ridiculous, really, being shaky and crap when nothing had really happened to her. Yes, her wrist was already swollen to twice its normal size and turning an impressive reddish-purple, and yes, she was bleeding from a shallow cut on her cheekbone where someone must have hit her, which to be honest she couldn't actually remember, but hell, that was basically a normal day for her. There was really nothing to be shaky over.

Except—

Except every time she closed her eyes, she could see that man crouched over the kid, the vicious smile on his face, and every damn time she saw it, she wanted to throw up again.

"It's not fair," she said quietly, as Lev sealed a bandage carefully over the cut under her eye. "It's not bloody fair."

"No, it's not," Lev said, his voice low.

"I thought—I thought maybe I could—if I brought him back here, maybe we could—" She swallowed back the sick and the choking tears. "But we can't. He's going to die. And there were people back there in the pleasure district, and—they wanted to— they were trying to—they must have known he was dying, and anyways, he's just a kid, like Olya, and—and they were going to—" She was babbling, and she couldn't seem to stop, and there was the sharp ache of tears behind her eyes. "He's going to die anyways," she choked. "No matter what I did, he was always going to die anyways."

"I know," Lev said quietly. "I know, Jez. But—at least he'll die somewhere warm, where no one's hurting him. At least you did that."

She squeezed her eyes closed, but the tears were leaking out anyways.

Damn it to hell. Damn everything to hell.

She stood abruptly, and Lev caught her before she could stumble.

Like he always did.

She turned and gave him a weary smile, because having him near was nice, and there was something in the warm comfort of his presence that made the horrors she'd seen that night a little more bearable.

"Thanks," she said.

He smiled back, and even though there was that tinge of sadness to it, his smile made the world seem just a little less hopeless.

"Are you going to be alright?" he asked quietly.

She managed a grin. "Well, considering nothing actually happened to me, figure I probably will be." She took a deep breath and straightened, and the grin faded from her face. "Um. Thank you."

"Go get some sleep, Jez," said Lev, with that faint, weary smile of his. "I'll wake you up if we need you, I promise."

She nodded, and made her way to her room, and even though she'd been one hundred percent sure that she wasn't going to sleep for probably the rest of her damn life, she couldn't even remember her head hitting the pillow.

20

There was a tap at the door to the conference room, and Lev looked up, startled out of his reverie.

"Come in," he said, and Tae pushed the door open.

Lev glanced at his com.

It had only been a few minutes since Jez had left.

"What's happening down there?" he asked.

Tae shook his head and dropped wearily into a chair. "They've made him comfortable, anyways. He probably won't last more than another day, but he's sleeping now, and he's not in pain."

Lev nodded. His muscles were tight, and he made a conscious effort to relax them.

He hadn't been able to make himself look at the child inside the bundle of rags Jez had been carrying. He probably should have, but he'd known, the moment he'd seen the look on Tanya's face, that the kid would die, and he wasn't sure he could handle it right now.

"How's Jez?" asked Tae after a moment.

Lev gave a small smile. "She'll be fine, I think. Give her time. It's —a lot."

"Yeah," said Tae quietly. He paused a moment, rubbing a hand over his face.

"What about you?" Lev asked softly. "You OK?"

Tae looked up and tried to smile, but there was a haunted look on his face that hadn't been there before. "I'm—yeah. I'm fine." He paused a moment, but Lev didn't say anything, just waited, and finally Tae looked down. "That could have happened here. Something like that, anyways. And it was my fault. I—I almost didn't get through Zhenya's blocker in time. I didn't expect it, and I should have." He gave a short, frustrated shake of his head. "I should have known. That's the second time Ivan's almost been killed, and it's been my fault both times. I thought I'd prepared for everything. I—"

Lev pulled his chair closer. "Tae," he said. "It wasn't you. None of us saw that coming. I should have assumed Grigory would have sent other people, and I should have foreseen that they might have asked for a server, instead of the people we'd set up as entertainers." He sighed. "There was a lot we should have done, but I didn't think of it, and we managed to pull it off, barely. Thanks to you and Jez and Radic."

"Ivan was armed," said Tae, his voice almost inaudible. "That whole time he was armed, I found out afterwards. He could have shot them dead, at any time. But—but he knew that would mean Caz and Peti and the others would die. So—so he didn't. He just stood there and let them—let them—" He swallowed hard, and trailed off.

Lev squeezed his shoulder. "I'm sorry," he said quietly, because he wasn't sure what else to say.

"I'm going to bed," said Tae shortly, getting to his feet. "See you in the morning."

Lev watched him leave, unease pricking up his spine.

Yes, they'd fooled Grigory once. Possibly twice, if they were lucky and Zhenya hadn't suspected. But—

But despite all their plans, Jez's quick thinking, and sheer blind luck, had been the only things that had saved them from disaster.

And the grim sight of the small, filthy bundle in the hangar bay—

Jez was right. There were some things that nothing could fix.

And they couldn't afford anything else going wrong.

It wasn't until Lev rolled over on his cot the next morning, groaning at the movement and blinking against a sun that was far too bright, that he saw the small, flashing notification.

It took him a moment to blink the sleep from his eyes enough to scan the message.

Then he froze.

Nephew, it said. *I've spoken to your friend, like you requested. I'm interested in speaking with you, too. It seems a shame for family to leave on the kind of terms you and I left on.*

He slapped his hand over the com, his mind racing.

What the hell could Vitali want with him?

To kill him, of course. And maybe that was all this was. But Vitali would know better than to try to bait him with something so obvious.

After a moment, he rolled out of bed and stumbled to the wash basin in the corner, the chill still lingering in his chest.

From the looks on the faces of the others as they gathered for breakfast, no one else had slept any better than he had. In fact, some of them looked like they hadn't slept at all. Galina's face had the drawn, greyish tinge of someone who hadn't seen a bed in at least twenty-four standard hours, and Tanya looked almost as exhausted.

"How's—" Jez began when she saw them, then bit off the question quickly, as if she'd just realized she might not want to know the answer.

Galina gave her a small, humourless smile. "He's—not going to make it to the end of the day. I'm sorry. But we were able to make him comfortable, at least. From the look of his leg, that was a bigger mercy than you think."

Jez managed a small smile, but it hurt him to look at it.

"That's—that's good. Thanks, Galya." She turned away, toying with her food, and Galina watched her with that tender, concerned look.

Lev forced himself to breathe out, something aching in his chest that wasn't pain, exactly, but hurt anyways. Someone who cared about Jez like that was what Jez deserved, honestly, and under the hurt, he was actually genuinely glad to see it.

His com gave a muted *ting*, and he glanced down.

He sucked in a quick breath.

"What is it?" asked Ysbel, leaning over. She wasn't sitting by the children, like she usually was, and her face was grave.

"I need to talk to you after this," he said in a low voice. "Alone, please."

She raised an eyebrow, but nodded. "I will ask Tanya to take the children after breakfast again, then."

Once everyone else had left the room, he met Ysbel's eye, and pulled up the notification on his com.

Nephew. We haven't spoken in a while. But I warn you, if you chose not to contact me, I will be very hurt. If you're interested in your friend and my continuing relationship, I would ask you to give me that basic courtesy.

Ysbel frowned. "What does he want?"

"I don't know." Lev sighed in frustration and shook his head. "Has he been in contact with you?"

The frown creased between Ysbel's eyebrows deepened. "Yes," she said slowly. "I haven't talked with you about it, because you asked to be left out of it. But he's been getting more demanding. He wants me to promise to hand over Masha. I told him it depends on what happens in the next few days, but—" She gave a small shrug. "I believe he's getting impatient. The more he thinks about getting Masha, I believe, the more he wants this, and he'll do whatever it takes to get to her."

Lev looked up, staring sightlessly at the wall.

Every muscle in his body was stiff.

He couldn't keep secrets from Jez, he'd promised himself that. He'd agreed with himself that that was one thing he wouldn't do. And Jez—well, she'd hate this. She'd agreed to it, because she'd been just as worried about the street kids as the rest of them were, but she'd made it very clear that she didn't want anything to do with it. And besides, after the way she'd looked this morning, he wasn't sure how she'd handle another blow right now.

But—

Well, but that was the thing. If anything, the last three days had convinced him they couldn't afford not to have a backup plan.

Ysbel was silent, waiting. She wasn't going to try to push him one way or the other, and he should probably be grateful for that, but instead he felt a small, shameful disappointment that he couldn't pin this decision on her.

Finally, he sighed. "Alright, Ysbel," he said quietly. "I'll talk to him, find out what he wants."

"And Jez?" asked Ysbel quietly, still watching him. Her gaze was unflinching, but he was too tired to try to hide anything anyways.

He managed a small smile. "I'll—I'll tell her. I'll talk to her and tell her."

Ysbel's eyebrows raised slightly, but she still didn't move, and finally he turned away, irritation giving an edge to his voice. "At least let's go somewhere we won't be walked in on in the middle of the conversation."

"You've changed, you know," said Ysbel at last, a hint of something in her tone.

He turned, frowning, and it took him a moment to realize what it was.

Respect.

For a moment, he wasn't sure what to do with her words.

"I haven't changed that much," he said, his voice a little rougher than he meant it to be. "I'm still the selfish bastard I was when you met me."

"No," she said quietly. "You're not. You say that, but the man I met in Masha's office however many months ago wouldn't have dreamed of giving up secrets, especially ones that might hurt him. I don't think there was anyone that man cared about enough to do that for."

He couldn't meet her gaze.

She, of all people, would know that.

"You know, Lev," she said, and the fondness in her tone made him look up despite himself. "I think you might end up as a good man after all, much as I've wondered at times."

Her words brought a comfortable warmth in his chest. He almost certainly didn't deserve it, but he found himself smiling at her anyways.

He followed Ysbel back to her room. She whispered something briefly to Tanya, who nodded and told the children that if they went to the kitchens, she'd get them something to eat, and the three of them slipped out.

Lev stared down at his com for a moment, trying to steady his heartbeat. The last time he had talked to his uncle, it ... hadn't been a good experience.

He tapped in a number, and waited a moment while the com buzzed.

"Lev." Vitali's tone was a mix of pleasure and lazy satisfaction, and the sound gave Lev an unpleasant jolt.

Funny how hearing the voice of the person who you last spoke to minutes before they tried to shoot you out of the sky did that to you.

"Tell me, how's my favourite nephew?"

"Vitali," said Lev, in the steadiest voice he could manage. "You asked to speak with me. I'm here. What do you want?"

"Ah, nephew. No small talk with your uncle?"

"Unfortunately, I don't believe you and I have a great many subjects to talk over that don't involve one of our deaths," said Lev.

Vitali, he'd realized the last time the man had been holding him hostage, was a man who was very easily amused, although not in the least easily deceived. Best to keep the conversation on topic.

"Lev. My boy. You know, I actually sent a message to your father after you and I parted ways."

Lev's stomach clenched, and he was biting down on his teeth so hard his jaw hurt.

He forced himself to relax. Betraying any emotion to Vitali would be a mistake.

"I hope you conveyed my regards," he said, keeping his tone pleasant. "And let him know the circumstances of your and my most recent falling-out."

"Ah, Lev." Vitali's voice was slightly harder now. "I would have, of course. But it turns out your family had moved, and he neglected to send me his forwarding address."

Lev let out a quick breath of relief, and for just a moment, silently thanked Masha. Whatever her personal failings, and whatever the lengths she was willing to go and the people she was willing to sacrifice to achieve her ends, she'd at least done what she'd promised when he'd joined the crew. More than she'd promised, honestly.

She'd gotten his family out of prison. And she'd hidden them somewhere that Vitali wouldn't be able to find them.

"I'm sorry to hear that," said Lev politely. "I'm sure he'd be disappointed to know he missed you."

"Enough," snapped Vitali. "You've always been too smart for your own good, haven't you? I try to avoid killing family, but for you, I'd make an exception. But right now, I'd just like to talk. And I'd like you to listen."

He paused a moment, and when Lev didn't interject, he continued. "Your friend offered to give me Masha if things went sideways, in exchange for my help in protecting certain people in Prasvishoni. Her offer intrigued me. Well, the entire situation intrigued me. I was always an admirer of her father, even if the feeling was one-sided." He paused again. "The question she didn't ask, though, is why I was here in the first place. You know, of course, what your little plot did to my relationship with several of my customers. I'm a businessperson first and foremost, and if one of my customers is willing to hire a team to rob me, well. Cutting off business with them is a matter of simple common sense. But business aside, Grigory Korzhakov and I have been personal friends for several years, since we were still young and trying to kill instead of be killed on the streets of Prasvishoni. And the last time we spoke, a few weeks ago, he told me he'd met you."

Lev and Ysbel exchanged a quick glance. Ysbel's expression was grim.

Grigory had mentioned that conversation to Lev, but that did nothing to assuage his unease.

Vitali chuckled. "You will never cease to impress me, Lev, but I am no longer surprised by anything you do. And so when I heard about the misfortunes Grigory had suffered, I knew who had to have been responsible. And when I thought about the potential fallout of your actions—" Lev could hear the slight smile in his voice. "You aren't the only one in the family who can make educated guesses, boy. Grigory would hunt you until he killed you. You had two options, and two options only—run and hope you'd escape, or turn and try to take him down. And you, nephew. You were always going to try to take him down. What better place to do that than the one planet that holds most of his investments, and brings in most of his income?"

"You were waiting for us, then," said Lev quietly.

There was something cold in his chest.

Another complication he hadn't anticipated.

"Of course. I was hoping I'd get a chance to pay you a visit, in return for the delightful visit you paid me." He paused again, and when he next spoke, his voice had dropped any pretence of amusement or good humour. It was the man Lev had always known existed under that cultured exterior, the man his father had so feared and loathed that he was willing to let his children go hungry rather than go to him for help.

"Since the day you left my compound, I swore I would hunt you down. I wanted to watch you suffer. I wanted you to watch your friends suffer. I thought there was nothing in the world I'd enjoy more. But then I spoke with Ysbel, and I realized there was one thing, one thing in the system, that would be more satisfying than what I had planned. And that was, letting you betray Masha to me." His cold tone took on the mockery of concern. "You wouldn't have thought up a plan like what you did to me on your own. You're smart enough to have, but you've always been a good boy. I knew that came from Masha. And when I talked to Grigory, he confirmed my suspicions. As I said, I don't like to kill family if I can help it. So I talked to your friend."

"Alright," said Lev, his voice steady, even though his hands were trembling slightly. "You spoke with her. Why do you need to talk to me?"

"You're very smart, Lev. I think you've already figured it out."

Lev closed his eyes for a moment.

He had, by the time Vitali had made it through the first two sentences. He'd had his suspicions even before he'd called.

"Perhaps," he said levelly. "But why don't you confirm it for me?"

Vitali chuckled, a low, amused sound. "If you insist. I called you to explain to you the stakes. You seem to think that you can tease me with an offer of Masha, and I'll sit waiting like a well-trained dog. But you see, I wasn't waiting for someone to find a way to hand me my prize. I was looking for a way to kill you. So I propose a deal." He paused a moment. "You will turn over Masha, and when I come to get her, I will make sure she knows who turned her in. You do that, and I will stop hunting the rest of your friends. Or, you don't accept my offer. And I will kill them slowly, and I will make you watch. As much as I hate to kill family, I hate it even more when family disappoints me."

Lev glanced up at Ysbel again.

Her face was pale, and as grim as he currently felt.

"I'm not looking for an answer right now," said Vitali. His tone had regained its old good-humoured amusement. "I wouldn't believe anything you told me anyways. You give me Masha, and I'll leave. Or, you don't, and—" he let the unspoken threat hang in the air.

Lev closed his eyes for a moment, glad that at least this time he didn't have to plaster a calm, amused look on his face.

First Evka, now this.

Apparently, everyone in his damn past was going to track him down and threaten to kill everyone he loved, because why the hell not?

"So," said Vitali at last. "I'll leave you to think on it. Don't feel bad. Your friend wanting to talk to me was a stroke of luck for you, really. I'd begun hearing rumours of your whereabouts, and I was only thinking of the best way to get to you. At the least, her offer put my plans on hold. So you've been remarkably lucky." Vitali chuckled again, and the sound sent ice through Lev's veins. "It was a pleasure to speak with you again, Lev. Please, consider my offer."

The com clicked off.

Lev let out a breath, and Ysbel did the same.

"Well," he said at last.

"Can he do it?" asked Ysbel brusquely.

He gave a small shrug. "It's possible he's lying. But I doubt it. He has the resources and the people to do almost anything he wants. He's on good terms with Olyessa. He could almost certainly buy her off, if he offered enough. We know she needs credits, and she depends on her relationship with him."

"So. It's Masha or the rest of us, as you said," said Ysbel. "Only not exactly in the way we'd supposed."

"You're—taking this very calmly," said Lev.

Ysbel watched him for a moment, face deadly serious. "Here is something I learned the hard way," she said at last. "You trust someone, if they earn your trust. You trust them with your life. Like I did with Masha. But if they betray you, you can't afford to forget that. They've shown you what they're capable of."

"You'd give Masha up, even if she played this job straight." He wasn't sure why the thought disturbed him. He'd been the one to push for a backup plan, after all, a way to protect themselves from her.

Maybe it was the look on Jez's face, the stubborn trust when she talked about the woman who'd lied to them and betrayed them weeks previous, listened impassively to the plans they'd willingly shared with her and then actively worked to subvert them.

But at this point, he wasn't certain what the alternative would be.

He sighed. "I'll—talk to Jez, explain the situation to her, and we'll see what we can do. Maybe she'll have an idea that I don't."

"And if you don't find a solution?" Ysbel asked.

"If we don't find a solution—" he paused a moment.

They'd worked together as a crew for months at this point, although it felt like years. It felt like he'd known these people his entire life. He felt like he'd worked with Masha for as long as he could remember, the constant, unspoken battle of wits, the tension between suspicion and trust, affection and antagonism.

But he'd let that lure him into complacency before, and it had almost led to their deaths.

Ysbel was right. He couldn't afford to underestimate Masha again.

"If we don't find a solution," he said slowly, "I suppose—we give Vitali what he wants."

21

"Tae? Are you in there?"

Tae jerked his head up, then pushed the heels of his hands against his eyes. There was a headache building behind his forehead from staring at the screen, but honestly, there wasn't much he could do about it at this point.

"I'm here," he called, and the door opened, revealing Lev standing in the hallway.

"Can I come in?"

Tae gestured with his hand to the empty room. "Not much happening."

Lev came in and sat down, and Tae looked him over surreptitiously. There was strain under his expression, and a tension in his posture that hadn't been there a few days ago.

Still, Tae was one to talk. He wasn't sure he'd been able to relax for one second since their near-disaster with Ivan.

"How's it coming?" asked Lev, pulling up a chair and peering at the holoscreen Tae had been pouring over.

"I don't know," said Tae. There was an unease stirring in his stomach, and he couldn't seem to get rid of it. "I've done everything I can, anyways. The account needs constant maintenance if I want it to mimic the security measures at the Svodrani Bank, and I can't stop until the funds come through."

"If it makes you feel any better, it looks like Grigory's found his credits. The bank is sending through the funds he's leveraged off his pleasure houses, from the look of it, so it should only be a day or so longer."

Tae nodded, trying to smile.

It was good news, but that still left a day or two of the constant tension-headache, wondering if he'd make a mistake, since any mistake, no matter how small, would be enough to doom him, or kill his friends.

Wondering if he'd done enough.

Knowing that no matter how much he did, it might not be enough.

"No word from Zhenya?" Lev asked.

Tae shook his head. "I haven't heard anything. I don't know if that's good or bad."

Lev raised his eyebrows wryly. "At this point, if it's not actually about to kill us, I'm going to go with good. I could use some good news, honestly." He leaned back in his chair, and for a moment, the strain and exhaustion in his posture was clearly visible.

"Jez?" asked Tae.

Lev gave him a small smile. "You know Jez. She says she's fine, and she looks like she's about to go completely mad. Galina's been talking to her, and I think it's helping. She took that kid's death pretty hard."

"I know," said Tae softly. He sighed. "Anyways, I'd best get back to —"

"Tae!"

He swore under his breath and hit his com. "What is it?"

"This is Artur. We've sent a group of people through the gates on schedule, but I'm getting feedback from one of the coms. I think the blocker's not working."

Tae swore again, and sighed heavily. "Sorry, Lev, I've got to go."

"This happen often?" asked Lev, eyebrows raised.

"About five damn times a day. If I'm lucky," Tae grumbled. He shoved back his chair and tapped the screen off on his com. "There's something about going through the city force-field that screws with the blockers, and if I had one damn hour to myself, I could fix it. But I don't, so instead I spend two hours every damn day trying to keep us from being spotted."

"I'm sorry," said Lev, his tone sympathetic, and Tae gave him a rueful glance as he headed out the door.

"Send me the coordinates," he muttered into his com as he took the stairs two at a time. "I'm on my way."

"Tae?"

He looked up quickly, and barely avoided running straight into Ivan.

"Where are you going?"

Tae gestured helplessly to his com. "More issues with the blockers on their coms. Hopefully it won't take long."

Ivan smiled at him, and something in Tae's chest unknotted slightly at the smile.

Yes, there was still a trace of that haunted look behind Ivan's expression, but his smile was genuine, and the familiar smile-creases at the corners of his eyes transformed his face, like they always did.

"Let me come. I just finished dish duty, and I wasn't going anywhere."

Tae found somehow that his face had relaxed into a smile as well, despite everything. "Sure. If you want to."

Ivan's smile deepened. "I did volunteer."

It wasn't a long walk from their building to the force-field entrance, which was the whole point of setting up where they had. Still, even walking quickly it usually took at least fifteen minutes, and Tae usually resented every lost second.

With Ivan walking beside him, though, it seemed much shorter.

The day was warm, as usual, and they pulled their scarves over their heads to shield them from the beating heat of the sun.

"Lev said probably just a couple more days before the money comes through," said Tae quietly as they walked.

Ivan smiled. "That's good to hear. I wouldn't mind seeing you actually get some sleep now and again. Some of us do it on a regular basis, you know."

Tae chuckled despite himself, and Ivan grinned.

"I guess that's the price you pay for being a genius. If you were average like me, you'd get a good night's sleep much more often, I imagine."

"You're not—" Tae broke off the sentence before he could finish it. He wasn't completely sure what he had been going to say, except to point out that someone who was willing to let himself be carved up with knives to keep a bunch of kids he'd never met safe was about the farthest thing from average Tae could imagine. And Ivan would just shake his head fondly and say something self-deprecating, like he'd done a million times already.

Ivan laughed softly. "I'm glad someone thinks so, anyways." He glanced up, then frowned suddenly.

"What—" Tae began, then Ivan grabbed him and shoved him bodily sideways into an alley. He stumbled, barely catching himself against the wall, and Ivan fell hard on the cobblestones next to him as the air at the entrance to the alley wavered from a searing burst of heat.

Tae scrambled to his feet and grabbed Ivan's hand, hauling him up. "Come on, this way," he said through his teeth, and they took off running.

Another heat-blast followed them down the alley, scorching the wall beside them, then they were out onto another street.

"Who was that?" Tae asked through gritted teeth.

Ivan shook his head. "I don't know. But my money's on Grigory's people."

Tae swore. "I thought Jez's gangster friends were keeping the streets clean."

Two more damn days before they should be able to just walk out of this, but no. He was out in the damn street getting shot at.

"I thought so too," said Ivan grimly. "Maybe the Blood Riots finally took the street."

"This way," Tae said, ducking into an alley, and Ivan followed close behind. They ducked down two more alleys, and then back onto the main street, and finally, he slowed.

"Did we lose them?" asked Ivan. He was breathing heavily.

Tae looked around quickly, his stomach tight.

Damn it, he didn't know, he had no damn idea, and he had to damn well figure it out, find a way to keep someone he cared about from being hurt, again—

Ivan stiffened. "Ahead," he said, his voice low and urgent. "Look down, and keep walking." He reached over and pulled Tae's scarf further down over his face, then adjusted his own.

Tae's heart, which was already pounding from their mad sprint, beat painfully fast. "Ivan," he muttered, panic choking the words in his throat. "I don't know—"

"Just follow my lead," said Ivan quietly. "I'll deal with it."

Tae closed his eyes for a moment, almost dizzy with panic.

"Tae." Ivan's voice was warm with concern. "Trust me, alright?"

He looked up, finally, into Ivan's dark eyes.

And finally, because he didn't know what else to do, Tae sucked in a breath and nodded, and Ivan stepped in front of him.

For a moment panic welled in Tae's chest again, because he'd almost let Ivan die twice in the past couple weeks, and he wasn't sure he could handle a third time, and then someone said gruffly, "Who are you? What are you doing here?"

"Getting out for some fresh air," said Ivan, his voice friendly and confident, and nothing like as shaky as Tae currently felt. "Had a fight with my boyfriend." From the edge of his vision, which he'd fixed firmly on the street, Tae saw Ivan gesture casually towards him. "Going for a walk, see if we can talk it out." His voice was slightly amused, and gave no hint whatsoever that he knew that the people in front of them would shoot him without thinking twice if they had any idea who he was.

There was a coarse snort of laughter. "Might be a long walk. He doesn't look very happy with you."

"Well, you know what they say. Blisters hurt less than broken hearts."

The boyeviki chuckled and stepped aside, and Ivan started forwards again, putting his arm casually around Tae's waist and pulling him close. And the motion was so natural that Tae found himself leaning into the warmth of Ivan's shoulder, and he had to stop himself with an effort.

At last, they reached the force-field entrance and slipped through, and Tae breathed a long sigh of relief. Ivan dropped his arm, and Tae looked up involuntarily. Ivan was watching him, that small smile on his face, and for a moment Tae's heart stuttered.

"That was a little more exciting than I'd imagined it would be," said Ivan, his voice amused. "Come on. Let's get the coms fixed for those ex-cons of ours." He frowned and shook his head. "And we'll have to let them know that the streets aren't as safe as we thought. I'll call Galina, get her to send someone to scout out a route our people can get in safely. I think we're going to have to nix putting on a show of customers for today."

He smiled at Tae and turned, but there was something about the thoughtless courage of his ridiculous gesture that made Tae look after him for a long moment before he could clear his head enough to follow.

22

Lev glanced down at his com for probably the twentieth time in the last hour, then leaned back against the hallway wall.

"Anything?" Ysbel asked quietly, stepping out into the doorway.

Lev shook his head. "Nothing yet."

The credits should have come through already. They'd received the notification showing the funds leaving Grigory's account. But even accounting for the time delay for the actual transfer, the credits should have appeared in their account already.

"Should we be worried?" asked Ysbel, lowering her voice further and glancing back into the conference room, where Tae was scowling down at his holoscreen.

"I—don't know."

The truth was, Lev was already worried.

If Grigory suspected something, Tae's friends were probably already dead. He glanced through the open door at Tae as well, then looked away quickly to avoid catching his eye.

"Grigory's people ambushed Tae and Ivan yesterday," he said quietly. "You heard?"

Ysbel nodded, and Lev bit his lip.

Why now? Why when things were so close? What was Grigory

playing at? And why hadn't the Rims warned them?

The rest of the crew had wandered into the conference room one by one over the last hour, waiting for news. He'd be the one to give it, assuming it came. Ivan and Radic had volunteered to keep things running downstairs, and Galina had stumbled to bed less than an hour ago. She was running this thing practically single handedly, handling the logistics of everything from the people to the kitchen schedules.

"Masha!"

Lev frowned. The voice came from the lobby.

There shouldn't be anyone in the lobby, except for Olyessa's guards.

"Masha?"

Masha came to the door, glancing around. She tapped her com to the guards' line. "I'm here. Did you need something?"

"Someone to see you downstairs," the guard replied, still calling up the stairs.

Lev frowned at the tone in his voice. It was off, somehow, but he couldn't put his finger on why.

"I'll be there in a moment," said Masha, after a pause.

Lev glanced down at his holoscreen again.

Still nothing.

He bit the inside of his cheek, and refrained from looking back at Tae.

Masha closed the door to the conference room carefully behind her, and walked briskly to the stairs. Watching her, he could see the faint tension in her posture, but honestly, he hadn't spent enough time around her in the past weeks to know whether this was new or if it had been there for a while.

Stupid. He should have been watching her more closely.

But somehow, since his conversation with Vitali, he hadn't been able to bring himself to, even in the few brief meeting he'd had with her since then.

In the back of his mind he heard her footsteps echoing off the high ceiling of the lobby as he turned back to his com.

He sucked in a quick breath, feeling suddenly dizzy with relief.

"What—" Ysbel began.

"Something's happening," he said in a low voice. "The funds coming through, I think."

Ysbel let out a short breath. "It's about time for something to go right," she grunted, the strain of the last few days clear in her voice. Lev closed his eyes for a moment, letting his own shoulders slump in relief. He hadn't realized how tense he'd been.

"Lev."

He opened his eyes, frowning. It was Masha's voice, coming through his com. He turned towards where she'd disappeared down the stairs.

"I'm afraid I'm going to need you down here, Lev. The others too, please. Quickly."

There was a strained urgency to her tone. Lev and Ysbel looked at each other, and Ysbel's face was pinched with sudden worry.

Lev gritted his teeth and shut down his holoscreen. "Masha wants all of us downstairs," he said over his shoulder into the conference room.

"Why?" asked Tae quickly.

Lev shook his head. "I don't know. But she said to hurry."

They stood, casting worried glances at each other, and started down the stairwell.

It wasn't until he was half-way down that Lev noticed Olyessa's guards were not where they normally were, standing in front of the entrance.

Instead, the six guards were gathered around a small group in one corner of the lobby. He couldn't make out the figures who were seated on the chairs, but he recognized the back of Masha's unmistakable pilot's coat.

He frowned, something niggling at the back of his mind. Something about the guards …

And then Tanya hissed in a breath, and he glanced up, and realized what had been bothering him.

They were dressed the same as Olyessa's guards had been. But these weren't Olyessa's guards.

And three more of them were on the landing, not too far from where he'd been standing, half-concealed behind the curve of the hallway. Their laser guns were in their hands, held loose, but they looked like they were ready to use them.

And Olyessa's guards, the six who'd been on duty this morning—

When he first caught sight of them, draped over the balcony ahead of him, he wondered, for a brief, disconnected moment, if perhaps they were drunk, or playing some sort of prank. And then his mind made sense of the limp droop of their bodies, the faint scent of burnt flesh, the slow, monotonous *drip* … *drip* … of blood, spattering and pooling on the polished stone floor two stories below, the sound so regular and so quiet that his brain had filtered it out.

He'd seen death, more times than he cared to think about. But still, he had to look away quickly, bile rising in his throat.

The guards behind them had come closer, following them at a safe distance as they walked down the stairs.

Masha. She'd finally done it, she'd finally betrayed them all that one final time—

But it didn't make sense. Not when they hadn't got what they were looking for yet. What could she possibly gain by selling them out now?

He'd heard the strain in her voice when she called them. It could have been guilt, but more likely this was as much of a surprise to her as it was to him.

They'd reached the bottom of the stairway by now, huddled together instinctively. Jez's pistol was in her hand, and Ysbel had something half-hidden in her palm that was almost certainly capable of transforming this entire place and everything inside it to rubble. But Olya was beside her, walking so close that Ysbel almost tripped over her at every step, and Misko was clinging to her trouser leg, and both their faces were pale and terrified, their eyes fixed on the bodies hanging over the balcony.

Ysbel wouldn't use her explosive, and Jez wouldn't start anything, not unless there was no other option.

They crossed the floor to where Masha was sitting. As they got closer, he could see her wrists were cuffed behind her back, but she turned and gave them a wan, strained smile over her shoulder.

"Lev. I apologize for not explaining what had happened more fully. However, I was informed that if anyone tried to put up a fight, there would be shooting, and I was confident that was an outcome that none of us wanted, considering—" Her eyes flicked briefly to the children.

Lev gave her a tight nod. "I understand," he said. Then he looked up across the circle of chairs that had been set up.

Somehow, he already knew what he'd see.

"Lev," said Grigory. There was a vicious, triumphant smile on his face, the same smile that Lev had seen once before, right before Grigory gave instructions for his boyeviki to torture a man to death in front of them.

"Hello Grigory," Lev said quietly, pulling up a chair. His legs were trembling slightly, and he was glad for the chance to sit down before it became apparent. There was a cold knot in his chest, and a dread weakening his joints.

"I'm glad you came without an argument," Grigory said, still smiling.

"What do you want?" asked Ysbel, her voice emotionless. "Why are you here?"

"Have a seat, all of you," said Grigory, gesturing expansively with one arm. "We can talk better if we're all relaxed."

"I'm sure you're smart enough to have guessed," said Ysbel, making no move to comply. "I'm holding the control down on the explosive in my hand right now, but the moment my finger loosens on the control, everyone dies. You included. Give me one reason why I don't take my finger off it right now."

"I'll give you two," said Grigory. He gestured to the children clinging to Ysbel's legs.

"You're going to kill them anyways." Ysbel's voice was flat and dangerous.

Grigory chuckled. "No. That isn't my plan currently. Why don't you sit, and you can keep your hand on your explosive, and we can talk this over."

Ysbel and Tanya exchanged glances, and then, slowly, they sat. The rest of the crew followed suit.

Grigory leaned back in his chair, watching them. "I'm impressed with what you did in such a short time," he said. "You almost had me fooled with your little con. I'd put in money, because I'd think I could call in all the debts, ruin you, turn Olyessa against you because you couldn't pull off what you promised you would. But you forget. I've been following your careers, ever since you came out of nowhere and destroyed my alliance with the government. Perhaps I underestimated you on the casino ship, but not a second time."

"What do you want?" asked Lev quietly.

Grigory smiled again. "I want, Lev, to convince you that there is no point in resisting. I want to explain to you how thoroughly you've lost."

"Not sure why you think we care, you bastard," drawled Jez. She was leaning back in her chair, posture mirroring Grigory's, but every muscle in her wiry body was tense, and she was holding the heat-pistol loosely on her lap. "Figure if we're all going to die, doesn't really matter, and I'll be honest, I'm getting pretty bored right now."

Grigory raised an eyebrow, but Lev saw the brief flash of annoyance that crossed his features. "That assumes I'm going to kill you."

Jez snorted. "What, found religion? Decided that the Lady doesn't like it when you murder a bunch of people? Was that before or after you killed those six guards up there?"

Grigory's eyes narrowed slightly. "I'm not stupid, Jez," he snapped. "I knew there was no way Ysbel wouldn't have a way to kill us all if I took you."

"You need to kill us," said Lev softly. "You explained that to me."

"You're right," said Grigory, the harshness grating in his voice. "But Ysbel would always pose a problem. And—" he gave a slight, brutal smile. "I'm not quite ready to take on Olyessa at the moment. And so I think I found a solution." He leaned back. "I've taken you at your own con. I've ruined you. Lev, look at your com, if you would."

Cautiously, Lev pulled up the holoscreen.

The bank account details were displayed on it, in full view of everyone. And—

He sucked in a quick breath and closed his eyes for a moment.

And it was empty. Every last credit, gone.

"Your tech boy did an excellent job of setting that up," said Grigory. "If I hadn't been suspicious, I'd never have told the difference between that and the real thing. You wanted me to put in my money, leverage my properties. That's why you put the limit on the account so high. And once you had my money, you'd simply close down the false account and disappear, and I'd be a broken man. But this isn't the first time someone's tried to pull a con on me."

His cruel smile had returned. "Would you like to know what happened to the account, Lev? I've already explained it to Masha. The transfer was bugged. As soon as my credits went into the account, it triggered a sequence that emptied every last credit out of your fake account and into a real account of my own. Everything you put into that account, along with everything Olyessa put in. I was watching the numbers just before you came down. I'm afraid she's not going to be very happy about how this turned out." He paused a moment, enjoying the looks on their faces. "Especially with her money gone, and her guards dead, and the eight of you disappeared."

Something like ice was forming in Lev's chest.

"You think she doesn't have tracking on us?" asked Masha calmly. "She'll be able to tell the instant we die."

Grigory smiled. "Oh, you're not going to die, not yet. You'll head off-planet. I'll order one of my pilots to take you somewhere in the outer rim, and you can do whatever you'd like after that. Until Olyessa catches up with you, I assume. Jez here can get a job as a pilot, if she'd like. Maybe one day she'll earn enough to buy her own ship again. Lev could be a university professor. There are plenty of outer-rim planets with small universities who would love someone of his calibre. The rest of you can live out your lives however you'd like. Maybe you'll even stay alive for a while. And what do you have to lose? You really think you could have changed anything in the long run?" he leaned forward. "So yes. I'm letting you go. But believe me, I haven't forgiven you. What I did will come out eventually, of course, but after a few months it won't be worth the risk for Olyessa to try to get revenge on me, instead of you, and that's worth enough for me to let you live. But you try to get involved again, in anything at all, it will be worth my while to hunt you down. Besides—" he smiled. "I think Tae here has some friends he'd hate to see hurt. I won't touch a hair on their heads, as long as you don't give me cause."

Lev just watched him. He wasn't afraid. He didn't even feel the despair he probably should be feeling. He just felt—numb.

Grigory put his hands on his knees and pushed himself to his feet. "I'd stay, but I'm a busy man. You've given me a very large gift, with all of Olyessa's savings, and I don't want to waste it."

He turned, and five bodyguards detached themselves from the wall and followed him out the door.

The other guards—the ones dressed to look like Olyessa's—stood back a little, postures relaxed, guns levelled.

Finally, Lev allowed himself to look at Masha.

Her face was drawn with strain, her jaw clenched. With an effort, she raised her head and met his eyes.

"It wasn't you this time, was it?" he said quietly.

She gave him a quick, tight smile. "I was hoping I wouldn't have to try to convince you of that. Grigory told me that I could convince you to come, or he'd take his chances with a shootout. And despite my faith in your respective abilities, I didn't have confidence that you would emerge wholly unscathed."

Lev nodded.

His brain was still trying to figure out logically how to deal with the situation without any input whatsoever from his emotions. Still, perhaps at this juncture that was for the best. Because if for one moment he let himself think about what this meant, let himself feel anything at all, the despair might crush him.

Ysbel looked around at the others.

Jez's eyes were closed, her posture slumped, expression haunted.

There were other things to worry about, too many to count, but for some reason, the sight of the blank hopelessness on the pilot's face hurt her.

Olya was clinging to her leg, and she put an arm around the girl's shoulders and pulled her close. Olya was very pale, and her lip trembled slightly, her small body shivering under Ysbel's arm. Ysbel managed to give her a small smile, even though she knew Olya was far too intelligent to be fooled by something like that.

"Well," she said at last, turning to Tanya. "I suppose it could have been a lot worse. We're all alive."

Tanya's shoulders were tensed, and Ysbel could see the strain in her face. "Alive? Perhaps. But—" she gestured helplessly around them. "The rest of them here? They're marked now. Olyessa will kill them."

One of the guards stepped closer, gesturing with his gun. "Go on. Grigory's ship is just outside the city forcefield. You have twenty standard minutes. If you want to bring anything with you, best start packing."

Masha got to her feet at last, her face bearing the same bland expression she'd worn almost since Ysbel had met her. "Well," she said quietly, "I suppose we'd best get going. Twenty standard minutes isn't long."

The guards moved forward, guns still at the ready. "We'll escort you back to the rooms," said one of them. "One at a time." He gestured at Masha with a jerk of his head. She hesitated, glancing back at them, then nodded and walked briskly to the staircase, two guards following. The other guards stayed where they were, guns trained on their little group.

Jez stood suddenly, quickly enough that she almost overturned her chair. The guards stepped closer at the movement, but Jez wasn't holding her heat gun. There were tears in her eyes, and something desperate and hopeless in her voice.

"Damn it to hell, we can't just leave. We can't just—there are people on this damn planet who are getting hurt, and we were going to—we were—" She stopped, choking on the words, and dropped her head to her chest, squeezing her eyes tightly shut.

Ysbel watched her, something tightening her chest.

"Jez." Lev's voice was gentle. He hesitated, then stood and rested a hand on her arm.

She spun on him. "I know, shut up, Jez, right? We can't bloody change anything anyways, so why the hell even try? We're just trying to keep our damn selves alive. Yeah, so we did it. Good for us. But you know what? I don't care about that right now!"

"No, Jez," said Lev quietly. "That's not what I was going to say. I was only going to say, I'm sorry. I'm sorry this is how things ended up. I'm sorry I didn't see this coming."

She swallowed hard and brushed her arm across her face. Her whole posture was slumped in defeat.

Ysbel turned away, unable for the moment to look at her.

It was like she'd told Tanya. This wasn't so bad. They were alive, after all.

She wasn't sure why she felt sick, instead of relieved.

"Aunty Jez?"

Ysbel frowned and glanced down.

Olya's face was fixed in determination, her eyes hard. "Aunty Jez, it's going to be alright," she said fiercely.

Jez turned, and tried to smile. "Yeah, Olya?"

"Yes," said Olya firmly. "Because my mama told me we were going to stop this stuff from happening. She promised. So—" she shrugged.

For a moment, there was silence.

Something clutched at Ysbel's chest.

"Olya," she said gently, although the words caught in her throat. "I'm sorry. Sometimes—well, sometimes your mama has to decide between keeping you safe, or helping other people. And you're very special to me, Olyeshka, you and Misko."

Olya looked up at her, face stubborn, and there was a glint of tears in her eyes. "Mama. But remember how you said you trust me? Remember how you said I was smart, and brave? You don't have to worry about me, mama. I—I want you to stop the bad things happening here."

"Olya—" she began.

"You will. Right, mama? You—you promised."

"I—" she looked up helplessly, unable to meet her daughter's gaze.

Tanya was watching her.

For a few moments, they just looked at each other.

"I love you, Ysi," said Tanya at last, quietly.

"And you believe we should do this," said Ysbel. Her voice was choked, somehow. "Even though right now, if we don't do anything, we get out alive."

"I do," said Tanya, even more softly.

Ysbel closed her eyes and breathed in deeply. Then she turned back to Olya, who was still watching her.

"My love," she said, trying to smile. "My Olyeshka. I can't promise I can fix this. But—I will try. Alright?"

The glow on Olya's face was sudden and brilliant, like the sun coming out from behind clouds.

23

Jez was almost vibrating with tension as the guards gestured them to their feet, slapped mag cuffs around their wrists, and herded them out the back way towards Grigory's ship.

They'd relieved her of her heat pistol when they'd cuffed her—at least the one she'd had in her hand. They hadn't found the one she'd shoved into the small holster in her boot, or the gutting knife slipped in the sheath on the inside of her thigh. Galya had shown her that trick—most guards wouldn't pat you down too thoroughly there, which gave you another chance to stab them in the gut.

Yet another reason she liked Galina.

"Go on," the guard growled, and she realized she'd slowed, and that there was a small grin starting on her face.

She was still swallowing back tears, honestly. But something was spreading through her body, something like the feeling she'd had in the alley back in the slums, when she'd picked a fight with about four people and all their damn bodyguards.

Maybe she couldn't fix all this crap, but she'd be damned if she gave up without a fight.

The ship was waiting for them outside the forcefield. The guards hustled them up the loading ramp and into the ship, and then closed the ramp behind them. Three more guards waited on board, and they shoved the *Ungovernable* crew into their seats. Jez ended up between Tae and Tanya. Tae glared at her as she shifted in her seat and managed to jab him in the ribs with her elbow, but honestly, he couldn't exactly blame her. Not like she'd asked to be cuffed and stuck between him and Tanya.

"Would you stop?" he muttered as she shifted again, trying to get comfortable.

She rolled her eyes at him.

Are you ready?

It was basically impossible to tell who was tapping out the message in her earpiece, but she turned and shot Masha a quick grin.

Remember, someone, probably Lev, tapped. *No one makes a move until we're out of atmosphere. Tae, you can reactivate the blockers on the coms even with your hands cuffed, right?*

Tae looked up briefly and gave a quick nod, but his face was tight with worry.

Don't worry, tech-head, she tapped, because honestly, it was easier than trying to lean over to whisper to him. *Figure we'll be fast enough that your buddy Zhenya won't even know we're coming.*

Zhenya is not my damn friend. She could almost hear the annoyance through his quick taps, and she grinned despite herself.

The guards watched them coldly, guns loose in their hands.

She could feel when the ship started up, the faint humming in her bones, the slight jerk as they lifted off. She shook her head. Bit of a crap pilot, if you could feel liftoff. It was supposed to be so smooth that the only reason you knew you were in the air was the sudden drop of your stomach.

She glanced across the small deck at Ysbel. The woman nodded, and Jez's grin widened.

Tae, are you ready?

Tae nodded.

Alright. On my count.

From the corner of her eye, she caught a glimpse of the concentration on Lev's face.

Honestly, he'd come a long way from the soft scholar boy who hated being shot at.

Three he tapped out.

Two.

One.

Jez exploded out of her seat. The guards jerked to attention, swinging their guns towards her, but Ysbel was already up, and kicked the legs out from the guard closest to Jez. The guard went down, and Jez took three running steps forward, bowling into another guard and sending the heat-gun blast into the ceiling and the two of them to the floor in a swearing, struggling heap. Jez ducked, managing to turn aside enough that the blow the guard aimed at her jaw struck her cheekbone, but it wasn't a huge improvement, to be honest. She rolled out of the way of another blow, but the guard grabbed her cuffed arms and jerked her back around.

Jez looked around quickly.

Ysbel had subdued the guard she'd knocked the legs from under by the simple expedient of a sharp kick to the temple, but the other guard was still standing, and was bringing her weapon to bear on Jez.

Jez twisted, trying to pull herself free of the guard's grasp. He tightened his grip, swearing, and his knee slammed into her back. She grunted as the pain knifed down her spine, her legs going weak and tears blurring her vision.

Damn it to hell.

The guard in front of her smiled, and through tears of pain Jez could make out the dark, menacing shape of a heat-pistol muzzle pointed at her face.

And then the woman's expression changed to one of faint surprise, and she collapsed gently to the ground.

Masha stood behind her, half-turned, a shock-stick in her cuffed hands.

Jez stared for a moment.

Hell of a shock stick to take someone down like that.

Still, if Ysbel could mod heat guns—

OK, she really needed to ask Ysbel to make her one of those.

Another jolt of pain shot through her side, and she yelped involuntarily.

Probably should focus on the fact that she was about to be killed by the maniac guard who'd gotten a hold of her arms, actually.

She braced her feet on the deck and kicked off, knocking him backwards. There was a satisfying *crack* as his head hit the deck, and then she slammed her own head backwards into the bridge of his nose. He gave a gargled shout of pain, then Tanya's boot connected with the side of his head, and he went limp.

Jez rolled painfully over, panting heavily. Every part of her hurt, and yes, hitting him in the face with the back of her head had been effective, but she was going to have a hell of a headache to show for it.

"You alright, Jez?" Lev asked in a strained voice.

"Define 'alright,'" she grumbled, wincing as she rolled painfully onto her side.

Tanya had shoved the man over with her foot and had her boot on the back of his neck. When he stirred, she pressed down a little harder, and he subsided. The other two guards were in similar postures.

"Tae," said Tanya. "If you have the blockers set, would you trade me off, please? I'm going to go look for something to tie them up with."

"If I didn't have the blockers set, we'd damn well be in the process of getting shot out of the sky," Tae grumbled, but he came over and did as Tanya asked.

By the time Jez had managed to get to her feet, gritting her teeth against the sharp jolts of pain shooting down her spine at every movement, Tanya had retrieved the knife from her boot and cut strips off one of the guards' coats. It was honestly pretty impressive, considering her hands were still cuffed.

"Did any of them get word off to the pilot?" asked Lev, glancing over at Tae.

"I don't think so," said Tae. "The blocker should have stopped internal lines as well as external, but I can check. Let me see your com, since I can't get to mine."

Jez snickered as Lev and Tae maneuvered themselves into a position where Tae could pull up the holoscreen on Lev's com.

Tae looked up long enough to glare at her.

"Careful there," she said. "Ivan might get jealous."

"Jez—" he said through gritted teeth.

Despite the tension, Ysbel was clearly trying to hide an amused smirk.

"No," said Tae after a moment. "Looks like they didn't get a call out."

Lev breathed a sigh of relief. "Good. Then I guess our next step is to hijack the ship."

"Don't suppose you thought about how to get us out of these?"

asked Jez, lifting her cuffed hands.

Lev's expression was grim. "I was counting on us using the maintenance tools. But unfortunately, it appears they're stowed in the cockpit."

Jez grinned. "Not like this is the first time I've escaped with my hands cuffed behind my back."

"Jez, what are you—" Lev started, but she'd already turned towards the cockpit.

"Masha? You coming?" she said over her shoulder.

Masha was watching her with a bemused expression, but gave a small smile, tightened her grip on the shock stick, and came after her.

Jez had to turn and crouch painfully to hit the door switch, and when the doors opened with a hiss, the pilot and copilot had already half-turned towards them.

Looks of blank surprise crossed their faces.

"You know," said Jez chattily to the pilot. "You spent a little more time learning your controls, wouldn't have nearly as much of a problem with lift-off."

There was a brief moment of dawning realization in the woman's eyes, then Jez bent and kicked out as hard as she could. The heel of her boot hit the back of the pilot's shoulder, and she slammed forward into the controls. The copilot halfway rose from his seat, then slumped as Masha's shock stick connected with his thigh. The pilot struggled upright, blood streaming down her face, as Masha turned, shock-stick between her clasped hands.

Lev appeared in the cockpit door just in time to see the pilot slump, unconscious, beside her companion.

He drew in a long breath, blew it out again, and shook his head. Then, at last, a slight, rueful smile formed on his face. "Well," he said at last. "Remind me not to pick a fight with either of you. I'll look for the maintenance tools."

Five minutes later, Jez's cuffs were off, and five minutes after that she'd broken the rest of them free.

"Tae, I presume your blocker has prevented word of what we've done getting out," said Masha, strain still apparent under her tone. "However, I imagine Grigory will learn what's happened soon enough. We have until then to stop him. At the moment, Tae's friends are safe. But as soon as Grigory finds out—"

She didn't finish the thought, but then, she didn't have to.

Jez cast a quick glance in Tae's direction. His jaw was clenched, and he was breathing too quickly.

She remembered, for just a moment, the kid from the pleasure district, that small, far-too-light bundle in her arms.

She gritted her teeth.

They were damn well going to make this work.

"Well genius," she said, turning to Lev. "Guess you better start making a plan. Because it looks like we're going to go pay Grigory a visit."

24

"Ivan. Come in," said Lev quietly over his com. "Come in, Ivan."

"Lev?" Ivan's voice was frantic. "Where are you? What happened? We found the dead guards, and the rest of you gone, and we thought—"

"We're fine," said Lev tersely. "Grigory found us, but we managed to get away. We're on our way back now." He paused. "Is Galina with you?"

"Yes."

"Alright. Listen, tell everyone in the house to be ready to get out at a moment's notice. They'll need to be able to find a place to hide. Then bring Radic and Galina and meet us at the force-field entrance."

"Is—is Tae alright?" Ivan's voice was strained.

Lev glanced over to where Tae sat on the edge of a seat, glaring at his holoscreen, face drawn and tense.

"He's … fine. Look, I'll tell you everything when we get there. We should be there in—" he paused, glancing at the coordinates on his com. "Fifteen minutes, give or take."

"We'll be there." There was sharp tension in Ivan's voice.

Lev tapped off his com. He closed his eyes for a moment, drew in a long breath, and ran a hand through his hair.

The number of lives riding on this ridiculous venture was growing too numerous to count—Tae's street kid friends, Ivan, Galina, Radic, the ex-prisoners who'd come to join them in the mock pleasure house—and their own, of course.

And that wasn't even mentioning the fact that, thanks to Masha, the *Ungovernable* was likely to be destroyed. Even if Jez survived their current absurd attempt, she might not survive that.

It seemed much shorter than fifteen minutes by the time the ship lowered gently onto the waiving grass in a dip between two hills that put them just out of sight of the city.

"Alright kids, we're here," came Jez's voice over the ship's com.

They gathered around the airlock, Ysbel holding Misko, Olya clutching her parents' hands tightly. Tae's face was grim.

Lev took a deep breath and hit the airlock, and light from outside flooded the deck.

"What, we all just going to stand here for a while, then?" said Jez, coming up behind him. She was limping heavily, and winced every time she had to move her right leg, but she wore that dangerous grin that usually meant whatever was coming, somebody was probably going to get kicked in the crotch.

Lev turned, and found himself grinning ruefully in return. "Let's go, then," he said.

Three figures waited for them just outside the gate. For a brief moment Lev felt a jolt of sharp, irrational panic, because their hoods covered their faces, and for all he knew these were Grigory's people, waiting to kill them—then one of the figures turned at the sound of their approach, and he recognized Ivan's slender form and let out a quick breath of relief.

"Tae!" Ivan strode quickly forward, grabbing Tae by the shoulders and inspecting him for injuries. "Are you alright?"

"I'm—I'm fine," Tae managed.

Lev wasn't sure what it said about how much his life had changed that he recognized the shaky relief in Tae's voice, the way his whole body relaxed, almost imperceptibly, at Ivan's touch.

And the sudden memory of the relief flooding through his body at Jez's touch, the concern in her dark eyes, was so unexpected and so sharp he almost gasped.

"Lev?" she said from beside him.

He had to close his eyes for a moment to regain his composure.

"I'm fine," he said.

It would get better, it just took time.

At any rate, if he didn't pull himself together, none of them would likely live long enough for him to find out if that was true.

Galina had come up beside Jez. Jez turned to her, smiling, and said something in a low voice, then brushed Galina's hair back from her face and kissed her gently.

Lev turned quickly away.

"What's the plan?" Radic asked quietly. Ivan looked up as well, although he left his hand on Tae's arm.

"We're going to have to get to Grigory before he figures out what's happened," said Lev grimly. "The hope is that we can hold him hostage in exchange for Tae's friends and the rest of our people at the pleasure house."

There was a long pause.

Finally Radic said in a flat voice, "We're going to try to kidnap Grigory."

"What, too easy for you?" Jez said over her shoulder. "I mean, we could try it with our hands cuffed behind our backs if you want. Although to be honest, figure I've done that enough times now."

"That—wasn't what I was—" Radic stopped, shaking his head.

Ivan turned to Lev, his face grim. "I assume you have a plan for this?"

"As much of a plan as we ever have for these damn things," Tae muttered.

Lev sighed. "We didn't have a lot of time to plan things out, to be honest," he said. "We're leaving the kids with the others at the pleasure house. We'll dress as servers, and try to sneak into the Strani house. That's where Grigory usually stays when he's in town. And then—"

"Then we figure it out when we get there," said Jez cheerily. "Figure that's what we usually end up doing anyways."

Lev sighed. "Yes. That is exactly what we usually end up doing anyways. In fact, I'm not certain why we bother with me making these plans."

"Ah, don't sell yourself short, genius," said Jez, grinning. "Think of all the places we wouldn't have ended up without your plans."

"That's my point," he muttered.

Jez grabbed Galina's hand and grinned. "Well," she said. "We going to do this, or what?"

25

Jez pulled her scarf over her head to form a loose hood as they made their way back to the pleasure house. Wouldn't do much to hide her face, but that was the best they had at the moment. She turned to Radic and winked. "Hey skinny. You figure we'll pull this off?"

He shrugged, grinning. "Can't be harder than breaking out an entire damn prison."

The street outside the house wasn't any busier than it usually was at this time in the evening, but with the bustle in the streets, it would be hard to tell if someone was waiting in ambush.

She glanced over her shoulder at Lev. "I'm going in. If I don't get shot, the rest of you come too."

"No," said Galina, stepping forward. Her face was grim. "I'm going. Jez, don't bother arguing. You can hardly walk, for the Lady's sake, and I almost lost you once already today. Stay here until I call."

She let go of Jez's hand and strode purposefully forward, heat-gun hidden in a fold of her jacket.

Jez stared after her, a wide, stupid grin on her face.

"I'm in," said Galina a moment later over the com. "I didn't see anything. Come on."

Jez blinked out of her slightly salacious daydreams, and they crossed the street to the entrance casually, or as casually as they could when Jez couldn't put any damn weight on her right leg.

Galina was waiting at the door, and she closed it behind them once they were inside.

"I don't want to stay here, Mama," Olya whispered. "I want to come with you."

Ysbel stooped to one knee and put her hands on her daughter's shoulders. "My Olya," she whispered. "I need you to do this for me. I need you to watch your brother and keep him safe, alright? I'm doing what you asked, but I need you to do this for me."

Olya nodded, her face pale.

The rest of the ex-convicts had gathered, and Tanya was talking quietly with the girl named Anya. Anya nodded, and then Ysbel pushed the children gently towards her. Olya grabbed her brother's hand tightly, and, with one last look over her shoulder at Ysbel, went.

Lev must have been explaining the situation to the others, because there were nods and the muffled sound of whispered conversation.

"Jez? You're hurt. Can you do this?"

She turned quickly. Galina had come up beside her, a bundle of server uniforms in her arms.

"Yep," Jez said with a grin. "If I let crap like this stop me, figure I'd never get anything done."

Galina gave her a fond, concerned look.

"Hey you two, you can make out after we kidnap the mafia boss," Radic whispered in an amused voice. "Come on, get dressed."

Jez turned to glare at him, and he shoved a server's uniform at her. "Here's one that looks just about tall enough and scrawny enough to fit you."

By the time she'd managed to strip out of her street clothes and into a server's uniform, swearing steadily and leaning up against the wall for support, the others were already dressed. Tae was averting his face, his expression a blend of annoyance and embarrassment.

"Jez—" he hissed through his teeth.

She grinned at him. "Thought after Dmitri you'd gotten over being such an innocent. Guess Ivan's got some things to teach you."

"Jez!"

"Come on, you idiots, we don't have time to waste." Ysbel's voice was amused. "Let's go."

"And where exactly do you think you're going?"

Jez spun, winced, and grabbed for the wall, swearing under her breath.

The lights in the lobby flickered on, and she blinked against the sudden gilt glare. Then she swore again, louder.

Olyessa's off-duty guards had returned from wherever the hell they went when they were off duty. And they'd clearly noticed the bodies draped from the balcony, because they were holding their weapons in a businesslike way.

Lev glanced at Masha, then sighed and stepped forward. "Grigory came in with his people. He did this. But we intend to take him down."

The guards looked at him, then at each other. "How do we know you're telling the truth?" one of them asked at last.

"Do you think if we'd killed the guards, we would have come back?" asked Masha calmly. "They've been dead for over an hour now. You can send someone to check. If we'd been trying to double-cross Olyessa, we certainly wouldn't have stayed here."

The guards looked at each other again, then spoke in low voices for a moment. One of them stepped away from the group and walked towards the stairs. She came down a few minutes later, and the guards conferred in low tones again.

At last, one of them looked up. "We won't kill you. But we're coming with you. Perhaps you're telling the truth, perhaps not. But there are six dead guards here, and Olyessa never really trusted you." He paused. "And, if you're going after Grigory, I assume you'd be happy to have more guns on your side."

Jez narrowed her eyes, but Radic nudged her.

"Kid, shut up. Unless you want to get us all killed."

Lev and Masha exchanged glances. At last, slowly, Lev nodded.

"Alright. You can come along. But you'll have to follow my instructions. If you can't do that, you may as well shoot us here."

Again, the guards conferred.

"Very well," the same guard said, at last. "As long as what you're doing doesn't hurt Olyessa, we'll follow your lead."

Lev and Masha exchanged glances again.

"I don't like this," said Tae in a low voice, his tone strained.

"Nor do I," said Lev wryly. "But it looks like we don't have many options. I don't think we're shooting our way out of this, not without getting our people killed, and I'm not sure we want to get on Olyessa's bad side right now."

"I agree with Lev," said Masha. "I don't see that we have a better option."

Reluctantly, Tae nodded.

Lev took a deep breath and turned back to the guards. "Thank you. Now—" he gestured to the pile of server uniforms. "I suggest you get dressed quickly. We'll have to move fast."

They left their skybikes at the outskirts of the pleasure district. Jez's gut clenched in a familiar sick feeling as she stepped onto the filthy, darkened streets, but honestly, she didn't really have time to think about that right now.

Get Grigory, save Tae's friends. Then they could worry about the rest of this crap.

The walk to the Strani House was only a few minutes, but the bruises along her back were stiffening, and she had to bite back a gasp of pain at every damn step. The guards followed, and maybe their guns were in their pockets, but Jez was pretty damn sure they were pointing at her crew.

Still, as long as they weren't shooting, she couldn't complain too much.

The streets were as busy as always, and the doors to the low, elegant shapes of the pleasure houses, with their garish flashing lights, swung open and closed as groups of people wandered in and out.

Jez fought back a shudder.

Galina was in the lead, and she beckoned them down a side-street and into a back alley.

"The servers' entrance is through here," she whispered. "Stay behind me."

Jez could see the tension in her body, and she bit her lip.

Galya hadn't had to do this. She wasn't on Grigory's hit list, never had been. And Jez knew what it was like to stand in front of something or someone that had haunted your nightmares, the past you could never really get rid of.

She stepped forward, ignoring the icy shock of pain at the movement, and took Galina's hand. Galina turned and gave her a wan smile, and something in Jez's chest twisted, but she managed a smile back.

And then they were there, outside a small, dirty door.

"Tae?" Galina whispered.

Tae gave a tight nod and stepped forward. He touched his com to the lock, pulling up a quick scan, then shook his wrist to reset the holoscreen and began typing rapidly.

"You OK?" Jez asked, slipping her arm around Galina's waist. Galina sagged against her for just a moment, and Jez could feel her trembling. She pulled Galina closer. "I'm sorry," she whispered. "It's going to be OK."

"I know," said Galina, her voice barely audible. "It's—it's alright. I'm fine."

Jez turned to her, face serious. "Look, Galya. You don't have to be fine. We're going to get in there and get Grigory, or at least try, but there's nothing about this damn place that's fine. You don't have to be alright about it."

"Just do it anyways, right?" Galina whispered. Jez nodded, and Galina leaned in for a quick kiss.

"Got it," said Tae, his voice tense.

Galina and Jez drew apart, looking at each other, and then Jez looked back over the rest of them.

She took a deep breath. "Alright then. We ready?"

"Do we … know what we're doing?" asked Ivan.

"Make it up as we go, I guess," said Lev, his voice grim.

She grinned at him, ignoring the dread tightening in her stomach. "That, genius, sounds like my kind of plan."

She took a deep breath as she stepped into the building, fighting down the nausea in her stomach. The entrance was dark, and she blinked, trying to adjust her eyes to the dimness.

In front of them, a narrow, cramped hallway led off to each side, and a filthy staircase in front of them led down to what must be a basement.

"Where the servers and entertainment are kept when they're not working," Galina whispered. Her voice was haunted, and Jez grabbed her hand and squeezed it.

"Galya. Let me go first."

"You don't know where you're going," she said, swallowing hard.

Jez shrugged, and tried to make her voice cocky. "Well, kick me if I take a wrong turn."

Galina's face was tight, as if she thought she should protest, but didn't actually want to. Jez gave her a quick wink, stepped past her, and started off down the hallway, trying to hide her damn limp and probably failing badly.

The smell of the place turned her stomach, unwashed bodies and decay and that faint rotting-meat scent she'd smelled in the alley, but she clenched her teeth and kept moving. The hallway turned, and beyond there was light and the sound of voices.

"Where will Grigory be?" she whispered over her shoulder.

"I'll send the specs through to your com," Lev whispered back. "Most of the guest rooms are on the second floor, but there's a large suite on the floor above. I suspect that's where he'll be."

She smiled grimly. "Going up, then," she said. "Tech-head, guess you better make sure he's in there."

He scowled at her. "What are you going to do?"

She grinned. "Me? Figure I'll give you a clear stairway to go up."

"What are you—" began Lev.

"Radic, you coming?" she said.

Radic heaved a long sigh, but he couldn't hide his grin. "Guess I don't have much of an option, do I?"

She smirked. "You always have an option. I just happen to know that this is the option you're always going to pick."

"Don't know why I put up with you," he grumbled.

"Well, I am pretty hot," she drawled.

Galina's face was grim. "There are going to be guards before you get to the main lobby. They'll be armed, and they'll be ready to shoot anyone who's making a disturbance. The people that attend here are the richest of the rich, and they don't come to get shot at."

Jez gave her a wink. "Sounds like my kind of job."

Radic pulled out his heat pistol, and she turned for the stairs.

"Jez. Wait."

She paused at Lev's voice, glancing backwards.

"Just—be careful, OK?" His face was tight with concern.

"Always am," she said.

He took a deep breath and managed a weak smile.

"Galya—" she began, then stopped.

There wasn't really anything she could say to make it better. Anyways, Galina's expression had hardened, and she looked ready to kill someone.

"Good luck," said Jez finally. Then she took a deep breath, pushed the door open, and stepped through.

It took a moment for anyone to notice them. They were dressed as servers after all, and it wasn't like anyone was actually expecting two lunatics to come barging through the kitchen, burst into the lobby, lob a smoke bomb into the first-floor balcony, and shout, "Everyone out! Damn place is on fire!"

Once they'd done that, though, people noticed them pretty quickly.

The guards started across the floor towards them, and Jez pulled out her modded heat pistol. Her first shot hit one of the artificial lights, and it melted, glowing metal dripping down onto the polished stone floor.

Someone screamed.

Jez grinned, and shot again. This time, one of the hanging wall tapestries caught fire.

More people screamed.

Guards were coming down the stairs two at a time, weapons raised, grim looks on their faces.

"Everyone out!" Radic shouted, his voice panicked.

People shoved past each other to get to the doors, faces terrified, fine clothes disheveled. Doors on the second floor, or at least the ones visible from the lobby, were flung open, and the patrons, some of them still half clothed, piled out almost on top of each other.

Jez tried not to think about the fact that no one in the whole damn house seem to be worried about the servers or the entertainment.

The picture of the kid in the alley flashed in her mind, and she swore softly.

This was a damn pleasure planet. What the hell did she expect?

The guards had almost reached them. She turned and let off another shot, melting a chair. The man who'd just risen from it screamed, beating at the sparks that caught on his trousers and jacket.

From the corner of her eye, Jez could see a rag-tag group of people in servers' uniforms, scarves pulled low over their faces, slipping up the stairwell, past the flood of humanity trying to push its way down.

A tall man shoved one of them, probably Tae, out of the way, and paused a moment to scream profanities at him, spittle flying from his mouth, his face a mix of outrage and panic. One of the guards turned, glancing in their direction, then, after a moment, started pushing her way through to the stairs.

Damn.

Radic was still shouting at the top of his lungs, although his voice was almost drowned out by the screams of the patrons and the shouts of the guards.

"Going to have to make a little more noise in here," she whispered to him, a tight grin on her face. He nodded, and his grim expression told her he knew exactly what that meant.

But hell. They'd come here to do a job, and if it meant getting shot at by guards, well, it wasn't the first time.

She aimed her heat pistol and melted a section of the floor directly in front of the guard who'd turned towards Tae. The woman stumbled and cursed, spinning around to find her attacker. Radic shoved Jez out of the way, and she hit the ground hard as a heat blast warped the air over her head.

"Careful kid," he muttered. "Don't want you to get barbecued just yet."

The guard was coming towards them, heat pistol still raised, but at least she wasn't looking at Tae and the others anymore.

Jez gritted her teeth against the pain and staggered to her feet. Someone bowled into her, knocking her back, and she swore loudly, grabbing for something to steady herself. Radic caught her arm and set her on her feet again, and she managed a quick grin.

Three more guards were heading their direction as well.

Jez snapped off one more shot, just to get their attention, and then she shoved Radic forward into the roiling mass of humanity fighting for the exit.

Radic gave her a grim smile over his shoulder. "We have a plan?"

She shrugged. "Out the door, I guess."

"You think we'll make it?"

She grinned. "Nah. But it's worth a try."

He glanced back once at the stairs. "Looks like the others got through, anyways. I don't see them anymore."

"Well, see, guess we win after all."

One of the guards had shoved his way through the press of bodies, and he caught Jez by the arm. She slammed the butt of her heat pistol against his wrist, and he grunted in pain, but his grip didn't loosen. "What the hell are you playing at?" he ground out. "If you think you can come into this house and—"

Clearly, a quick chat wasn't going to help this situation. She spun her pistol, aiming for his head, but someone grabbed her gun arm, jerking it back painfully, and the gun dropped from her nerveless fingers.

Damn.

Radic had been pushed away from her by the crowd, but he yanked out his own gun, trying to bring it to bear. The guards holding her were too close, though, and if he fired, he'd be just as likely kill her as them.

"Radic!" she shouted. "Get the hell out of here."

"Jez," he called through gritted teeth. "You've got to—"

And then someone grabbed him from behind as well, yanking his arms back. He struggled, but it was no use.

Damn it to hell.

They were both going to die here. She'd guessed that going in, but it was different when you were actually staring into the muzzle of the damn heat-gun that would kill you—

And then the alarms on the guards' coms began to wail, the ear-splitting noise blaring through the packed lobby. There was a moment of hesitation, then the guards exchanged glances, faces grim. The guard holding Jez shoved her, and she fell, hitting the ground hard.

Around her was a dizzying mass of hurrying feet, and she curled into a ball on instinct to keep from being trampled. Someone stepped on her hand and she bit back a curse, and a foot kicked hard against her bruised back. She gasped in pain, vision going momentarily woozy, and then a hand grabbed her by the shoulders and hauled her to her feet.

"You OK, kid?" a familiar, worried voice asked in her ear. She staggered, caught her balance, and looked over at Radic.

"What happened? They find the others?" Her voice was tight.

Radic shook his head. "Doesn't look like it." He gestured to a corner, where the guards were huddled together, looking both irritated and confused. "I don't know for sure, but I think Tae happened."

She felt her shoulders slump in relief.

"So. I guess we head up?" he said.

She glanced around quickly. The lobby was now almost impenetrable, and fights were breaking out as people tried to shove through to the doors. The tapestry she'd set on fire was still smouldering, and had set its neighbour alight as well, and one of the lights hung crazily from the ceiling.

She raised an eyebrow. "Well, figure we've distracted them. Might as well see what's happening upstairs."

26

When Tae pushed his way out into the lobby behind Galina, he came to a sudden, involuntary halt.

The Strani house had been turned into a scene of mass chaos, people screaming and shoving, guards cursing, and what looked like a tapestry on fire.

He shook his head for a moment in stunned disbelief.

"If you let that girl do what she's good at, she's very good at it," said Ysbel, her voice amused.

"Let's go," said Lev. His voice was grim. "We can't afford to waste this."

They stepped out into the mass panic that was the lobby.

A shoving flood of people streamed down the stairway, fighting for the exit. Smoke was rising from one of the tapestries, and he could hear Radic's panicked voice shouting, "Get out! Everyone out!"

Tae gritted his teeth.

"Let me," said Ysbel grimly. She stepped to the front of the group, and there was something about the look on her face that made people part around her.

They reached the stairwell, and Tae kept his head down, swearing softly as they pounded up the stairs.

They had to make it. They had to. He couldn't stop and think about what would happen if they didn't make it.

Someone shoved him, and he staggered as a man screamed out insults. Ivan caught him before he could fall, face grim, but from the corner of his eye, Tae saw a guard looking in their direction.

Damn it.

"Ysbel, they've seen us," he hissed.

She glanced at him over her shoulder. "There's not much we can do about it at this point," she muttered. "If we get in a shootout, we get in a shootout."

It was just possible, with Ysbel's modded weapons and the chaos below, that they'd survive a shootout. But Caz and Peti and the others wouldn't, because they'd be dead the moment one of the guards recognized them.

His heart was pounding so hard it felt like it was choking off his breath.

And then the guard swore and spun around, yanking her heat pistol up and firing off a shot at something across the room.

Jez. It had to be Jez.

Lev looked up sharply, face pale.

"Come on," said Galina from behind him, her voice strained. "We can't help her by getting caught. Let's get this done."

The crowd thinned out as they reached the second story, and by the time they reached the third floor, they were pelting up the stairs at full speed.

"What now?" Ivan gasped as they reached the third floor landing.

"Tae," said Lev. "You're going to need to hack in, check how many of Grigory's people are in there." His face was bloodless.

"Wait," Tae gritted. He leaned against the wall, panting, and pulled up his com. He'd already hacked into Grigory's system, this should only take him a moment—

He typed the last command and hit enter. And then a shrill alarm sounded from the lobby, and he sighed in relief.

The guards were running for a spot in the corner that had absolutely nothing remarkable about it, except that he'd just pulled in urgent instructions to his com that every damn guard in the lobby was needed, immediately, in that exact spot.

Wouldn't last for more than a couple minutes while they tried to figure out what had happened, but it should give Jez a chance.

There was a sudden relief in Lev's posture, and he shot Tae a look of wordless gratitude.

Tae pushed himself upright, face set. "Alright. Let's go."

Lev led them quickly to a hallway, barely visible from the main stairway. "Tae," he said quietly. "Can you do a scan? I need you to confirm he's in here, and how many guards he has with him. And I'll need you to set up a block so that they can't call out for help." He glanced around at Olyessa's guards, who'd followed them up the stairs and were now standing grimly behind them, weapons drawn and ready. "If we can get in quickly and overpower them when they're not expecting it, it's just possible we can pull this off. But there will be shooting. Grigory won't be unprotected."

The guards nodded grimly.

Tae closed his eyes for a moment and drew in a long breath. "I've got tracking on Grigory's people, but that's all. If he's holed up with one of the street gangs or something, my scan won't pull that."

Lev nodded, forehead creased in a frown. "It will have to be enough."

Tae nodded, and pulled up his holoscreen.

He was half-way through setting a block when footsteps pounded up the hallway behind them. He spun around, but Galina and Lev's matching gasps of relief were enough to tell him who it was.

"Hey tech-head," Jez whispered. She was sporting a black eye and limping badly, but she was grinning, as usual. "We miss the fun yet?"

Radic leaned up against the wall, panting and muttering something about getting too damn old for this.

Galina closed her eyes for a moment in relief and put her arm around Jez, pulling her close.

"How's it coming?" Ivan whispered, crouching down beside Tae.

"Give me a couple minutes," said Tae, his voice tight.

Ivan nodded. "Let me know if there's anything I can do to help."

There wasn't, but the fact of his presence was somehow soothing, and Tae found himself relaxing slightly, his fingers finding the commands he needed a little more easily than before.

"There," he said finally.

Lev glanced over quickly. "You have it?"

"I have the blocker, and I've set it into everyone's coms."

"And the scan?"

Tae shook his wrist quickly to reset his screen. "Just doing it now."

Lev crouched down to watch as the scanner worked. At last, a diagram of the room at the end of the hallway popped up, populating with green dots, one red dot in one corner of the room.

Tae felt his shoulders slump in relief.

"Grigory?" asked Lev, pointing at the red dot.

Tae nodded. "And the others are his people. Guards or his boyeviki, I'm not sure. My scan isn't sophisticated enough to tell them apart."

Lev nodded, frowning. "Well," he said at last, "there's eight of them. That's not ideal. But we'll have the element of surprise, so it's something." He turned to Ysbel. "Alright. We'll need—"

"You'll need to put your weapons down, right now," said a man's voice.

Tae looked up quickly, something cold gripping the pit of his stomach.

Olyessa's guards had spread out to surround them, heat-guns levelled at the heads of every member of the crew.

Slowly, Lev got to his feet, hands spread to show he wasn't holding a weapon. "What is this?" he asked, voice a measured calm. "We're going after Grigory, not Olyessa. This isn't anything we didn't tell you about. And we'll need your weapons to pull it off."

One of the guards grabbed him and spun him around roughly, shoving the heat-gun into his back. "Drop your weapons," she snapped.

Tae glanced quickly around at the others.

Their grim faces told him everything he needed to know.

Slowly, he did as he was told, and heard, from behind him, the sound of the others doing the same.

"Get up," said the guard holding Lev. "Hands where we can see them."

They obeyed.

Tae's chest was tight with a sort of panic, and every breath was an effort.

One of the guards tapped her com and muttered something in a low voice, and a moment later the door to the room clicked and swung gently open.

The guards gestured them inside.

Grigory sat in one corner, leaning back casually, his bodyguards forming a loose half-circle around him. He smiled as they stepped inside, a lazy sort of smile.

But the guards holding them weren't looking at him. They were looking to the other side of the room.

Tae knew, somehow, what he'd see, even before he turned.

A plump, grandmotherly woman, with a lined face and cold eyes, watched them from a chair in the other corner, a satisfied smile on her face.

Olyessa.

"Masha," she said, in a rustic, rural drawl. "It's so good to see you all. Grigory and I were watching with interest to see what you'd do. And you didn't disappoint." She gestured to her guards. "Bring them all the way in." She spared a glance for Tae. "Grigory's already killed the street kids. He did it the moment my guards told me you'd come back, unfortunately, so we'll need something else for leverage, I suppose."

Tae stared at her for a moment, trying to make sense of her words.

He felt, somehow, distant, and numb, and very, very cold.

She was still talking, but he couldn't really hear her anymore, and he couldn't really feel the floor holding him up, or the guard's grip on his arm. He felt like he was falling, and there was nothing to catch him, and he'd be falling forever.

27

Ysbel's breath was coming too quickly, but she managed a quick glance at Tae.

He looked like he was going into shock, face sick, eyes glassy, jaw clenched unnaturally tight.

But there was nothing she could do for him at the moment.

Tanya's expression was stricken, but she caught Ysbel's eye and managed a small smile.

Ysbel drew in a deep breath.

The children were safe, at least. They had that. And if she was going to die, she'd at least die with Tanya. Really, it was more than she'd expected.

It was one thing to con a weapons dealer, even one as dangerous as Vitali. But trying to pull a sting on the mafia?

It had always been a crazy idea. Impressive, really, how close they'd come to succeeding.

"Well, this is certainly unexpected," said Masha. Her voice managed to convey bland surprise, but her posture gave her away. "I had thought you two weren't on speaking terms."

Grigory turned to her, and his smile did nothing to disguise the hatred on his face. "Masha," he said. "We have you to thank for that.

You must think I'm very stupid. You honestly thought you could take me down, didn't you?"

"It appears to me that we very nearly did," murmured Masha. "Considering that if it weren't for Zhenya, I'd have every credit from your pleasure houses in my account right now."

Grigory's eyes narrowed further. "You've always had a high opinion of yourself, haven't you, Masha? But there was one good thing that came from your scheme. Olyessa and I have made up." He smiled at the woman sitting across the room. "Getting rid of you was something that would benefit both of us. It drove us to negotiate, and it turns out we can do business together quite well. Under the table, of course. There are still advantages to being seen as rivals."

He turned back to Masha. "Which is why I was willing to let you go and take the fall for the scheme falling through. If things played out like I'd hoped, both your disappearance, and Olyessa's subsequent 'discovery' of the truth, would have made a decent smoke-screen for our dealings. And you would have stayed alive, at least for a little while. But you could never leave well enough alone. Still, it's probably better this way. I'll sleep better when you're dead."

"I see," said Masha, her voice crisp and cutting. "You'll work together until you can't take anything else without dividing it between you. And then you'll kill each other over who gets the bigger portion. And Olyessa didn't mind that you killed her guards, I take it?"

Grigory's smile broadened. "Oh, that may come in the future. But we'll let the future take care of itself. And as you well know, those six were guards you'd managed to compromise, Masha. As always, I have nothing but respect for how quickly you work."

"Olyessa. Did you always plan to double-cross us?" asked Lev, voice strained.

Olyessa smiled at him. "Not at first, no. When I thought you could pull it off, then I had every intention of honouring my bargain. But then Grigory sent me a message, telling me he'd figured out the scheme and offering to talk, and I decided it would be smarter to go with the winning proposition. I didn't get where I am now by backing losing bet." She shifted in her seat to face Masha. "Masha, you did me a good turn after all. I see substantial benefits to both Grigory and myself with this alliance. So I am grateful. But really, it's better this way. You're much too dangerous to keep alive."

Masha took a small step forward, a smile playing at the corners of her mouth. Her posture was tense, but for the first time, Ysbel realized it wasn't tense from fear.

She frowned.

"I'm very afraid, Olyessa, that you will be disappointed with the bargain you made," Masha said, and there was a note of something unfamiliar in her voice.

"I'm very happy at the moment," said Olyessa easily, but now there was the faintest hint of concern behind her expression.

Masha ignored her, and turned to Grigory. "Grigory Korzhakov," she said.

This time, Ysbel did turn to stare at her.

Masha's calm, bland tone was gone. Her voice was sheer ice, words cutting like knives.

"Grigory. You killed my family. And I watched you do it. I watched every scream, every sob, every plea for mercy. I saw all of it. I was seven years old at the time. I doubt you remember it, to be honest. It was just one of several in that week, wasn't it? I learned later that it was the week you expected payouts, and of course my parents wouldn't pay. They were religious, you know, my parents. Prayed to the Lady three times a day, said grace over every meal, never picked up a weapon, never harmed another person. They couldn't have paid the mafia. It would have gone against every single thing they believed it. The mafia knew them, but they always turned a blind eye. Never hurts to have someone praying to the Lady, does it? But then Zorya murdered her way to the top, and she wanted to set a precedent. She didn't want people like my parents to inspire others to defy her. So she sent you. When my parents refused to pay, like she knew they would, you killed them."

Ysbel stared at Masha, the faint taste of bile in the back of her throat.

She'd never heard this story.

No wonder Masha was willing to do anything to bring Grigory down, even betray her team. Ysbel couldn't honestly say she wouldn't have done the same in Masha's place.

At least, once she might have.

She glanced around at the others, their faces the grim set of people who know they're going to die.

This crew had become her family, as certainly as her children and her wife were.

She understood Masha. She could even, almost, sympathize. But Masha had taken herself out of the group of people Ysbel would die to protect when she betrayed them on Grigory's ship. And she was dangerous. She was perhaps the most dangerous person in the room at the moment, and that was a high standard to meet.

Perhaps it was too late to save Tae's friends. But they still had one option left to save the crew.

She glanced towards Lev. He met her eye and gave a short nod, although his face was paler than usual.

She'd set the message to Vitali into her com days ago.

The only thing left was to send it.

She tapped her com against her thigh, swallowing down the faint sickness in her throat.

It wasn't like they had other options at this point.

Masha turned, and for just a moment her eyes met Ysbel's. Ysbel kept her gaze steady, but even here, even now, she couldn't read Masha's expression.

Grigory's head was cocked slightly to one side, watching Masha with faint interest. At last, he chuckled. "You're right, I didn't remember that. When I figured out who you were, before I sent my people to go pick you up from Prasvishoni, I had to go back and look it up. Wasn't memorable enough to note down on my com chip at the time. I knew it might sour you on my offer, but I gambled that you'd be interested enough in keeping away from the government that you'd agree anyways. Because, as I'm sure you know, the reason we killed so many people that week was that the government gave us the go-ahead. They pulled the police out, and only sent them in afterwards to do clean-up." He leaned forward. "Of course, every gamble brings its risks, and even the best gambler can lose. Once." He smiled, and the menace in the smile made Ysbel shiver slightly.

"So yes. I know who you are, and I know what happened to your parents. Do you feel better now that you've said it? Now that you've faced me? Or were you hoping your story would make me pity you?"

"Neither," said Masha, and again Ysbel was struck at the cold disdain in her voice. "I told you so you would understand why this was worth it."

Grigory frowned slightly. "What was worth it?"

Masha smiled, a slow, icy smile that chilled the blood in Ysbel's veins. "Look at your credit account, Grigory," she said quietly. "You as well, Olyessa, since you decided to cast your tokens in with his."

"What are you talking about?" Now the worry was clear in

Grigory's voice.

"Go ahead," said Masha. "Take a look. It's not like you don't have us at gunpoint."

His frown deepening, Grigory pulled up the holoscreen on his com and typed something into it. There was a long moment of silence, the tension in the room thick enough to breathe.

And then Grigory's face went slack with a mixture of shock and horror.

He swiped desperately thorough screen after screen, and then, at last, he stopped, sagging. He looked, suddenly, like a very old man.

"What is it?" Olyessa snapped.

"Look for yourself," said Grigory, in a hollow voice.

Olyessa pulled up her own holoscreen, movements sharp and quick and nothing at all like the calm, grandmotherly persona she normally affected.

She stared at the screen for a moment, then slumped back in her chair, hand clutching the arm of her seat as if it was the only thing that kept her from falling over.

"What did you do?" asked Grigory, in that same hollow voice. "What did you do, Masha?"

Masha smiled then. Her eyes were narrowed slightly, and there was a hint of cold, merciless triumph in her face, and for the first time, Ysbel understood why people were afraid of Masha.

"I had Tae create the false account, you knew that," she said, and her voice would have been pleasant, if it hadn't held that hiss of hatred. "But you didn't see what he placed in it with his security protocols. The moment you put your money into the account, his bug was triggered. Every credit in that account was corrupted, beyond repair. And more than that. If you look through your financial records, you'll find that it traced back to the source of the funds, and corrupted them as well. Considering Olyessa's funds were in that account, it did the same to hers. And although she didn't leverage every asset she had in order to get the necessary funds, like you did, I made very certain that the amount of funds I asked her for would have been enough to break her. And I made certain that she had enough funds tied up in my enterprise that she'd have to leverage at least some of her assets in order to keep her … business, if that's what you'd prefer to call it, running."

She turned to face Grigory. "You, Grigory, are finished. You have nothing. A dock-worker walking the street is richer than you are right now. You're a broken man. Your organization is broken. This house isn't yours anymore, and nor are any of the other pleasure houses you owned. And if my records are correct, the few houses Olyessa owned were the assets she chose to leverage in order to keep her enterprise running." She turned, so she was looking at both of them.

"I have a feeling that the person who owns those loans now is going to call them. Because that's the other thing that happened when you pulled your credits from that account—it set up a signal to the Svodrani banking system. It set up an alert that your credits were bad, and everyone with access to the accounts will see that. You're finished, Grigory. As is Olyessa. There's nothing left for you."

Grigory swore, his voice a choked snarl. "I'll kill you, Masha. I'll kill you right here." He was already going for his heat pistol.

"Stop." Masha's voice rang out sharply, and she turned to the bodyguards. "He's not going to be able to pay you. Any wages you were owed, they're gone now. And perhaps you're loyal to him as a friend. If so, more power to you. But I swear to you, he'll never recover from this. Are you really willing to take his orders now?"

The guards behind Grigory stirred uneasily, and from the corner of her eye, Ysbel saw that the guards flanking Olyessa were doing the same.

"There are crumbs left in this empire of his," Masha said, voice thick with disdain. "You can hold on with that old man, drooling and slavering through the rubble trying to find something worth saving, or you can turn over a new leaf, hope that whoever steps in where he left off decides to grant you mercy that you don't deserve. But if you help Grigory kill the person who took him down, I don't think whoever that is will be grateful."

Grigory grabbed his weapon, pointing it at Masha with shaking hands. Ysbel swore.

Perhaps Masha had taken Grigory down, but this place was about to turn into a bloodbath. If Vitali's people didn't show up soon, there wouldn't be anyone left to save.

One of the bodyguards snatched the weapon from Grigory's hand. Grigory spun, his face twisted and ugly with rage. "How dare you," he began, in that same choked snarl, and grabbed for the bodyguard who'd taken his gun. The bodyguards swung the butt of her gun down towards Grigory's temple, but another guard caught her arm in one hand, and with his other fist, knocked her backwards.

Grigory was on his feet, reaching down into his boot for another weapon.

Two clicks through Ysbel's com.

She glanced quickly around the room. The others were back against the wall, mostly. That was good. And Masha—

She took a deep breath.

Masha would be exposed to the door, the moment Ysbel stepped back.

The door burst open in a ball of flame, the hinges twisting and warping, the door itself sagging half-melted on its hinges, and a group of navy-clad figures, faces obscured, burst into the room.

Masha turned, and for half a second, her eyes caught Ysbel's.

And then Ysbel stepped back, leaving Masha in full view.

"What is the meaning of this?" Masha snapped, her voice sharp.

The figures had already spread out around the outside of the room. There were at least fifteen of them, although in the chaos it was hard to tell exact numbers.

One of them spoke. Their face was obscured by the mask, but there was a hint of dry humour in their voice.

"Masha. Vitali Dobrev sends his regards. Lev called us in, told us where you'd be. Sold you out for favours. He and his friend Ysbel, of course."

There was a moment of complete silence.

Ysbel found she couldn't meet Masha's gaze, and she didn't want to meet Jez's.

This had been the only option. After everything, this had been the only feasible option to keep the crew alive, keep them from dying in the inevitable firefight with Grigory's guards.

But there was a knot in her stomach, tight and hard, and she realized she must not be as certain of that as she might have been.

"What do you want?" Masha seemed to have recovered herself, because her posture was erect, her voice almost steady.

"You, Masha." There was still that dry humour in the voice. "Vitali wants you." The figure looked around at Grigory and Olyessa, the bodyguards who'd paused mid-struggle, still not certain whose side they were on.

"Go on," said the navy-clad figure, gesturing to the door. "We don't want you. Mister Vitali has no reason to start fights with the mafia. We only want her."

There was a long pause. Then, at last, Grigory pushed himself to his feet. His face was still contorted with rage, his expression deadly.

"I have no objection," he hissed. "Only I would ask that for old friendship's sake, Vitali makes her death long and painful."

He jerked a head at his bodyguards, and reluctantly, they followed him.

Olyessa stood as well. The woman's face bore no trace now of the kindly, grandmotherly woman she'd appeared a few minutes earlier. The cold hate that shone from her eyes made her look almost demonic.

"You planned on double-crossing me from the beginning, Masha," she said in a low, icy voice.

"Yes. However, it is good to know that my assumption, that you would turn on us the moment it appeared beneficial, was borne out," said Masha.

Despite everything, she was still Masha, unruffled and unruffleable, her voice calm, her bearing competent and self-effacing. But Ysbel had seen the woman behind that mask, for the first time.

And for the first time, that calm voice sent shivers through her.

Grigory had just reached the door when the first of Vitali's people stepped towards Masha, heat-gun drawn.

What happened next happened so fast that Ysbel's eyes hardly had time to follow.

The figure grabbed for Masha. Masha twisted away, ducking under the figure's outstretched hand, and when she straightened, she was holding a gun. The movement was fast enough that Ysbel couldn't tell if she'd grabbed it from the guard, or if she'd had it hidden somewhere on her person. For a split second, she wondered if the room would be turned into a firefight after all.

And then Masha turned. Her face was grim, but still calm, and there was a deadly, pitiless look in her eyes.

"Lev," she said quietly.

He turned.

She fired.

Everything seemed to have slowed to half-speed—Lev, crumpling to the ground, Jez yanking her arm from the person holding her and springing towards him as Masha fired a second time.

The gasp of pain from Jez as the shot aimed at Lev hit her, the horrified look on her face as she fell. The momentary shock in Masha's expression, instantly hidden.

And then time seemed to start again. The figures in blue leapt forward, guns drawn. Masha turned, and they fired, how many of them Ysbel couldn't tell.

Tae grunted in pain, collapsing against Ivan, and Ysbel tried to shove Tanya behind her as heat blasts whined through the air.

And just as the figures reached Masha, the woman caught Ysbel's eye one final time.

She raised her heat gun.

There was no time to move, no time to run, no time to duck out of the way. Ysbel only managed to push Tanya a little farther behind her.

And then Masha pulled the trigger.

28

Jez lay on the ground, eyes closed. The room was a wash of noise, and she was having a hard time distinguishing one sound from another.

There was something warm underneath her.

Lev.

She'd seen him fall.

She'd seen Masha look at him, and raise her gun, and pull the trigger, and she wasn't sure if she'd ever forget that sight for as long as she lived.

However long that ended up being. At this stage, she wasn't sure it would be all that long.

People were shouting and screaming and swearing, and she could hear Grigory's raised voice. "What just happened?" he was shouting. "What the hell—"

"Get out of here, both of you, unless you want to be caught in the damn crossfire," someone else snapped.

There was the unmistakable hiss and sputter of heat gun blasts, and a grunt of pain, and she couldn't tell who it was from.

"Get out!" the voice snapped again. "Get out, I'll take care of the Masha woman. We're not taking her alive."

Another heat blast, a strangled shout of pain.

Pain washed through Jez's own body, hot and cold at the same time, and she found she didn't really want to move. She didn't really want to think, she just wanted everything to stop, for just a minute.

And then, finally, the room grew still.

She kept her eyes shut, because she was pretty sure she didn't want to open them right now.

And then, at last, a voice. Calm, and collected, and ever-so-slightly amused.

Masha's voice.

"They're gone."

Jez stirred, and blinked her eyes open.

"Jez?"

She turned slightly, and found she was looking into Lev's face. He wore a wry expression.

"Jez. I don't mean to be rude, but your elbow is in the middle of my stomach."

She managed a snarky grin. "Sorry, genius."

She tried to roll off, winced, and bit back a curse, and his expression turned immediately to one of sharp concern.

"Jez? Are you alright?"

"'M fine," she muttered, managing to push herself into a sitting position. "I just got the hell beat out of me on the damn ship, and then again downstairs, and I don't heal as quickly as all that."

The pain radiating through her back, where Grigory's stooges had kicked her, was almost enough to make her lightheaded.

Damn. She was going to be sore tomorrow.

With a moderate amount of effort and a substantial amount of swearing, she made it to her feet, and then she had to reach out and catch herself on the wall before she fell over again.

Galina appeared at her side, steadying her, and Jez sighed in relief and relaxed against her.

Galina was a hell of a lot more comfortable than the wall.

"Well," said Ysbel, at last. "I think that was effective."

"I hope so," said Masha.

Jez took a deep breath and glanced around the room. The figures in navy blue were gone, except for one. And that one had pulled their face covering down and was running fingers through their hair.

Jez stared.

"I'm very confident we fooled them, at any rate," said Zhenya.

Tae, who was slumped in one corner, leaning against Ivan as if he didn't quite have the strength to stand, jerked his head up.

"What the hell—" he began through his teeth, his voice shaking.

Zhenya smiled. "Don't worry, Tae. Your friends are alive." They shrugged. "I was the one Grigory put in charge of killing them, and he trusts me implicitly. I can assure you, they're perfectly safe."

"I—What—" Tae's face had gone bloodless, and he seemed unable to form a complete sentence.

Zhenya chuckled. "Tae. I've always liked you. And as I told you, I have no interest in killing street kids unless it's absolutely necessary. After the arrangement Masha and I worked out—" They glanced at Masha, and shrugged. "There was no need."

Tae sagged in relief, and Jez sucked in a long breath, feeling suddenly lighter than she had in a very long time, even with her whole damn body aching like she'd basically climbed into a meat pulverizer and turned it on.

Lev was shaking his head. "Masha, I have to hand it to you. The look on Grigory's face—"

"Wait," interrupted Ivan, looking back and forth between Lev and Masha. "Wait. You mean—what you said about the credits—"

"Yes," said Masha, with a slight smile. "Everything I said about the credits was true. He played perfectly into our hands." She glanced around the room.

"That means—" Ivan trailed off, his face slack with disbelief.

"Yes." Masha's voice held a hint of that same coldness it had held when she was talking to Grigory, and Jez gave a small shiver. "As I promised. Grigory is completely destroyed. Olyessa as well. By this time tomorrow, both of their organizations will be nothing more than rats fighting over bones. With no assets to use to borrow funds, no way to pay the boyeviki or grease the wheels of the government —" She smiled, and her smile was utterly merciless. "We've done exactly what I promised we'd do. We've taken Grigory down."

Jez watched her. Honestly, Masha was right, they'd pulled a damn good con. But—

She shivered slightly, and Galya looked up at her in concern.

"Jez? Are you alright?"

"I'm fine," she said, trying for a grin.

But there was something about the look on Masha's face. Something about the look on her face when she'd turned to Lev, aimed, and pulled the trigger. And yes, it was a rigged gun, and yes, they'd planned it that way, and yes, Lev was fine, they were all fine.

But there had been one moment, that moment just before Masha pulled the trigger. That moment where Jez had realized, irrevocably, that Masha would have done it, even if the gun were real. Even if things had changed, and their plans had fallen through, and the gun in her hand was real, Masha would have pulled that trigger.

She'd always doubted it before.

But now—well, there was nothing to doubt anymore.

They were all alive. Everything had turned out exactly the way they wanted it to. But there was something icy in the pit of Jez's stomach, and she wasn't sure that even Galina holding on to her could make her feel warm again.

29

Masha glanced around the room.

She'd expected to feel triumphant, or at least pleasantly satisfied.

Instead, her muscles were shaky with a sick, desperate relief.

They'd all survived this, somehow.

But when she'd turned and grabbed the heat gun.

She'd been almost certain the weapon she'd grabbed was the rigged one. But—not completely certain.

And she'd pointed it at Lev and pulled the trigger anyways. She hadn't even hesitated.

She'd seen the look on Jez's face when she'd done it. Jez had known it. In that moment, Jez had realized.

She wasn't sure how much of the sickness in her stomach came from relief that it had worked out anyways, and how much came from the way Jez had looked at her as she lunged towards Lev.

She drew in a long breath.

Not that it mattered now.

The boulder she'd shoved over the cliff with the heist on Vitali was tearing down the mountainside now, and there was no way to stop it. Her only option now was to keep ahead of it long enough to do what she had to do.

"I'm sorry. But can someone explain to me exactly what just happened?"

She turned to where Ivan was standing, his arm protectively around Tae.

Tae's face was still sick with shock, and something twisted in her stomach at the sight. She managed to smile anyways.

"Ivan. I believe you know Zhenya," she said.

"Yes. We've … met." Ivan's voice was cold.

"When Lev informed me Vitali was willing to let the rest of you go and protect Tae's friends if you'd hand me over, I agreed that, with the risks we were taking, we needed a backup plan. I was understandably reluctant to be killed, but I assumed Vitali's offer could be used to our advantage. So, I contacted Zhenya, and after some negotiation, they agreed to facilitate the plan."

"So—" began Ivan. "Those people in blue weren't Vitali's people after all?"

"Oh, they certainly were," said Masha lightly. "They were Vitali's hired guns, and they came in here to kill me. And they watched me kill Lev and shoot Ysbel, and they watched the rest of you fall in the crossfire, from guns that Zhenya had provided them. They were set with a brilliant modification Tae designed that cut the power to the heat sink, so the blasts wouldn't have the heat power to kill.

"They took some time to install, but they're simple to disable, and I've already done that from my com. By the time they reach Vitali to bring the news, the guns will function as normal. They saw you die, as did Grigory, as did Olyessa, and I'm certain Vitali has been told. Once again, we are presumed dead. And while I'm certain they'll realize their error eventually, it gives us time to prepare our next move."

Ivan's eyebrows had raised listening to her recital, and now he shook his head slowly, relief and anger fighting in his face.

"So you almost gave me a heart attack watching Tae get shot, and you almost gave Tae a heart attack thinking his friends had died. You didn't think to tell us this?"

Judging from the protective way his arm tightened around Tae, his anger was less about his own fright, and more about the way Tae had slumped against him in despair before Zhenya had spoken.

"I'm sorry, Ivan," Masha said, removing her gaze from Tae deliberately. "The plan was still in the initial stages. I didn't foresee Olyessa joining forces with Grigory, and I believed once the plan was set, I'd have time to inform the rest of you. I did not believe it would be necessary for Zhenya to join Vitali's people to pull this off. And I certainly had no way to foresee that Zhenya would be instructed to kill Tae's friends, nor that they would choose not to do so."

She glanced at Zhenya. "I assume you'll hear if Grigory believed what happened?"

"Of course," said Zhenya. "Although I suspect within twenty-four standard hours, he'll no longer be in a position to hurt you. Nor will Olyessa. But I've come to understand how, in a profession like yours, you'd want to keep off the sensors."

Masha nodded. "Thank you."

"Wait," said Tae. "How do we know that Zhenya won't go straight back to Grigory?"

Zhenya turned and smiled at him. "Tae. You know me better than that, I hope. Grigory is finished. You finished him. He'll never come back from this." They shrugged. "Why would I go back on my bargain for a man who will almost certainly be dead in a few standard weeks' time?"

They turned to Masha. "Masha. You and I have some catching up to do, I think. I have some loose ends to tidy up, but I'll call you on your com later."

She nodded, somehow managing to keep her expression pleasant, and Zhenya slipped out the door.

"So," said Jez at last, once Zhenya was gone. She was clearly trying to sound jaunty, and failing badly. "If those bastards lost everything, what happens to the pleasure houses now?"

Masha turned and gave her a slight smile, even though looking at her sent a small stab of pain through her chest. "I believe that's up to the new owners."

Jez looked at her for a moment, then dropped her eyes, a small, humourless smile on her face. "Well, so much for taking down the damn pleasure planet."

Galina's eyes narrowed. "Masha," she said, and there was a controlled anger in her voice. "I agreed to help you take down the pleasure houses. But you've just sold them to the highest bidder. These new owners, are they as bad as Grigory? Olyessa? Do you think they might think twice about leaving children to die in alleyways, or will it just be a matter of profit to them?" There was a bitter harshness to her words.

Masha raised an eyebrow, biting back a small smile. "As for whether they're better than Grigory, opinions may differ," she said. "Although I personally believe they are. The owner is a shell company, the shares of which are held by another shell company, which in turn is held by a partnership made up of two other shell companies. I won't bore you with details. But the ultimate owner of these pleasure houses, Galina, is you."

Galina stared at her.

"If you'd like," Masha amended. "It is myself, currently, but I believe you would be the person best suited to oversee taking them down. If that is what you want."

Galina was still staring, her face gone suddenly bloodless, and it appeared that Jez was supporting her now, rather than the other way around.

"Are—are you telling the truth?" asked Galina finally. Her voice was hoarse. "Please. Don't lie to me about this."

"I'm not lying, Galina," Masha said, with a slight smile. "I can sign the documents over to you tonight. Ownership will not come through until the banks on Prasvishoni open for business tomorrow, which—" she glanced at her com, "I believe will be early afternoon tomorrow here."

Galina swallowed hard, and for a moment Masha wondered if she'd actually faint.

Jez was staring at Masha, too. They all were, in fact.

"Masha," said Lev carefully. "How did—"

"You don't imagine I took all the funds that Olyessa provided and put them into that account, do you?" she asked.

It was always slightly gratifying to see Lev surprised.

"When she transferred the money, I repurposed the bug Tae created, that Jez used to steal information from Olyessa's man on the casino ship. It drained Olyessa's account, and I used the excess funds to purchase the shares in the leveraged pleasure houses." She paused a moment. "Galina. I assume you've thought about how you'd go about dismantling this place?"

There was a long, long moment of silence.

Finally Galina said, "I've been thinking about that since the day I left this hell-hole." Her voice was so quiet that it was barely audible, but there was a hard edge to it.

Masha nodded in satisfaction.

If Galina didn't have the entire pleasure district closed down by this time tomorrow, she'd underestimated the woman.

"Well," she said at last. "I believe it wouldn't be a bad idea for us to get some sleep while we can. If we want to take advantage of our brief respite, it would be best to get off-planet as soon as possible. I have a few things to take care of here before we go, but the rest of you may as well get some sleep. I have a feeling we won't be getting much sleep very shortly."

"Wait," said Jez, her expression changing to one of horror. "Wait. My ship. Olyessa can—she can just—"

Masha glanced at her quickly.

She still couldn't quite meet the pilot's eyes.

"Jez," she said. "As I promised, you will not lose your ship. The system she installed on your ship was nothing but a forgery. I swapped the chips out while we were still on Olyessa's base."

"You—" Jez turned to glare at her. "OK then, why the hell did you let her put it on? And let me think that—think—"

"Because I needed your reaction to be genuine, so that Olyessa would believe it," said Masha quietly. "And I needed Olyessa to have some connection with the ship. Since she installed the chip, the *Ungovernable* has been broadcasting the location of her base to a number of people I once worked with very closely. People who have a vested interest in rooting out Olyessa's encroachment in the government. They've been biding their time, but I believe that the moment they hear that she's been weakened, they'll pounce. I very much doubt Olyessa will find much peace on her base at present."

Lev was watching her with that calculating expression of his.

"Masha," he said, after a long moment. "This job has been, against all odds, a success. But I'm afraid that our contract with you has ended. We came, before, because we trusted you. That's no longer the case. This job was to ensure that, despite the fact you set us up, Grigory would not be able to track us down and kill us. And it appears we've done that. And so—" He spread his hands. "I'm afraid this is where we part ways."

She looked at him for a long moment.

That moment when she'd pointed the heat gun at his head and fired.

She hadn't been certain she'd grabbed the modded gun. And she'd pulled the trigger anyways.

"Lev," she said, forcing the tremor from her voice. "As always, you're welcome to go your own way. But—" She shrugged slightly. "We've created the largest power vacuum the system has seen for a very long time. There will be war. There will be people dying in the streets of Prasvishoni, and in the outer settlements. Tae's friends from university. Certainly they won't stand by, not based on what I saw of them. Ysbel's students. I'm sure even in the apartments where we left them, a street war like that will suck in Caz and Peti and the rest. Possibly your family, even as distant as they are from the capital, currently."

She turned, so she was facing all of them. "And, of course, that's not the only thing. There is still the matter of the gas. You've breathed it in. Misko and Olya breathed it in. Yes, we've bought ourselves a short respite. But it's only that. We were not able to completely destroy the institutional knowledge, and with a person as intelligent as Lev's former professor—it's only a matter of time."

"So we've condemned our friends." Tae's voice was tight with hurt and anguish and anger. "And what now? You think that will make us come with you?"

"We've only condemned them if we don't step in and stop it before it begins," said Masha quietly.

"And you have a plan to do that." Lev's voice was flat and hard.

She nodded, and gave him a small smile. "I do. However, without your assistance, it will be impossible. As I've said from the beginning, I chose you all very specifically."

There were a few long moments where no one spoke. Finally, Lev turned in disgust, and she could see the anger in his movements.

"We'll discuss it," he said shortly. "We'll talk it over, and let you know in the morning."

She said nothing, just kept her pleasant smile.

He gestured to the others with a sharp jerk of his head. "Come on. She's probably right that it would be a good idea to get some sleep, anyways."

The rest of the crew filed slowly out of the room. Jez cast a glance over her shoulder as she left, and the look on her face cut Masha.

When the others were gone, Lev turned back to her. "Masha," he said quietly. "As always, you played this well. But we are not your pawns, not anymore. If we come, it will be on our own terms."

She met his eyes. There was a hard challenge in them.

She'd chosen him because he was, as he put it, very, very smart.

And he was no longer on her side.

But she didn't drop her gaze, and finally, he turned away, stepping through the ruins of the door.

She waited until his footsteps moved off down the hallway. Then she sank down into Grigory's chair.

Every muscle in her body ached with exhaustion, and the rush of adrenalin from earlier that day had faded, leaving her muscles weak and shaky.

She looked around at the luxurious room and repressed a shudder.

She'd prefer to spend as little time in this place as possible. But she had business to take care of, and here she was unlikely to be interrupted by any of the crew.

At last, grimacing, she tapped her com.

Zhenya answered immediately. "Masha. I was waiting for you."

"They're gone," she said, and was distantly surprised at how weary her voice sounded.

"I'm just coming back from checking in with Grigory," they said. "I'll be there in five standard minutes."

By the time Zhenya opened the door and stepped into the room, Masha had managed to straighten, holding herself as if she were exactly what she appeared—a simple, competent, mid-level government employee.

"Masha," said Zhenya with a slight smile, pulling up the chair Olyessa had been sitting in. "So. Shall we discuss the terms?"

"The terms, Zhenya, are exactly what I described to you," she said, her voice sharp.

"I saved you from the shootout, and you paid me an obscene amount of credits," Zhenya said, still with that slight smile. "That was the bargain. You convinced me it was a good one when you made it clear that you'd already ruined Grigory. But then you called a second time, a few hours back. To bargain for one last favour."

"Yes," she said, shortly.

"The lives of a group of street kids," said Zhenya. Their smile widened slightly. "You know, I was glad you did. I prefer not to kill street kids if I can help it. I would have, because it would have made things much easier, to be honest. I had to work very hard to convince Grigory to trust me without showing him proof the children were dead. But as I said, I was happy to have an excuse not to. Besides, I must admit, I find Tae quite fascinating. It would have destroyed him, and that would have been a shame." They paused a moment. "But you, Masha. I thought you were all transactional. You had me convinced, you know. And then this. Save Tae's street-kid friends. And rather than hold it over him, let him think I'd had a change of heart."

"I still need them," said Masha. "I still need leverage to use against Tae."

Zhenya raised an eyebrow. "Oh, I can think of several other things you could use as leverage against Tae. In fact, any single member of your crew would be enough. You know that as well as I do. Tae is extremely loyal. All you had to do is convince one of them to come with you, and Tae wouldn't have been able to bring himself to leave." They shook their head. "But then again, I'm telling you things you already know, aren't I? You saved those street kids because you didn't want to see Tae hurt."

She gave them her coldest stare, but she knew well enough that her non-answer was answer enough.

Zhenya sat back in their chair, smiling slightly. "So. Those are the terms I'd like to discuss. You promised me a place in your scheme. I take you up on that offer."

"And what exactly do you want?" asked Masha. There was a tightness in her stomach that made her feel slightly sick.

She'd worked across from Zhenya before. They were a survivor, and they were clever. Far too clever for her to be able to trust them.

"I'll watch your next move, Masha," they said at last, still with that faint smile on their lips. "I'll watch. And I'll tell you when I decide I'd like in." They pushed themselves out of their chair, their movements graceful. "And remember. I know where those children live. I'll be able to keep tabs on them, no matter where you hide them. I know a lot of people, Masha, perhaps not as many as you do, but enough. They're alive as long as you keep your side of our bargain."

They watched her for a moment, then turned and slipped from the room.

Masha watched them go, an icy chill lingering in her chest.

She'd given them far too much. Zhenya had a pull over her now that she couldn't afford to give to anyone. And she'd known that from the moment she tapped their number into her com and told them she had another proposal.

But she'd seen the look of hurt betrayal on Tae's face, back in the casino ship. And she hadn't been able to bear the thought of seeing it again.

She shivered.

This was exactly what she'd been afraid of. That in the end, she wouldn't be able to put the fate of the system ahead of the fate of these people who she'd brought together to use as tools, but who had somehow become her crew.

She could have pulled that trigger.

But she couldn't have borne the look in the faces of the others afterwards.

She closed her eyes for a moment, trying to push back the cold terror.

She'd find a way to make this work. Somehow. She'd put too many years of planning and preparation into this to let it fail, and she'd find a way.

But—

But this had complicated her plans in ways she'd never counted on.

Zhenya was very, very clever. And she had no idea what they were after.

30

Jez glanced down at Galina as they stepped into the almost-abandoned lobby of their mock pleasure house. Galina's face was set and bloodless, her whole body practically vibrating with tension.

They'd stolen some skybikes from the pleasure district, and Tae had hot-wired them, and honestly, she was pretty damn sure that even Tae hadn't felt bad about that, considering the kind of absolute bastards who frequented the pleasure district.

Masha wasn't back yet, but she was pretty sure that Masha would be able to get herself back here just as easily as the rest of them had.

The thought of Masha was a hard, painful knot in the back of her brain, and she didn't want to touch it. She didn't want to think, for one second, about Masha.

About what she'd done.

About what she could have done.

She shook her head. The thing was, everything had worked out exactly how they'd wanted it to, in the end. Even if it wasn't exactly how they'd planned it, it had all worked out. And maybe she'd been wrong. Masha was good at faking it, hell, that was basically Masha's entire personality.

But—

She shivered slightly.

But she was pretty damn sure she wasn't wrong. And the thought was enough to make her sick.

She shoved the memory away. She'd deal with it later. When she had time to.

When she had time to think about the fact that the woman she trusted—who she actually liked, who honestly, she trusted as much as she'd ever trusted anyone in her whole damn life—would have been willing to kill the man who'd become maybe the best friend she'd ever had.

She took a deep breath. "Hey. Galya," she whispered. "You OK?"

Galina looked up at her and tried to smile. "I'm—I'm just a little stunned, I think," she said quietly, but her voice was shaking.

Jez put an arm around her and pulled her up against her shoulder, and for a moment, Galina's body relaxed into hers. Jez closed her eyes and breathed in Galina's smell and held her, and something inside her hurt, just a little.

Yes, she'd told Galya she didn't do relationships. And hell, she didn't. She'd never done relationships, because before all this crap, when she'd been a smuggler flying solo runs, the thought of having someone who you were stuck with, who you couldn't get away from, who trapped you, basically, was maybe the worst thing she could imagine.

But—well, but—the thought of coming back every evening to something like this, to someone whose shape and feel was as familiar to her as the controls of her ship, who she didn't have to fake anything around, because they actually liked her, the real her, as stupid and impulsive and crazy as she was, who smiled when they saw her and leaned into her when she held them—

She cut off the thought, and found, for some reason, she was blinking back tears.

Galina drew in a deep breath and looked up at Jez. There was a small, weary smile on her face, and Jez leaned in and kissed her, and yes, Galya was sexy as hell, but there was something comfortable and comforting in her kiss, something that made the world seem a little more bearable.

"We should probably let everyone else know what's happened," said Lev, from behind them.

"Probably not a bad idea," said Radic. Even he sounded tired. "Considering they probably think we're all dead and they're next." He tapped his com. "Alright all you idiots, cut your slacking and get into the lobby."

There was a moment of startled silence, and then various shocked profanities began to filter through the general com line.

Jez looked over at Radic. He winked at her, grinning. "Come on," he said into the com. "We're not answering any questions until you get your lazy butts up here."

It took the rest of their rag-tag group of ex-convicts a surprisingly short amount of time to assemble, and less time for Olya and Misko to ensconce themselves in Ysbel's and Tanya's arms.

When they had, Radic turned to Galina. "You want to explain?" he asked softly. "Or do you want me to?"

"I'll do it." Galina's face was set, that expression that made Jez want to hold her until the tension drained from her body, want to make everything OK somehow.

But the thing was, Galina could do that all by herself. Always had been able to.

Galina stepped forward, glancing around the ragged group of them. Their eyes were fixed on her, and Jez felt a small spark of pride as she watched her.

"There's—a lot that's changed in the past few hours," said Galina, her voice just loud enough to carry.

Jez leaned back against the wall and watched her explain, and tried not to think about the ache growing in her chest. Because of course Galina was staying here. Jez had known that from the moment she'd realized what Masha was saying, back in Grigory's private room in the Strani house.

It would take some time for the properties to get transferred over. But Galina would stay, and she'd shut them down, and she'd figure out what to do for the people who'd been used here in the houses— the entertainment, yes, but also the cooks and the servers and the cleaners. The people who'd been dragged away from everything they knew and forced into something designed to rip their humanity from them. But the thing was, people weren't like that. You couldn't take away someone's humanity, no matter how much you tried. People were still people, no matter what you did to them, and the only people who lost their humanity were the ones who gave it away freely trying to take someone else's. And Galina would do something about it. Hell, she was born for it.

And Jez would fly away, with Masha and the others. Because that's what she was born for.

The crew hadn't had a chance to talk it over yet, but that's what they'd do. They all knew it, she'd seen it when she looked at them. Maybe with more time to prepare, Lev could have come up with an alternate plan. But Masha had been right—starting tonight, or maybe tomorrow if they were lucky, the system was going to devolve into civil war, and the centre of it would be fought right down the streets of Prasvishoni.

And the truth was, none of them could leave the people they cared about there to get hurt.

"Anyone who'd like to stay and help, I'd be honoured to have you. But it will be long, and difficult, and I don't expect it from any of you unless you want to. Take the evening. Think about it. You can tell me in the morning." Galina paused a moment, as the others turned to each other and the quiet buzz of conversation began, then stepped back to stand beside Jez. Jez gave her a quick smile, and Galina took her hand and squeezed it.

"I don't know about the rest of you," said Ivan, looking around at them. "But I feel like I could sleep standing up."

Tae smiled at him wearily, then turned to the others. "Come on. We can talk in the morning."

Jez smiled slightly. He knew as well as she did what they'd decide.

As the others dispersed, the crew filed up the stairs, huddled together in a group as if they didn't really want to get too far away from each other.

When they reached the hallway upstairs, Jez didn't turn off at her room, and Galina didn't seem to mind. At Galina's room, Jez hesitated at the door. Her heart was beating a little faster than it should have been, and there was something sick in the back of her throat.

"Galya," she said quietly. "Can I come in for a minute?"

Galina nodded and pushed the door open. She sat on the bed, still holding Jez's hand, and after a moment, Jez sat beside her.

"I guess this is goodbye, then," said Galina finally. She was looking down at their twined fingers, and her voice was subdued.

"Yeah," said Jez, and for a moment they were silent. Her heart was beating so quickly she thought it might make her sick. "Galya," she said at last.

Galina looked up.

"Galya. I—" She swallowed hard, trying to make the words come out. "Look. I know I said I didn't do relationships—but here's the thing. I—you—" She took a deep breath. "I thought maybe, when—when all this is done—I mean, look, I thought we got along pretty well, and maybe—maybe after I get back—"

Galina looked up at her, and there was something so sad in her face that Jez knew, the moment she saw it, what Galina's answer was going to be.

"Jez," she said, cupping Jez's hand in both of her own. "I haven't met someone like you, ever. You're—you're something special. And I wish I could—I wish—" She closed her eyes for a moment, and Jez's chest twisted painfully.

"I really like you, Jez. I like you more than I've liked anyone in a very long time." Her voice was quiet, and Jez could hear the hurt in it, and somehow that made it even worse. Galina glanced up and tried to smile. "But look at us. This, here, doing this—this is what I'm good at. This is what I've always dreamed of. And I've seen you. You'd go mad if you had to stay on the ground. You belong in the sky, Jez. I've seen you there. I've seen the look on your face. It's what you were born for."

"I—I could—I don't know, I could fly runs, and then come back here and spend some time," said Jez. Her voice was choking, just a little. "We could make it work."

Galina looked up at her again. She was blinking back tears, and suddenly Jez was too. "No, Jez," she whispered. "You wouldn't be happy. I wouldn't be happy. I need someone who can be here, with me, and I know you'd try, but I couldn't watch you tear yourself to pieces. And you deserve someone who loves what you love, who can see the same things you do when you sit in the cockpit and stare out to space, like you can see all the way into heaven." She squeezed Jez's hand in both of her own, and Jez closed her eyes for a minute, because damn it to hell, she hadn't planned on crying, and it was actually kind of pathetic, honestly, but she couldn't seem to help herself.

"Yeah," she said finally, when she could speak again. "Yeah, guess you're right. Anyways, I've always been kind of crap at relationships, so—" she shrugged, and tried to smile.

Galina shook her head fiercely. "Stop it, Jez. That isn't what this is about. You say those things about yourself all the time, and they're not true. You're kind, and you're caring, and you're brave, and when anyone else in the world would run away, you stick around. Whoever you find, whenever you find them, is going to be very, very lucky. And I wish it was me, Jez. I honestly wish it could be me. But if we were together, one of us would be miserable, and that wouldn't be fair to either of us."

Damn it to hell, it had actually been easier before Galina had started saying nice things about her. "Yeah," she said finally. "Thanks. And—well, and thanks for the past few weeks. It was really good."

She couldn't look at Galina, because she was pretty sure if she did, she'd just break down and start crying, and she didn't want to do that right now.

She pushed herself off the bed, and Galina stood too, quickly.

"Jez," she whispered. And finally, reluctantly, Jez turned to look at her. Galina leaned in and kissed her, gently.

"You mean a lot to me, Jez," she said, finally. "I—I wish—"

And then Galina turned away, blinking back her own tears.

Jez stepped out the door and wandered down the deserted hallway. Finally, she slipped into the conference room, closing the door behind her, because she wasn't quite sure she was ready to go back to her room alone right now.

She looked around for a moment, then collapsed onto the couch, staring out at nothing.

She didn't feel like crying anymore, not really. She felt empty, like someone had taken a spoon and scooped out all of her insides, leaving nothing but a shell.

The thing was, Galina was right. They'd both known that. And honestly, this was exactly the kind of thing she always looked for— someone hot who'd spend every moment possible with her for as long as they were together, but no strings attached. She could leave when she wanted to, and it wouldn't even matter.

But—well, but something had changed, somehow, in the past few months. Since she'd started flying with the crew. Maybe she still didn't completely understand all that crap, but somehow, the thought of being alone again wasn't nearly as attractive as it had been, once. And somehow she found herself actually wanting people who would stick around. Wanting a person who would stick around. Someone who could be what Ysbel was to Tanya. A person who meant home, no matter where you both were.

She swore quietly to herself.

That was the worst part of it, in the end. She finally wanted what everyone else in the system wanted, apparently. But she was still her. And so she'd never actually be able to have it. First there was that fiasco with Lev, where she'd almost lost him for good, and now Galina.

Galina hadn't said any of those things, of course. She'd said all sorts of nice things, and honestly, Jez would have assumed that she'd like that more than someone who basically pulled out a heat gun and threatened to shoot her, which was what some of her ex-lovers had done.

But the thing was, insults and threats she could brush off. Galina's words, she couldn't. They were kind, and nice, and they crept down inside her. And they told her that yes, maybe she was all those things Galina said, but … it still wasn't enough. It would never be enough.

She would never be enough.

That kid she'd brought back and tried to save, and who had died anyways.

Masha, who she'd managed to convince the others to trust, and who could have killed Lev.

Galina.

She tipped her head back against the back of the couch, too tired and empty to cry.

"Tae."

Ivan's hand on his arm was comforting, and even in the dim light of the hallway leading to the rooms, Tae found he'd turned towards him without thinking.

Ivan's eyes were warm and dark, and there was a familiar concern on his mild face, and, like always, Tae's muscles relaxed just a little, the tension in them bleeding away, and he was smiling, even though he was so tired he could hardly think.

"You're going with Masha, aren't you?" Ivan asked softly.

Tae closed his eyes, and for a brief moment he felt the sick panic of earlier in the day, when they'd walked into Grigory's room and he was sure he'd killed Caz and Peti and Mila and Luka and every damn one of the street kids, whose only crime had been that they knew him and they needed him.

Ivan swore softly, his hand tightening on Tae's arm. "Tae. I'm sorry, I wasn't thinking. You haven't even had time to call your friends yet, for the Lady's sake. Sit down and give them a call, because the look on your face right now is enough to give me nightmares. We can talk later, I'll wait."

Tae gave him a grateful look and sank down against the wall. His hands were shaking as he hit the button on his com. Ivan had slid down beside him, and the warmth of Ivan's hand on his shoulder was honestly the only thing keeping him from passing out.

The com buzzed for an endless few moments. And then Caz's face, sleepy and worried, appeared on the holoscreen, and Tae sagged back against the wall, lightheaded with relief.

They were alive.

And it hadn't been him who saved them, after all. Every damn person in this crew had risked dying to keep them safe, and for some reason the thought made something catch in his throat.

"Tae?" Caz asked, his voice thick with sleep. "What is it? What's the matter?"

"Nothing," said Tae, when he could speak again. "I just—I wanted to make sure everything was alright."

Caz frowned at him. "Yeah, everything's fine. What happened?"

Tae took a long breath. "It's—a long story. I'll tell you soon. I— didn't mean to wake you."

"It's fine," said Caz. He glanced over at Ivan. "Who's that?"

Tae found he was smiling again, without quite realizing it. "A friend. I met him a few months ago, and he's been helping us out. Ivan, Caz."

"Nice to meet you, Ivan."

"And you. Tae talks a lot about you," said Ivan. There was a smile in his voice, like he was genuinely happy to be introduced to a bunch of rag-tag street kids.

Kids who he'd never met, who he'd been willing to let himself be killed for.

Caz studied Ivan for a moment, and when he turned back to Tae, he had a slight, amused smile on his face, and Tae wasn't entirely sure why. "You look tired, Tae."

"Yeah." Tae rubbed a hand over his face and blinked back his exhaustion. "Look, we're … probably going to be coming back there soon. I'll—I'll see you all then."

"Sounds good. Goodnight, then," Caz said, through a yawn, and again, Tae felt almost lightheaded with relief.

Caz and the rest of them were alive. Somehow, he still wasn't certain how, they'd survived this.

And it wasn't even just that. Caz looked well-fed, for once, and the tiredness on his face was that of someone woken out of a sound sleep, not someone who hadn't been able to sleep soundly for months because he couldn't afford to let down his guard for even one moment.

"'Night," said Tae, and tapped off his com. He turned to see Ivan smiling at him.

"Will you be able to sleep now?" Ivan asked, that warm amusement in his voice.

Tae took a long breath and nodded. "Yeah. Yeah, I think I will, now."

"Good." Ivan paused. "I'm glad I got to meet these friends of yours, even if it was over a holoscreen."

Tae realized he was watching Ivan, and he probably had been for a lot longer than was really polite. His face heated, and he looked away quickly. "Yeah," he muttered. "I'm glad you could meet them too."

Ivan pushed himself to his feet and offered Tae his hand. "You've already decided, haven't you?" he asked quietly, as he pulled Tae to his feet. "You're going with Masha."

Tae looked up at him, and Ivan's eyes caught his and held them.

He swallowed hard. "Yeah," he said. "I—I don't know what else I'd do. My friends are there, and I can't very well—I can't—"

Ivan's smile was warm, and Tae found he still couldn't look away. "I know. You can't leave someone you care about to get hurt."

"Look, I just do what anyone would do," he muttered, but there was something about the way Ivan's eyes held his that tightened something in his throat, and he found it was hard to speak.

"So I just wanted to let you know," said Ivan. "I'm coming too. Back to Prasvishoni, with the rest of you."

Tae blinked. "You—Ivan, you don't have to—"

"Tae." Ivan stepped closer and put both his hands on Tae's arms, turning Tae to face him.

For no reason he could fathom, Tae's breath was coming far too quickly, his heart pounding an unsteady rhythm against his chest. Ivan was standing very close to him, and there was something about the pressure of his hands that formed a tight, warm knot in the pit of Tae's stomach, and his brain didn't seem to be working the way it should be.

Ivan's dark eyes were studying his face. "Listen to me, Tae," he said finally. "You said you wouldn't leave a friend to get hurt. And I'm not going to either, alright? If you don't want me to come, just tell me. But if you think there's even a possibility that I could help you? I'm coming."

"I—" Tae's mouth was dry. He swallowed hard. "I … do want you to come. If—if you want to. I don't—you don't have to—" He wasn't sure what had happened to his voice, and why his words seemed to be coming out tangled.

"Tae." Ivan smiled that smile again, his eyes never leaving Tae's. "I told you. If there's any possibility at all I can help—I'm coming. OK?" He paused, and his eyes still held Tae's, and there was an intensity in them as he watched Tae, and for half a second Tae's thoughts went back to that moment on Grigory's ship, his back pressed into the arm of the couch, Ivan's mouth on his—

He closed his eyes and wrenched his thoughts away with an effort.

He was being ridiculous, honestly.

"I—I should probably get to bed," he said, looking away quickly before his eyes could get caught again, although his throat was so dry he wasn't sure how he managed to form the words.

Ivan gave a small, rueful smile, and released Tae with what felt almost like reluctance. Although to tell the truth, Tae was pretty certain he couldn't trust anything his senses were telling him right now, considering how the whole world seemed to have gone slightly fuzzy. "You're right. You look like you need your sleep. And we'll probably be busy tomorrow." He paused a moment, then rested his hand lightly on Tae's shoulder again for the briefest of moments. "See you in the morning."

Then he turned and walked off down the hall, and Tae stared after him, and he wasn't sure why his knees felt shaky enough that he had to put a hand on the wall to steady himself. And he wasn't sure why he was smiling, and he wasn't sure why that ache in his heart that had been there ever since he left Dmitri standing at the gates of the university seemed to have shrunk, just a little.

He only knew that for the first time in a very long time, he felt utterly and inexplicably and absurdly happy.

"Mama?"

Ysbel looked down at Olya, who was clinging tightly to her hand. "Yes, my love?" she said, smiling despite herself.

"You won, didn't you? You stopped Grigory, like you said you would?"

Ysbel exchanged glances with Tanya over Olya's head, and smiled. "Well, I wouldn't necessarily say that. But your mamochka and I helped, anyways."

Olya breathed in a deep sigh of contentment. "I knew you would," she said, and there was a certainty in her voice that filled Ysbel with a sort of deep happiness that was almost painful.

"Well. You and your brother need to get to bed. Come on," said Ysbel, opening the door to the children's adjoining room. "In you go, and change into your pyjamas, please. I'll come in a minute to tuck you in."

Tanya lifted a drowsing Misko down from her hip and pushed him gently forward after Olya. "Go on then," she said.

"I want mama to put me to bed!" Misko proclaimed sleepily.

"I will come put you to bed, I promise," said Ysbel. "But you need to get changed."

He nodded, and Tanya gently closed the door. When she looked up, she was watching Ysbel, and there was a soft look on her face.

"They love you, you know," she said quietly. "They've always loved you—I told them about you every single day we were in prison. But now—" Her smile widened, and her eyes were slightly misty. "Now they are getting to know you. Not like some hero they tell stories about. Like a mother."

Ysbel's eyes were misty as well, and she leaned over to kiss her wife. "I suppose that's why they act like little monsters when I try to get them to behave?" she grumbled.

Tanya chuckled. "Honestly, Ysi, it is. They're not trying to impress you anymore. Because they know they don't have to. They know you'll love them no matter what they do."

Ysbel swallowed down a lump in her throat and blinked back tears. "I do, you know."

"I know that. And they know it too, now."

Ysbel sighed, and put her arm around Tanya, holding her tight and leaning her head against her wife's. She closed her eyes for a moment, letting herself relax against Tanya's shoulder, feeling Tanya lean into her.

"Mama! Mama, we're ready!"

"Mama, Misko pushed me! I was ready first, but he pushed me and he grabbed my nightshirt away!"

"I did not! Mama, Olya's lying!"

Ysbel sighed and grimaced, but she was smiling despite herself. "I'm coming," she called. "And Misko, if you pushed your sister, you're going to have to tell her you're sorry."

She cast a rueful glance at Tanya. "I'm sorry. I'll be back when they're in bed."

Tanya smiled up at her, and even though they were both older now, and even though so much had happened and so much time had passed, her smile was the same smile that Ysbel had fallen in love with so many years before. "I'll be waiting for you," she said softly.

And Ysbel turned away quickly to hide the sudden tears in her eyes.

Because perhaps that was what love was all about, really, if you came down to it. They could have their fights and their disagreements, and Ysbel could try and fail and try again to be the kind of wife that Tanya needed, and Tanya could get angry and frustrated and stressed, and the children could fight and cry, but at the end, when the dust had settled, they'd be there. Waiting for each other. Loving each other, no matter what happened.

She cleared her throat and pulled the door to the children's room open. "Alright you two, what's going on?"

But she couldn't make her voice harsh, even if she'd wanted to.

***

Lev paused a moment, running his fingers through his hair. He grimaced at the wall at the end of the corridor.

When had he become the kind of person who paced?

He was going to turn into Jez sooner or later, the way things were going.

At any rate, he couldn't seem to sit still, not with the thoughts chasing each other through his head.

They'd won. At least, they'd done what they'd set out to do. But—

He turned, and paced back down the corridor.

There was that kid Jez had brought back. There were people in the pleasure houses tonight who wouldn't live to see the morning. Yes, they'd won, but there was a bitter aftertaste to the victory.

And Masha.

He shook his head in frustration. He should have thought of this. He should have seen the path she was leading them down, but he'd been fully occupied in trying to keep them alive.

Which was, of course, exactly what Masha had counted on.

They were with her again, for another mission, the end goal of which he had no real idea. But they'd do it anyways, because what choice did they have?

He paused in front of the door to the conference room. Really, he should be trying to get some sleep, but he wasn't going to sleep tonight, he could already tell. He might as well do some research, get them prepared for whatever Masha was dragging them into next.

He'd pushed the door open and stepped inside before he noticed Jez. She was laying back on the couch, her head tipped back, eyes closed, and for a moment he almost tiptoed back out of the room, leaving her to sleep.

Then he noticed her hands clenching and unclenching restlessly, the way they did when things were too much for her to handle, the stiffness in her posture, the way her face twitched slightly, as if she was in pain and trying to hide it.

He paused a moment, then stepped quietly out the door.

He made his way down the stairway to the darkened lobby, and over to the doors that led into Jez's makeshift gambling hall. He tapped the light on his com, and by its dim glow, he sorted through the bottles behind the bar until he found the one he was looking for. Then he turned and stepped back out into the lobby, and almost bumped into Masha.

"Hello Lev," she said quietly.

"Masha." He kept his voice cold.

There was a moment of silence. At last she gestured down at the bottle in his hand, a question on her face.

"Jez," he said shortly.

She nodded, and for a moment they stood there, neither meeting the other's eye.

He took a deep breath and turned to go, but her voice stopped him.

"Lev." She paused, and there was something in her tone that made him turn back. "Lev. Is Jez—is she alright?"

He frowned.

Masha's face was shrouded in shadow in the darkened room, but there had been a note of something in her voice, almost desperation.

"She's—I think she's alright. I don't know. I'm going up to check on her now," he said at last. He hadn't meant to say it, he'd meant to say something sharp and cutting, but somehow he hadn't been able to bring himself to.

"Thank you," said Masha, softly.

He looked at her for a long time. Then, at last, he turned back to the stairwell.

He tapped at the door of the conference room this time, and when he pushed it open, Jez had raised her head.

"Hey genius," she said dully.

"Hey, Jez," he said. He came over and sat beside her, and handed her the bottle wordlessly.

She looked at it, then back at him.

"You looked like you might need it," he said, smiling despite himself at the look on her face. "I brought it in case you wanted to get drunk. Or—" He looked at the ceiling, as if trying to remember something. "Or, what did you say last time? We could both get drunk and have sex, that might help?"

She stared at him for a moment, then finally broke into a weak chuckle.

He grinned back at her.

"Thanks," she said at last. She pulled the top off the bottle with her teeth, and Lev coughed, blinking back tears at the sharp fumes of alcohol wafting from inside.

She glanced over at him and rolled her eyes, then put the bottle to her lips and tipped her head back.

He leaned back against the couch, but a few moments later she lowered the bottle and, after a brief hesitation, replaced the cap, placing it on the ground beside her.

He gave her a questioning look.

She managed a small smile. "Guess I don't feel like getting drunk as much as I thought I would."

He gave a small shrug. "That's fair."

For a few moments, they sat in silence.

"Do you want me to leave you alone?" he asked at last, quietly. "I can go somewhere else if you want."

"No." She turned to him, something desperate in her face. "No, please. I—" She closed her eyes for a moment, her whole posture slumping. "I mean—I mean, sure. You probably have plenty of stuff to do anyways."

Her voice trembled slightly, and it made something inside him hurt.

"Jez," he said, turning a little so he was facing her. "Look. I have no idea how to be a good friend, I know that. But I'm here for as long as you want me, OK?"

She looked up at him, blinking hard. "You—you don't have to—" she started.

He shook his head and put up a hand to stop her. "I want to," he said quietly. "Please. Like I said, I don't know a whole lot about this, but I'm pretty sure that's what friends do."

She studied him for a long moment. Something tightened around his chest again, like it always did when he was looking into her eyes. But when at last her face relaxed and she dropped back against the couch, close enough that their shoulders touched, her eyes closed in a sort of weary vulnerability—the tightness in his chest loosened just a little.

It hurt. It might never stop hurting, really. But Ysbel had been right about one thing, at least.

It was worth it.

It was worth whatever it cost, just for this. For him to be able to sit here next to her when she was hurting, and maybe make it a little better. For her to be able to lean against him when she was too weary to pretend anything, and trust that he'd just be there, nothing else. Just be there, for as long as she needed him.

"Genius?" she said after a few moments.

He turned towards her. "Yes, Jez?"

She'd opened her eyes, and was staring straight ahead. "You think any of this is worth it? In the end?" she asked in a low voice. "I mean —we do all this crap, but what difference does it make?" She stopped, swallowing hard. "Guess I'm just not sure what the point is anymore. I used to think it was pretty simple—we do crap to make things better. But turns out that's all crap. We work so hard to do this, and what do we even change?" She turned to him, finally. "I—I guess I don't know what the right thing is anymore. Guess I've always been kinda stupid."

He reached out, and after a moment's hesitation, rested his hand on her shoulder.

"Jez," he said. "You were the one who trusted Masha, when none of the rest of us did. You talked me into telling her about Vitali, and it kept us all alive."

"That's what I mean, though," she said, her voice dull. "I trusted her. I—I don't know, maybe I still trust her. But … I saw her face in that room, Lev. She would have killed you. She would have shot you, if it came to that, and she wouldn't even have thought about it twice."

Jez's words brought a spark of unease in the back of his brain.

Because she was right, he knew it deep down. Masha would have shot him. She wouldn't have hesitated.

And yet—

"She didn't, though," he said. "She didn't, and we all survived. And Jez—" He turned to her, face serious. "Somehow I doubt that Zhenya had a change of heart about Caz and Peti and the others."

She frowned at him. "You mean—you mean, you think Masha—"

"I don't know," he said. "But I think so." He paused. "I don't think we should tell Tae. I don't know if he could handle it right now."

Jez leaned back again with a faint chuckle. "Yeah. This has been kind of a lot, I think."

"It has," he said. "It's been kind of a lot for all of us, I think." He leaned back as well, so their shoulders were touching again, and there was something comforting in the warmth of her.

"You said you don't know what the right thing is anymore," he said finally. "I guess—well, I guess I never really did know. But I've been thinking about it a lot, since—well, since everything that happened on Grigory's ship. I'd almost convinced myself that anything I did would be worth it, if I got what I wanted in the end." He shifted, so he was looking at her. "But the thing is—I saw you. And you don't believe that. There are things you won't do no matter what, because they're wrong. And—and I realized I'd never had that. A line I wouldn't cross. I thought I had, but when things went wrong back in the university, I would have stepped over it and not thought twice. And since then I've been thinking about it, trying to figure out what's the right thing and what's the wrong thing, even in a place like this, that's maybe the closest thing to hell I can think of."

She sat up a little, turning towards him as well. "Yeah, genius? And what did you figure out?"

He smiled slightly. "I haven't figured anything out, not really. But —but I think the difference is, when you have a choice between doing something kind, and just walking away, because it's too much and nothing you do will make a difference anyway—you do the kind thing. When there's something wrong, and someone's getting hurt, and you can't fix it, you do something anyways. Maybe that's how people like Grigory win—because everyone knows no one can fix everything that's wrong with the system, so you might as well just embrace it. But—but maybe that's how things change, too. Enough people who won't stop doing all those little, stupid, pointless things.

Maybe that's what changes everything, in the end."

She was watching him, a frown creasing her forehead.

Finally she turned away. "Yeah," she said quietly. "Yeah, I guess maybe you're right."

"It's worth it, Jez," he said, still watching her. "I think, in the end, it's worth it. Because maybe you're right. Maybe we don't change much. But we change something. And maybe sometimes the people we trust aren't trustworthy. But the thing is, maybe that's better than just never trusting anyone. Better than just walking away because it seems hopeless. Better than just looking out for yourself, and screw everyone else."

"Better than just being alone," she said softly.

He gave her a small smile and leaned back next to her, and for a little while they sat in silence.

Finally, she turned her head to look at him. "For what it's worth, genius," she said softly. "I think you're actually pretty damn good at this friend thing."

Masha walked slowly up to her room, and closed the door behind her.

Lev wasn't in his room yet—she'd watched him turn down the hallway in the other direction.

He was probably in talking to Jez.

She closed her eyes for a moment.

The look on Jez's face when she'd seen Masha point her gun at Lev and pull the trigger.

She took a deep breath.

Just as well, really.

The same reason it was just as well she hadn't told Tae about her bargain with Zhenya. She could have. It would have cemented his loyalty, or if not that, at least his guilt.

But it was better this way. Better that he didn't trust her, that he believed she'd sell him out in a heartbeat if it advanced her agenda.

She wouldn't let herself think the next thought.

That maybe, if they didn't trust her, they'd be able to see through her plans and keep themselves alive.

Things were moving too quickly to stop now. Everything was falling into place. And this crew would get hurt. Possibly killed. There was no way around that, no matter how much she wished there was.

Maybe, if she'd known what she knew now, she'd have planned it differently, she'd have found a different way. But in those long, long years, while she smiled pleasantly and kept her head down and worked for the government that had killed her parents, and made her plans, planting the beginnings of the schemes that were just now beginning to bear fruit, she'd thought of the people she'd need for this as tools—no more, no less. Important, yes, but not more important than anyone else in the system. Just another life, in a system where lives were worth less than space-junk.

She sighed reluctantly.

Best get this over with before Lev came back.

She tapped her com. It buzzed for a few moments, and then a voice came through her earpiece.

"Masha. Is that you?"

"Yes. I'm calling to let you know that I've done what I promised. Grigory is finished, and Olyessa as well. It's time for you to start your part in all this."

Her voice was steady and calm. She'd had years of practice keeping it that way, no matter what was happening around her.

"I'm impressed. Some of us thought you wouldn't be able to pull it off." There was a slight pause. "Everything went well, I assume? No additional complications we need to know about?"

For a moment, a picture of Zhenya flashed in her mind, the faint smile on their face as they watched her.

"I'll watch your next move, Masha. I'll watch. And I'll tell you when I decide I'd like in."

If anyone else knew about her bargain, they'd take precautions.

And Tae's street-kid friends would die.

"No," she said at last, in that same calm voice. "No complications to speak of. We can proceed as we'd planned."

"Good. Then I will expect to see you soon."

The com clicked off.

For a few moments Masha stood there, looking down at her com. Then, at last, she sank down onto her bed, jaw clenched tight, staring sightlessly ahead into the darkness of her room.

THE END

ENJOYED THE BOOK?

I HOPE YOU'VE ENJOYED Trojan Horse, the sixth book in The Ungovernable series. Thank you for reading!

I have a small favour to ask you: Would you please leave a review? It may seem like a silly thing, but reviews are very important to authors like me, as they help other people find my book, which in turn helps me to keep writing. Even a line or two would be unbelievably helpful.

If you haven't read it yet, Zero Day Threat is the first book in the series. The seventh book is Security Incident.

In the mean time, if you subscribe to my mailing list, I'd love to send you an exclusive short story prequel featuring Jez Solokov, *Devil's Odds*. I'll also let you know about future launch dates, giveaways, and pre-release specials. And I always love to hear from my readers, so feel free to drop me a note!

If you'd like claim your free short story and subscribe to my newsletter, head over to my website: www.rmolson.com

Also, feel free to connect with me on Facebook: https://www.facebook.com/rmolsonauthor

or Instagram: https://www.instagram.com/rolson_author/